Artemis L█ █ SO-ASO-948

1. Song of the Moon
2. Kiss of a Star*

*Kiss of a Star will be released in 2011.
Check www.catherinebanks.com for updated
book information.

SONG OF THE MOON

AN ARTEMIS LUPINE NOVEL

Catherine Banks

Song of the Moon
An Artemis Lupine Novel

This is a work of fiction. Names, characters, places and incidents either are the product of the author's imagination or are used fictitiously. Any resemblance to actual persons, living or dead, events, or locales is entirely coincidental.

Cover design, logo and artwork by Avery Banks
Photograph by Larry Snook
Book design by Catherine Banks

PRINTED IN THE UNITED STATES OF AMERICA

ISBN: 1448659434
EAN-13: 9781448659432

www.catherinebanks.com

To the reader:

Thank you for purchasing and reading my book. As an author I feel I should explain why I write.

I write because I enjoy it, not to become famous or rich. Ideas and stories flow through me and beg me to write them down. I am at the mercy of my characters and their wishes, not the other way around.

An author's main payment is to hear people tell them how much they enjoyed the book. Maybe someday I will be listed among someone's top ten favorite fantasy authors, but until that day I will continue to write my stories for the enjoyment it brings me and, hopefully you, the reader.

Thank you again,

Catherine Banks

*To Avery for believing in me and
creating a beautiful logo and cover.*

*Thank you to Heather Donovan, Lauren
Snook, my parents and everyone else
who helped me.*

CHAPTER ONE

Today is our third day away from home. Darren, my father, decided that we needed a vacation from our small town life by getting away from the drama around us. I don't know what drama he was talking about, but it was nice to get away. Darren sang along quietly to the song on the radio as we drove towards our third destination: South Lake Tahoe.

The first day, well technically night, had been Las Vegas with bright lights and non-stop gambling. I'm not actually twenty-one, but somehow Darren got fake ID's that allowed both Bret, my best friend, and me to gamble and drink. Vegas had been fun, but the men were very abrasive, throwing offers at me like I was a street walker. Darren had, of course, protected me, but Bret was the one to make them back off. Bret is my best friend of thirteen years and is the star quarterback of our high school football team. He just accepted a full ride scholarship to Notre Dame for the upcoming semester. It is the main reason he had come with us, so that we could have one last trip together before he left California for Indiana.

Our second day was spent in Reno, which is a smaller version of Vegas minus the bright lighted streets. We went to a rodeo, much to Darren's dismay, and then gambled more of Darren's savings away.

That was yesterday though. Tonight we get to enjoy Tahoe. Bret silently stared out the back passenger window of Darren's Nimbus Grey Metallic, VTEC Honda Ridgeline. The townspeople made fun of Darren for buying an import truck, but I loved it. What's more reliable than a Honda? I drive a small blue Honda Del Sol. Bret hates my car telling me, "It's a death trap waiting to happen." I ignore his domestic car loving mentality and enjoy driving the small car with my targa top off every summer.

I felt my eyes starting to droop and then Darren cleared his throat. "Welcome to South Lake Tahoe."

I turned to the left and stared out at the perfect blue water. "Wow! It's beautiful," I said. The mountains which lined the lake still held on to a thin layer of snow making the scene twice as lovely.

Bret sat up straight and asked, "Do we get to go swimming?"

Darren laughed. "Of course! I would never bring you to Tahoe and not let you enjoy the lake. That's like taking you to San Diego and making you stay away from the beach."

I started bouncing up and down on the seat excitedly. "I can't wait to jump into that lake!"

"You won't be jumping in. You'll be flying in," Bret said as he laughed.

I scoffed. "Like you could catch me!" I knew he could catch me easily, but it was fun to roughhouse with him. We spent a lot of time wrestling and goofing around. He easily out muscled me, but that's to be expected since I'm a small girl and he's a football player. It just makes me feel better to play tough sometimes.

Darren laughed quietly. "Now children, remember we are supposed to be acting like adults."

Bret shrugged. "You said we only had to act in our early twenties and I guarantee any guy in his early twenties would try to throw Artemis in the lake."

I rolled my eyes. *Boys are so weird.*

Darren sighed. "I don't think you two will ever grow up."

Bret and I shrugged in unison and then laughed together.

Darren finally stopped in front of a large hotel. "This is my favorite hotel, so no screwing things up. You can use an underground tunnel to go from this hotel to the one across the street."

"Awesome!" I said

"That means there are twice as many restaurants for us to eat at," Bret said with a smile on his face.

Darren and I groaned at Bret. "You always think about food," I complained.

"Come on! It's been like four hours since lunch. I know you are hungry too," Bret said.

I started to deny his statement, but my stomach growled loudly giving me away. I sighed. "Guess I can't deny it now." I looked down at my stomach and whispered, "Traitor."

Darren shook his head smiling. "Come on. Let's get checked in and put our bags away and then we'll get some food."

Darren pulled into the valet parking line and handed the valet the truck keys. I stepped out of the truck, jogged to the back, and opened the compartment in the bed to get out my duffel bag of clothes. I hate those girls who pack five bags of crap for only being gone three days, so I make sure to pack as light as possible. I started to sling my bag over my shoulder when Bret took it from me. He slung it over his shoulder with his. I smiled at him and followed him and Darren into the hotel.

Darren checked us in, and then we followed him to the elevators. No one was waiting so we got the elevator to ourselves. I breathed slowly trying to fight my paranoia of imagining the elevator reaching the highest floor then plummeting back to the first level, killing us. Bret put his arm around my shoulders and rubbed my arm to calm me. Darren rolled his eyes at me and pushed the button for the tenth floor.

I groaned. "*Tenth* floor?"

Darren shrugged. "At least it's not the top floor. There are fourteen."

I snarled. "Four more isn't that big of a difference."

Darren smiled sideways. "It is when you are falling to the ground. Four less floors may be the difference between death and being permanently paralyzed."

I started breathing faster and turned my face into Bret's side. Bret shook his head. "Darren was that necessary?"

Darren scoffed. "She is such a baby about heights. One day she'll have to get over them."

I shook my head. "It's not the heights, Dad, it's the elevator. I would more than gladly take the stairs up. I just hate the thought of plummeting to my death in this tin can."

Bret rolled his eyes. "But you drive the Del Sol and feel safe. Isn't that kind of backwards?"

I shook my head. "Nope. *Nikkou* is very safe." (*Nikkou* is the Japanese word for "sunshine" and my little car always makes me think of the sun.) Darren rolled his eyes as the elevator door opened. I ran out from under Bret's arm and sat on the tile of the tenth floor. "Oh thank God, we made it."

Bret picked me up under the arms and set me on my feet. "Come on scaredy cat. Let's go."

Bret and I followed Darren as he wound the way down the hallways towards our rooms. Darren stopped next to two doors. "That one is your room and this one is mine." He handed Bret a keycard and then walked into his room without another word to us.

Bret turned to our door and opened it with the keycard. I walked in before he could and looked around the room. It was a large room with two queen sized beds and a gorgeous view of the mountains. I walked into the bathroom and giggled happily. A large jetted tub sat to the side waiting for me to get in. I turned on the bath and then walked out to the bedroom. Bret was flipping through the channels on the television and then he groaned. "All that is on is some breaking news story."

I shrugged. "Let's watch it."

Darren burst in through the side door that connected our rooms and took the remote from Bret, turning off the television. "No TV! I told you that before we left!" His voice was raised, he was breathing heavily and his face was flushed.

"Why are you so angry?" I asked.

Bret shrugged. "It's alright. Whatever you want, Darren. I was just curious what the breaking news story was."

Darren shook his head. "You aren't allowed to watch TV. I told you we were getting you both away from the drama and watching TV won't do that. Now dammit, enjoy yourselves without the TV!"

I stared at my dad as he tried to play off his anger and become playful. I wasn't buying it. "I'm taking a bath." I grabbed my bag and walked into the bathroom. I could hear Darren and Bret talking quietly, but I focused on relaxing. I set my bag down in the area with mirrors, grabbed a towel and set it next to the tub as I climbed in. I settled into the hot water and turned on the jets. I love hot baths and any free time I had was spent in the tub. I let my body relax with the gentle humming of the jets. In a matter of minutes my mind began to wander and my subconscious took over.

My breath steamed out in front of me as I ran through the thick forest. The other five people around me panted and sucked in air as we fled from our pursuers. The three wolves chasing us yipped in delight at hunting and fear made me trip on a tree root. I increased my speed, dodging around the trees as fast as I could. I knew I only had to run faster than the last three people. I increased my speed dodging in and out of the trees. I knew I couldn't run my fastest or I would increase my chances of hitting one of the trees and ending up in the claws of those pursuing us. The sounds of the others grew fainter as I dodged around more trees. My shirt was plastered against my chest from sweat and the pressure of the wind. I heard movement beside me, but moved too late. A large animal slammed into my side, sending me flying sideways. I wrapped my arms around my head to protect it as I slammed into a tree and slid to the ground.

The animal stood over me snarling and snapping its teeth, but made no move to hurt me. I moved one arm to my stomach and one to my throat to try to protect my most vital parts. I opened my eyes and gasped. A wolf the size of a horse stood over me snarling. I had never seen such a beautiful animal before. The wolf's jet black fur reflected the moonlight as its muscles flexed. The wolf sat staring at me with its deep amber eyes. It seemed strange to me for so much hate to be emanating from such a beautiful creature. I reached out and stroked the soft furred neck and the wolf quieted. I slowed my breathing as I stroked the wolf. I looked down the wolf's body and saw the male sheath and smiled. "Hello boy. Why don't you change and let me see how beautiful you are in human form?"

The wolf snarled and I pulled back my hands. The words seemed to come out even though I wasn't sure of their meaning. "I only meant that you are so beautiful in wolf form that I have no doubt that you are gorgeous in your other form as well." The wolf stepped back and stood up on its hind legs. I scooted backwards to get farther away from him and watched in amazement as the wolf's body rippled like water and became human. The man before me smiled and walked forward. I couldn't help but stare at his naked perfection, although I kept my gaze above his belly button so as not to offend him. "What's your name?" I asked.

The man smiled and held his hand out to me. He spoke with a voice like honey and said, "Ares."

The dream ended as quickly as it had started. I sat up and stared at the wall in front of me. I slowed my breathing as I focused on reality, and then sighed heavily. It was the same dream I had been having for the past week. I wished it wouldn't end in the same spot every time. I wanted to know what happened next.

Bret knocked on the bathroom door. "Are you alright, Artemis?"

I inhaled one more big breath then called back, "Yes, I'm fine. Just fell asleep in the tub." I climbed out of the now lukewarm water and dried off quickly.

Bret sighed. "Well hurry, I'm starving."

My stomach growled in agreement and I groaned. "Alright. Sorry." I threw on a pair of jeans and a low cut t-shirt then ran my brush through my shoulder length black hair before throwing it up into a ponytail. I pulled open the door and ran into Bret's chest.

He stumbled backwards and smiled at me. "Shit, you caught me off guard."

I smiled back. "Don't lie. You know I'm just stronger than you."

Bret rolled his eyes. "Yes, you, a five foot two, hundred and ten pound girl, is stronger than me, a six-foot, hundred and eighty pound guy. Not likely."

I shrugged. "It's okay that you don't want to admit it. I know the truth."

Bret sighed and motioned towards the door. "Let's go eat." I hurried out the door to find Darren, who stood against the opposite wall waiting for us. He acknowledged us with a smile and then started walking down the hall towards the elevators. I tried to listen to the boys' conversation, but all I could think about was the wolfman of my dream.

Darren interrupted my thoughts by pushing me into the elevator. I frowned at him, but ignored his taunting. *Could the man be real?* I shook my head. *Of course not. There aren't men who can turn into wolves or vice versa. That's all just fantasy. Wait... wouldn't he be a werewolf then?*

Darren cleared his throat making me look up at him. "Are you alright?" he asked.

I nodded my head. "Sorry. I fell asleep in the tub and I'm still trying to wake up."

Darren rolled his eyes and changed topics. "I was thinking we would go to a steak house."

I licked my lips hungrily. "Steak sounds great!"

Darren frowned at me and Bret laughed. "I swear if we took red meat away from you, you would end up eating one of us just to get your fill."

I wrinkled my nose in disgust. "I don't think you would taste too good."

Darren rubbed his temples. "Let's not discuss eating each other." He walked out of the elevator as soon as it opened and led us through the now crowded hotel. A line of at least thirty people was formed at the steak restaurant, but Darren walked up to the front and the hostess nodded her head as he spoke to her. She walked into the restaurant quickly. Bret and I walked up to Darren who stood, looking smug. The hostess came back and waved us in, smiling happily. Darren walked in and sat down at the largest booth. Two waiters came up and handed us menus and took our drink orders without even asking for ID.

I turned to Darren. "Why are they treating you like royalty?"

"The owner is a long time friend of mine," he said. A short very muscular man with a three inch tall, bright green Mohawk walked over to our table. He had on a nice, very expensive looking suit that fit every curve of his body. Darren smiled wider, but it seemed to almost look like a grimace. "Koda! I didn't think you would be here! I thought you were still in Germany."

Koda smiled wide, flashing perfectly white teeth. I stared at his face and guessed him at about twenty-five, but that made no sense to me since Darren was close to forty. "We came back from Germany a few weeks ago. I'm sure you know why."

Darren frowned. "Yes, yes I do." Darren's sudden mood change made me stare at Koda longer. He was very handsome and looked very strong. Darren shook his head and smiled again. "Where are my manners? Koda I'd like you to meet my daughter, Artemis and her friend Bret."

Koda turned his attention to me and stared at me in shock. His bright blue eyes pierced through me as he stared into my own. He slowly reached his hand out towards me and I took it shaking hands like Darren had taught me. His skin was extremely warm and I felt a small tingle rush up my arm and to my head. Koda smiled and shook my hand back with an equally firm, yet gentle shake. "It is a pleasure to meet you, Artemis. I have heard so much about you."

I frowned. "Unfortunately, I cannot say the same. But it is nice to finally meet one of dad's friends."

Koda dropped my hand abruptly, making the tingling disappear, and turned to Darren. "She hasn't heard about me?"

Darren swallowed hard and started to look nervous. "I have not told her of my past life."

Koda's lip twitched in a snarl. "That is very interesting indeed." Koda turned to me, smiling again. "If you want some time away from your father and friend please feel free to find me. I am always around this restaurant and, if not, my staff can reach me at any time, day or night." He took my hand again and kissed the back of it. "And I would be more than happy to show you around."

Bret stiffened beside me and I smiled nicely at Koda. "Thank you Mister..."

Koda shook his head then winked at me. "Call me Koda."

I smiled wider. "Thank you, Koda, but we are only here for one night and I'm sure the boys have a lot planned."

Bret relaxed back against his seat and Darren let out the breath he had been holding. Koda shrugged. "As you wish, but the offer is open any day."

Koda smiled at me then stepped closer to Darren and whispered quickly into his ear. Darren's face fell and he nodded once, very short and quick as if he were afraid to make any other movement. Koda walked away without glancing back. The waiters came back and took our orders. Darren smiled quickly and shook his head. "It has been too long since I've seen him. So, how does gambling for a few hours, then a trip to the hottest dance club in town sound?"

Bret smiled. "Awesome!"

I groaned. "A dance club? Why don't you just stab me in the eye with this fork?"

Bret and Darren talked excitedly about the night to come, but I couldn't listen to them. I stared in the direction Koda had disappeared and wished I could find a way to speak to him further. I remembered the strange tingling and wondered what had caused it. My ruminations ended as our food came and I ate my medium rare steak quickly. I ate the fries and salad as fast as my steak then downed my beer. I looked at Darren and Bret. "I need to use the restroom. I'll be right back." I started to get up then realized I had no clue where the bathroom was.

Darren noticed my problem. "Straight back and to the left."

I walked in the direction he had told me and felt butterflies as I realized it was the same way Koda had gone. I turned right down a dark hallway and ran into the back of Koda. I hadn't seen him in the darkness. He spun around and his shock turned into a warm smile. "Hello, Artemis. Get tired of your friend so soon?"

I laughed. "Hi, Koda. Sorry, I was just going to the bathroom and wasn't paying attention."

Koda shrugged. "No harm done."

He stepped to the side to allow me to pass him, but I stayed still. "Koda, what did my dad mean about not telling me about his past?"

Koda's eyes squinted in anger. "I'm sorry Artemis, but it's not my place to discuss your father's past with you. Your father will have to tell you."

I sighed. "Alright." I continued past Koda and into the bathroom. I hurriedly went pee then washed my hands and walked out of the bathroom. Koda stood in the same spot as before, talking quietly on his cell phone. I hurried to the table where Darren and Bret had already finished their food. "Time to gamble?" I asked.

Bret nodded his head. "Let's go!"

Darren rolled his eyes. "So eager to waste my money?"

"It was your idea." I pointed out.

Darren laughed. "True, very true."

We started to walk out of the restaurant when I felt someone's hand on me. A quick rush of heat raced up my arm, making me gasp. I spun around and stared in shock at Koda. He dropped my arm and the heat stopped. "My apologies, Artemis, I didn't mean to frighten you."

I smiled. "It's alright. No harm done."

His smile widened at my reminder of his comment. He held out a small piece of white paper. "Take this. If you ever need anything feel free to call me."

I slowly took the paper and nodded my head. "Th...Thanks."

He winked at me. "No problem." I couldn't help but stare at his backside as he walked away. Darren cleared his throat and I hid the piece of paper in my hand and turned to him.

Darren asked, "What was that about?"

I shrugged. "He was just saying bye."

Darren stared at me for a second then shrugged. "He's a nice guy." We started walking out of the restaurant again and I put the piece of paper in my pants' pocket. There were so many questions about Darren that I wanted answers to. Maybe I would call Koda and see if he could answer them. Darren stopped in the middle of the gambling area and turned to us. He pulled out his wallet and made three piles of bills. He handed one pile to me and one pile to Bret before pocketing the third pile for himself. "Now make this last at least two hours."

"I'm sure I can do that, but Bret will probably spend it in ten minutes," I said sarcastically.

Bret rolled his eyes. "You only spend it slowly because you play slots."

I shrugged. "I think slots are fun."

Darren laughed. "Play nice kids. I'll meet you back here in two hours." He walked away quickly towards the blackjack tables.

I turned to Bret and smiled. "See you in two hours."

He rolled his eyes again. "Have fun with the slots."

"I will," I said. I walked slowly towards the slot machines when I got the feeling that someone was staring at me. I looked around, but couldn't see anyone. I shrugged it off and walked faster towards the five cent slot machines. I felt a warm tingling sensation spread over me and turned to my right.

Koda stood a few feet away from me talking to someone whose back was towards me. Koda's eyes widened when he saw me and he whispered something to the man he was with. I smiled at Koda and waved, starting to walk away when the man turned around. I gasped and stopped moving. The man with Koda smiled politely at me, but I stood dumbfounded. He was the man from my dreams, the werewolf man.

Koda walked quickly to my side and whispered, "Breathe!"

SONG OF THE MOON

I inhaled a big breath and then stopped breathing again as the man walked towards me. I started to ask his name when Darren grabbed my arm and yanked me behind him. The man growled softly at Darren and I gasped at his wolf-like growl. I shook my head, clearing my thoughts. *I'm just projecting my thoughts into what I want to hear.*

The man seemed angry and stood in a loose stance usually taken when preparing for an attack. "What are you doing Darren?" His voice was tinted with anger as he glared at Darren.

"Leave my daughter alone," Darren said with menace in his voice as he pushed me father behind him and away from the man.

The man smiled. "I haven't done anything and you know I would never hurt our kind, especially not one as beautiful as her." My cheeks instantly flushed.

Darren's lips twitched up in a snarl. "Are you here for what I think you are here for?"

The man frowned. "Darius sent us here to continue our mission, yes."

Darren sighed then walked backwards and grabbed my arm. "Come on, Artemis. We're leaving."

I shook my head and stared at the gorgeous man in front of us. "I don't want to leave." I could feel the man's dangerous potential and yet I could tell he was good. How did I know this? I have no idea.

Darren looked from me to the man and then back again. He shook his head and dragged me away by the arm. "We are leaving."

I grabbed at my stomach so that I wouldn't reach out towards the man from my dreams like I wanted to. The man blew a kiss at me and I felt my blush intensify. I forced myself to turn away from him and followed Darren. Darren grabbed Bret and we hurried to our rooms. We traveled in silence until we reached our rooms, and then Darren turned to us suddenly. "I can't explain this, Artemis, but you two need to trust me. We have to leave, now."

I nodded my head and hurried into the hotel room to pack my bag. Bret grumbled about being on a streak as he packed his bag too. I turned to walk out of the room and stopped dead. Koda stood at the end of the hallway by the elevators staring at me. I dropped my bag and hurried to him. He frowned. "I wanted to make sure that you did as your father says and leave. Do not come back."

"Who was that man? I...I've had dreams about him," I said nervously.

Koda's face dropped in shock and he shook his head. "Just leave. If you want to call me later you can, but do not try to call me for at least two days."

I started to ask him why when the elevator opened and Koda hurried inside staring at the back of the elevator. The elevator doors closed a few moments before Darren spoke from his room. "Where's your bag?"

I turned around and smiled. "Sorry, I was trying to catch the elevator and dropped it by the door." I rushed back down the hallway and grabbed my bag as Bret followed me out, shutting the door and handing Darren the keycard. Darren watched me curiously, but didn't say anything. We took the elevator down and Darren paid the front desk clerk. I walked quickly towards the doors which led to the valet area, but I felt someone looking at me again and turned around, raising my eyes to the second story of the lobby. The man from my dreams stood on the upper level staring at me. He started to move towards the escalators and Koda and another man grabbed him and held him back. I hurried out the door and inhaled the cool refreshing night air. Darren walked out just as the valet brought the truck up.

I threw my bag to Bret and climbed into the truck, quickly shutting my door and putting on my seatbelt. Darren climbed into the truck and started it, sighing as the motor started up. I looked back in the hotel and saw the man and Koda inside the lobby. Koda was holding onto the man's arm and talking sternly to him. The man was yelling at Koda, but he stopped in mid-rant and turned to look at me. I stared into his beautiful blue eyes and wanted nothing more than to have him hold me.

Darren yelled, "Artemis!" I stopped moving and realized that I had unbuckled my seatbelt and was opening my door. I slammed the door closed and put my belt back on facing forward. Darren put the truck in gear and raced away from the hotel leaving Koda and the mystery man behind. We drove in silence for an hour, and then Darren pulled into a small diner. We got out and I numbly followed them into the diner. Darren ordered a burger for me and shoved a soda under my chin.

I drank absentmindedly as I thought about the mystery man. Who was he? Why did I feel so strange when I was near him? The news chiming on the television brought my attention back. I stared at the news reporter as his sad face told me that it wasn't going to be a happy report. "We know you all have heard of the devastation that is sweeping the Orient. It started in Japan and spread through China at an alarming rate..."

Darren yelled, "Can we change the channel?"

Our waitress came over smiling politely. "I'm sorry Sir, but there are more people here that want to watch it than those who don't."

Darren sighed loudly and stood up dragging me with him. The news reporter continued. "We just learned that Russia has been..."

Darren shoved me out of the diner so hard and fast that I fell on my face on the concrete outside. Bret rushed to my side and picked me up in his arms. Bret growled. "What the hell is wrong with you Darren?"

Darren shook his head. "Get in the truck!"

Bret set me down in the truck and got in the backseat. I stared at Darren in shock. "What's happening? Why won't you let us watch the news? What's going on?!" I screamed at Darren, knowing he was up to something.

"Just do what I say." He started the truck and took off out of the parking lot, spraying gravel from his tires as we raced out on to the highway again.

I felt my anger rising at Darren and my body began to heat up. I turned to yell at him then felt my body starting to twitch. I grunted in frustration as I had a seizure. Bret screamed, "Darren!" Darren pulled over and Bret held me down against the seat so I wouldn't thrash around and hit my head. Darren grabbed a cold water bottle, unscrewed the lid and splashed it on my face. I closed my eyes and focused on the cold feeling, willing myself to calm down. My body slowed its convulsions and then stopped altogether. Bret sighed. "I wish I knew what the hell caused those."

Darren just stared at me with anger and worry filling his eyes as I regained control. I whispered, "You can let go Bret. I'm fine now."

Bret sat back in his seat and Darren started driving again. We listened to the radio in silence the rest of the way to town.

We hurried to the house and I climbed straight into bed. Bret followed me in and closed the door behind him. He set our bags down and sat on the bed next to me. "I'm sorry we had to leave so early," I said to Bret.

Bret shrugged as he settled himself next to me. "It's not your fault, Artemis."

I rolled over and laid my head on his chest. We had been sleeping like this for so long that I barely thought about it. I focused on the beat of his heart and closed my eyes. Bret softly rubbed my back and I fell asleep.

The rain poured like a giant waterfall down my face as I scanned the forest. I wiped at the rain, but nothing helped. I put my hands over my eyes and screamed in frustration. I tensed as a wolf howled nearby, answering my scream. I walked backwards into the cave, pressing my back against the wall. My heart hammered against my chest, threatening to break through. I wiped the water from my eyes and stared at the black opening of the cave. Lightning flashed allowing me to see outside and my entire body stilled. A large black wolf stood in the doorway smelling the ground. The wolf turned its head towards me and sniffed three times quickly. I tried to slow my breathing, but the adrenaline was pumping too quickly to allow it. The wolf walked into the cave and whimpered. I shook my head and closed my eyes. The sound of bones snapping and popping echoed in the cave. I hugged myself tighter, fear consuming my rational thinking. A familiar male voice whispered, "It's alright. I won't hurt you. I'm Ares."

I sat up in bed and focused on slowing my breathing down. I looked around the room and realized I was in my bedroom, not a forest, and Bret was sleeping soundly beside me. I crawled over the top of him and walked into the bathroom. I flipped on the light and stared at the blank wall where a normal household would have a mirror. I opened the wooden medicine cabinet and took out my nighttime contacts. I forgot to put them in, in my hurry to get to sleep. I took out the ones already in and threw them in the garbage. I let my eyes rest for a minute without any contacts in, and then put eye drops in to refresh my eyes. I slowly put in the nighttime contacts and sighed.

It took me a while to be able to put contacts in since we didn't have a mirror, but I learned to do a lot of things without mirrors. So much so, that I never even look at one when away from home. Bret thought it was weird that I didn't have a mirror, but to me it was just how I was raised, like the kids who didn't have televisions. I closed the medicine cabinet and walked out into the living room. The TV was turned to the news, but Darren wasn't there. I heard him shooting his gun in the distance and knew he was out target shooting or coyote hunting. I sat down and turned the news up so I could hear it.

CHAPTER TWO

The news reporter's face was saddened and he spoke in a monotone voice. "Just two hours ago devastation wrought the town of South Lake Tahoe." I gasped. "So far no survivors have been found within a ten mile radius." I stared in shock at the television channel, not wanting to believe what was being reported.

Bret walked out of the bedroom rubbing his eyes. "What are you doing?"

I shushed him and pointed at the television. "Everyone is dead in Tahoe."

He stared at me in shock. "What?"

I patted the seat beside me and said, "Watch." He sat down next to me and stared at the television.

The reporter began speaking in his monotone voice again. "At full dark, something began to kill people. We do not know what it was, but the bodies were found exactly like those in Japan and Russia. Their throats torn out and..."

Darren ran into the house and turned off the television. Bret jumped up. "What the hell are you doing?"

Darren pointed his finger at us. "I said no television!"

"Now you are being stupid, Dad. Something is happening and we need to know. Why aren't you letting us watch the news?"

Darren shook his head. "I can't tell you. Just trust me that you do not want to watch the news."

I snarled at him. "I do want to watch the news! I want to know what is going on!"

"It's not safe, especially not after tonight. Now go to bed," Darren said in his no back talk allowed tone. He was mad at me, but I hadn't done anything that bad. I knew I wasn't supposed to talk back to him, but he had never been this angry before. I wanted to argue more and find out what had happened in Tahoe, but Darren was not someone I liked to see mad.

I groaned at him and stomped to my room. I think at times like this it's perfectly normal to act bratty. Bret followed me in and he laid back down and stayed silent. *Something is going on and I am going to find out what. Whether Darren likes it or not, I need to know what is going on.* Bret hummed softly and rubbed my back lulling me to sleep before I wanted to fall asleep.

The sun shining in my room woke me up. I stretched and yawned, feeling refreshed. I looked beside me and realized Bret was gone. I listened and heard bacon cooking which let me know that Bret and Darren were in the kitchen. I hurried to the bathroom and changed my contacts to the daytime prescription. Apparently my eyes were so bad that I needed two different sets of prescriptions. I rushed to the kitchen and found Bret sitting at the kitchen table. I sat down next to him sipping the hot chocolate that was on the table for me. Darren finished the bacon and set it on a plate in the middle of the table. I started to reach for a piece and he smacked my hand. "You wait for the rest of us."

I groaned. "But it smells SOOOO good!"

He smiled and started making scrambled eggs. I bounced my leg as I waited impatiently for my food. Darren scraped the eggs into a bowl then placed it on the table. Before I could move he smacked my shoulder. "Wait!"

I groaned and started bouncing both my legs at the same time. Darren opened the fridge and tossed Bret the butter tray and then the bottle of syrup. Darren then opened the freezer, which was on the bottom of the fridge, unlike most refrigerators, and took out frozen waffles.

I started bouncing on my chair. "Come on! Hurry!"

Darren rolled his eyes at me as he put ten frozen waffles in the microwave. I watched anxiously as the microwave table spun in small, slow circles. I felt my mouth watering as the eggs and bacon sat waiting on the table. The microwave dinged and I jumped up. Darren growled at me and I sat back down, sipping my hot chocolate. Bret laughed at me as I waited until Darren gave us each a waffle then he smiled. "Go on."

I grabbed four pieces of bacon from the plate and spooned two large spoonfuls of eggs next to the bacon. Bret was holding the butter tray and spreading the butter on his waffles slowly. I groaned and started bouncing my legs again. He handed me the butter with an exaggerated slowness. I yanked it from his hand and slapped butter on my waffle then took the syrup and poured it all over my plate dousing the waffle, eggs and bacon with syrup. I set the syrup bottle down and looked up to find Darren and Bret staring at me in shock. I giggled nervously then started eating. I shoveled the food in my mouth as fast as I could chew. I groaned happily at the delicious food and ate without any more noises until my plate was empty. I sat back and sighed in contentment, resting my hands on my full stomach.

Darren rolled his eyes at me and continued to slowly eat his food. I picked up my hot chocolate and sipped it slowly like a dessert. I stared out the window next to the kitchen and wished I knew what was going on with Darren. I tried to think of a way to ask him when Bret did it for me. "Darren, what the fuck is going on?"

Darren stared at Bret in shock. "Well Bret I think that is the first time I have heard you cuss."

Bret frowned. "It won't be the last time if you don't answer my question."

Darren sighed. "There is a lot of bad stuff going on in the world and I am trying to keep you two out of it so that you can enjoy your last week together."

I stared at Darren and for some reason knew he was lying. It was like a punch in the gut. I started to say something, but Bret interrupted me. "Well if it might interfere with our safety, I think you should tell us."

Darren said, "You're fine for now. I promise that I will tell you, if it gets to that point. Now go enjoy the day."

I stood up and walked past Darren and out the back door. Bret followed me and together we walked out to the open fields that lay behind my house. This is the one place of country I still had. On TV they always showed the industrialized parts of the world. None of that interested me. Just give me open fields or forests and I'm happy. I was about to head towards the forest when Darren called to us, "Don't go to the forest. I saw a group of wolf tracks in that area this morning. I'm not sure if they are passing through or not, but just don't go that way."

I nodded my head and walked the opposite direction farther into the open fields. Bret followed me, staying silent, but close. I could hear the mooing of our cattle in the distance and the neighing of my horses. I started running through the open fields just enjoying the feel of the early morning sun and wind on my face. Bret ran beside me. I smiled at him and increased my speed. He easily caught up with me and we ran for a few more minutes. I collapsed to the ground and closed my eyes.

Bret laid down next to me and asked, "What do you think is really going on with Darren? Why would he want to keep this all hidden from us?"

I shrugged. "How should I know?"

Bret stroked the side of my face with his hand. "If anything does come I'll protect you."

I rolled my eyes. "Shut up Bret. Nothing is going to come."

A high pitched voice yelled from the road near the field. "Bret! Bret, what are you doing?!"

I groaned and opened my eyes. "Skankzilla is calling you."

Bret rolled his eyes at me. "Yeah, I hear her." He sat up more so that she could see him and waved. "Hey guys."

Guys? I sat up and the two guys and two girls that had been smiling and waving at Bret from a lifted Chevy Blazer frowned at me. I smiled at them knowing they hated that Bret spent so much time with me.

"Oh, you're busy I see," said the girl whom I call "Skankzilla". I could hear the discontent in her voice.

I retorted, "Actually we are just hanging out. Shouldn't you be getting back to your corner? Wouldn't want some other skank to take it."

She flipped her blonde hair behind her back and turned away from me. Bret sighed. "She was just kidding! What are you guys up to?"

J.D., one of Bret's best friends spoke up. "We're going to the lake. You two wanna come?"

Skankzilla sighed and asked, "Why did you invite her?"

I stood up and put my hand on my hip and flipped my hair behind my shoulder in an imitation of her. "Because if you don't invite me Bret won't come, Skankzilla. And we all know how bad you want Bret's balls in your mouth."

The skank frowned at me. "That's just disgusting, Artemis."

I shrugged. "You're the one that does it." I wasn't usually so abrasive, but she rubbed me the wrong way.

J.D. and the other three people in the truck laughed loudly at Skankzilla. She screamed in frustration and turned away from me. Bret sighed and whispered, "Do you always have to get her all riled up?"

"It wouldn't be any fun if I didn't. Besides, what did I say that wasn't true?" I walked towards the truck and smiled up at the two boys in it. "Hey J.D. Hey Billy. One of you strong boys wanna give me a boost?"

They both started to reach towards me, but Bret grabbed me. "I got her guys."

J.D. rolled his eyes. "Yeah, Bret. You've always got her."

In reality all of the kids just put up with me because Bret was my friend. If they had their choice I would be the biggest loner ever. Billy smiled kindly at me and moved over so I could sit in the front beside him. Bret started to sit beside me and I shook my head. "Go sit in the back with Skankzilla. I'm sure she needs some consoling after my insults."

Bret rolled his eyes at me, but did what I asked. J.D.'s girlfriend Jessica smiled at me. "Hey. Chicky." Chicky was Bret's nickname for me, not sure where he got it from, but it stuck.

I smiled back at her knowing she was just being nice. "Hey, Jess."

Billy started the truck and drove off towards the lake. I put my seat belt on and watched the landscape go by as we drove. Billy turned country music on the radio and everyone started singing along except me. I ignored the rowdy teens and watched the fields. Billy asked, "So, how was your trip?"

I shrugged. "It was alright. We gambled and drank and had fun. And Bret tried to get in a fight in Las Vegas."

J.D. asked, "What happened?"

I turned to Bret and nodded my head. "You can tell them."

"When we were in Vegas, these older guys were trying to proposition Artemis." Bret said without hesitation.

Billy kept looking at me out of the corner of his eyes. All of them did this, like they couldn't let me out of their sight. Like they were *scared* of me. I didn't understand it because I had never done anything to any of them, but I was used to it by now. Bret continued telling them all about our adventures. The lake started to become visible and I got excited. I loved the water and couldn't wait to get in it.

Billy parked the truck and I hopped out before anyone else and ran down to the new dock the townspeople had built. I threw off my shirt and pants and ran straight off the dock and into the water without making the dock squeak. As I went under the water I swam farther out pushing against the water and loving the feel of it on my skin. I could hear the rest of them jumping into the water and surfaced when I knew I was far enough away that none of them could jump on me.

I turned around and gasped as Billy splashed me with water. I splashed him back and we started a girls versus boys splashing war. Of course the boys always won, but I like to think that we let them win. Boys have very sensitive egos. Billy splashed me with water and I launched myself at him pushing him under the water. He pulled me down with him and I went willingly, glad that for once one of them was treating me like a friend. I started to swim up when Billy pulled me against him and kissed me under the water. I froze in shock as he went up for air. I sat under the water not comprehending what had happened when Bret pulled me up. I gasped for air and stared at Billy.

Bret yelled, "What the hell did you do to her?!"

I shook my head and put my hands on Bret's chest. "No, Bret. It's okay. He didn't do anything. I was just seeing how long I could hold my breath." *And wondering why Billy had kissed me and why it had felt so strange.*

Bret frowned at me, then shrugged. "Sorry Billy."

Billy smiled. "No prob. We know you are protective of her. Just like a big brother."

Bret flinched at the words and I ignored him. I dove under the water as far down as I could go. I swam right to Billy's legs and pulled him under the water. His arms flailed as he tried to stay up, but ended up failing and went under. I surfaced before he did and swam a few feet away. Billy came up sputtering and smiled at me. Bret glared at me and I shrugged at him trying to look innocent. The girls started fighting with individual boys and, as I suspected, Skankzilla went to Bret. I floated on my back enjoying the sun on my face. I heard the water moving and turned my head to see Billy floating next to me. He spoke softly, "Hey."

"Hey Billy. Nice day, huh?"

He nodded his head and then turned serious. "I'm sorry Bret's leaving."

I shrugged. "Yeah, but it's great for him."

He nodded his head. "Yeah, but bad for you."

I stopped floating and treaded water so I could look at him better. "What do you mean?"

He dropped down too and smiled. "Artemis, we know how you feel about him."

I shook my head. "No, you don't."

He rolled his eyes. "So you're trying to tell me that you don't like him?"

I frowned. "Of course I like him, but not like J.D. and Jess like each other. You said it right. He's like my big brother."

Billy flinched. "Don't tell that to Bret. You'll kill him."

I shrugged. "I've never told him any different."

He frowned. "So you've never done anything with him?"

I laughed. "No! I've never done anything with anyone." I suddenly felt embarrassed and turned away.

"It's okay Artemis. I know it's hard for you here. Since everyone treats you bad." Billy said softly.

I shrugged. "I'm used to it."

Billy moved closer to me and said, "When Bret leaves you can spend time with me, if you want to."

I turned around and stared at him in shock. "You're not afraid of me?"

He smiled. "A little, but I'm tougher than Bret and he can handle you so, I figure I shouldn't be too scared."

Skankzilla screamed and pointed behind me. "Oh my God, do you guys see those bears?"

I turned and looked in the direction she was pointing and gasped. "Those aren't bears, they're huge wolves!" Two gray wolves and one beautiful black wolf were standing on the sandy edge of the lake drinking. They looked up when they heard her and I felt drawn to them. I started swimming towards them and they turned to stare at me. The black wolf in the middle took a step forward and the other two snarled at him. He stopped moving and they all started to turn away. I called to them, "Wait! Don't leave!"

Billy grabbed me. "What are you doing, Artemis?"

I shook free of him and swam faster towards them. "Please! Wait!" I recognized the middle one and knew where I had seen him before. He was the wolf in my dream last night. He was Ares, the mystery man in my dreams and the man at the casino. The wolves ignored my pleas and ran into the fields and then disappeared into the forest. I sighed and Bret grabbed me in his arms. I growled, "Put me down."

"What were you thinking?!" He shouted at me.

"You wouldn't understand." I pushed off of him and swam towards the shore. The girls were already dressed and headed towards the truck. I put my clothes back on and my shoes and started walking.

Billy caught up to me. "Where are you going? Come on, I'll give you a ride home."

I shook my head. "No thanks. I'll talk to you later Billy."

He stared at me as I started running down the road. I heard Bret grunt and stopped running. I yelled, "You go with them! I need time alone!"

Bret started to shake his head as he tried to put his pants on and I ran down the road as fast as I could. Dirt kicked up behind me as I sprinted towards home. I felt stupid for even believing that wolf had been Ares. *A werewolf? How stupid am I? I have a wild imagination.* I stared in shock at my house. *How did I get here so fast?* I shrugged and walked up the steps of the front porch.

Darren opened the door before I could reach to open it and stared at me. "Where's Bret?"

"With his friends. I left early to come home."

He shrugged. "Okay. Now what are you doing?"

"Taking a shower and then eating lunch. Is that okay with you?" I asked angrily.

He raised his hands as if surrendering. "Yeah, yeah kid."

I hurried into the bathroom and undressed. *What the hell is wrong with me? I keep having wolfman dreams then I think I see the man that is from my dreams. Koda said I couldn't call him for two days. Why not? Oh shit. Is he still alive?* I started to get nervous and wanted to call him, but breathed slowly, letting my body relax again. *I can wait until I'm done. If he is dead...* I swallowed hard... *rushing won't do anything.* I would have rather taken a bath, but I needed a shower after swimming in the lake. I climbed into the hot stream of water and washed my body and hair absent-mindedly. *Why had I felt so strongly that the wolf was Ares? It was stupid to even consider that my dreams were real, right? But how was he in my dreams? Why was he in my dreams?*

"Artemis, are you alright?" Bret called through the door.

I sighed. "Yes Bret. I'm fine. I thought I told you to hang out with your friends?"

He sighed heavily leaning against the door. "I know what you are doing." I stared at the wall waiting for his answer. He continued. "You think by pushing me away it will make it easier on you when I leave."

I sighed. "Yeah, well what am I supposed to do?" I turned off the shower and wrapped the towel around myself. I opened the door and looked up at Bret who stood frowning at me. I walked past him and into my room to get dressed. Bret shut the door behind me waiting in the hallway as I got dressed as slow as possible.

When I walked back outside Bret was still scowling at me. I put my hands on my hips. "What?"

He frowned. "Looked like you and Billy were pretty friendly at the lake?"

"He was just trying to be nice since you are leaving and everything. He offered for me to hang out with him, so that I wouldn't be lonely."

Bret rolled his eyes. "Right, so you wouldn't be *lonely*. What a dirtbag!"

I frowned at him. "Why are you upset? Most of the time your friends won't even talk to me so, shouldn't you be happy that he is being nice to me?"

Bret scoffed. "I'm sure he'll be real nice once I'm gone."

I stared at Bret and realized what was going on. "You're jealous."

Bret's face twisted from shock to sadness. "No I'm not. Why would I be jealous of Billy?"

"Because you think that when you leave I am going to hook up with Billy and then when you come back it won't be the same between us."

Bret played with a string at the end of his shirt. "That's not it. I just ... I just don't want him to hurt you."

I smiled. "You mean emotionally, right?"

He smiled back. "Well not physically. I think you could take Billy if you wanted to."

I rolled my eyes. "I could take you if I wanted to." I pushed his chest and he fell backwards onto the floor.

He swept my legs out from under me, making me fall to the ground on my back beside him. He rolled over and before he could do anything else, I punched his chest and arm. His face was lit up with a giant smile as we wrestled in the hallway. We both admitted defeat when we were breathing heavily and sweating. Bret stood up and then held out his hand to help me up.

I folded my legs under me and stayed sitting as I looked up at him. "Tell me the truth, Bret."

Bret's face turned serious making him look older and a little handsome. "I don't want to leave. I want to stay here with you." I started to protest but he squatted down, grabbed my arms and shook his head. "I'll play for one of the colleges close to here. We can live in my parent's house and..."

I shook my head. "Bret, Notre Dame is an amazing opportunity. I'll make new friends."

"I don't want to be away from you Artemis. I lov..."

I pushed him away and ran from the house. *I am not doing this right now.* I could hear Bret calling after me, but I didn't want to deal with him and his stupid attempts at making me more than his friend. I just didn't see him that way. Bret was catching up to me and I knew I couldn't outrun him so I stopped. He stopped a few feet behind me trying to catch his breath. I focused on my own breathing and realized that I wasn't even winded, but I normally never got winded. Bret said it wasn't human for me to be able to run so fast or long without getting winded, but I just told him he was just mad that I'm in better shape than he is.

I started to turn around to look at Bret when I heard a soft growl from beside me. I turned my head slowly and saw one of the wolves from the lake standing in the forest. The black wolf. Bret grabbed my arm before I realized I was moving towards the wolf. The wolf snarled loudly and I knew he was snarling at Bret. Darren appeared beside me and yelled, "Get in the house!" I hadn't even heard him run up to us, so I jumped when he yelled.

I started to protest leaving, but Bret picked me up in his arms and started running. I tried to fight Bret, but he was a lot stronger than me. I twisted in his arms so I could see the wolf as he watched us leave. Darren raised his gun and aimed at the wolf. I screamed, "NO!" and pushed myself from Bret's arms. He stumbled as I made him lose his balance and I ran to Darren. He had his finger on the trigger, gun aimed at the wolf. I ran as fast as I could into Darren making his gun go off high in the air and he fell to the ground. I jumped up and looked to the forest hoping the wolf was fine and smiled when I saw him standing proudly in the clearing. The other two wolves from the lake came to him and together they ran off into the forest. I turned on Darren. "What the hell are you doing?! That wolf didn't do anything!"

Darren snarled. "That wolf is dangerous! He needs to be killed!"

I shook my head. "You were the one that taught me that predators are not always dangerous and shouldn't be shot just because they *might* harm your animals. He was just sitting there!"

"He growled at you!" Darren yelled at me, his face blushing with his anger.

"He growled at Bret, not me and he was just standing there," I said as I glared at Darren. "I can't believe you were going to shoot him. You are not the man I thought you were." I started to get angry and felt my body temperature rising. My hands started shaking and I sighed as the first of the convulsions brought me to my knees. I fell to the ground on my back and started to twitch hard.

Darren yelled, "You bastard!" in the direction the wolves had gone then stared into my eyes.

"Artemis, breathe honey. Slow your breathing and calm yourself. You can work through this. Focus on happy thoughts."

I clenched my teeth together and closed my eyes. I tried to slow my breathing and pictured how beautiful the wolves had looked at the lake and Ares' smiling face from my dreams. My body slowed, cooled down and then stopped twitching. Bret started to pick me up in his arms, but I pushed him away, standing on my own. I brushed my backside off and ran towards the house. We had no clue why I had the seizures and Darren refused to take me to the doctors. I threw clothes, contacts and my toothbrush in my backpack and ran back out of the house. Bret was following me and I stopped running to wait for him. He caught up to me frowning. "Where are you going?"

I snarled. "Away from my father."

"Are you coming to my house?" He asked smiling.

"I hadn't really thought about it actually," I said quietly.

He smiled wider. "You know you are always welcome to stay with me."

I stared at his smiling face and felt sadness overwhelm me knowing that in a week I would no longer have him. I would be alone, just like the first week of kindergarten. I started to tell him I couldn't when Billy drove down the street. I waved at him and he stopped the truck, waving back at me. I smiled at Bret. "I think I'll go hang out with Billy for a while."

Bret's smile fell and a quick anger replaced his happiness. "Fine. Do whatever you want." His anger faded and he rubbed the back of his neck in his nervous gesture. "If you want to stay the night at my house I'll leave the door open for you. I think I'll go hang out with the guys for a while if you won't be with me."

I could see the hope in his eyes that I would go with him and smiled reassuringly. "I'll meet you at your house for dinner, 'kay?"

He nodded his head and attempted a smile. "Alright. I'll see you at six."

I stood on tiptoe and kissed his cheek. "Bye Bret."

He smiled at me with a little gleam of hope in his eyes. "Bye Artemis."

I ran to Billy's truck and hopped up into the open door. I threw my bag in the back before turning to him. "Hey Billy. You know you have perfect timing?"

He laughed. "Well that's a first." He looked at my bag. "You going somewhere?"

"Just running away from home for a little while. Not like my dad won't know where to find me, but I need some space." Billy's face fell as he realized I meant Bret's house. "So Billy, you want to go somewhere? Bret's hanging out with the guys for a while and I'm not supposed to be back at his place for dinner 'til six."

Billy smiled. "We could go to the mall."

I nodded my head. "Great! I need to do some shopping."

Billy nodded his head clearly overjoyed. "Cool." He started the truck back up and drove away down the road towards the highway. I buckled my seatbelt and sat back against the seat. Billy talked about his after high school plans and I tried to pay attention, but all I could think about was the wolves. I had never seen wolves come so close to humans before, especially twice in one day. Billy must have noticed my wandering mind because he turned on the radio and didn't talk the rest of the way to the mall. We parked on the top level of the parking garage and walked towards the mall.

I smiled reassuringly at Billy and asked, "Do they have cell phones in here?"

Billy shrugged. "I don't remember. I have one you could borrow, though."

"Thanks. I just need to make a call tomorrow."

"No problem." He opened the door for me and I walked in and inhaled the smell of cinnamon. Billy laughed. "It's the cinnamon bun place. It's like two feet from the department store. If you want we can get something there?"

I licked my lips realizing that I hadn't eaten after my shower. "Actually I think I need to get food, like more than a cinnamon bun."

Billy rubbed his stomach and said, "I'm always hungry."

"What is it with boys and always being hungry?" I asked.

He shrugged and then flexed his arms, showing off his muscular biceps. "It's from all of the working out and growing big."

I nodded my head. "That must be it. Working out your big egos."

He rolled his eyes. "Come on, there is this great Chinese food place in here I love."

I shook my head. "No way. I need meat!"

He laughed and put his hand on the center of his chest. "A woman after my own heart!" We walked through the department store to the exit, which led to the rest of the mall. I dodged around people as I hurried to the food court, which was about fifty feet away. I turned and looked at all of the places surrounding me, trying to figure out where to go. Billy started pointing out places. "There's the fast food burger place or the burrito place that makes giant burritos that are like *ten* pounds! You can get an all meat burrito I bet."

I licked my lips at the thought of spicy shredded beef in a burrito. "Burrito place it is." He led the way to the burrito place which thankfully had no line in it. I ordered the largest burrito of spicy shredded beef, rice, sour cream, refried beans and cheese they could make. Billy ordered his burrito then got us chips and salsa with our drinks as well. We sat down at an empty table and started in on our chips and salsa. I moaned happily. "I forgot how much I love chips and salsa!"

"My mom always keeps chips and salsa around at the house. We could watch a movie afterwards and chow down on some more chips and salsa there if you want?" Billy said with a nervous smile.

I shrugged then talked around a chip in my mouth. "Maybe, it depends on how I feel after shopping. I generally get tired from dealing with the Barbie girls here."

Billy frowned. "What Barbie girls?"

I looked around us and saw at least ten blonde haired, big-chested, slutty dressed girls and laughed loudly. "Look around us Billy. It's like an 'I wanna be Barbie' convention."

He looked around us and smiled. "I guess I see what you mean."

I scoffed. "As if their looks weren't bad enough, these girls all act dumb and talk in high pitched voices." I changed my voice to as high pitched as I could get. "Like *ohmyGod* Billy! Did you see her hair? It is like *totally* last summer."

He laughed loudly at my mocking and shook his head. "So, why is it that you have been the outcast in our group when you are so much fun to hang out with?"

I shrugged and tried to hide the pain from my face. "I think because Bret forced me on everyone so they didn't get a chance to decide if they liked me or not. Then you have Skankzilla who wants Bret so bad that she will do anything she can to try to get rid of me."

Billy looked nervous as he dipped a chip in the salsa. "Yeah, she definitely hates that Bret is with you."

I felt my face wrinkle in disgust. "I told you that I'm not *with* Bret! We are just friends. I told you that at the lake."

He shrugged. "You don't have to lie to me Artemis. I see the way you are together."

I shook my head. "You obviously don't. Bret is my friend and that's all. Ugh. I hate it when people assume we are together."

He smiled and asked, "So you guys aren't a couple?"

I shook my head. "NO! He is just so damn protective of me that he makes everyone think that."

Billy smiled wider. "Oh. Well I'm glad I know now." I finished eating my burrito and finally felt full. Billy finished his burrito with a sigh. "Man that was good."

I nodded my head. "Yep. Definitely hit the spot. So are you ready to shop?"

He smiled. "Always!"

"Are you one of those guys who is a secret shopaholic?" I asked after laughing at his enthusiasm.

He put his head down in a bashful manner. "Maybe."

I laughed. "Great. I think I'm coming here for a relaxing time and you're going to be going to all of the sales."

His eyes got big and he looked around the mall. "There's a sale?! Where?"

I rolled my eyes. "Come on tough football player. Let's shop!" I stood up and he followed me throwing away our tray of food on the way.

I started to walk past the teen clothing store with a giant SALE sign and Billy cleared his throat. "Ugh, I wasn't kidding about being a shopaholic." I laughed and followed him into the store. He rushed right to the discounted racks and started pulling out t-shirts with the clothing store's logo on them. I had to admit that Billy did have decent taste in clothes. He cleared his throat and I looked up from the floor that I had at some point started looking at. He smiled. "What size are you?"

I frowned. "Why?"

He sighed. "Just play along."

I sighed back at him. "Medium."

He nodded his head then turned back to the discounted racks. I walked over to one of the display stands and sat down on it. It was definitely going to be a long day of shopping. Billy walked across the store with a pile of clothes over his shoulder to another rack which had sunglasses. He put on a pair of the old style aviators and I couldn't help, but laugh. He turned to me and frowned. "You don't like them?"

I shook my head. "No!" I walked over to the sunglass rack and found a nice pair of sunglasses and put them on him. He looked in the mirror and smiled. I nodded my head. "I like those."

He reached over to the girls' side and handed me a pair with diamonds on the side. "Put them on." I frowned and put the sunglasses on. I had never really been a big fan of sunglasses so I didn't own any. I tilted my head to the side as if I was modeling them and he nodded his head. "I like those. They look good on you."

I blushed. "You think so? You don't think they make me look..."

He moved closer to me and whispered, "Hot? Yes definitely." I turned to face him and he kissed me on the lips, sending an unpleasant shock down my spine. He pulled away from me smiling and took the glasses off my face. "I'm buying you these."

"I have my own money Billy."

He shook his head. "Nope, I picked the store so I'm buying."

He walked over to another rack and started looking at belts. I sighed. "I'm going next door to get my shopping out of the way while you are finishing up."

"Okay. I'll meet you in there. I think I'm almost done."

I laughed at him as he scowled at a pair of jeans trying to decide if they were worth it with the ten percent off or not. I hurried to the store right next door and walked in. It was my favorite place, a jewelry store. I didn't wear jewelry, but I loved looking at everything. I walked down to the men's jewelry spot and looked at the necklaces. They were all chains and reminded me of rappers you see on TV. I rolled my eyes and then found the necklace I had been looking at since I found out Bret was leaving. I smiled at the clerk who stood silently waiting for me to ask for help and pointed at the necklace. "I'd like that one please."

She smiled. "That's a nice one." She took it out and put it in a box. I watched the silver chain with the football on it sparkle and hoped Bret liked it. It would be my last present to him before he left. I paid for it and walked outside and almost ran into Billy.

He smiled and looked down at the bag. "Gift for Bret?"

I sighed. "My going away present for him. Something so he'll remember me."

Billy rolled his eyes. "Like anyone could forget you."

I smiled at him and started walking towards the exit. He walked quietly beside me and opened the door for me. I looked down at his hands and gasped. "How much did you spend?"

He shrugged. "A couple hundred dollars. Not much."

I gaped at the ten bags he was holding. "Oh my God. I don't think I've spent that much in five years of clothes shopping."

He rolled his eyes. "Are you sure you're a girl?"

"Are you sure you're not gay?" I asked.

He frowned. "Would I have kissed you if I was gay?"

I fought the frown that wanted to form and forced a playful look. "You did just question if I was a girl."

He rolled his eyes at me then started walking to his truck. I walked beside him and smiled at how easy it was to be around him. I felt for once, normal. We were almost to his truck when we heard screeching tires. I turned my head and saw Skankzilla driving J.D.'s truck and swerving out of control. Billy jumped in front of me to protect me from the careening truck. I tensed waiting for impact, but nothing happened. I opened my eyes slowly and saw the truck had stopped just inches from Billy. He exhaled and turned around to face the truck. "You almost killed us!"

Skankzilla shrugged. "I wasn't aiming for *you* Billy."

Bret was frowning angrily from the passenger seat and shook his head. "I can't believe you just said that. Are you alright Artemis?"

I patted my arms and legs and nodded. "Yeah. Billy saved me by blocking Skankzilla's path to me."

Bret's forehead creased further in anger. Billy stepped in my view of him and looked me over. "You sure you're alright?"

I laughed. "Billy I'm fine. If anyone would have been hurt it would have been you for jumping in the way. You could have died."

He smiled. "Well I couldn't just let you get hurt. I had to protect you." He kissed my cheek and I felt the blush spread across them. He turned around and yelled, "Don't ever let her drive again!"

Bret glared at Billy as he walked to the truck. Bret hopped down and walked towards me. "You having fun with Billy?"

I shrugged. "Actually yes. We ate then we shopped..." Billy whistled and I turned just as he tossed the sunglasses he bought me towards me. I caught them easily and put them on smiling at Bret. "You like them?"

He nodded his head. "Yes. They look good on you."

Billy called, "That's because I picked them out."

Bret snarled. "So you and Billy dating now?"

I frowned and pushed the sunglasses on top of my head. "Bret, I have to make friends, right?

You'll be gone in a week. And we just talked about this."

He scoffed and then glared at me. "Friends? *Right,* more like bed buddies."

I shoved Bret in the chest as hard as I could, making him stumble a few steps backwards. "Don't ever say something like that about me again! You know I'm not like that! I can't believe you said that. Here! Take this." I tossed the bag with his necklace in it at him and walked away. Bret started walking towards me and I turned around and yelled, "Screw you! I've been your friend for over ten years and never *ever* done anything with you. How dare you assume that I'm with him for a few hours and I'm screwing him! If that's what you think of me then you should just leave for Indiana now."

Bret called, "I'm sorry Artemis! Wait! Please!"

I hurried to Billy's truck where he stood with the door open. I pulled my sunglasses down so he wouldn't see me crying and hopped up into the truck. He shut my door and got in the driver's side, starting the truck quickly and pulling out of the parking lot. We wove our way down the parking garage while I cried as silently as I could. Billy put his hand on top of mine and rubbed small circles on it trying to be soothing. His touch began making me nauseous so I patted his hand to let him know it was alright and turned to face the passenger door. I let the tears fall then shook my head. *I am not going to let him ruin my day.* I turned to Billy. "Sorry about that Billy."

He rolled his eyes. "Bret is a jerk to you and you apologize to me? That's a little backwards Artemis. I can't believe he said that to you."

I shrugged. "He's just upset. I'm sure he feels like a jerk especially after seeing the necklace." I thought about it and realized that I didn't want to see Bret... "Is it okay if I come over and eat chips and salsa and watch movies?"

Billy smiled wide. "Yeah! My parents are still out of town so we'll have the place to ourselves."

I smiled. "Cool. So, what are we watching?"

He shrugged. "I have like a thousand DVDs so I'll let you pick."

The trip passed quickly and we stopped in front of his house. I climbed out of his truck and grabbed a couple of his bags. He opened the door and waited for me to go in. I called over my shoulder, "Where do you want the bags?"

He whispered, "Here is fine." I jumped since I hadn't realized how close he was. He laughed. "Sorry. I whispered so I *wouldn't* scare you."

I smiled. "It's alright." I set the bags down in the entryway and walked to his kitchen. I had been to Billy's house a few times to watch movies with everyone. I took out a soda for each of us and Billy took out the salsa and got the chips down. We walked to his living room and I gasped. A new gigantic TV sat taking up his entire living room wall. "Holy crap!" I exclaimed. "How big is that?"

He shrugged. "It's a seventy-three inch. We are going to get the eighty inch next month."

I turned to my right and gasped again. The wall was an array of shelves of DVDs. "What order are they in?"

"Release year."

I walked to the wall of movies and started going through the titles. I finally decided on one of my favorite movies. "Here."

He looked at the movie then up to me again. "This one?" he asked. "Are you sure?"

I nodded my head smiling. "It's one of my favorites. You don't like it?"

He laughed. "No, I love it! It's just that I thought you would pick a comedy or something..."

I finished, "Something girly?" He nodded his head and I laughed. "Nope, I like action movies."

"Alright, *300* it is." He walked to the stand which held the DVD player and what seemed like every game console ever made and put the movie in. I sat down on the couch and opened up my soda and ate a chip with salsa on it. He turned the lights off and sat down beside me as the previews started to play. I relaxed into the couch and felt the stress on my shoulders. Billy sat back against the couch beside me and clicked the menu button to start the movie. I smiled excitedly as the movie started to play. I could practically say each line along with the movie, but I kept quiet so Billy could enjoy the movie as well. Halfway through the movie a message blinked at the bottom of the screen. Billy sighed. "Breaking news alert again."

I turned to him and asked with a shaky voice, "Can you turn to it?"

He shrugged. "Sure. I'm surprised you want to after how much has already gone on."

I frowned harder. "I haven't heard anything. Darren has been keeping me and Bret away from the television so we haven't heard about what's going on at all."

Billy's mouth fell open. "So you don't know what's happening?" I shook my head. "Then you need to watch this." He hit pause on the movie and changed inputs to go to the news.

The reporter was the same monotone reporter we had seen at the diner. His face seemed more solemn than before. "Another attack and another country completely decimated..."

I turned to Billy. "What is he talking about?" He shushed me and pointed at the television. Pictures started flashing on the TV of a city with buildings on fire and hundreds of dead bodies everywhere. I gasped. "What's happening?" The look on my face shifted from curiosity to disbelief.

The reporter came back on screen. "The entire country of Mongolia is completely devoid of human life." The bodies in every town have all been found left in the same state of mutilation: their throats ripped out and their blood drained. Some even seem animal ravaged, but we believe that may be from scavengers who smell the decaying corpses. We haven't been able to find a single shred of evidence as to the cause. Scientists are baffled, saying that they do not believe this is some type of disease, but no answers have been found as to what or *who* has been causing this. Video surveillance is unable to pick up anything either. So far the following places have been hit... Japan, Russia, North and South Korea, Nevada and now Mongolia."

I gasped. "Oh my God! Why wouldn't Darren let us know about this?! It's kind of important."

Billy shrugged. "I don't know."

The shock slowly set in, "We were just in Tahoe. What if we had been there..." I remembered Darren making us leave so quickly from Tahoe and then it had been massacred. *Could Darren be in on it?* I shook my head dismissing that thought. I stood up. "I have to go."

Billy stood up and followed me to the door. "Okay, but will you come back?"

"Not tonight. Thank you for a great afternoon." I put on my best smile and put a hand on the doorknob.

He held up one finger. "Hold on. I got you something." He walked over to his bags and rummaged through them. I twitched nervously as he came back with a small white box. He handed it to me. "Here, I thought you would like this."

I opened the little white lid and gasped. A silver chain with a silver wolf hanging from it glittered in the white box. I stared at the small wolf and whispered, "It's beautiful."

He kissed me lightly on the lips. "You can come by anytime you want."

I smiled at him and kissed his cheek. "Thanks. I love the necklace, and I'll hold you to that offer." I ran from the house to his truck and grabbed my backpack. It still didn't feel right when Billy kissed me. *Was it just me since I hadn't been kissed before?* I ran down the road, past the feed store and the side street that led to Bret's house and out of the town's cozy little feeling to my house. Darren sat on the front porch cleaning one of his shotguns. I frowned at him as I walked up the steps. "You shoot one of the wolves?" I asked nervously.

He shook his head then sighed. "I wasn't going to kill the wolf Artemis. I was just going to scare it a little." He looked at the necklace box and sunglasses on my head and smiled. "Bret get you those?"

I shook my head. "No, Billy did. Bret and I aren't speaking right now."

He frowned. "Not speaking? When have you ever not been speaking? What happened?"

I groaned. "I don't want to talk about it. I *do* want to talk about what's been going on that you've been hiding from us. Why didn't you tell us that people are dying or being killed? That's kind of important, Dad! Especially when it happens at a place right after we leave."

He flinched. "I know. I was just trying to keep you kids happy and not worrying about what was going on."

I shook my head. "You knew about the attack in Tahoe. How?"

"I can't tell you that." He said sternly.

I groaned. "You are always keeping secrets from me, you have ever since I was born. Why?"

He shook his head. "I can't tell you. I'm sorry. If I tell you it will put you in danger and I want you to be safe and happy."

I sighed then turned around when I heard someone running down the street. Bret was running up our road with his necklace shining in the sun. I groaned. "Great. Just freaking great."

Bret looked down at my necklace box and frowned, but turned to Darren. "What the hell Darren? Why didn't you tell us what was going on?"

"I've heard this, so I'm going inside to pack better." I walked away leaving the boys to talk and went to my room. I pulled out more pairs of underwear and a couple of pajama tops and bottoms and shoved them into my backpack.

I heard Bret come in my room, but ignored him and zipped up my bag. He whispered, "So, how was your day?"

I shrugged. "It was great until my best friend called me a slut and I found out my dad has been hiding things from me."

Bret sighed. "I'm sorry Artemis. I didn't mean what I said."

I raised my hand stopping him and looked up into his eyes. Tears had started to well up in mine. "Don't apologize for something you meant."

He wrapped his arms around me. "I didn't mean it!"

I shrugged and pulled out of his embrace. "Whatever. I'll be at Billy's if you need me." I started to walk out of the room and Bret grabbed me by the arms and kissed my lips hard. I felt the strength he had in his hands and knew I couldn't fight him off even though his kiss sent my stomach rolling.

He pulled back from the kiss and whispered, "Please don't go over there. I'm better than him. Stay with me. Please."

I stared up at his face and knew that if I didn't go with him that it would crush him. Yet the disgust I felt each time I was kissed by him or Billy was too much to deal with. "I'm sorry Bret. I need some time alone."

Bret frowned. "You can't go out alone with the wolves constantly showing up."

I snarled at him. "I can do whatever I want. Besides, I'm sure you need time to go see Skankzilla." I pulled away from him and walked out of the house. If it had been any other girl than Skankzilla I wouldn't have cared since I didn't like him in that way. Why her? Why my nemesis?

Darren called after me, "Where you going?"

I yelled, "Away from you!"

"She's trying to go somewhere alone," Bret said angrily.

Darren frowned at me. "You going to the stable?" I nodded my head. Darren quickly put his gun back together and handed it to me. "Take this then. Just in case you need it."

SONG OF THE MOON

I slung my bag over my shoulders and took the gun and the box of shells sitting next to Darren. "Thanks."

I walked away from Bret, who was frowning in frustration at Darren for not stopping me, and through our field. The stable sat in the center of our property and was basically an empty building for the horses and cows to use to get out of the sun, rain or snow. The trees swayed slightly in the breeze and birds and insects chirped and clicked and built an endless stream of music as I walked. I raised my arms to the wind and reveled in the feel of it against my skin. The outdoors had always drawn me more than buildings. The forest felt like a friend waiting for me to walk with. And I could feel the moon's presence like a buzzing in my veins, though I couldn't see her. I jogged through the pastures past grazing cattle until I finally came to the stable. The building was dark brown instead of red and I could see a few horses dozing inside under the shade. I approached slowly making kissing noises so I wouldn't frighten them. The horses bobbed their heads and waited patiently for me to come to them. I stroked the three horses' heads and crooned and cooed to them. Two feral cats stared at me from their perches on the beams. Cats had never liked me or Darren so the only cats that we got were the feral ones who ate mice in the stable. In the back east corner was a ladder that led up to the small loft.

I climbed up and shook out the bedroll to make sure there weren't any creepy crawlies hiding within the folds. The horses nickered and snorted and talked to each other relaxing my nerves. I set the gun against the wall and opened the necklace box. The wolf charm sparkled in the sunlight that was streaming through the windows. I picked the charm up in my hand and screamed in pain as it burned my fingertips. I dropped the charm and stared at the red blisters now present on my fingertips. The silver burned me? I held my palm out flat and laid it against the charm and screamed again as the charm burned me. "What the hell?!" I cradled my hand against my chest and squinted against the tears trying to squeeze out. *Something isn't right.* I needed to get cream for the burn or it would get infected. "So much for my alone time." I muttered as I used the bedroll to put the necklace back in its box and close the lid. I grabbed the gun again and grimaced at the pain from holding the gun against my burn. I climbed down from the loft and ran through the pastures towards Bret's house.

I hadn't forgiven him, but I needed to take care of my burns and I didn't want to see Darren or Billy. *How could I explain that the necklace burned me?* Bret's house came into view and I saw him sitting on his back porch talking on the phone. As soon as he saw me he hung up and ran out to meet me. "Hey."

I frowned and looked down at the ground. "I haven't forgiven you, but I hurt my hand and need to treat it before it gets infected. So, even though I'm still mad at you can I please stay the night?"

Bret nodded his head and held his hand out for the gun. I gave it to him and gritted my teeth as I released the cold metal from my burnt hand. I followed him into the house and into the bathroom. He tried to help me with it, but I told him to leave. I sat down on the toilet and stared at the wolf-shaped burn on my palm. I squeezed burn ointment on it and wrapped gauze around my hand. I smeared some ointment on my fingertips and walked out to the living room where Bret was watching a movie.

I kept quiet the rest of the night so that I wouldn't start any more trouble between us. I leaned against Bret as I started to get tired. He put his arm around me and rubbed my arm as he watched the movie. I rested against his familiar body basking in his familiar cologne. I used to hate cologne, but Bret's had just become his smell. I shivered and Bret walked to the closet and got a large afghan out. He laid down against the back of the couch and I laid down in front of him as he wrapped us up together.

He put his arm out and I laid my head on it in the perfect curve of his elbow. This had become such a common occurrence that I could be practically incoherent and still do this. Although doing it now felt wrong somehow. I shook my head and ignored that thought.

I was almost asleep when I heard two gun shots. Bret jumped up and we ran to the window to see what was going on. Billy stood a few feet in front of Bret's house facing away from us and aiming his gun into a clump of trees. I stared into the trees and saw the reflection of amber eyes. Wolves. I ran to the door, flinging it open and ran outside. The wolves had started to walk towards Billy, snarling. I ran in front of Billy and put my arms out in front of me, "No. You three leave!"

The wolves stopped and stared at me. I instantly recognized the three wolves as the ones that had been around the area today. They looked extremely large, but were always too far away for me to be able to tell. The middle one was obviously the alpha and took a step forward so I mimicked him by taking a step towards him. Billy started to grab me, but I waved him away. Bret whispered loudly, "What are you doing?"

"Trying to show the wolf that he is not dominant to me. I am alpha here, not him," I answered quietly.

Bret groaned. "Great, you're going to make the wolf attack you."

I shook my head at him then squared my legs and stared straight in the wolf's eyes. He stared back at me, unwilling to be seen as submissive. One of the other two wolves nudged the alpha in his side. The alpha's hackles rose and he snarled. I stayed perfectly still and for once wished I had a tail so I could show that I wasn't scared of him. The other wolf nudged the alpha and the strangest thing happened...the alpha sighed. The alpha snapped his teeth at me and then ran off into the trees with his two pack members. I turned to Billy and saw the white of his face. "What's wrong? They weren't really going to hurt you Billy." I reached out to him and he backed away.

"Don't touch me Artemis," he said quickly as he backed up.

I stared at him in shock. "Why are you acting like you are afraid of me? All I did was use some of my nerdy research to show the head wolf that I wasn't afraid of him. I did it to save your life. It's not like I *talked* to the damn wolf."

Bret stood beside me and stared at Billy. "Dude, what is your problem?"

Billy shook his head. "You can't expect me to believe that you just used common wolf knowledge to show you were tougher. You *had* to have been communicating with him."

I rolled my eyes. "Right, communicate with a wolf. Have you lost your mind?"

He shook his head. "I'm sorry Artemis, but I can't see you anymore." I frowned at him and was about to say something when he tossed me a large box. "Here, now you don't need mine."

I stared at the box and read the label. "Pay as you go cell phone. Uh, thanks."

He nodded his head then ran down the street away from us. Bret folded his arms across his chest. "No wonder the wolf was going to eat him. Billy's a puss."

I nodded my head and walked back inside the house, opening the cell phone box as I went. I put the phone together and plugged it in so that I could use it to call Koda tomorrow. Hopefully he would answer. Bret turned on the news channel and we laid back down on the couch under the afghan. I sighed in contentment against his arm as my body warmed back up.

The monotone news reporter came on the channel looking as somber as ever. "What I am about to show you is very disturbing. If you have small children or sensitive individuals you should make them leave the room." I looked back at Bret and he shrugged, staring at the TV.

"A cell phone caught footage of an attack in London. We aren't sure how the video got to the internet, but sources believe the boy had set his phone to automatically send when he was done recording. Please, brace yourselves for what you are about to see." A new grainy video came on the screen showing a dark London night where two men were surrounded by people as they prepared to fight. Just as one of the men arched back to throw his punch two of the people in the circle around them started screaming and were thrown across the road and into a building. Their bodies made disgustingly, loud, wet thuds as they hit the brick wall. Everyone started looking around unable to see what was going on. Four more people in the circle disappeared screaming only to land a few blocks away on the cement, no longer breathing.

White mist appeared around one of the fighters and he screamed in pain then was flying through the air. The second fighter and the boy with the phone started to run, but three more patches of mist appeared in front of them. They started to back up and then the mist sped forward wrapping around them and their screams stopped with a loud crack and a strange hissing sound. I turned to Bret and saw he had the same shocked and scared expression on his face. The news reporter came back on. "As you can see, it appears that the strange mist is causing these deaths, but we aren't sure how the mist is capable of doing the physical damage we have seen done to the bodies. Some have had their throats torn out, some have had their necks broken and others have been found completely drained of blood. We will continue to keep you updated as we learn of new developments."

Bret turned off the television and I shuddered against him. He wrapped his arms around me and I wrapped the blanket tighter around us. I closed my eyes, willing them to forget the horrified expressions frozen on the victims' faces as they were thrown through the air. *What could cause this? What is the mist?* I shivered at the thought of what this could mean for us and closed my eyes. Bret stood up and carried me to his bedroom. He gently laid me down then climbed in bed with me. I got into our sleeping position with my head on his chest and sighed as our bodies heated up the sheets around us and the heavy comforter made me feel even more secure. Bret hummed a soft song as I fell into a deep sleep.

The *branches stung as they hit my face. I ran as fast as I could, trying to keep up with Darren. He dashed and dodged and jumped over and around trees and bushes. I started to fall behind him and yelled for him to wait, but he ignored me. I could hear the wolves getting closer and I knew I didn't want to die. I increased my speed, but the wolves continued to gain ground. I could see Darren just ahead in a clearing and a small spark of hope seeped through me. I ducked under a low tree branch then stopped running. Darren's body twitched and convulsed then fur sprung out from under his skin. The wet splitting sound made me cringe in disgust, but what stood in Darren's place replaced my disgust with awe. A medium-sized brown wolf stood over Darren's shredded human skin. I stared at this wolf and gasped as its eyes turned to me. "Dad?" The wolf nodded its head and then bound away as the wolves following us pounced on top of me.*

I screamed and sat upright. I looked around and realized I was safe in Bret's bed. He opened one eye and looked at me sleepily. "Dream?" he asked with a yawn. I nodded my head. He pulled me back down and hugged me against him. "'S alright. I'm here."

I relaxed against him and tried to shake off the bad feeling. I wasn't sure I *was* alright. *It was just a dream. Darren can't become a wolf. That's crazy.* I nodded my head making myself firmly believe what I said and closed my eyes.

SONG OF THE MOON

"Artemis. Artemis honey, wake up," Bret whispered in my ear.

I groaned. "Five more minutes."

He laughed softly. "Breakfast is ready."

I inhaled and smelled bacon and eggs. I licked my lips hungrily and sat up. "Well let's go!" I jumped out of the bed and jogged to the kitchen. I stopped in the entryway and gasped. "You cleaned?"

He walked past me and nodded his head smiling. "I knew it bothered you, so I cleaned."

I looked around the immaculate kitchen and smiled. "It's great Bret! I can't believe you did such a good job. I'm impressed."

He bowed at the waist and draped a hand towel across his arm. "A table, m'lady?" I curtsied and walked to the small dining table, where he pulled out a chair for me and I sat down in it. He laid the hand towel across my lap and pushed my seat in.

I inhaled the smell of the delicious looking food and licked my lips. He sat down across from me and nodded his head. I started shoveling food on to my plate and groaned in happiness when I saw the homemade waffles. I drowned all of my food in syrup and butter and started eating. I ate slowly enjoying the food and tasting everything in my mouth and chewing thoroughly. Darren sighed behind me and I growled. I turned around and he smiled at me. "Guess her eating your food slow means she likes it more than mine."

Bret shrugged and I glared at him mouthing, "Traitor." He rolled his eyes at me then smiled at Darren. "Come sit down. We just started eating."

Darren sat down next to Bret and looked at my plate. "I can see that."

I rolled my eyes at him and kept eating. Darren quietly spooned food on his plate while I started to eat my food faster. Bret cleared his throat. "The wolves were back again."

Darren stopped moving and stared at me. "What happened?"

I ignored him and kept eating. Bret sighed again. "They were being aggressive to Billy and he shot at them, but he apparently missed. Well Artemis ran out and yelled at them to leave and the head one the?" Bret turned to me. "The alphy?"

I sighed and set my fork down. "The alpha. The alpha male took a step forward and tried to show dominance to me and I did it right back to him. He was contemplating what to do when his two pack mates nudged him and I swear to God he sighed."

Darren frowned. "Sighed?

I nodded my head. "Yes, he sighed and then he snapped his teeth at me and they left."

Darren groaned and put his head in his hands. "Oh, no. He snapped his teeth at you?" I nodded my head and he groaned again. "Shit! I knew this would happen one day, but why now. Dammit!"

I stared at him in shock. "What are you going on about?"

He looked up slowly at me and sighed. "Nothing."

"Why are you being so secretive all of a sudden?" I asked angrily. Darren ignored me, eating more of his food. Apparently this was a battle I couldn't win right now. "Fine, be that way. I'll be leaving after I finish eating." Bret started to eat faster and I waved my hand at him. "I'm going alone."

He sighed. "You shouldn't go alone with the wolves out."

Darren scoffed. "She'll be fine. They won't hurt her." We both stared at Darren and he shrugged. "She showed him she was dominant. If he wanted to hurt her, he would have done it then."

I nodded my head. "He's right Bret. Wolves aren't smart enough to plan a later attack." Darren scoffed again and rolled his eyes. He saw us looking at him and resumed eating. I shoveled the rest of my food into my mouth and walked to the plugged in cell phone. I waved at Bret and Darren. "I have a cell phone if you need to reach me. I'll be back for lunch."

I handed Darren the piece of paper I had written the phone number on.

Darren frowned at my bandaged hand. "What happened to your hand?"

I pulled my hand away. "Nothing."

I ran out of the house carrying the phone in my pocket. I ran through the town ignoring the younger boys' calls and the stares of Billy and his group of friends. I knew by now he had told them what a freak I was for being able to communicate with the wolves. Boys are so dumb sometimes. I knew I would definitely have no friends when Bret left and that actually made me sad. I sighed and increased my speed, pushing my limits to get to the lake as fast as possible. I finally got to the lake, thankful to find no one there. It was too early in the morning for anyone to want to try to swim. I sat down on the dock at the very end so I could dangle my legs in the water. I took out the cell phone and the piece of paper with Koda's number on it and took a deep cleansing breath. I quickly punched in the numbers and hit send.

The phone rang four times before someone answered. "Hello?"

I stopped breathing for a second then exhaled. "Koda?"

Koda sighed. "Artemis."

I nodded my head then realized he couldn't see me. "Yeah, how'd you know?"

He laughed. "Only four people have this number and two are with me and the other is a man so it kind of narrowed it down. What's up? Are you alright?"

I sighed. "No, I need to ask you some questions."

He was silent on the other end for a full two minutes before finally talking again. "Ask and I'll see if I can answer or not."

"Why am I dreaming about your friend?" I asked quickly before I lost my courage.

"What are you talking about?" He asked softly.

"I've been having these weird dreams and the man that was with you has been in them. I have had them for the past week and a half."

He whispered, "Exactly how many days?"

I thought back to when I had the first one and answered, "Ten days."

He groaned. "Shit. How do you know it was my friend and not just you dreaming about someone who looks like him?"

I asked, "Is his name Ares?"

Koda went silent again. I couldn't even hear him breathing. His voice boomed back making me pull the receiver away from my ear. "What happened in the dreams?! Tell me every little detail!"

"Calm down," I said into the phone.

He growled. "I don't have time to be calm. Now answer my questions." I quickly explained my dreams to him. He groaned softly. "Hold on one minute."

"Alright," I said with a sigh. He talked quietly away from the phone, but I couldn't understand what he was saying. I heard a man with a thick British accent talking back to him, but still couldn't understand what they were saying. I kicked my feet around in the water as I grew impatient.

Koda came back on. "Alright. I can't really say anything to you except that they are just dreams."

"Why are you being so secretive with me?"

"It's your father's fault. If he had told you about us, there wouldn't be a problem. Shit, you would probably be with us right now." I felt my breath whoosh out of my lungs and tried to think about what he had just said. Koda grunted. "Shit. That was too much information."

I inhaled and asked, "Is your friend's name Ares?"

Koda groaned. "Yes, that's all I'm going to say though."

I nodded my head. "Fine. Well I did have another dream last night as well."

Koda sighed in exasperation. "Tell me." I explained the dream about my father and he sighed again. "You've been in contact with wild wolves."

It wasn't a question, but I answered anyways. "Well, sort of. There was a group of three wolves at the lake and I swore one of them looked just like the wolf in my dreams that turned into Ares and I just felt compelled to go to him. Well his other two pack mates pushed him away. Then this morning the same group of wolves were being aggressive and I showed the alpha a sign that I was dominant and he was debating what to do when his pack mates nudged him and I swear I heard him sigh. Then they left."

Koda scoffed. "He sighed. You know it's not very smart to show an alpha dominance when you aren't."

"What should I have done? Let him eat Bret's friend?" I said defensively.

He laughed. "It might have been funny."

"The asshole would have deserved it. He thought I was *communicating* with the wolves. How stupid is that?"

"Look Artemis. I can't really tell you much and I'm sorry for that. I do have a feeling that we will be seeing you soon though."

"I have two more questions."

He groaned. "What?"

"Do you know what the white mist is and if it is going to come here?" I asked.

He exhaled. "You have to keep this completely secret. Even from you friend, okay?"

"Okay."

He whispered quickly, "I do know what the mist is and I promise it will not come for your town and you will be perfectly safe. Consider the wolves and your dreams a good omen."

I sighed as the heavy weight was lifted from my shoulders. "Okay. One more thing. Why does silver burn my skin?"

Koda spoke in another language fast and loud. I assumed he was cussing, but couldn't be sure. "I can't say anything. Just don't touch silver. Did any of it get in your blood?"

"No, just burned my palm."

"Good. Don't worry Artemis. Soon you will be experiencing a lot of different things. I'll see you soon."

I yelled, "How soon?"

"A few weeks probably. We'll find out for sure next week."

"What happens next week?" I asked.

He laughed. "Can't tell you. Bye Artemis."

"Wait! Why did you know that we had to leave Tahoe and how did you get out okay?"

"Bye, Artemis," he said again.

"Bye, Koda." I pressed the end button and stared at the phone in my hand. Why was everyone so secretive? I hate secrets and surprises. I remembered that Koda had said they would be coming soon and felt butterflies flip around in my stomach at the thought of seeing Ares again. "Just what I need, a crush on some older guy who won't be interested in me." I walked slowly back home and didn't care how late it was when I got there. It would only take me ten minutes at the most to get home anyway. *Stupid small town.*

I heard someone walking behind me and stopped and turned around. Billy stood smiling behind me. "What is it Billy?"

"I'm sorry I overreacted today," he said softly.

I scoffed. "Right. Calling me the wolf whisperer was just a small overreaction."

"I just said I was sorry." He started to move closer to me and I held my hand up.

"I thought you said we couldn't see each other anymore Billy? Why the change?"

He smiled. "I changed my mind. I don't want to be away from you."

I remembered what Bret had said about him being a horndog and asked, "Is it me or my body you don't want to be away from?"

He stopped moving and the smile left his lips. "What's that supposed to mean? I haven't tried anything with you."

I shrugged. "From what I've heard you think mostly with your smaller head and you're just being nice today so you can pressure me tomorrow."

Billy snarled. "That bastard will say anything to keep you to himself! I swear I am going to kick his white ass!" He started walking quickly down the road to Bret's house. I knew I should stop him, but this was actually a fight I wanted to see. We arrived at Bret's house quickly and Billy yelled from the yard, "Come out come out wherever you are! You pussy ass liar!"

I stared in shock at the angry Billy who was somehow more attractive now. Bret walked out of the house with no shirt on smiling. "Hey bro, what's up?"

Billy shook his head. "Don't call me bro! You tell Artemis the truth right now or I'm going to whip your ass!"

Bret shrugged smiling smugly. "I did tell her the truth! I'm better than you."

Billy looked at me. "You didn't tell me that part."

I shrugged. "It didn't seem important at the time."

Billy turned around and glared at Bret again. "Tell her the truth!"

Bret smiled. "You aren't better than me. That's the truth."

Billy charged up the steps and slammed into Bret, knocking him down on the ground. Billy was one of the strongest football players on the team. I had seem him bench pressing and couldn't even add up all the weights that were on the bar. Billy started punching Bret in the face. Bret shoved Billy backwards and jumped up. Darren walked calmly out of the house and past the fighting boys to stand next to me. "What's going on?"

"Not much. Bret said Billy was a horndog and that he is better and now they are fighting," I said.

Darren smiled. "So, they're fighting over you?"

I frowned and then thought about it. "Shit! Now you tell me!" I ran over to the boys and threw myself between them. Bret threw a punch that barely missed my face. "Hey!" I yelled as I ducked down. Bret at least had the decency to blush. "Look, I didn't really think this through. Now stop fighting."

Billy shook his head. "Not until he tells you the truth!"

"Fine. Artemis he isn't a horndog. He's a freaking spineless virgin!"

I stared at Bret in shock. "Why is that a bad thing? I'm a virgin."

Bret's face fell. "No, it's different for girls."

"You're one too." I said quietly, nervous of his answer.

Bret sighed. "No, I'm not."

Billy smiled smugly. "He's been telling you that so he had a better chance of screwing you."

Bret punched at Billy and I kicked Bret in the shin. "We are done Bret!" I ran into the house and grabbed my bag. I walked out of the house furious and shaking with anger. "I should let my dad kick your ass!"

Darren smiled and waved bye to me. I walked away with Billy walking beside me silently. We got halfway through town and I stopped walking, turning to look at Billy. "Why didn't you tell me about Bret?"

"What was I supposed to say? 'Hey Artemis, Bret's really just trying to get in your pants, but he is lying to you to do it'?"

I smiled. "Yeah that would have worked."

He scoffed. "Right, and then I wouldn't have him as a friend anymore because I broke the guy code."

I rolled my eyes. "The guy code. Stupid!" I realized I had no clue who Bret had slept with or anything. "Billy, who has Bret slept with?"

He cringed. "You sure you want me to answer that?"

I gasped. "Skanzilla! That's why she is always hanging on him and hates me so bad. Because he's been screwing her! That bastard!" I felt my body heating up more and groaned as I fell to the ground and started convulsing.

Billy held me down and whispered, "Breathe Artemis. Come on, stop the seizure."

I gritted my teeth and focused on calming myself down. The twitching finally stopped and I exhaled. The doctors always thought I was lying when I told them that I could stop the seizures, but obviously they were wrong. I looked up at Billy and asked, "How'd you know?"

He smiled. "Bret told us in case he wasn't there and you needed help."

I smiled back at him. "Thanks. You can let me up now."

He kissed my lips softly. "I don't want to let you up."

I suddenly felt pinned and my body started to heat up again. I thrashed against him, but he held me down. I screamed in anger and fear of being trapped and pushed against him lifting him up off the ground. *TRAPPED!* I fought with my mind to make it realize that I wasn't trapped, but nothing worked.

Darren appeared over the top of me and saw the fear in my eyes. "Billy get off of her!" Billy stepped away and Darren backed up too.

I sat up slowly and slowed my breathing down so I wouldn't hyperventilate. Billy shook his head. "What happened?"

Darren rubbed the back of his neck, a mirror of Bret's nervous habit. "She got scared and well...its hard to explain."

"Sorry." I said, embarrassed.

"Are you okay now?" Billy asked. I nodded my head and he smiled. "Good. Now let's go." I let him grab my hand and pull me up to a standing position. Once I had my balance I kissed his cheek. He smiled wider. "What was that for?"

I smiled back. "For being understanding about my...uh...stuff."

He shrugged. "You're too much of a catch to let a few minor things bother me."

I started walking away with Billy when Darren cleared his throat. I turned around to glare at him. "What?"

"When will you be home?"

I shrugged. "Why do you care?"

He frowned and spoke in his 'don't talk back' tone, "Artemis."

I sighed. "Tonight. You and I have things to talk about anyway."

He cringed. "What stuff?"

I smiled. "Things Koda and I were discussing."

He growled. "What did he tell you?! And when did you talk to him?"

I shrugged and turned away, dragging Billy along with me. "Interesting things. Bye Darren."

Billy walked with me as I skipped like an elementary school girl. "What was that about?"

I smiled and started walking instead of skipping. "Apparently my dad has been withholding information about my past so I have to make him sweat a little." Darren and I had never been close. He provided for me and I never starved or anything like that, but he had never been emotionally open to me. I'd never felt loved by him. He didn't act like he loved me. I'd always blamed it on my mother's disappearance, but maybe it was more than that. I needed to get out of the town and away from Darren as soon as I could.

We arrived at Billy's house to find J.D. and Jess sitting on the porch. Billy smiled at them. "What's up guys?"

Jess and J.D. stared at us in shock for a second before smiling. Jess held up a bottle of whiskey. "We come bearing gifts."

Billy licked his lips then looked at me. "You don't have to drink if you don't want to."

I shrugged. "I've never tried it before."

Jess laughed. "Oh, girl, you are in for a great night!"

We walked into the house and sat down around the kitchen table. J.D. grabbed four red plastic cups and poured some of the alcohol into each glass. I sniffed the cup and gagged. It was horrible smelling, like rubbing alcohol.

Billy laughed. "Don't smell it! Just down it."

I stared at the brown liquid. "Down it?"

J.D. tipped his cup up and gulped down the drink in one swallow. "Woo!" He yelled.

Jess smiled. "Like that." She held up her cup towards me. "Ready?"

I lifted mine up and hit the side against hers. "I guess." I looked at the liquid one more time then tipped the cup up and swallowed. The liquid burned my throat and I exhaled and set the cup down. "Whoa."

Billy poured another round and raised his cup. "Cheers!"

We all hit cups then downed the alcohol. My stomach felt warm for a moment as the liquid settled then the warmth disappeared. J.D. frowned. "You sure you haven't drunk before?"

Jess giggled beside me. "I'm a lightweight no matter how much I drink!"

Billy snorted. "You're just a lush!"

Jess rolled her eyes. "You're a boozer!"

I could see the difference in Jess already, but I didn't feel any different. J.D. poured another round and we touched cups then downed yet another drink. Billy took out a deck of cards and taught me a drinking game which consisted of taking as many shots as corresponded to the card you pulled. Jess and J.D.'s eyes became glazed over and they started acting drunk. Billy was slurring his words and smiling a lot. I frowned as I realized I didn't feel any different. I went to the bathroom for the fifth time and as I walked out of the restroom ran into Billy. He wrapped his arms around me and I felt instantly disgusted as his alcohol breath stole my fresh oxygen. He tried to kiss me and I pushed him away heading for the door.

Billy frowned and followed me. "What's wrong? Aren't you having any fun?"

J.D. scoffed. "No 'cus we're drunk and she's not. Artemis has been holding out on us."

I rolled my eyes and smiled at Billy. "I have to see my dad, remember?"

"Are you coming back tonight?" He asked.

I shook my head. "No, but you can come over in the morning and I'll make you breakfast."

He pulled me against him in a hug. "That sounds great."

I pulled away from him feeling released and grabbed my backpack. "Bye."

He let me go and waved as I walked down his porch steps. Once I was in the night completely I stopped and inhaled. I had always loved the night time. It was like more sights and sounds and smells came alive in the dark. I stared up at the half moon and smiled. The full moon would be here soon. I could feel her song flowing through my body like a second pulse. The full moon always made me feel safer and more powerful. As if that made any sense. I jogged across town towards my house and inhaled loudly trying to separate the different smells. I reached the house much faster than I had wanted to and looked up at the moon one last time before walking up the porch. Darren sat in one of the chairs staring at me. I smiled. "Hey, Dad."

"What did he tell you?" He asked with a big frown on his face.

"Nothing really. He said that if I had known about our past that I would probably be with them right now. Then he said that they would be coming to visit in a few weeks and we would know for sure in the next week."

Darren frowned. "Why would they visit? They have no reason to come here." He groaned. "Unless it's to discuss a punishment for me not telling you. Dammit."

I shrugged. "I'm not worried about it. He said that mist won't be harming our town so I'm not scared anymore."

Darren smiled. "The mist would never come near our town with me here. Bastards."

I frowned. "You say that like the mist are people. What the hell is it?"

He shook his head. "If you knew they would *definitely* come for us."

Darren's evasiveness proved that he was hiding something big. I needed to find a way to get out of the town and soon. Someway, somehow I would leave. I took out a frozen bean burrito and popped it in the microwave. I heard Darren come in and ignored him as he sat down on the couch and turned on the TV. The microwave dinged scaring me. I took out the burrito which had split open and hurried to my room. I sighed and ate my burrito slowly. A quiet chiming made me stop eating. I looked down at my pants and remembered I had the cell phone still. I took it out and stared at the number. "Koda." I smiled then frowned wondering why he was calling. I flipped open the phone and answered, "Hello?"

The person on the other end was silent for a second and then sighed heavily. His voice made me shiver in delight. "I thought you were a figment of my imagination at the hotel, but everything is the same."

I felt my hands shaking and my heart beat pick up as I recognized the voice. "Who is this?"

He laughed softly. "Do you really need to ask?"

"No. I...I'm just confused."

"I know you are and it's your father's fault. You would be able to understand the connection an alpha male has with a new female if he had told you."

"Alpha male? You mean like wolves? What are you talking about?" I asked, clearly confused.

He scoffed. "That's what I mean. You have no idea! I can't talk long because Koda will have a cow if he finds out that I am talking to you since it breaks all the rules, but I had to hear your voice. I had to know that you weren't just a girl in my dreams that I made real at the hotel."

I gasped in shock. "You've been dreaming of me?"

He laughed quietly. "Yes, every night for the past ten days. I can't explain what's going on between us because I'm not completely sure. Has Koda told you that we are coming to get you?"

"Get me? Where are you taking me?" I asked, suddenly nervous, though I wasn't sure if it was a good or bad nervousness.

"We are taking you with us to where you belong. You do not belong in that town with those...*people*. I'm not sure how long before we get there, but I will come for you. I have to go."

I felt my heartbeat becoming frantic. "Wait! Don't go! Please!"

"Don't worry. I will speak with you again and I will see you soon as well. Sweet dreams, little wolf lover."

"Bye, Ares," I said quietly. I'd wanted to say more, but it didn't seem right. I turned the phone off and tossed the left over burrito and plate in the trash can. Paper plates are very convenient sometimes. I took my pants and bra off and climbed into bed under the covers. I played his voice over in my head and smiled knowing he was coming for me.

CHAPTER THREE

The rest of the week went by quickly with Billy coming for breakfast every morning in place of Bret and us spending the entire day together. He was extremely understanding and fun and luckily hadn't tried to kiss me again. Darren grumbled a lot, but didn't say anything to us. The news stories continued on the television with no new leads. Darren watched the news and told me that he would let us know if anything new came up. I didn't worry because I knew Ares was coming for me. I never told Darren because it seemed like he didn't like Ares. I had gone without worrying almost a full week until Friday night, when Bret ran into our house. It was just before eight o'clock and the sun was starting to set, casting purple and red hues across the sky. I could feel night coming like a chill creeping up my arms to my neck. Bret spoke quickly to Darren and Billy, then turned and ran from the house.

Darren sighed and turned to me, "Apparently there is new information we need to hear. Everyone is gathering at the pub." We walked quickly from the house towards the pub.

The town's streets and buildings sat deserted with an unnatural silence. The only light and noise was coming from the pub. Children were placed in a separate room, left to play, so that they wouldn't watch what was happening. I stood in front with Darren as the news reporter began talking. Billy had walked to the back with the other teens.

The reporter, a man with a deep voice and salt-and-pepper hair, sat in front of a stone wall wearing jeans and a t-shirt. He whispered and looked around warily, "The scene here in Washington is chaos and devastation. Some are calling it the end of the world. Revelations and doomsday. I don't know what to call it, except gruesome. It started three hours ago at full dark. Humans started falling down, their throats cut or ripped out by something with claws. Some found in dark alleys with their blood completely drained from their bodies and two small puncture wounds on their necks. No one has been able to catch a glimpse of the attackers as they move faster than the wind and just as quietly."

The cameraman crept forward showing the hundreds of bodies littering the streets of Washington. Blood ran down the drains like rain. Cars were turned upside down and some were even on fire. The street lamps cast a halo around a group of three teenagers' bodies lying on top of each other.

The reporter cleared his throat making the cameraman turn back to him. "It appears to be the same situation as what is happening all over the world, but we appear to be the only survivors in town. We don't know if the attackers are moving on, or have stopped. I wish we could be more help, but..." The reporter was seen suddenly flying through the air, screaming as he sailed into the side of a building, smacking it with a solid thud.

The cameraman panned around frantically, trying to see what had done it, but nothing was visible. We all watched as he stared down a dark alley, his breathing speeding up. He swallowed hard and whispered, "Fuck." It looked as though the mist sped forward and wrapped around him, but the camera fell and the screen went black as we heard his screaming begin.

Darren turned off the television and turned to everyone with sad eyes. "We have to start our plan."

Glen, the oldest in town, nodded his head. "Darren's right. Something killed those people and its getting closer."

Darren spoke before any of the others could. "Tomorrow morning, meet at my place at five. Bring your guns. If we all know how to use a gun we might stand a chance against them. Or at least go down swinging."

I walked back to the rest of the teenagers who sat in the back of the room, whispering quietly. "Hey guys." The three girls and four boys looked up at me. I sighed. "Come on. It's not that bad. We are in such a small town that I doubt these things would come after us, whatever they are."

Trixie, Skankzilla's youngest sister, shook her head. "No. Did you see what happened? Whatever it is will find us. It was like fog. How can fog hurt you?!"

Bret sighed and stood up. "Artemis is right. We just have to get ready and prepare for any possibility. Nothing is invincible."

Skankzilla rolled her eyes. "Of course you agree with her. When haven't you agreed with her?"

I ignored her comment because it didn't matter anymore. I would leave soon and this would all be over with. The children came in from the other room and were reunited with their families. The quiet whispers of each family showed how scared each was. Each group began to disperse to their homes, to get ready for bed. Billy led me from the pub out to the dark night. I pulled away from him and inhaled the sweet smell of night and basked in the moon's glow. I closed my eyes and stopped walking. I love the night.

Billy laughed. "I swear, if I didn't know better, I'd say you were a vampire or something."

"Yes, let me suck your blood." I said in a mock accent.

Skankzilla smiled. "I bet he has something you could suck."

I turned to her and let my anger loose. "Shut up you dirty whore! I've had enough of you!" I started to move towards her, and then smiled. "You know what...it's not worth it. I'll be out of here in a week anyway."

Billy frowned. "A week? Where are you going?"

I was about to answer him when Darren came up. "Tomorrow we are waking up early to start preparing, so we need to go home."

"What are we preparing for?" I asked.

Darren sighed. "Come on girl, let's get home."

Billy kissed my cheek then waved. "Later, Chicky."

I smiled at him. "Later, B."

Bret growled behind us. "Great, she already found someone else."

I ignored his comment and started walking towards home. Darren smiled and spoke to the teens, "Five a.m. we are doing shooting practice. I expect you all to be there with your gun of choice."

Bret saluted Darren. "Yes, sir."

Darren shook his head and walked after me. He smiled at me as I walked beside him towards the house. The streets were still eerily empty, but a soft glow fell from each house's porch light. We walked in silence, as we always did at night, enjoying the smells and noises only available in the dark. I looked up at the moon and smiled. Only a few more days until the full moon. Darren had said the reason I was named Artemis, Goddess of the Moon, was because I had been born on a full moon, and every milestone I ever reached was on a full moon. I think he just wanted to make me feel special.

We arrived home and I hurried to bed. The image of the three dead teenagers was still in my head. I sighed and prayed Koda was right and the town would be okay, even after I was gone.

SONG OF THE MOON

"Artemis, get up." Darren said.

I opened my eyes and looked at the dark sky. "Dad, it's still night time. I just went to sleep."

He laughed. "Come on lazy. You just have to shoot once, to show that you can handle your gun, and then you can come back to bed."

I sighed and got out of bed, changing into my jeans and putting a bra on under my shirt. I hurried through my morning routine and walked out to the kitchen, where Billy, Bret and Darren were eating breakfast. I smiled at Billy's excited face. Billy patted the chair beside him, but I shook my head and took my normal chair across from Darren. I ate the eggs, bacon and toast which were already on my plate. Bret had added strawberry jelly to my toast as usual, which made me feel sad that we weren't really friends anymore. The milk was a little warm, but still delicious. Darren and Bret placed their plates in the sink and started towards the door. I sighed and followed their leads. Billy followed behind me. I pulled on my boots and grabbed the hunting rifle Darren had given me last year for Christmas. Bret held his hunting rifle down by his leg. We had been taught since we could walk that you never point a gun at something you aren't willing to kill. Billy followed us with two revolvers. I looked at Darren's empty hands and asked, "Where's your guns, Pop?"

"I'm teaching, not shooting. I'll practice later tonight." Darren answered.

Bret shook his head. "I don't understand how you and Artemis can see those targets at night."

Darren and I shrugged then walked out the door with Billy and Bret following closely behind. The entire town was sitting on our front lawn, waiting to start the lessons. The children had already started playing in the tree house and swinging in the tire swing my father built for me and Bret. Bret smiled at the children and nudged me with his arm. "That used to be us."

I nodded my head, and felt a twinge of sadness at the thought that I wouldn't see Bret again for a long time, if ever. "Yeah, used to be." I walked away from him, with Billy following me, around the back of the house to the shooting range Darren had set up. Darren believed that everyone needed to know how to use a gun in case of emergency. Now, with the threat of some unseen monster, it was even more important.

I stood at the mark for the first target and chambered a shell. I sighted down the barrel at the beer bottle that had been set up and exhaled. I pulled the trigger and smiled as the bottle shattered. I heard Trixie say, "Wow" from behind me. I lowered my gun and walked to the back porch setting my gun in the safe and locking it with the key. Bret walked to the next mark and aimed his gun. He pulled the trigger shattering another bottle just like I had. Skankzilla clapped her hands and cheered, "Yay, Bret!" I fought the urge to take my gun back out and end her miserable existence. Bret pointed his gun at the ground, ignoring Skankzilla, as he walked towards me. He motioned at the gun safe and smiled. I unlocked it and waited while he put his gun inside. Billy waved at me. "I'm going to go listen to your dad." I nodded my head and walked into the house. Darren rolled his eyes at us and began instructing the rest of the town who did a lot less shooting than Bret and me. I walked inside the house with Bret following closely behind. I sat down on the couch and turned on the television flipping through the channels in search of cartoons. Bret sat down behind me, stretching his long arms along the back of the couch. I groaned as every channel was a news alert. The light in my head clicked on and I stopped on one of the channels. Bret leaned forward beside me, his mouth dropping open.

The reporter spoke softly, standing in the middle of Oregon, surrounded by dead bodies. "The scene here is a duplicate of every other city. No one saw it coming and whatever has done this has vanished with the morning light. Every human found is dead. Hundreds are missing. The only clues as to what monster has done this are the claw marks we found on one body left beside a dumpster in an alley. Police from surrounding states have come to investigate this tragedy. Thousands are dead, leaving us to wonder what or whom is doing this. We found one surveillance tape which showed us this. Please be warned, this tape contains graphic scenes not suitable for some audiences."

The view changed to a grainy surveillance camera. A man stood pressed against a brick wall as a large dark shape moved towards him. It looked like mist, but moved unlike any mist I had ever seen. The mist covered the man, who screamed in terror. A sharp crack resonated through the alleyway, and the man stopped moving. The shadow disappeared. The reporter from our local news came back on, "This is replayed footage from New York. We have been told that there are indeed no survivors living in New York City, or any of the surrounding cities. The President has issued a warning to all states, saying, 'We need to prepare for the worst. There is no way to tell where it will strike next.' The reports are conflicting, but with the mist and claw marks, we do know that something is killing and *kidnapping* humans. Yes, you heard right, not all of the bodies are accounted for. We can only assume that with no signs of any of their personal belongings that they've been taken."

Bret stood up and ran outside. He yelled for Darren who came running into the house. I changed the channel to another station that showed the same scene all over again. Darren sat down beside me shaking his head. "Shit."

I felt my body begin to shake with fear, and Bret pulled me up, wrapping his arms around me. He whispered, "It's going to be alright Artemis. I'll be here for you."

Darren stood up and walked outside, telling the rest of the town what had happened. I pushed Bret away. "It won't matter, because neither of us will be here. I'm leaving in a few days, and so are you."

He frowned. "I love you, Artemis. Why can't you see that?"

I felt the tears in my eyes and turned away, walking to my room. I laid down on my bed facing the wall, and closed my eyes. Bret climbed on the bed behind me, and pulled me against him. I shook my head and tried to pull away from him, but he held me tight. I whispered, "I can't Bret."

Bret nodded his head against the back of mine. "I know that you feel betrayed, but I love you. I always have."

I sighed. "You're my friend, Bret. That's it. I can't date my friend. It never works out. Especially when that friend has been trying to screw me."

Bret shrugged and hugged me tighter. "What doesn't work about this?"

I pushed against him. "Just leave."

He sighed and stood up. "Fine, but just know that I'll wait for you. I love you."

I waited until he shut the door, and closed my eyes. I focused on relaxing my body and fell into a deep sleep.

Billy softly shook me awake. I opened my eyes to the dark and rolled over so I could see him. He whispered, "Your dad is outside shooting right now, but you need food."

I nodded my head as my stomach growled loudly. Billy snickered. "It's been doing that for fifteen minutes so I figured I should wake you up."

I looked out the window and saw the dark sky. "What time is it? How long have I been asleep?"

Billy stood up. "It's eight o'clock and you've been asleep for a long time. I'm sure you will be awake all night now."

I stretched my arms and legs then sat up throwing my legs over the edge of the bed. Billy extended his hand to me and I took it standing up. He pulled me against him and kissed my lips. I stood frozen as he pulled away and smiled at me. He laughed. "What's wrong?"

I pulled away from him. "I can't Billy. I'm leaving soon."

He smiled. "So, that means I can't get a few last kisses in?"

Bret walked into the room and glared at Billy's arms around me. He pushed Billy off of me and kissed my lips hard. I pushed against his chest, but couldn't do anything. He pulled back and asked, "Who's do you like more?"

I groaned. "Why? Why are you doing this?"

Bret reached for me, but I dodged his hand running towards the door. Bret grabbed me around the waist and pulled me back hugging me against him. "Just admit that you liked mine more. Just admit that you want me to do it again without him here."

Billy yelled, "Let her go Bret!"

I shook my head and fought against Bret, but he was much stronger than me. I suddenly felt trapped, and fought as hard as I could against him. I kicked at him and tried to elbow him, but he juggled me around so that I couldn't make contact. I pushed at his arms and they started to give. He exclaimed, "What the hell?!"

I pushed his arms off of me and ran away into the kitchen. I turned back towards them and panted and fought to control my emotions. I was no longer trapped and felt better, but I had a strange urge to fight Bret. Bret walked into the kitchen staring at me in shock. "What is going on with you Artemis?"

Billy smiled. "Obviously she doesn't want you touching her."

I shook my head and held out my hands. "Don't come near me, either of you. I don't...I felt trapped."

Darren walked into the house and stared from Bret to Billy to me and back. "What's wrong?"

"I was holding her and she started attacking me and got some burst of strength. She pushed my arms away and says she felt trapped." Bret said.

Darren frowned and stared at me, but talked to the boys. "Bret and Billy, I think you both should leave."

Bret frowned. "Why? She's fine now. I think I just scared her."

Billy scoffed. "No, he kissed her and she didn't want him to."

Darren set his gun down on the table and walked towards me. I took a step back and hit the wall. I shook my head as the urge to run tried to take over. I whispered, "Stop."

Darren stopped moving and whispered, "You want to run, don't you?"

I nodded my head and stared at him in shock. "How'd you know that?"

He sighed. "I can't explain right now." He turned to the boys. "Look, you know I've never had a problem with you being here before, but we have family matters to discuss."

Bret nodded his head. "I understand." Billy nodded his head too. Bret walked towards me and stopped a few feet away, raising my instinct to flee two notches higher. Bret asked, "Can I get a hug or are you going to go all crazy again?" He finished the last part trying to hide the hurt in his face.

I shook my head. "Both of you, please, just leave. I'm sorry."

Bret smiled. "Night, Chicky. Night, Darren."

Billy waved, with an obvious look of concern on his face. "Bye, Chicky."

Darren watched them leave. I plopped down into one of the kitchen chairs and put my face on the table. "Dad, what's happening to me?"

Darren rubbed his face with his hand. "I can't tell you everything yet, but you are coming into adulthood. It's a transition period for our family that few others here have to go through. It's because of your interactions with Ares and Koda. You are going to have to stay indoors for the next week and I'm going to have to forbid anyone from coming over here until your transition is finished."

I gasped, "But Bret is leaving in a few days!"

He sighed. "I'm sorry."

I stared at him in shock and disbelief. "What are we?" I asked, fear creeping up my spine.

He smiled. "We're human, but with a little extra spice in our blood. I told you I can't explain it yet. You'll understand in a few days."

I asked, "Are we like the things that have been killing all of those people? The mist?"

Darren shook his head angrily. "NO! We are nothing like those things. I promise, in a week or so, you'll know everything." He sighed heavily. "Whether you like it or not."

I stood up, wanting to ignore the jumbled new information in my head, and walked to the television. I turned on the TV. "Dad, there's another video."

He walked over and sat on the couch beside me. The news reporter showed video of a city being wiped out by the mysterious monsters. No new information was available, and the same signs had been shown. Claw marks, two puncture wounds, blood completely drained and broken necks. I wondered what these things were, but knew Darren wouldn't tell me. "Can they be killed?" I asked Darren.

He smiled a purely evil smile. "Yes, but not very easily."

"Why won't you just tell me what they are?"

"I fear that speaking their name will bring them to us. They have spies everywhere and can be almost anywhere. I would rather they left our town alone, but I fear they will be here much sooner than I wanted." He picked his gun up off the table and walked towards the door. "I'm going shooting, but stay here. If either of the boys come back, don't let them in."

I shrugged. "Whatever you say, Dad."

He smiled. "That's my girl. I'll be back in a few hours. Do some chores or something to keep yourself occupied."

I laughed and nodded my head. "Alright." I stood up and headed towards the kitchen. I turned on the water, and started doing the dishes. I could feel that something was going to change my life. *But what? What are these things, and how does what I am relate to it?*

I kept myself busy for the next two hours cleaning the kitchen and scrubbing the floors, but I grew bored. I hated staying inside the house. I went to my room and cleaned everything. I started a load of laundry. I walked into Darren's room, but was careful not to touch any of his books or research. He was always researching something, but I never knew what, because he kept his door closed and told me I couldn't go in his room. However, curiosity overrode the warnings in my brain, and I picked up a stack of papers and read the title. "Lycanthropy and Its Effects on Humans, by Darren Smith." I gasped. *Dad had written this? What the hell is lycanthropy?* I sat down and started to turn the first page when I heard the front door open and close. I set the papers back down and hurried out of his room, closing the door quietly. I ran into the bathroom across the hallway and turned the water on, splashing my face. I grabbed the towel and walked out of the bathroom, drying off my face.

Darren frowned. "The cows are missing, but your horses are fine."

I nodded my head. "Thanks."

He smiled. "Yep. Hey, you want to play a board game?"

I stared at him in shock. "We haven't played a board game together since I was ten."

He nodded his head again. "I think it's time we played one then."

I shrugged and walked towards the closet that held all of our games. Darren had always kept an abundance of board and card games around in case of bad weather. I pulled down Risk and set it on the table. He locked his gun up in the safe and walked back smiling. I pulled out the board and set it up. We played for a few hours, but I started to grow sleepy again. I yawned and stretched my arms. "Why am I so sleepy?"

He smiled. "It's all part of the transition. Don't worry. When the full moon gets here you'll be as good as new." He tried to smile, but it didn't reach the corners of his mouth. I nodded my head and walked to the bathroom to change my contacts. I hurried to my bedroom and fell asleep faster than ever before, dreaming of wolves running together in a pack, playing and hunting.

I stretched my arms as I woke up with the sunrise. I sat up and looked around my room. Everything was where it should be, but something felt wrong. I walked to the bathroom, changing my contacts and then toward the living room. I stopped moving when I saw the television. Darren sat watching the news report of another attack. This one was in Nevada again. Darren sighed as he heard me walk up. "You better sit down for this kid. Someone got a glimpse of the beasts."

I sat down quickly and pulled my legs up wrapping my arms around them. A cell phone video popped up on the screen. Two men were fighting in front of a bar with people forming a circle around them. Suddenly a black shape jumped on top of the fighters, clawing and biting them. The men screamed and all of the people started to run away. Mist moved towards two people that had started to run away and stopped them.

I stared at the black figure, as the phone focused on it. The men who had been fighting were no longer moving, and blood was gathering in a massive pool around their bodies. The black figure tore a chunk of meat from one of the men's sides and tilted its head back swallowing. The video panned out and you could see the rest of the massive black figure. I shook my head as I realized what it was. "A wolf? NO WAY! Wolves don't get that big." *Well except for the three that have been around here.*

Darren said nothing as the video continued playing. The wolf dropped its head and looked at the person recording it. I stared in awe at the wolf with its black fur and perfect amber eyes. I gasped, "ARES!"

Darren turned to me and frowned. "What?"

I shrugged. "Nothing."

I stared back at the wolf as it stalked towards the person recording him. The wolf walked with such pride, such power. I shivered as it stared directly into the camera and howled loud and long. I started gasping for breath and felt my body start to convulse. Darren growled. "Fuck. That piece of shit."

I fell off the couch and continued to convulse unable to get air. My bones began aching and felt like they were trying to separate. I closed my eyes and could see a white wolf with a blue mane and purple eyes. I stared into the wolf's eyes and realized it was me. *Impossible, I don't have purple eyes.* The wolf me nodded her head, tilted her head back, and howled loudly, shaking my entire body. I felt Darren's hands on my body seconds before cold water covered me. I gasped for air and stood up staring at Darren's infuriated face. I shivered and stared at him in shock. "How did we get to the creek at the edge of our property?"

He smiled. "I had to stop you. It's not time yet."

I growled, and the sound vibrated my chest, sounding like a wolf. I pictured the wolf with purple eyes and felt my body warming up. Darren grabbed me and snarled in my face. "You aren't allowed to change yet."

My body cooled and the vision of the wolf disappeared. I collapsed into his arms and asked, "What's happening to me?"

Darren stroked my hair and whispered, "It's alright. Just sleep. You'll understand when you wake up." I nodded my head and relaxed, as he picked me up and carried me to the house, and to my room. I started to get up to change my contacts, but he just rolled me over, so I could take them out. He whispered, "You won't be needing those."

I curled up under the covers, not having the energy to ask anymore questions, and fell asleep. I dreamt of Ares and pictured his gorgeous face. I could see him in front of me running through the forest. I ran after him as fast as I could, but my human legs wouldn't keep up with him. He turned to me and howled, summoning me to him. I tried to reach him, but he was too far away. Another howl broke through my dream, waking me up. I sat up on my bed with sweat running down my face. The windows were dark, so it was still night. I inhaled and smelled wolves.

I ran from my room to Darren's, but he wasn't there. I ran to the gun safe and unlocked it, taking out a gun and loading it. I grabbed a handful of shells and put them in my jeans pockets. I walked quickly to the back door and stopped moving. Darren stood on the porch with his hands to his sides with no weapons. On the ground twenty feet away from him stood three giant wolves. I instantly recognized the middle wolf. "Ares." I whispered quietly. I pushed open the door and walked out, setting the gun on the porch and taking the shells out of my pockets. I started to walk past Darren to Ares, but Darren grabbed me, pulling me against him. Ares snarled at us, but I felt no fear.

Darren snarled back sounding just like Ares. "She's my pup. You can't take her like this. She hasn't changed yet." I felt anxious at Darren's words and wanted to go to Ares. I pulled away from Darren, but he grabbed me, holding me tighter. Ares walked forward and sat on his butt tilting his head to the side. Darren shook his head. "No, Ares. She can't be yours. I don't care if she is the one who answered your call. She's not ready. She doesn't even know yet."

I looked up at Darren and smiled. "They said that was your fault."

He frowned. "You've talked to them?"

I shrugged. "I've had dreams about Ares and he's had them about me. I had to talk to them."

Darren sighed and looked at Ares. "If you want to see her reaction, then go ahead."

Ares stood up and shook his body. I held my breath as his body rippled like water and turned human just like in my dreams. Darren ran into the house and returned quickly with a pair of pants which he tossed to Ares. Ares put the pants on then smiled at me. His blue eyes sparkled like crystals. He took a step towards me, and I looked at Darren. "We're werewolves, aren't we?

Ares frowned. "Why haven't you told her? The full moon is tomorrow."

Darren sighed. "I didn't want to scare her. She has no idea what she is. She thinks she is human."

Ares snarled. "You would rather her be scared shitless when she changes for the first time? That is the worst way to find out."

Darren snarled. "She is my pup to do with as I please."

Ares shook his head. "I am alpha to you and she is my *passt genau*. I am taking her. I will teach her the ways of our kind."

Darren pushed me behind him and squatted down in an attack stance. "You will not touch her. She will not become like you."

Ares snarled. "And what am I?"

Darren spit. "A monster."

The two wolves behind Ares growled and took a step forward. Ares held up his hand and they stopped moving. Ares sighed. "I understand you don't agree with what is being done. Neither do I, but I am following my alpha's orders. If I could, I would stop it."

Darren sighed. "What do you want with her Ares?"

He smiled at me as I looked around Darren. "She is mine. She answered my call."

"What call?" I asked.

Ares took a step towards the porch and Darren growled. Ares sighed. "I'll stay here, but not because you are dominant to me. Keep pushing it and I'll remind you who is dominant."

Darren sighed and walked to one of the chairs on the porch a few feet away from me. Ares cleared his throat. "I sent out a call through the video that only my true match could answer. You answered me. I was still in Nevada when I heard you."

I shook my head. "I don't understand. What are we? I mean are you really a werewolf?"

Ares smiled. "I'm a lycanthrope, also known as a werewolf."

I gasped and turned to Darren. "Your papers in your room. They were talking about lycanthropy."

Darren sighed. "Yes, because I am a lycanthrope as well, and you, being my child, have had the disease passed on to you."

I stared at Ares and asked because I had to be certain, "I'm a werewolf? How is that possible? I thought werewolves were myths?"

Ares snarled. "There are many myths that are true, but the humans forced us into hiding a few centuries ago. We have just been waiting for the right time to come out and take over."

I stared at him in shock. "You are killing all of these innocent humans because of what other humans did centuries ago? How can you do that? They had nothing to do with it."

Ares frowned. "You think these would be any different? You think that if I were to show myself to the humans of this century that they would not hunt us down? You are very naïve and it is your father's fault for not teaching you our history."

Darren sighed. "I just wanted her to have a normal life. I had no idea when you would be returning. I had hoped that she could live out her life until she was an adult without changing, but when she saw the news, she started showing the signs. And then you had to call her and speed up her process. I had to force her change back once."

Ares bowed his head. "My apologies for that. But I had to know if she was my match or not."

I took a step down the porch towards Ares. He smiled at me, but Darren growled making me stop moving. Ares ran up the porch in a blur of tan skin grabbing Darren by the throat and holding him up, choking him. "I warned you already. I am the alpha here, not you. Do not hinder her again."

I ran to them and pleaded, "Please don't kill him!"

Ares dropped Darren back into the chair and smiled. "I would not kill him. He is your father and just needed a small reminder."

I stared at his handsome face and couldn't help but look over his muscular body. His light tan skin was the color of caramel and his perfect blue eyes were like a June sky. I reached out toward him, and almost touched him, when I heard the wolves behind us snarl. I turned around and saw Bret standing on the side of the house with his rifle aimed at the wolves. Ares snarled and the two wolves moved towards Bret.

I screamed, "NO!" and ran as fast as I could to Bret, standing in front of him.

He dropped the gun down immediately and stared at me in shock. "Artemis, what the hell are you doing? Don't you see the wolves? They are the same as the ones that have been killing people."

I looked back at the wolves still moving forward and Ares close behind me. I turned to Ares. "Tell them to stop moving. He won't shoot them. Please."

Ares sighed and held his hand up. The two wolves stopped moving, sitting on their butts, staring at Bret angrily. I reached for Bret's gun, but he backed up. I shook my head. "Bret, give me the gun or they will kill you."

Bret reached towards my face and asked, "Why are your eyes purple?"

I heard Darren speaking to Ares. "I made her wear contacts because they changed when she hit puberty."

I ignored Darren, and turned to Bret. "Look Bret, there is a lot of shit I can't explain right now, but if you don't give me the gun, they are going to kill you."

Bret stared at Ares and the two wolves and shook his head. "They are going to kill me anyway. I can see it in his eyes."

I turned to Ares and snarled. "You won't touch him."

Ares snarled back at me. "You are not dominant enough to make such statements."

I shook my head. "I don't care about dominance. If you try to hurt him, I will die protecting him."

Ares shook his head. "Do not threaten me, pup."

I sighed. "Please Ares. I am asking you as a submissive. I am pleading with you as the one who answered your call."

Ares smiled. "Only if you promise to leave with me."

I looked up at Bret's shocked face and turned back to Ares. "Only if you and all of your people leave this town unharmed." *Good thing he doesn't know that I was already planning on leaving with him.*

Ares sighed and rubbed his temples. "I should have known you would be smart. Very well, if you leave with me, we will leave this town unharmed including this boy."

I reached down and grabbed Bret's gun out of his hand before he could react. I ran over to the gun case, and locked it inside before Bret could reach me. He spun me around and shook me. "What have they done to you? Have they brainwashed you?"

I felt the tears falling down my face and shook my head. "I'm sorry, Bret. I had no idea about any of this. I have to go though."

Bret stormed towards Ares and glared at the shorter man. "Who the fuck is he that you would leave me for him?"

Ares smiled up at Bret. "She's my one and only, destined since she was born to be mine."

Bret spit on the ground beside Ares. "That's a bunch of shit. We've been together since we could walk. She is mine, not yours."

Ares smiled wider, but it made the hair on the back of my neck stand up. "Would you put it to a test?"

Darren stood up and walked quickly to Ares. He dropped to his knees and begged, "Please don't do this to him. He does not know anything about us. Please, Ares."

Bret stared at Darren in shock. "Why are you groveling to him? He's just another man."

Ares laughed. "Just another man! How funny."

I grabbed Bret's hand and pulled him to me. "Just leave, Bret. You have to move on. I'm sorry, but I won't be here. It's for the good of the town."

Bret shook his head. "You're not making any sense. Why would you leaving benefit the town?"

Ares smiled and motioned at the two wolves. "Because your town is just another one to be destroyed. She has bargained for your lives, can't you see that?"

"I won't let you leave with him." Bret said angrily.

I smiled and hugged him standing on tiptoe and whispered, "I have always known you were my best friend, but this is bigger than us. I have to protect everyone, including you." I pulled away and backed towards Ares.

Bret shook his head. "No, don't leave me. I am the one who is supposed to protect you, remember?"

I smiled. "We always knew it would end with me protecting you, Bret. You just never wanted to admit it."

Ares extended his hand to me smiling, "Come, my Moon Goddess. Let me take you away and show you your true nature."

I smiled back at him and took his hand. The

instant our skins touched an electric shock went through our bodies. I collapsed forward falling into his arms. He picked me up and held me against his bare chest. "I'll treat you like a Queen."

I looked one last time at Bret's distraught face then relaxed as Ares began running. I heard the two wolves following closely behind us. I expected his running to be bouncy, but it was smooth. It was like we were standing still, with the air whizzing past us. They ran for a few hours taking us into a thick forest. When they finally stopped running Ares set me down on the ground. I wrapped my arms around myself and sighed. Tears escaped from my eyes before I could stop them. Ares sat down beside me and wiped the tears away with his thumb while he rested the rest of his hand against my cheek. I leaned into his hand enjoying the warmth. He whispered, "You will be happy again soon. I promise."

I nodded my head and turned away from him. The two wolves stared at me with curious expressions on their faces. I turned to Ares and asked, "Why are they looking at me like that?"

He smiled. "They want to know how it's possible that you do not know what you are. And why you have not changed."

I shrugged my shoulders, "I don't know. My father never changed in front of me, so until you changed I had no idea."

One of the wolves shook its head, I heard popping and snapping. It sounded like bones breaking. I cringed as I watched his head reform into a human head. His green Mohawk was a dead give away. I smiled. "Koda!"

He smiled at me as I stared at his human head on the giant wolf body. "Hey, Artemis."

I smiled. "I should have known you would be here. Why aren't you changing back all of the way?"

Ares rolled his eyes. "He is trying to save you from embarrassment. If he changes completely, he will be naked and we have no clothes with us for him to change into."

I blushed. "Oh."

The other wolf shook his head and changed it to human. He looked exactly like Koda, but had a blue Mohawk and spoke with a British accent. I recognized him as the other man from the hotel. "She's blushing. That is very cute, Love."

I turned away from them and walked a few steps away. Ares snarled. "Nice job, Matt."

"What? You can't tell me that it's not cute that she blushes like a human." Matt said.

I turned around and snarled at them. "I am a human!" I clamped my hands over my mouth and turned away again. *Holy shit. What is happening to me?*

Ares whispered, "It's okay that you are scared."

I shook my head. "I'm not scared. I just want to know what's happening." Okay, I was scared, but I didn't want to admit it.

Ares spoke softly to me. "You are going to change for the first time when the full moon rises tomorrow night. Your body is going through your transition phase and during that phase you can be a little bit temperamental."

"Great! So it's like getting your period all over again."

Ares smiled. "Sort of. How old are you, Artemis?"

I looked at his face and gauged him at about twenty three. "Seventeen. Well, I'll be eighteen tomorrow."

Ares smile fell slightly at the corners. "You're turning eighteen?"

I nodded my head. "Yep. I'm hoping to make it a couple more years too."

Koda and Matt laughed, but Ares just regained his full smile. "It would be a truly amazing feat for you to hold off your change on your eighteenth birthday, but I do not think it will be possible. You're getting a double whammy of full moon and eighteenth birthday."

I shrugged. "Can't hurt to try."

Matt laughed again. "I like her. She has a much older soul than her human years."

Ares nodded his head. "It has to do with the fact that she is my match."

I sighed. "I don't understand this whole match thing. I mean, I don't even remember answering your call or whatever. I started having convulsions after I saw you on TV and my dad stopped them by throwing me in the creek. I went to sleep, and when I woke up, I could smell wolves. When I went outside, you were there."

"You must have answered before your dad threw you in the creek."

The memory of my wolf self howling played in my mind and my eyes widened. I asked, "So, what happens now?"

Ares stood up and held out his hand for me. I stood up without his hand brushing off my pants. Ares smiled at me and walked towards Koda and Matt. "Now we continue moving towards our destination. Once there, we will take you to a special place to wait for your first change."

I shook my head. "I won't change tomorrow night."

Ares smiled. "We'll see about that, but we must hurry."

I looked at Matt and Koda in their wolf bodies and human heads, and at Ares, and sighed. "Why is this happening to me? Why couldn't I just have a normal life?"

Ares frowned. "Your father said you were an outsider anyway."

I laughed. "An outsider to everyone but Bret and Billy."

Ares snarled. "You have to forget about them. You will never see them again."

I stared in shock at him. "What? Why? You promised not to kill them!" I felt my anger boiling up and my skin started to turn hot. I took a step towards him and growled. A deep wolf growl came from my throat, but I didn't cringe.

Ares growled back. "Do not try to fight me Artemis. You are completely human until you change, and I don't want to hurt you."

"Then answer my questions." I snarled at him.

Ares snarled back at me, taking a step towards me. I fought my body and stayed still, not stepping back from him even though I could feel the pressure building against me. "I will only let your aggressive gestures last so long. I understand that you are not used to the werewolf way, but I am your dominant, and you must treat me as such. Your friends will be alive and fine, but you will not be allowed to visit them or anyone else. After you have your first change, your food instincts are a little off."

I stopped snarling and stared at him in shock. "You mean that I might end up trying to eat them?"

Ares nodded his head. "Exactly."

I frowned. "Aren't humans the top of the food chain?"

"Humans were never the top of the food chain," Ares answered angrily.

"What is?" I asked.

"We are." Ares answered.

I decided to leave the food chain topic alone, and walked towards Koda and Matt. "How old are you three?"

Koda frowned. "You don't want to know."

"Try me."

Matt laughed. "Just wait until you know everything about us before we tell you our age."

I sighed. "Fine, be secretive. See if I care! Now let's go. I'm starving."

Koda smiled. "Me too."

I looked at him and realized he was trying to make a joke. I laughed and turned to Ares. "So I guess you'll be carrying me again?"

Ares shrugged. "Would you rather ride one of them?"

I looked at Matt and Koda and asked, "Would one of you let me?"

Koda stepped forward and nodded his human head. "Of course. Hop on." He coughed and I cringed as his face snapped and popped and extended into its wolf form.

I shook my body. "At least you look natural again, but that's disgusting to hear."

"Wait until it's your body doing it." said Matt.

Ares snarled and Matt quickly changed his head back to wolf. I reached out towards Koda and stopped mid way. I looked back at Ares. "Are they still them?"

He tilted his head to the side in a very canine like manner. "You mean are they still thinking like themselves or are they thinking like a dog?"

I nodded my head. "Yeah. If I pet him is he going to try to bite me?"

Ares shrugged. "Depends on what kind of mood he is in."

I looked into Koda's eyes and said, "Don't bite me." I reached forward and stroked his fur with my hand. "It's so thick."

Koda laid down so I could get on to him easier. I climbed up and grabbed a fist full of his fur enjoying the feel of it in my hands. He stood up slowly and started walking. I tucked my legs up slightly to get a better hold, since he was too large to ride like a horse. Koda crouched down and then sprang forward in a full run. I held on tightly, leaning forward so the wind and branches wouldn't hit me. We ran much faster than before and came out of the forest in a few minutes to a flat grass field. Koda slowed, and Ares walked to stand beside us. He looked around, then nodded his head. Matt walked forward into the open field and looked around carefully. He got to the middle of the field and howled loudly. I watched as five wolves ran from the trees on the other side of the field, and walked up to Matt. They smelled each other's faces and then sat down on their butts. Matt turned back to us and nodded his head. Koda and Ares walked together towards the group. I lay down flat on Koda's back trying to hide as much as possible in his fur.

We reached the group and Koda sat down making it harder for me to hang on, but I gripped his fur tighter not wanting to fall. Ares still in his human form said, "Greetings, fellow wolves. We come to seek shelter in your town."

Another man who had changed forms answered, "Greetings, Prince Ares. Of course you may stay with us. You need not even ask our permission."

"Thank you, Gregory, but I wanted to be polite and not insist you let me stay with you." Ares said in a lighthearted tone.

My grip slipped through Koda's fur and I hit the ground making an "oomf" sound as I landed. The other man growled. "What do you have with you?"

I peeked around Koda and Ares smiled at me. "It's alright Artemis. Come here."

I walked slowly toward Ares eyeing the other wolves cautiously. "Are you sure they aren't going to hurt me?"

Ares smiled and held out his hand. "You are one of us, and you are mine. They will not harm you." I took his hand and hurried the rest of the way to his side. He said, "Gregory, I would like you to meet Artemis, my *passt genau.*"

Gregory, the only naked man, shook his head in disbelief. "Your match? I did not think it was possible for a wolf to find a match."

Ares smiled and kissed the back of my hands sending chills up my spine. "Neither did I, but we had been dreaming of each other. I sent out a call and she answered from a state away. Her father did not tell her about our kind and kept her away. She has yet to change though."

Gregory stared in shock at me. "How old?"

"Seventeen, eighteen tomorrow."

Gregory shook his head. "Amazing. It must have something to do with her not being around our kind."

Ares nodded his head staring at my face. "That's what I assumed. Her father has even refused to change in front of her. She had no idea that werewolves even existed until a few hours ago when I came to her."

I couldn't help but look at Gregory's body. He was muscled like Ares and naked. I started to look lower, but Ares tapped my face making me look at him. He whispered, "I assure you that there is nothing special for you to look at on him."

I blushed and turned away from both of them. "You can't get mad at me. I hadn't seen a naked man before you changed at my house."

Ares snorted. "Don't lie. I could tell that you have slept with that boy."

"Define slept with. I have been asleep in the same bed with him, if that is what you mean, but I have never even kissed him, more than a kiss on the cheek."

Ares sighed. "Now is not the time to discuss this. We must hurry to your place. The full moon comes tomorrow, and she will need her rest."

I nodded my head. "Especially if I'm going to stop the change."

Gregory shook his head. "You can't stop it."

I glared at him, no longer unable to meet his eyes. "Do not tell me what I can or cannot do."

Ares laughed. "See Gregory. She is perfect."

Gregory smiled. "She is something, great Prince. Hurry and follow me then."

He changed back to a wolf, his body popping and snapping as it changed. I cringed at the sound and moved towards Ares, but he was changing too. I ran to Koda and hopped up on his back as he started to stand up. I clung to him as he ran with the others.

CHAPTER FOUR

We ran for a few hours through the trees before coming to a clearing. The large clearing was filled with little log cabin houses and one large concrete warehouse building. Adults and children of various races walked around smiling, talking and laughing as our pack of wolves ran by them. I stared in shock, not believing that this sight wasn't scaring them. *How can this be normal? Are all of these people werewolves? I* shuddered at the thought of so many werewolves being in one place. *Aren't werewolves supposed to be angry and bloodthirsty?*

Our group stopped in front of the largest house and the men changed from wolves to human. I kept my face burrowed in Koda's fur as they walked inside so that I wouldn't have to look at their naked bodies. Koda turned his head to me and nudged my arm. I looked up and he snorted. I slid from his back and walked forward until I was on the steps of the house. I could hear Koda's body popping and snapping and cringed with each sound. He made a stretching noise and said from very close behind me, "Come on. Everyone went to get clothes so that they wouldn't embarrass you anymore."

I felt the blush on my cheeks and was glad

that I didn't have to look at him. I walked into the house quickly before anymore naked men showed up. When I was inside the doorway, I stopped. The house had a very warm feeling. The entryway had rows of pictures of people and wolves with a chandelier made of deer antlers hanging over the doorway. The living room sat off to the left, the bedrooms to the right, and the kitchen was straight ahead. I frowned at the set-up and then shrugged. *Not my house to decide how to set it up.* I loved how normal everything looked and hoped that my life wouldn't have to change too much.

Ares walked out of one of the bedrooms in a pair of blue jeans and nothing else and I stared at him as he walked towards me. His flawless caramel skin begged for me to lick it and his piercing blue eyes would be perfect staring down at me while he...

I broke the thought off and turned away as a burning blush roared up my cheeks. I felt Ares behind me and desperately wanted to turn around and touch him, but I stayed still, digging my fingers into my arms to hold myself together. *You don't even know this guy and you're already thinking about doing things you have never done with any other man before.* I swallowed hard. *Man. He was definitely a man.*

"Artemis." Ares whispered behind me. If his voice was a physical element, it would be velvet.

I swallowed hard. "Yes?"

He moved closer to me so that a large thought would make us touch. "Are you alright?"

I nodded my head quickly then sighed. "I...I..."

Ares wrapped his arms around my waist and I moaned at the feel of his burning skin against mine. He placed his lips next to my ear and asked, "Would you like me to give you some space?"

I tried to say yes, but my mouth said, "NO!" I spun around in his arms and stared at his gorgeous face. His rugged physical features reminded me of the men who often camped in the nearby mountains.

If he had wanted to, he could have been a model. I felt the muscles of his arms against me and his chest muscles as he wrapped his arms around me. My eyes rolled in the back of my head. He laughed quietly and set me down in a chair walking across the room. I stared after him and fought my body to stay in the chair. He smiled and I smiled back at him.

Matt whistled from the doorway and spoke in his thick British accent, "Wow, she really is all bonkers fer ya. I can't believe you have *a passt genau.*"

Ares smiled and nodded his head. "She's perfect. Well, except that she hasn't changed yet."

I frowned. "I'm not going to change."

Ares shrugged and smiled. "Whatever you say."

I smelled steak and licked my lips. "Are we going to eat soon? I'm starving." Ares started walking towards me and wicked thoughts about parts of him I wouldn't mind nibbling on instantly sprang to mind. I shook my head trying to clear it and asked, "Did you put some type of spell or something on me?"

He whispered from behind me. "No. It's just how we are together."

I groaned. "Great. Just great."

Matt and Koda walked into the room and sat down on the love seat. They were both wearing only pants like Ares and it took all of my willpower to look away from their bodies and stare at my hands as I sat down on the farthest seat of the couch. I pressed myself into the corner trying to hide and disappear even though I knew it was impossible. I stayed staring at my hands even when someone sat down next to me on the couch.

Matt whispered, "What's wrong, Love?"

I looked up slowly making sure to avoid staring at his body and go straight for his face. "I don't really want to answer that truthfully."

Matt smiled. "Is it because of how we're dressed?" I looked back down at my hands as another blush spread over my cheeks. Matt laughed.

"It's alright. We won't get mad if we catch you looking at us."

"It's not that, well it sort of is, but that's not completely it." I said quietly.

Someone else sat down on the couch beside Matt. Koda asked, "You can't tell me you haven't seen your guy friends with their shirts off before."

I felt my blush deepen and shook my head. "I didn't really have any friends besides Bret and I never paid attention to the guys anyway." *And I guarantee none of them had bodies like yours.*

Matt snarled. "Was Bret the one trying to shoot us?"

I sighed and looked up at him. "Yes. You can't hate him for that, though. I've never seen wolves your size until we watched the videos on TV and then to see two of them at my house." My throat constricted as I thought about never seeing Bret again. After taking a deep breath I continued. "Bret has always vowed to protect me, and he was just worried for my safety. He didn't shoot you, right?"

Matt shrugged. "I didn't say I hated him. I just don't like humans in general."

I grimaced. "You don't like me?"

Matt smiled sweetly. "Love, you aren't human. Your father made you believe you are, but you are a werewolf." He stared at my eyes and shook his head. "And something else, because I have never met anyone with purple eyes before."

I frowned. "What are you talking about? I don't have purple eyes." Koda and Matt stared at me in shock. I shook my head. "I don't know what you are talking about."

Koda called, "Ares." Ares walked over and stood in front of me. I stayed staring at Koda. Koda said, "Ares, you need to take her to the bathroom."

I looked up at Ares' face, waiting for his reaction. Ares frowned. "Why? Are you not feeling well?"

Koda shook his head. "Ares, she doesn't know what her eyes look like."

Ares looked down at me in shock. "What color are your eyes Artemis?"

I shrugged. "Brown. At least that's what Bret always told me. Darren never had a mirror in the house and I never really thought about it. Whenever I walked by a mirror I just never looked into one."

Ares picked up my hand then turned it over staring at the burn from the wolf necklace. "What happened?" He asked softly.

I sighed. "Billy gave me a necklace with a wolf pendent and the wolf burned my hand."

Ares asked, "Silver?" I nodded my head and he whispered, "Don't touch silver." He pulled me to the bathroom down the hall. We passed Gregory, who stared at us in shock. Ares pushed the bathroom door open and pushed me in front of the mirror. I stared at him, not sure what he wanted.

Ares sighed. "Look in the mirror."

I turned my head and looked at the mirror and gasped. I put my hand up to my face and rubbed my cheek. I knew I looked like my mother because Darren had told me, but I hadn't realized how much I looked like her. I stared in shock at my dark purple eyes. I turned to Ares and asked, "This isn't some illusion is it? Is this really what I look like?"

"Yes, Artemis. That is what you look like. Didn't you own a mirror?" I shook my head and ran my fingers through my thick black hair. I felt the tears running down my face before I saw them in the mirror. I turned away from the mirror and sat down on the floor holding my face in my hands. Ares sat down next to me and wrapped his arms around me. "It's alright Artemis. Everything will be alright."

I stopped crying and rubbed my eyes with my arms. "I'm sorry. It's just that I haven't seen my face before and I didn't realize how much I look like my mother. I thought this whole time that I was just ugly and that's why everyone treated me like an outsider." I stopped talking because I felt like I was being arrogant to say that I thought I was beautiful.

SONG OF THE MOON

Ares tilted my head up with his finger under my chin and smiled. "You're very beautiful Artemis. I'm sure the reason they treated you like an outsider has nothing to do with your looks. I'll explain it to you later, but we need to eat."

I nodded my head and stood up. I turned to him and asked, "Do you know of anyone else who has purple eyes? And why is it that I feel like I have known you my entire life, when I have only known you a few hours?"

He smiled and ran a fingertip along my jaw line. "I keep telling you that you were destined to be with me. I'm not making it up. And yes, I have met someone with purple eyes, but it has been a very long time since then."

I asked, "Does everyone have someone to answer their call?"

He shook his head. "No. The one that did had to wait a long time to find the person who answered."

I asked, "How long did you wait?"

He shook his head. "Not yet. Wait until we explain everything about our culture to you."

I sighed. "Fine. But can you explain it soon?"

Ares laughed. "Of course." He walked from the bathroom back to the living room where everyone was sitting. I followed him and sat down in my spot in the corner of the couch.

Gregory brought out three plates of burgers and set it down on the coffee table. Gregory smiled. "Dig in!"

Matt and Koda jumped from the couch and grabbed two burgers each. Ares stood up and grabbed two also then all three sat down on the floor and began eating. I stared at the normal setting of guy friends eating burgers in a living room and wondered if all things about werewolves were the same. *Well except for the body changing part.* Ares looked up from his burger and frowned at me. "You need to eat."

I sighed and stood up grabbing one burger and sat back down pressing myself harder into the corner of the couch. I took a small bite from the burger and groaned in pleasure. "This is the best burger I have ever tasted!" I ate the burger quickly then grabbed another from the table scarfing it down too. Gregory handed everyone cups of soda then sat back down. I swallowed mine quickly sighing in happiness when I was done. I felt a burp coming and fought to hold it down, but Koda burped loudly below me so I let mine out. I burped loud and long and laughed when I was finally done. "Excuse me."

All of the men stared at me in shock then started laughing loudly. Matt said, "Koda, she beat your burp like you were still a pup."

Koda smiled. "Looks like we may have a good burping contest with her around." I blushed and looked down at my hands. Koda groaned. "You embarrass too easily. I know you don't know us, but we really aren't bad, and we aren't trying to embarrass you. Just treat us like we're your friends.

I stayed looking at my hands, no longer embarrassed, but now sad. *I wonder what theory Ares has about why I didn't have any friends.*

Koda sighed. "What did I say wrong?"

I looked up at him and smiled. "Nothing Koda. I just didn't have any friends besides Bret, so I don't really know how to act around a group of people."

Koda frowned. "But your friend was the all star football player. You would go everywhere with him."

I stared at him in shock. "How did you know that?"

Koda smiled. "I can recognize the type."

"Sure I went with him everywhere, but he was the only one that wanted me there, and no matter how hard I tried to fit in, it never worked." I laughed bitterly. "I'm sure they are ecstatic that I'm gone."

Ares shook his head. "They might be, but Bret won't."

I smiled. "I wish I could see their faces when they make a comment and he tears their heads off. Well, for the next day or two, until he leaves." I sighed. "He was always sticking up for me." I looked at Ares. "It wouldn't be possible for me to go back and explain everything to him, would it?"

Ares smiled. "Maybe someday, but not soon. You are in for a long couple of weeks of dealing with the transformation and the new things that come with it.

I nodded my head. "Sure. Will you explain everything now?"

Ares nodded his head then looked at Gregory. Gregory asked, "What do you know about werewolves?"

I shrugged. "Only what I've seen in movies."

All of them groaned. Gregory shook his head. "I don't understand why your father was so stupid not to tell you about what you are. Alright, I'll explain from the beginning. There are three ways to become a werewolf. One is to be bitten, which injects the Lycanthropy disease. The second is to be cursed by a witch, which sort of implants the disease in your body. The third is genetic, where you receive the disease from either the sperm or egg."

I stared at him in shock as he continued his editorial. "You were born which means that either one or both of your parents were werewolves. We obviously know your father was one, but aren't sure about your mother what with your purple eyes and all." Ares cleared his throat and Gregory continued. "Werewolves are special from humans not only in the fact that we can change shape, but also that we move fast and heal much faster than humans. We don't live forever, but if we find someone who will tie themselves to us, then we will live an endless number of years. Basically, if one of you dies, the other dies, too. Luckily, it's difficult to kill us. It's really the only drawback."

I felt my jaw drop open and looked around at the men around me. "You...you're all old aren't you?"

They all frowned at me as I looked at all of their handsome faces and sculpted bodies. I looked at Ares last and asked in a voice barely louder than a whisper, "How old are you?"

Ares smiled. "I honestly don't know how old I am. I tried once to go back and figure it out, but I always lose count around the time of the Battle of Actium in Greece. I was old by human standards then, though."

I felt my jaw drop open. "Why are you interested in a seventeen year old then? Isn't that kind of like being a pedophile?"

Ares frowned deep, his forehead furrowing together and anger stretching his eyes tight. "I am not a pedophile! The rules are different when you live for hundreds of years. I am technically only in my mid twenties. And besides, you are the one who answered my call. No matter what your age, you would be the only one for me. If you had been an infant, I would still have taken you and cared for you until you were old enough to truly love me like we are meant to."

I felt my face fall in shock. "Love?" *What the hell is he talking about?*

Ares sighed. "You don't get it. You and I are destined to be together for eternity. We are the only couple that does not have to be bound to live forever. You and I will live an endless number of years and if one of us dies the other will not."

I stared at the ground. "I did not mean to upset you, but fifty was old to me. How can you not expect me to be upset that you are over two *thousand* years old?"

Koda cringed. "Don't tell her my age. I may be younger than Ares, but not by her standards."

"You might as well tell me. If I am really going to live for eternity, I will find out later." I said.

"Later. Keep going Gregory." Koda said.

Gregory smiled. "When someone is bitten they change at the next full moon, the same as with being cursed by a witch. But when you are born, you don't change until you hit puberty."

I stared at him in shock and shook my head. "That's wrong. I hit puberty at thirteen."

All of the men turned and stared at me. Ares asked, "Thirteen? Have you ever stopped your transformation before?"

I thought about it and shrugged. "I don't know. I didn't know I was a werewolf until you came, remember?"

Ares snarled. "I'm really starting to dislike your father more and more. Have you ever had an instance where you thought you were having a seizure or heart attack or something?"

I thought back through my childhood and then remembered everything. I felt my eyes widen and said, "Shit. You've got to be kidding me." They all stared at me waiting for me to answer. I groaned. "When I was ten, yeah ten, I had what appeared to be a seizure at school. My dad refused to take me to the doctors though, which pissed off the town. Then I kept having them. Not everyday or anything, but once every few months. The last three years I've had them about every month, sometimes three times a month. Like once when I was thirteen, when I hit puberty, I started getting the shakes really bad. Darren kept me home from school and I fought my body to stop the shaking. Then when I was fifteen, I had another seizure episode at school in the middle of the cafeteria, but obviously it wasn't a seizure. One time I was at the lake with Bret and this girl slapped me in the face. I punched her back, but then fell on my hands and knees and started seizing." Gregory's eyes were wide in fear as I continued. "Yesterday I started seizing, but Darren threw me in the creek, which stopped it."

"Holy shit." Koda said.

Matt nodded his head. "Love, you are amazing."

I looked at Ares who was smiling happily at me. "What does this mean, Ares? That I have been fighting my transformation since I was ten?"

Ares nodded his head. "I believe so. I don't know why you started before you hit puberty or why you were able to stop them for so long. No one has ever stopped their first transformation before. And it is very unheard of to stop any of them."

I asked, "Can you stop them?"

He nodded his head. "I can, but not all of the time."

I shivered. "Oh, god. Why didn't Darren tell me this before? I felt like I was handicapped or something with the seizures."

Ares snarled. "I think you may get your wish to visit your town. I need to speak with your father."

"You aren't going to hurt him are you?" I asked nervously.

Ares smiled. "Not if you don't want me to."

I shook my head. "I don't. So when we go back do I get to speak with Bret?"

Ares snarled. "With supervision."

I snarled back. "I don't need supervision."

Ares shook his head. "I won't let you see him alone."

I stood up glaring at him. "You cannot tell me what to do. I may be stuck with you the rest of my life, but I don't have to bow to you just because you have some stupid title among the werewolves."

Ares stood up and growled at me. I flinched, but didn't take a step back. I felt something pushing at me and looked around, but there was nothing. I felt a thick substance, like mud, spread around me seeping upwards until it covered me and I couldn't breathe. I fell to the floor gasping for breath as Ares stood over me pushing his power over me. I looked up at his eyes and if I had had any breath would have gasped. His eyes were completely black, like the pupil had expanded to cover everything. He snarled. "I am dominant to you and although you do not understand our ways, you will not try to belittle me."

I began to see grey spots as my body tried to black out with the lack of oxygen. I shook my head and rolled over on to my stomach. I felt a flame flare inside my core and focused on it. It flared higher and higher until it filled my entire body up. I looked up at Ares and smiled as I realized I had my own magic. Ares stared down at me in shock as I pushed with my hands and the internal flame at the invisible mud covering me. The internal flame extended past my hands and pushed the mud back enough for me to breathe. I gasped for breath and pushed harder with my power. Ares shook his head and I watched in amazement as his eyes cleared back to normal. The invisible flame from me snapped back inside and only a small flicker like a candle flame stayed inside me. I collapsed against the ground and closed my eyes in exhaustion.

No one spoke or moved for ten minutes. Ares finally cleared his throat and spoke. "Well, that was interesting."

"Did she just use magic against you?" Koda asked.

Ares laughed. "Yep. Darren has been holding out on us. I thought he had been bitten, but apparently he comes from a line that was cursed, or he was cursed. That bastard. Now I really have to speak with him."

I sat up slowly and looked up at Ares. "What just happened?"

Ares smiled. "When you are cursed by a witch, or come from a line which is cursed by a witch, you gain magical powers. Apparently when I used my powers on you it let yours emerge."

I shook my head and laughed. "Werewolves, witches and now magical powers? You've got to be kidding me."

Ares frowned. "You've seen us change and you felt what just happened. You can't honestly think I am making this up?"

I sighed. "No. It's just a lot to take in. Are there any more mythological creatures I don't know about?" Everyone nodded their heads smiling. I groaned. "Great. So, when do I get to know which ones are real?"

Ares shrugged. "When we come across one."

I sighed. "Okay, fine. Look, I'm tired. Can I go to sleep?"

Ares smiled. "Of course. I'll show you to your room."

Ares extended his hand to me and I took it following him past the bathroom and into one of the four doors down the hallway. He held the door open for me, so I could walk in. The room was small, just big enough for a bed and a dresser, but it was inviting. I sat down on the bed and smiled at the feel of the soft mattress. Ares closed the door behind him and turned to me. I felt my heart speed up as I realized that we were alone in the room together. He smiled at me and shook his head. "Don't get nervous; I just want to talk."

I slowed my breathing down and crossed my legs on the bed. Ares leaned against the door and frowned. "You really have to watch how you act. I know I told you that I was going to give you slack about treating me as Prince, but I am dominant to you. If you had been any other werewolf I would have punished you severely for what you did."

I sighed. "I'm sorry, but I have to speak with Bret alone."

Ares shook his head. "It is out of the question Artemis. I can't allow you to be alone with that human. If he hurt you, I would never forgive myself."

I frowned. "Bret would never hurt me."

Ares sighed. "You may think that, but when humans find out what we are, they turn into different people. It makes me wonder who the real shifters are." He said almost to himself.

"Bret would never hurt me. He has always been my protector. It would be kind of hypocritical to protect me from everything then hurt me himself."

Ares frowned. "You'd be surprised."

"Can't we at least try to compromise?"

Ares smiled. "Alright. What do you propose?"

"Well since you won't let me meet with him alone, can I choose who goes with me?" I asked.

"Who did you have in mind?"

I shrugged. "Koda or Matt?"

He nodded his head. "Koda."

I smiled victoriously. "And he stands in the back of the room while I talk to Bret."

Ares shook his head. "No. We may be fast, but I won't take the chance on him hurting you before Koda can get there."

"Fine, after I tell Bret what I am, and Koda sees his reaction, he will stay in the back."

"Only if Bret's reaction is decent."

I nodded my head. "Fine."

Ares nodded his head. "Fine."

I raised my pointer finger. "One last thing."

Ares groaned. "What?"

I stopped smiling keeping a serious face. "Koda won't repeat what is said to you or anyone else. Everything that is said stays in that room."

Ares snarled. "What is it that you will say that you don't want me to hear?"

I looked at the ground. "Just agree."

Ares sighed and rubbed his face. "Fine."

I smiled at Ares and wondered if things would work out. *Could I be happy with him? They seemed okay so far, but it takes a while to find out how people really are. Can I really believe that there are other mythological creatures running around?* I sighed and shook my head.

Ares sat down on the bed beside me and smiled. "I promise that I will work my hardest to make you happy. I know that this must be hard for you."

I rolled my eyes. "No, learning that I'm not human and that I was destined to be with a man I don't know and having to deal with the fact that I'm going to have to stop my transformations all the time because I'm a werewolf isn't hard at all."

"If your father had done the right thing and told you about us, this wouldn't be that difficult for you. He and I are going to have a long talk when we go visit them."

"Fine, but if you kill him I won't forgive you." I said with as much anger as I could muster.

Ares smiled. "I won't kill him. Promise." I smiled back at him and tensed as he leaned towards me. He lifted his hand, and reached towards my face, causing my heart to speed up even faster. His hand was an inch away from my face when someone knocked on the door twice. I stood up quickly, moving to the window which looked out at the village. I felt the blush on my cheeks and shook my head so that my hair fell around my face. Ares sighed. "Come in."

The door opened and Koda said, "Ares, the King is here."

Ares groaned. "What is he doing here?"

Koda laughed. "Not sure, but he is requesting to speak with you."

I stayed facing the window not wanting to go anywhere or talk to anyone. Ares stood up from the bed and walked to stand behind me. "I know you are tired, but I would like you to meet the King."

I sighed and asked without turning around, "Will you keep your agreements about our visit?"

Ares laughed softly. "Yes."

I turned around slowly and nodded my head. "Alright."

Ares smiled and kissed my cheek. "Thank you."

The blush erupted on my face before I could even blink. Ares walked out the door leaving me alone with Koda. He smiled and shook his head. I held up my hand at him. "Don't even say anything."

He held his hands up in surrender. "I wasn't."

I growled and walked past him out of the bedroom. When I got down the hallway, Koda started laughing in the bedroom. I blushed darker and walked faster towards the living room. Matt stood by the entrance and smiled at me. "Ready, Love?"

I shrugged. "What's one more werewolf?"

He frowned. "What's that supposed to mean?"

I shook my head. "Nothing. Forget about it." I squared my shoulders, and walked past Matt, to stand beside Ares, but stopped halfway when I saw the man he was talking to.

To say he is a large man is a lie. *He's ginormous.* At least six and a half feet tall, he towered over Ares' five foot five frame easily. His body looked like a professional wrestler and I was just waiting for him to yell, "I'll crush you!". I had never been intimidated by anyone before, but he definitely intimidated me. His dark hair hung to his shoulders and his beard hung to his belly. I instantly thought of a biker and wondered if he had been living here this whole time as one. Ares turned to me, smiling reassuringly, and reached his hand out to me. I thought about rejecting his hand, but knew I would feel safer if he held mine. *How childish is that? I* walked quickly to Ares' side taking his hand and pressed myself against his side.

Ares cleared his throat. "Darius, this is Artemis, my mate."

Darius smiled, but it didn't make him any less menacing. "Your mate? I thought you said you were waiting for the one who would answer your call?"

Ares nodded his head looking down at me with gentleness in his eyes. "I did."

Darius stared at me for a second then his eyes bulged in surprise. "This child answered your call?"

I glared at him. "I'm not a child."

Ares nudged my arm to quiet me. "Forgive her, Darius. Her father decided that he was not going to tell her about us until she changed for the first time, so she knew nothing of us until I came to get her."

Darius stared at me in wonder. "She answered your call without having her first change?"

Ares nodded his head. "We have learned that she has actually been fighting her changes since she was ten years old."

Darius shook his head. "Impossible. No one can fight their first change."

Ares shrugged. "Apparently, she can. She has done it numerous times already. Tomorrow will be the ultimate test though."

I rolled my eyes. "I keep telling you that I will not change tomorrow. Why won't you believe me?"

Darius snarled. "Because it's impossible."

I shrugged. "We'll see. I'm still going to try."

Darius laughed. "She does seem to be a perfect match for you Ares."

Ares nodded his head smiling at me. "She seems so, so far."

I tensed beside them, unsure of what they meant, but Ares rubbed his thumb across my knuckles, calming me.

Darius sighed. "Well, I am just on my way through. We are going to the meeting place."

Ares nodded his head. "I have one stop to make after tomorrow night, and then I will be through. We should probably be there in three or four days, depending on how things go tomorrow night."

Darius nodded his head and looked at me appraisingly. "Does she have magic?" Ares nodded his head. Darius snarled. "Why do you have purple eyes, pup?"

I shrugged. "I have no idea. I didn't even know I had purple eyes until a few minutes ago.

Ares smiled. "She has, literally, been kept in the dark."

Darius frowned and seemed like he wanted to say something else to me, but shook his head. "Well, I better get going."

Ares nodded his head then bowed to Darius. I looked behind me and found Matt and Koda bowing, too. I curtsied and looked at the ground as Darius walked past us and out the door. Ares stood up and so did I. He turned to me smiling. I dropped his hand and moved away from him. "What?"

He laughed. "You really are amazing."

I shook my head. "I don't know what you mean."

He smiled and moved towards me making me stare at his naked upper body. "I know you don't understand. You will soon though."

I turned towards the windows as I felt the sun coming up and sighed. "The sun is here."

Koda stared at me in shock. "You can feel when the sun comes up?"

I nodded my head. "Since I can remember. I have always loved the moon and it's like an alarm in my head goes off when the switch between moon and sun is about to happen."

Ares stared at me in shock for a moment and then whispered, "Oh, Goddess, she might be her."

I turned and looked at him. "Who?"

Koda shook his head. "She can't be her."

Matt nodded his head. "She has the right powers and abilities."

Koda shook his head. "But she is obviously not full werewolf."

Ares shook his head. "The prophecy says she'll be a mixed blood."

I walked slowly away from them towards the bedroom. Ares called, "Where are you going?"

I turned around. "You probably aren't going to explain it anyway and I'm tired. I need to sleep."

Ares smiled. "Of course." He walked towards me making my heart speed up again. He smiled wider and when he was close enough whispered, "I hope your heart speeding up isn't because you are frightened of me."

I shook my head. "No, not frightened in the regular sense."

He smiled and bent down towards me. I tried to move away, but my body wouldn't let me. He bent over my lips with just a breath between us and whispered, "I know you are fighting your feelings, and I understand, but if you would just let go it would be truly amazing." I went to answer him, but he stopped me by kissing me on the lips. I stayed tense as his lips pressed softly, but warmly against mine. My body wanted to wrap my arms around him and kiss him back, but my brain refused to admit that I could have any feelings for this man I had just met hours before. He pulled away and laughed. "You are a fighter. I admire that. Now go on to sleep. We will be in the rooms beside you if you need anything."

I turned quickly away from him without another glance and walked as fast as I could without jogging to my room. I slammed the door shut and threw myself onto the bed. My lips burned where he had kissed me as I buried my face in my pillow. I shook my head back and forth. *I can't have feelings for this old half man, half wolf. I just met him hours ago. Shit.* I groaned and rolled on to my side closing my eyes. *Things will work out. I can control myself long enough to find an escape plan.* I pulled the covers over my head and hummed the song my father had always sung to me as I drifted to sleep.

"Artemis. Artemis, wake up." Koda said softly.

I opened my eyes and looked up at Koda's smiling face. "Hi, Koda."

He laughed softly. "Hello. It's time to get up."

I looked out the window and saw that there was no light coming through. "Is it night-time already?"

He nodded his head. "You slept through the day. The only reason I am waking you now is because your stomach has been growling loud enough that we heard it in the other room. Ares thought it would be best if you ate before you fought your change as well."

I nodded my head and stood up stretching my arms over my head. I squealed as I finished my stretch and smiled. Koda laughed. "I see you're calmer today."

I shrugged and smiled. "I figured that being nervous all the time and thinking about things I can't change is stupid. I am just going to relax and learn to enjoy how my new life is." *Until I can think of a plan to escape from you.*

Koda frowned. "What was that?"

I stared at him in confusion. "What do you mean?"

He sighed. "You flinched as you finished saying that. That usually means that you are lying or thinking something bad."

I felt my eyes widen and turned away from him. *Shit. Why the hell is he so perceptive?* I sighed. "I'm sorry, it's just that I can't believe I am saying this and feeling so comfortable with you all when I don't even know you."

"I know how you feel, Artemis. I helped a wolf that wasn't told about being a werewolf until one month before his first change. He was scared and it was in the eighteen hundreds when the werewolf and witch hunts began. At least for you, things are a lot better and will be getting much, much better soon."

I turned to him and asked, "What do you mean, 'soon'?"

He smiled. "The preternaturals or mythological creatures as you like to call them, are taking the world back from the humans."

I stared in shock at him as I remembered the London and Las Vegas scenes. "You're killing all of the humans?"

He shook his head and waved his hands at me. "No no no no no. Okay, we kill some, but we capture most of them."

I snarled. "So you can eat them later?"

Matt walked into the bedroom laughing. "Now that's original. Of course not, Love. We are taking them as slaves. It's the only way for them to live as humans. Either you are a slave or you become one of us."

I growled and felt my power rising inside me. "That is ridiculous! Who are you to decide how they live?!"

Matt snarled at me. "They decided to kill us centuries ago. To avoid that fate, we were forced to hide in sewers and nearly starve."

I shook my head angrily, my power radiating off of me in waves and slapping against Koda and Matt. Every time a wave would hit them they would take a step back. "It was not these people, but the people who lived during that time. It would be like the African-Americans forcing Caucasians into slavery because of what happened hundreds of years ago. That's ridiculous, because we live peacefully together, no matter what color the other is. How do you know it wouldn't be the same for you?"

Koda laughed. "Are you serious? Do you honestly think the humans would live peacefully with a werewolf? They would be too worried that we would hurt them."

I growled loudly and moved towards the bedroom door. Matt blocked me, making me snarl and growl louder. "MOVE!" I felt my body starting to shake and stopped growling. I stayed perfectly still and breathed slower taking big, deep breaths. Matt and Koda stared at me in shock as I kept my body calm and collected. I sighed and looked up at Matt. "I said move."

Matt moved to the side and I hurried past him into the kitchen. I opened the fridge and found lunchmeat and took it out, swallowing the pieces of turkey and ham whole. Koda and Matt watched me from the doorway as I finished the two packs of lunchmeat. I opened the freezer and pulled out a block of ground beef. I put it in the sink and turned the water on scalding hot to defrost it as quickly as possible. After watching me for a few more seconds, Matt walked away from the kitchen and out of the house. I ignored Koda, as I waited anxiously for the meat to defrost. I poked at the meat and smiled as it started to give way. I heard the front door open, but ignored it, continuing to poke at the block of beef. I started dancing from side to side as I grew antsy for the meat to defrost. I snarled and flipped the meat over to allow the water to defrost the other side. I felt someone standing next to me but ignored him. *Nothing matters but food right now.*

SONG OF THE MOON

Blood started to run down the sink and I pulled the meat out holding it in my hands. I licked my lips hungrily and looked around for a plate. Ares, who was standing beside me, handed me a plate. I took the plate quickly and placed the meat on it. I sat on the ground, and started eating the ground beef. I groaned in happiness as I swallowed the beef and blood. Someone's hand reached towards my plate and I snarled and pulled the plate away. The hand disappeared, and I went back to scarfing down the food. When I had finished the ground beef, I stood up and put the plate in the sink. I went back to the fridge and took out the milk. I turned for a glass, but Ares was already handing one to me. I took it and poured a glass of milk, then swallowed it quickly. I put the milk back and put the glass in the sink, before sighing in contentment. I looked around at the three men staring at me, and felt self-conscious. I wiped at my mouth and ran to the bathroom to see if I had food or blood on me. My face was clean, so I walked back out into the living room where they had moved and begun to whisper together. I sat down on the couch and stared at my hands, as they finished talking.

Ares cleared his throat making me look up at him. "How are you feeling?"

I shrugged. "Fine. Why?"

"You don't know what just happened do you?"

I shrugged. "I started to get shaky and I calmed myself down, but then I was really hungry so I ate."

He laughed and turned to Koda and Matt. "You see? She has no idea what just happened."

"You want to explain to me what happened?" I said angrily.

"You just stopped your transformation again. This time you stopped it so fast that the only need you had was food. Usually you are extremely tired when you stop it too, but you stopped it so fast and so early that you aren't tired."

I stared at him in shock as I comprehended what he said. I smiled at him and laughed. "So, I stopped the transformation again?" He nodded his head. I smiled wider. "I told you I could."

Koda snorted. "Just because you said so doesn't mean you can. If I hadn't seen it with my own eyes, I would have told them they were crazy."

"Oh. Well, can we go see Darren and Bret now?"

Ares shrugged. "I guess it is safe, since you didn't change."

I stared at him in shock. "You thought I was going to lose control and try to eat Bret, didn't you? Is that the main reason you wanted Koda with me?"

Ares nodded his head. "You would never forgive yourself if you hurt him."

I nodded my head solemnly. "You're right. So, does this mean I can meet with him alone?"

He sighed and rubbed his temples. "You are so pushy, but since it's your birthday, I'll let you."

I smiled at him and walked towards the door. "Come on. Let's go. You can decide when we get there." I walked out the door and stopped in my tracks. Bret stood a few feet away from the door staring at me in shock. I shook my head and whispered, "Bret? What are you doing here?"

His surprise turned into a wide toothed grin as he picked me up spun me around. "Oh thank God you're alright. Come on let's get you home." I shook my head as he set me down and started to pull me down the porch. I grabbed his arm and pulled him back. He stared at me in shock. "Come on, Artemis."

I shook my head. "Bret, you need to leave, now. It's not safe for you here."

"Why? Because of all of the big wolves around? I can handle myself. I need to take you out of here." He said fiercely.

Ares, Matt and Koda walked on to the porch and stared in shock at Bret with his hand on my arm, and mine on his. I sighed and placed my body in front of Bret's. "Just listen to me for a second, okay?" Ares, Matt and Koda nodded their heads in unison. "He thinks you are going to hurt me, and he came to save me. You can't hurt him for that."

Ares shook his head. "No, but he can't go free."

I shook my head. "He doesn't know anything. He hasn't figured it out."

Bret pushed me to the side and asked, "Figured out what? Why do I feel like I am missing some big secret?"

I smiled and turned to Ares. "See? He doesn't know. Just let me take him home. You want to talk to my dad anyway, right?"

Matt snarled. "You plan on telling him anyway. Then he will know how to get here. We can't let him go."

I snarled back at him and put myself in front of Bret again. "You are not going to hurt him."

Koda smiled. "We never said we were going to hurt him."

I snapped my teeth at Koda. "You aren't going to kill him either."

Ares waved his hands in the air. "Calm down Artemis. We aren't going to kill him. But he can't go free. He is going to have to stay with us."

I looked from Ares to Koda to Matt and back to Ares. "Why do *I* feel like I'm missing something now?"

Ares sighed. "If I tell you, you are going to freak out."

I shook my head and took a step back pushing Bret back with me. "Then it's definitely no."

Bret asked, "What is going on Artemis?"

I snapped. "I'm trying to save your life Bret. Just shut up and let me handle this." He stared at me in shock, but didn't say anything. Ares and Matt took a step towards me while Koda took one to the side. I snarled and crouched down. "Please stop. I don't want to fight you."

Ares stared in shock at me. "You are willing to fight us over him?"

I nodded my head. "He has done nothing wrong and you are trying to do something horrible to him."

Ares smiled. "You don't even know what it is."

I snarled. "No! You told me that he would be unharmed."

Ares nodded his head. "Yes, but that was when he was at your town. Now he knows the way here and will tell the others."

Bret shrugged. "Why would I tell anyone about this place? Just let me take Artemis back and we'll forget about it."

Ares shook his head. "She can never go back."

I felt a tear fall down my face and shook my head. "Shut up. All of you, just shut up!"

I heard someone behind us and spun around to see Koda coming towards us. I growled loudly and jumped in front of Bret as Koda ran towards him. Koda smashed into me, sending me flying through the air. I felt my body hit the wall and shook my head to clear my daze. I jumped up and saw Matt and Ares holding Bret. I snarled loudly and snapped my teeth at them as I moved towards them. I felt my body begin to shake and sighed. I breathed slowly and stopped the shaking. I looked up at Bret's face and stopped moving. He stared at me with a mixture of horror and fear on his face.

Bret asked, "What's wrong with you?"

I shook my head. "Nothing Bret."

He shook his head at me. "You aren't human are you?"

I looked at Ares and snarled. "Let him go. Please!"

Ares dropped Bret's arm and moved towards me. "Artemis. I didn't want this to happen."

I shook my head and moved away from him. "Bret you need to leave."

Bret shook his head. "Whatever you are, I...I can deal with it. Come home with me."

I laughed bitterly and shook my head. "It's never been my home, Bret. I can't go back there again. You're right, I'm not human. That's why I never fit in."

Bret asked, "If you aren't human, then what are you?"

I looked up at Ares' worried face and sighed. "I'm a werewolf."

Bret laughed loudly and said, "Yeah, right. So, really though. What's going on with you?"

I looked Bret in the eyes. "I'm a werewolf, Bret. So are the three men around you."

Bret looked at three men holding him who were all shorter, but more muscled. He shook his head in disbelief. "No way."

"Bret. You remember Ares was there at my house, right?" Bret nodded his head. I went on, "So were Koda and Matt, just not in human form."

I watched as Bret comprehended what I said. "The wolves? The giant wolves?" His face grew more worried as he looked at the men holding him.

I nodded my head. "Yes. And I'm one of them, but I haven't changed shape yet."

Bret shook his head. "Then how do you know that you are one of them?"

I looked at Ares who nodded his head. I groaned. "Because my dad is one." Bret's face fell and he stopped talking. He stared at me for a full minute before shaking his head. I walked towards him, but he backed up as much as Matt and Koda would allow. I stopped walking and looked at the ground. "I would never hurt you." I looked back up at him and smiled.

Bret shook his head. "You can't be a werewolf I can't be in lov..." He stopped talking and looked up at me. I let the pain and shock show on my face. He sighed. "I won't believe you are a werewolf until you change."

I groaned. "I'm not going to change. I refuse."

Bret smiled. "Then it's alright. We can go on with our lives like normal."

I groaned again. "Don't you see Bret?! I'm not normal. I don't belong with you and your friends. I belong here with other wolves. Eventually I'll change and I know that. I won't be able to hold it off forever. When that happens I don't want to be near you. I could kill you."

"I don't believe you. If you don't love me or don't want to be with me, then just tell me. Don't make up these crazy lies." Bret said with pain pinching his face.

Ares laughed. "Damn, you are persistent. Would you rather I changed and showed you?"

I snarled at Ares. "Don't even think about it."

Ares snarled back. "Do not threaten me. I have the power to force you to change if I want."

I snapped my teeth at him. "Let Bret go, and you and I can finish this."

Ares shook his head. "I already told you that we can't let him go. He knows too much."

I shook my head. "No way. You are going to make him a slave or something and I won't let you."

Ares growled. "You wouldn't be able to stop me, even if that was what I was going to do."

Koda cleared his throat, "Prince." Ares looked at Koda and stopped snarling. Koda smiled. "Perhaps I should just get this over with so we don't have to stand here and talk all day?"

Ares nodded his head smiling. "Okay." I took a step forward as I saw Koda open his mouth. I watched in amazement as fangs extended. I finally knew what they were going to do and ran forward. I dodged around Ares as he tried to grab me and lunged at Koda. Koda grabbed Bret around his arms and bit into his shoulder. Bret yelled in pain as Koda bit down harder drawing blood.

I screamed, "NO!" and charged into Koda knocking him backwards and away from Bret. Koda landed with a large thud as I rode his body down to the ground. I pushed off of him running back to Bret. Matt was kneeling beside him and I charged forward smashing into him and sending him flying backwards into the side of the house.

Ares snarled at me from the other side of Bret. "Stop Artemis. It's too late now. He's already infected."

I shook my head and charged forward, picking Bret up in my arms and running as fast as I could. I had to fight to keep a hold on Bret because he was too tall to be carried easily. I could hear someone following me, but I didn't care. My only concern was getting Bret to safety. I ran faster and weaved in and out of the trees trying not to hit one. I saw a clearing and ran for it. I set Bret on the ground and ripped open his shirt. I stared in shock at the wound which was still bleeding. I placed my lips over the wound and sucked as hard as I could. Bret screamed in pain as I sucked his blood and another bitter tasting substance into my mouth. I sucked until my mouth was full then turned and spit. I clamped my mouth over the bite again and sucked. Bret screamed with every suck and thrashed his legs.

Ares sighed beside me. "It's no use Artemis. Even if you suck up what is there, some has already gone into his bloodstream. Look at his eyes."

I pulled back from the bite and spit what was in my mouth. I looked at Bret's eyes and gasped. They were wolf amber and glowing. I shook my head and let the tears fall. "No! No, I can stop it."

Ares reached towards me and I snarled at him. "Get away!" I clamped my mouth over Bret's bite and sucked as hard as I could making Bret scream in pain. No more bitter taste came and I stopped sucking. I spit what was in my mouth out and stared at Bret. He breathed slowly staring at me with amber eyes. I cried harder and hugged him. "I'm so sorry Bret. I'm so sorry. I could have tried harder. Now you are going to be like me and never be able to go back to our town. Never finish football."

Bret laughed. "It's alright Artemis. I don't care about that as long as I have you."

Ares growled. "She is not yours."

I pushed off of Bret and shoved Ares in the chest. "I am not yours either you asshole! You think after you take my friends humanity away, that I am going to stay with you?!"

Ares frowned. "I did not bite him."

I snarled. "But you let Koda. You could have told him not to, and that makes you just as liable. It was your plan all along to have him changed, wasn't it? That was what you didn't want to say to me. You bastard."

Ares sighed. "I'm not going to fight with you anymore tonight. He is changing already and there is nothing you can do about it."

Bret stood up behind me and grabbed my arm hard. I looked up at his black eyes and said, "Bret, just calm down. You can fight the change."

Bret snarled. "I'm hungry."

I smiled. "Well, let's go get you some food."

Bret shook his head then inhaled above my head. "I have food here."

I felt my mouth drop open as I realized he was talking about me. Ares moved forward so that he was standing beside me and Bret. "She is not food." Ares said in a strained voice

Bret turned to Ares and snarled. "She smells like food."

The tension in the air was growing thicker. Ares shook his head. "You do not know what food smells like. Come with me and I will show you real food."

Bret snarled and pulled me against him. "You just want her to yourself. No!"

Matt and Koda jogged into the clearing and came to stand behind Ares. Koda whispered, "What's going on?"

I cried softly and whispered, "Bret wants to eat me."

Matt and Koda looked from me to Bret to Ares and back to me. When they settled back to me their faces held more of a softer look. Matt said. "Love, I'm sorry. This has never happened before."

Koda nodded his head. "Never. Maybe it's because you haven't changed yet."

Matt nodded his head. "That's it. You need to show him who is dominant to convince him that you aren't food."

"So I have to fight him?" They nodded their heads. I looked up at Bret who was staring intently at Ares in a battle of wills. I groaned. "Shit." I yanked my arm from Bret's arm and ran away from him as fast as I could. I heard rustling and yelling, but kept running. When I was far enough away that they couldn't see me clearly I jumped up the nearest tree and climbed up. They came running and pushing each other searching for me. *Why are Ares, Koda and Matt pushing each other?* I didn't have time to decide because Bret passed under me. I jumped down from the tree on to his back forcing him to the ground. I drove my knee into his spine as he fell making him scream in pain. He rolled over and I jumped up straddling him. I bent to press my knee into his throat when someone slammed into me and grabbed me. I grunted from the impact and said, "STOP!"

The person stopped and I looked up to see Matt's excited amber eyes. I shook my head. "Matt, what the hell are you doing?"

He inhaled loudly then sighed. "Sorry. You got us all excited when you ran away like that. Our wolf sides kicked in."

I groaned and pulled away from him going back for Bret who was standing up now. He smiled and licked his lips. I shook my finger at him. "I am not food. I am your alpha."

He snarled. "You are not dominant to me!"

Ares appeared behind him. "I am." He grabbed Bret around the neck and proceeded to choke him until he passed out. He laid Bret on the ground and wiped his hands off against each other to symbolize he was done.

I snarled. "I was supposed to dominate him. Now he is still going to think I'm food when he wakes up."

Ares shrugged. "He won't wake up for a few days anyway. We'll worry about it then."

Koda ran to us. "You really have to learn not to run like that. I got all excited and almost ate you."

"You were nowhere near me. None of you knew where I was," I said with a suppressed laugh.

Ares looked up at the tree branches above us. "Yeah, how did you get up that tree so fast?"

I shrugged. "My life depended on it."

The three men laughed loudly at my joke and the tension disappeared. Koda reached down and picked Bret up under his arms. "We better get back and put him in the hibernation room."

Ares nodded his head. "We'll leave him here while we go talk to Darren."

"I'll stay here with Bret," I said.

Ares shook his head. "He tried to eat you. I'm not leaving you here. You have to come with us."

I groaned. "Why are you always so pushy? Can't you just suggest that I go with you and then let me decide?"

Ares thought in silence for a minute before speaking. "Then I suggest you come so you don't get eaten."

I nodded my head. "Sounds like a good idea."

Ares laughed. "You agreed with me for once."

"Trust me it won't happen again. Besides, as soon as I can, I'll be leaving." The words left my mouth before I could stop myself.

Ares and Matt stared at me in shock. Ares asked, "What do you mean by that?"

"Nothing. Forget I said it."

Ares grabbed me by the arms and stared into my eyes. "I am sorry that we turned your friend. You have to forgive me."

I laughed bitterly. "I told you that I wasn't going to stay with you."

Ares face fell into sadness pulling at my heart. "How can you say such a thing? Do you not feel for me?"

I stared at his handsome face and desperately wanted to kiss him, to heal the pain I had caused. I shook my head. "I refuse to admit anything."

SONG OF THE MOON

The pain in his eyes made me flinch, but I held my ground. Ares asked, "Do you want to leave? To go back to your father and the little town you came from when Bret won't be there?"

I groaned and looked at the ground. "I can't believe you allowed this to happen."

Ares whispered, "If I had known how you would react I would not have let it happen. I figured you would be happy that your friend is now like you, and will live almost as long as you."

I shook my head. "But he is in love with me. The day before you came, he was trying to make me his girlfriend. Don't you get it? You have just prolonged his life, to watch me be with you."

Ares smiled. "So you admit that you have feelings for me?"

I shook my head. "I didn't say that. What I am saying is that I do not love him in that way. And that you would not even let us try, because you believe I am destined to be with you." I rolled my eyes at the thought of destiny.

Ares frowned. "Why do you roll your eyes?"

"Destiny is not something I believe in. I believe that we make our own destiny, not that it is pre-set for us."

Ares shrugged. "Either way, you still answered my call, which means that you are essentially mine. You can call it whatever you want, but you and I are meant to be together. I am sorry that your friend will have a tough time dealing with that, but it is the truth. It is why your father could not stop me from taking you. He could feel the connection between you and me when you came out the door."

I frowned. "What if I do not love you? What if I never love you?"

Ares smiled. "Just give it time, and do not strangle your feelings. You will see."

I looked at the ground. "It's really irritating that I can't be mad at you for very long."

Ares nodded his head. "I'm sure I will find out how that is soon enough."

I looked up at his face and asked, "Will you let Bret stay with us, or will you send him away?"

Ares shrugged. "I'll leave that up to you and him to decide. If he thinks he can handle staying and seeing us together, then he is welcome to join us, but if he wishes to stay with the wolves in this village, then I will let him."

I nodded my head and started walking back toward the village. I called over my shoulder, "We better get him to your hibernation thingy."

Koda and Matt picked Bret up and carried him behind me. Ares walked beside me, smiling. I tried my best to ignore him, but couldn't help glancing at him occasionally. He never looked at me, but every time I glanced at him his smile seemed to get bigger. It took us longer to get back because I was walking, but I didn't care. When we made it to the clearing, I stopped moving and tilting my face up to the full moon, closed my eyes. Koda and Matt continued past me with Bret leaving me and Ares alone. I put my arms out to the side and inhaled as deep as I could. I loved the smell of the forest and the night. I opened my eyes and bathed in the warmth of the moon pulling my arms back down to my sides. I turned to Ares and smiled.

He had his face upturned to the moon and his eyes closed, breathing deeply. He opened his eyes and smiled at me. "You enjoy the moon, too, I see."

I nodded my head. "The moon makes me feel at peace."

Ares nodded his head. "Me, too. Of course, I should have assumed someone with the name of the Goddess of the Moon would like the moon."

I laughed. "Yeah, but I guess my connection to the moon is more because of my werewolf side."

Ares shrugged his shoulders. "We are the Children of the Moon. Our power to change comes from the moon. I have always liked the moon's glow. It's much better for your skin to moonbathe than sunbathe."

I laughed and took a step closer to him feeling a strange pull. I thought about fighting it, but remembered him asking me to not strangle my feelings. He stared at me in shock and nervousness and did not move. I took another step closing the distance so that only one foot of space separated us. I looked up at his uncertain face and smiled. He smiled back at me, but stayed perfectly still, his breathing speeding up slightly. I slowly reached a shaky hand out to him and placed it on his chest. His muscle flexed then relaxed as I stroked down his chest and across his chiseled abdominals. His skin was so hot against my hand that I had to keep moving it, or it was too much. I ran my hand back up his stomach and across his chest and up the side of his neck to rest on his face. I stared a little longer at his sky blue eyes and realized that there was a slight slant to the corners. *I wonder if he is part Asian.* I started to stand on tiptoe to reach his lips when I heard something moving through the trees. I quickly dropped my hand and turned around towards the sound.

Ares stepped around me so that he was standing beside me. A small grey wolf cub covered in blood walked from behind a tree to stare at us. Ares squatted down and opened his arms as if inviting the wolf for a hug. I watched in amazement as the wolf's body snapped and popped and twisted to form a small boy. The boy ran to Ares and collapsed into his arms. Ares cradled the boy and whispered to him. "What happened?"

The boy shivered against Ares and whispered, "The humans figured it out. They. They killed my pack."

Ares asked, "Are you hurt?"

The boy shook his head. "It was my pack's blood. I hid under the bodies so the humans wouldn't kill me."

Ares stood up with the boy still in his arms and walked towards Gregory's home. Gregory opened the door before we got there and took the boy from Ares' arms. The boy turned to Ares. "Prince, wait."

Ares stayed still and waited for the boy to speak. The boy cleared his throat. "One of them there is a wolf. He is helping them find us. They have guns and knives with silver. Stay downwind of him."

Ares nodded his head. "Do you know his name?"

The boy snarled, "Darren."

I gasped and shook my head. "It must be someone else."

Ares asked, "What did he look like?"

The boy sighed. "I didn't get a good look, but he had her hair."

The boy pointed to me then gasped. "Is she with them? Is she going to kill us?"

I shook my head. "No, I'm not with them and won't hurt you."

Ares smiled at the boy. "It's alright, she's my *passt genau.*"

The boy nodded his head. "Okay." Gregory took him inside and shut the door. Koda and Matt walked up the porch steps to stand beside us.

I looked at Ares. "What's pause...gee...now?"

Ares laughed at my poor attempt to speak the words he had just done. "It's *passt genau*, German for what you are to me."

"What does it mean, Ares?" I asked again.

He smiled. "Perfect match."

I fought to frown, but my mouth formed a smile. I shook my head and asked, "What are we going to do about the humans and that werewolf?"

Ares frowned. *"You* aren't going to do anything. You are still very human. Until you change you aren't doing any fighting."

I groaned. "Ares, I have to go. What if it's my dad?"

Ares sighed and rubbed his temples. Koda said, "I think she should stay here. You will be too worried about her to focus on the fight."

Matt nodded his head. "I agree with Koda."

I sighed. "Fine. You go off and battle the humans and leave me here alone to worry. I'll just find things to break while you're gone. And fight my change."

Ares smiled. "You would worry for us?"

I nodded my head then hissed, "Damn you!"

Ares laughed and grabbed me, pulling me against him. "Koda is right, I would worry too much about you if you went. You worrying for us will be a lot less of a problem. Please stay here. If it is your father, I will try my hardest to simply restrain him and bring him here. But if it comes down to it, and I must, I will kill him."

I nodded and relaxed into the warmth of his body, leaning my head against his chest. "I understand. Be careful."

He pushed me back and kissed my lips softly. I kissed him back and then quickly pulled away, running into the house and shutting the door. My lips burned even hotter than before as I leaned against the front door. Gregory and the boy sat in the middle of the living room. The boy had been given clothes much too big for him, but he sat playing a card game with Gregory, smiling. *How can he be smiling after his pack was killed? I would be devastated.*

Gregory saw me and smiled. "You want to play?"

I shrugged my shoulders. "I guess I should. They are leaving me behind."

Gregory shrugged. "Ares would be too focused on your safety to worry about his. It's better this way."

I groaned and sat down beside them. I turned to the boy and said, "Hi, I'm Artemis."

He smiled at me. "Jason."

I smiled back at him as Gregory passed out cards. I watched as he dealt us each thirteen cards and asked, "What are we playing?"

Gregory smiled. "Thirteen."

I sighed. "I don't know how to play."

Gregory laughed. "It's alright. We'll teach

you."

I listened intently as Gregory explained the game to me. The game was like war, where you had to put a card down which was higher in either number or suit and the first one out of cards won. I arranged my cards from lowest, three, to the highest, two then started playing. Gregory put down the three of clubs, the lowest card in the game. I put down a three of hearts which was higher in suit so it beat his card. Jason put down a king, making Gregory and I groan. Gregory put down an ace then I put down a two. Jason and Gregory groaned.

Jason said, "Pass."

Gregory nodded his head. "Pass."

I smiled and laid down a six card straight. Both groaned again and said, "Pass" in unison. I put down a pair of fives and Jason laid down a pair of eights. Gregory passed and I put down a pair of tens.

Jason sighed. "Pass." Gregory nodded his head and waved his hand for me to go. I put down my final card, an ace and raised my hands in the air. "I'm out."

Jason groaned. "I thought you said that you haven't played this?"

I smiled. "I hadn't played this before. It's a very fun game though. Can we play again?"

Gregory smiled. "Sure."

Jason turned and looked at me frowning. "Why are you nervous?"

I looked down at him and frowned. "Why do you think that I am nervous?"

His eyes went wide. "Aren't you a werewolf?"

I nodded my head. "Yes, but what does that have to do with why you think I am nervous?"

Gregory smiled. "Jason, she hasn't had her first change yet."

Jason's eyes went even wider. "What?! How is that possible?!"

I smiled and shrugged. "I didn't know I was a werewolf until yesterday and apparently I have been fighting the change since I was around your age."

Jason gasped, "No way! Asena's children were the only ones who were supposed to be able to do that."

I frowned. "Who's Asena?"

Jason and Gregory stared at me in shock. Gregory asked, "You don't know who Asena is?"

"I told you that I didn't know I was a werewolf until yesterday. Your speech last night was the first I have heard about us."

Gregory sighed. "I thought they were joking and just wanted me to talk. Alright. I'll have to tell you our story then."

I smiled. "Okay." I adjusted myself so that I was a little more comfortable before he began.

Gregory cleared his throat. "All of us that are born werewolves are descendents of the Mother of all werewolves, Asena. She herself was not a werewolf, but...I'm getting ahead of myself. A village was raided by soldiers, killing everyone but one infant, who the general took pity on and only gave the infant cuts on his arms and legs. Asena, a great she-wolf with grey fur and sky-blue mane saved the boy and nursed him back to health. The boy eventually impregnated her and she gave birth to ten boys. Those ten boys were half man, half wolf. The very first werewolves. They ruled over the Empire, but many of the boys became bored of their home and left to explore the world. They went to Iceland, Germany, Scotland, England and many other places. The men would mate with women in those countries, thus passing on their half wolf traits to their offspring. That's how we came about. There are some who came from Greece who claim that they are descendants of Lycaon who tried to trick Zeus into eating human flesh and then was turned into a wolf by Zeus, but I don't believe that. They are just descendants of Asena like us."

I stared in disbelief of the story he had just said, but strangely it made sense. "Why are you killing all the humans now?"

Gregory frowned. "During the medieval times in Europe, there was a rash of wolf killings. Instead of realizing the reason there were so many more wolf kills was that the wolf population had gotten out of control, they started the search for werewolves. Unfortunately for some of us, we really did exist and lived in Europe at that time. I don't know how the notion of werewolves got into their heads, but they started looking. Soon after that they started searching for witches as well. I had many witch friends who died. It was horrible. We all went into hiding then. Some of us managed to come to America and start over here, but others went into the sewers with the vamp...with the others."

I shook my head. "What were you going to say?"

He shook his head back at me. "I can't tell you that part yet. I'm sure soon, but not yet. Anyway, the others decided it had been long enough and we planned our take over. I give it three months before the world is completely taken over by us preternaturals."

I shook my head. "What's a preternatural?"

He sighed. "I'm telling you too much already. Preternatural means exceeding what is natural or regular. All races that possess gifts, as you humans call them, are called preternaturals. Basically, anyone that has characteristics that surpass natural human abilities is a preternatural."

I nodded my head. "Like witches."

Gregory smiled. "Yes, like witches. Now let's play some more thirteen."

I smiled and nodded my head. "Alright. How long do you think it will be before Ares is back?"

Gregory smiled. "I'm not sure, but you don't have to worry about Ares. He is the toughest of us. Did he tell you that's how he became prince?"

I shook my head. "We haven't really talked much." I felt a blush starting and shook my head.

Gregory sighed. "Well, I will let Ares tell you about the ways to become powerful." He picked up the cards on the floor and started shuffling them. I turned and saw that Jason was staring at me curiously.

"What is it Jason?" I asked.

He looked down. "Nothing."

I laughed. "You can ask me whatever you want. I promise I won't get mad."

Jason looked up and smiled. "I was just trying to remember where I saw purple eyes before."

Gregory frowned. "Enough Jason."

Jason sighed. "Alright."

I frowned at Gregory. "What? Why can't he tell me where he has seen purple eyes before? It might help me find my mom."

Gregory shook his head. "Sorry. We can't tell you that. When Ares wants to he will."

"Whatever. Let's play." I said to change the subject.

We played for a few more hours, but the sunlight started to peek through the curtains and I couldn't stay awake anymore. Jason fell asleep on the floor snoring softly. I stood up and started to walk back to my room when I felt Ares. I threw the front door open and ran out on to the front porch. I looked around, but couldn't see him anywhere. I inhaled and could smell him. *How the hell do I know it's him? Is this one of those weird things about being tied to him? I know he is here. Where is he?* I continued to scan the yard and turned as Gregory came out.

"What is it Artemis?" He asked me looking around too.

"Ares is here, I can feel him and smell him, but I can't see him."

Gregory inhaled then nodded his head. "You're right. He must be close for me to be able to smell him too. Come on, let's go look for him." I followed Gregory down the porch steps still frantically searching for Ares. Gregory led us towards a large white warehouse and stopped me at the black metal door, "You can't come in here. I'll be right back."

I inhaled deeply and jumped up and down. "He's in there. Hurry."

Gregory stared at me strangely, but walked in the large warehouse shutting the door tightly behind him. I paced back and forth in front of the door as I waited. People passed me with odd expressions on their faces, but I ignored them pacing back and forth and back and forth. Ten minutes passed and I started to get worried as I reached for the door handle, the door swung open nearly hitting me in the face. Koda looked around and finally saw me standing next to him. He frowned. "What are you doing here?"

I sighed. "I can feel Ares and smell him. What's wrong? Is he hurt?"

Koda laughed and grabbed my shoulders stopping me from jumping around. "He's fine Artemis. Calm down. I'll go get him for you."

"Why can't I come in? Gregory went to get him for me ten minutes ago."

Koda sighed. "Just stay here and I'll get him."

I snarled and crossed my arms over my chest. "Fine, but you better hurry."

Koda shut the door behind him as he went back inside. I picked up my pacing route again as I wanted yet again for Ares to come out. I walked a few feet away from the door then spun around as I heard it open. Ares stared at me in shock then smiled and walked quickly towards me. I walked as fast as I could without running to him wrapping my arms around his neck as he wrapped his around my waist. "Are you okay?" I asked frantically.

Ares nodded his head inhaling my hair. "I am now."

I sighed in happiness and pulled back to kiss him on the lips softly. He kissed me back pressing harder. I pulled away and asked, "What's going on? Why didn't you come see me?"

He frowned. "I was talking to our prisoner."

I gasped, "Is it my dad? Was it him that was taking the humans to find the wolves?"

Ares pulled away from me and nodded his head. "Yes, but your dad is not the prisoner I have. Darren got away before we could catch him."

I sighed. "Does that mean you are going to go after him?"

Ares shook his head. "I ran into Darius again and he said he will take care of it." I started to say something, but he held up his hand. "He promised not to kill him until you and I spoke with Darren."

"Thanks." I realized that I still had my arms wrapped around his neck and pulled away from him blushing.

Ares laughed. "I wondered how long it would take you to pull away from me. I don't understand why you won't just enjoy it?"

"Because I shouldn't have such strong feelings for you so soon. It's not normal."

Ares smiled. "We aren't normal anyway. And by the way, Bret is doing well. We should be able to let him out tomorrow, to spend time with you."

I smiled. "That's great. Thank you." I sighed and looked back up at Ares. "Is it true that you are one of the strongest of the werewolves?"

Ares frowned. "Has Gregory been telling you stories?"

I shook my head. "He explained about Asena and Lycaon, but said it was your choice to tell me about how you became prince and how that works."

Ares smiled and extended his hand to me waiting for me to take it. "I'll explain everything back in the house."

I took his hand reluctantly, but once our skin touched I felt much better. We walked in silence back to Gregory's house and into my bedroom, so Jason could sleep. I sat cross-legged on my bed, with my back against the headboard, as Ares closed the bedroom door. He sat down cross-legged facing me and smiled. "Alright, here it is. I come from a family of kings and queens who ruled humans in Europe. Of course, my ancestors are from Asena and that is where my slanted eyes are from." He noticed my shocked face and whispered, "Yes, I saw you looking at them." He shifted on the bed before continuing.

"Anyway, I technically was a prince in Europe, but in the order of werewolves to be king or queen is by fighting. I fought my way up to Prince one hundred years ago and have stayed there because no one has tried to fight me for that place. Darius just became king a few years ago after defeating our old king."

"His wife, who happens to be my mother, got her place because her husband, the old king, made a decree that a king could choose his own queen or have the queen he wanted kill the old one or keep the current queen. Unfortunately for my mother Darius chose to keep her." Ares snarled as he finished his explanation.

I gaped at him, "Darius killed your step-dad and is sleeping with your mom?"

Ares snarled. "No one said they were doing anything like that. Although, sometimes the ruling pair do end up becoming a breeding pair. That is not the case with my mother and Darius."

I shrugged and couldn't help smiling a little. "Whatever helps you sleep at night."

Ares sighed. "Anyway, I killed Darius' son to become prince and I think that was his motivation to become king."

I asked, "Are you going to fight him to be king?"

Ares laughed bitterly. "Someday, but not anytime soon."

I stopped talking and stared at his thoughtful face. "Have you ever done modeling?"

Ares smiled and nodded his head. "I actually did. When I lived in London, I did some modeling for money. Why would you ask that?"

I blushed. "Don't make me say it."

Ares crawled forward on his hands and knees until his face was just in front of mine. "I love that you blush for me."

I looked up slowly and my breath caught in my throat. *He is too handsome.* I reached out slowly and stroked the side of his face with my hand. His muscles were hard as he clenched his jaw. I smiled. "Why are you clenching your jaw?"

He slowly relaxed his jaw and whispered, "I am trying to hold myself back."

I shook my head. "From what? I don't understand." I ran both my hands down the sides of his face and felt him clench his jaw again. I leaned forward and kissed the right side of his jaw softly. "Stop clenching your jaw."

He relaxed his jaw then leaned forward kissing me on the lips. His lips were burning hot and all I wanted was to kiss him back. I wrapped my arms around his neck and kissed him back letting him feel how much I wanted him. He grabbed my legs and uncrossed them pulling me down the bed so that I was lying under him. Our lips melted together as we kissed. I felt his joy and it was suddenly my own. *Why had I been so reluctant to give into him?* I heard the door open, but did not stop. Ares tried to pull away, but I held him in place kissing him harder and flicking my tongue across his lips. He groaned and pulled away from me jumping off the bed. I smiled at him then turned to the door. Bret stared at me in shock and I watched as the hurt sank into his eyes. I sat up quickly and shook my head. "Bret. I...I didn't know you were there."

Bret shook his head looking at the ground. "I should have knocked, I'm sorry."

He turned away to leave and I jumped off the bed running to him. "Please don't...I'm sorry. I don't know what got into me."

Ares sighed. "I'll leave you two to talk." He started to walk past me, but I saw the sadness in his eyes.

"Ares, what's wrong?" I asked.

Ares shook his head smiling. "I know you are young and inexperienced, so I won't hold tonight against you."

I groaned. "What did I do?"

Bret sighed. "You are trying to please both of us and can't Artemis. You tell me that you don't know what came over you, that you weren't in your right mind, but that means that you are telling Ares that what happened wasn't what you wanted. Either way you are hurting one of us. Just tell us the truth, don't try to please us."

I groaned and turned away from both of them. "I don't know what to say. Did I enjoy kissing Ares, yes, but I didn't want it to happen in front of you Bret."

Ares cleared his throat. "I know that you want to talk, but I can't let you two be alone while he is still adjusting to his instincts."

Bret growled. "I would never hurt her."

I scoffed. "No, not hurt me, just eat me."

Bret stared at me in shock then turned to Ares. "Did I try to eat her?"

Ares shook his head. "No, but you were saying that she smelled like food and that *you were* going to eat her. You didn't hurt her or touch her though."

Bret grimaced. "And that's because you protected her, right?"

Ares nodded his head. "Yes, but you were not in your right mind."

Bret sighed. "I don't want to talk to her in front of you."

I turned to Ares. "Can we use the same deal that I had set up with you before?"

Ares groaned. "I don't know why you are trying to be secretive with me, but I'll agree to it. KODA!"

Koda appeared in the doorway without making a sound. "Yes?"

Ares smiled. "These two need to talk, but they can't be alone so you are going to stay here and make sure he doesn't try to eat her again." I cleared my throat and Ares sighed. "And whatever they say you can't tell me."

Koda frowned. "Are you sure about that last one?"

Ares looked at me and smiled. "For her I'd do almost anything." He walked towards me then looked at Bret and sighed. "Good night Artemis."

I kissed his cheek quickly. "Good night Ares." He smiled and walked out of the room towards his bedroom. Koda sat in the chair which was beside the bed.

Bret walked towards me slowly with his hands out, but when he was close enough to touch me he dropped his hands. "I'm sorry I tried to eat you."

I laughed. "It's alright Bret. I know it wasn't really you. I'm sorry I got you into all of this and you ended up becoming one of us."

Bret shrugged. "There are a lot of upsides to being a werewolf especially since they are taking over the world now."

I groaned. "Don't remind me."

Bret laughed. "I know. I'm torn about how to deal with it as well. At least our town is okay."

I nodded my head. "Yeah." I looked up at his face and realized that I no longer thought of him as very attractive. *I guess when you have to compare him to the God of War he isn't really that handsome. Still attractive, but no contest. Okay, Ares isn't the mythical God of War, but he is very handsome.* I groaned. "I'm sorry about everything Bret. I didn't want any of this to happen. The plan was that I would leave and the town would go on like normal while I started my new life with Ares. You would stay home and fall in love with one of the local girls and live happily ever after."

Bret shook his head smiling. "I already fell in love with one of the local girls."

"Bret, I can't be with you. Whether I like it or not, Ares and I do have a connection. I can't explain it, but I crave...I...uggh! I don't want to talk to you about this, but I want you to know."

Bret sighed. "I can see how you two look at each other. I know you have feelings for him."

I shook my head. "It's deeper than that. We are connected so much that when he feels sad I feel sad. It's why I could feel him yesterday. He was worried and I started getting worried. I thought he was in trouble and had to find him." The truth to that statement shocked me. Until then I hadn't even been aware of that fact.

Bret stared at me in shock. "That's not possible to be like that."

Koda scoffed. We turned to look at him and he shrugged. "Sorry, but you two do not know about the connections our kind can have. If Artemis's father had taught her, she would have felt similar to that with Darren. She could have been connected to him like Ares, but obviously not the physical attraction part."

I shivered in disgust. "Thanks for that visual."

Koda rolled his eyes. "Don't you understand? If you form a connection with another werewolf you feel what they feel. Now of course you and Ares' connection is a lot different because your ties are like when you bind yourself to someone, but without the death factor. What I'm saying is that although Ares and Artemis's connection is very unique, you can have a much smaller version with any werewolf you wanted."

I nodded my head. "I understand."

Bret shrugged. "Whatever you say. The point is that I love you Artemis and that won't change. I know you are with Ares and can't be with me, but I want to be close to you. I want to stay with your group."

I asked, "Even if that means having to see me *with* Ares?"

Bret sighed. "Yes. I will have to deal with it."

I smiled and hugged him tightly. "Thank you for staying with me."

Bret hugged me back and kissed the top of my head. "Anytime."

Koda stood up. "Alright, time to go."

SONG OF THE MOON

Bret kissed my cheek quickly then walked out the bedroom door. Koda smiled. "Good night, Artemis."

I smiled back at him. "Night Koda." I waited until Koda closed the door to throw myself on my bed burying my face in my pillows. *Why me? Why do I have to deal with two men? What happens if I start to develop feelings for Bret? Oh God!* I shook my head and started thinking about Darren. I tried to focus on my thoughts, but sleep overtook me.

CHAPTER FIVE

I woke up slowly, although I wasn't sure what had woken me up. I tried to roll over, but something held me down around my waist. I started to panic and looked down to see an arm lying over my stomach. *An arm?* I rolled over and bumped noses with Ares. I jumped out of the bed and snarled. "What are you doing?"

Ares woke up and smiled at me. "Good morning. Did you sleep well?"

"Ares what are you doing in bed with me?"

He whispered, "I heard you crying and you sounded scared, so I came in here to check on you. You wouldn't stop shaking and I was worried that you were going to shift for the first time so I laid down next to you to take the transformation from you. When I laid down you stopped shaking and crying and went quiet. I was too worried about you changing though so I stayed with you."

I stared at him in disbelief. "How do I know you're telling the truth?"

He smiled. "If I wanted to sleep with you I wouldn't sneak in here. You know that I have been behaving myself and letting you decide what happens between us."

I sighed. "I know that. I'm sorry. You just caught me off guard. And how can you take my transformation?"

"Only those with enough power can take someone's transformation. It's one of the ways I became prince. I took my opponent's transformation from him and changed myself when he couldn't to kill him. We are a lot easier to kill in human form."

I stared at him in shock. "You killed to get to your spot?"

He nodded his head. "I had to. I have to take the throne away from Darius and free my mother. I already told you that." -

I sighed and nodded my head. "I know."

He patted the bed. "Come back to bed, it's still too early."

I shook my head. "No. Get out."

He groaned. "You were fine just a minute ago."

I snarled. "I was asleep and didn't know you were there."

He smiled. "You said my name."

I gasped. "No I didn't. You're lying."

He held up three fingers in a boy scout salute. "I swear on my mother's grave that you did."

I blushed. "Great." I turned away from him and heard the bed move as he stood up.

He wrapped his arms around my waist and placed his face next to mine. "It was very sweet to hear you say my name in your sleep."

I blushed deeper and tried to pull away from him, but he just spun me around to face him. He kissed my lips softly and crept backwards towards the bed. "I promise I will do nothing, but cuddle with you while we sleep."

I blushed a shade darker. "Alright, but if you try anything you have to leave."

Ares smiled widely and nodded his head. "Promise." He lay down and scooted back so there was plenty of room for me to get on. I climbed into the bed and laid down facing away from him. He spooned his body to mine and sighed in contentment. "It's no different than you sleeping in the same bed with Bret."

I closed my eyes and relaxed against him as our bodies warmed up the covers again. "It is much different than sleeping with Bret." I whispered.

He kissed the back of my head then wrapped his arm back around my waist pulling me tighter against him. I tensed for a second, but then relaxed. I felt safe again and fell into a deep sleep.

Ares shook my arm. "Artemis get up."

I groaned and sat up. "What? I'm up."

He pulled me back off the bed holding me in his arms. "Someone is here."

I opened my eyes and stared at a dark shadow in one corner of the bedroom. "What is that? Why is that shadow so strange looking?"

Ares snarled. "Why are you here? And why sneak in?"

I watched in amazement as a man stepped out of the shadow making it disappear. I gasped. "Holy shit. How did he do that?"

The man bowed at the waist and smiled at me revealing fangs. "My apologies for sneaking in Ares. I wanted to see your *passt genau* while she was not hiding her feelings for you."

I snarled. "Word travels fast I take it."

Ares sighed. "Victor this is Artemis. Artemis this is Victor. I almost killed you before I smelled you, you know?"

Victor laughed and it made me shiver, thinking of sexual things. Ares snarled. "Knock off the voice powers."

Victor bowed at the waist again. "My apologies. Your *pass*...Artemis has an aura I seem drawn to test."

Ares sighed setting me down on my feet beside him. "I know what you mean."

I stared at the two of them and asked, "Why are we suddenly friendly with the weird guy with fangs who appeared out of a shadow?"

Victor blinked then asked, "She does not know about us yet?"

Ares shook his head. "I have much to tell you old friend."

I gasped, "Friend? This freak...no offense...is your friend?"

Ares snarled. "Be nice Artemis. He is not a freak, just a jerk. And yes, he is my friend."

"Great. Well I need breakfast." I said.

Ares nodded, "I'm hungry too."

Victor smiled flashing his fangs again. "I could eat."

Ares snarled. "You be nice too Victor. She knows nothing of you, so stop."

Victor sighed. "Very well, but I really could use something to eat."

I walked from the bedroom with them following me. Koda, Matt and Gregory stood at the end of the hallway ready to attack. I smiled. "Sorry boys, but it's a friend of Ares apparently."

Koda and Matt smiled at Victor as he walked out. Victor shook their hands. "Hey Matt and Koda. How are my favorite twins doing?"

I stopped walking and turned back. "Twins? You guys never told me that."

Matt shrugged. "You were a little preoccupied with Ares to notice Love."

I stared at Matt's face and his blue Mohawk then turned to Koda and gasped. "Holy shit! You guys are identical twins minus the different colored Mohawks!"

Koda smiled shaking his green Mohawk. "I was the first one to do the Mohawk, but he had to copy me."

Matt rolled his eyes. "I didn't even know you had one. I was in London while you were in Germany with Ares. There's no way for me to have known."

I shook my head at the siblings and walked to the kitchen where Gregory had started taking out food. I saw a bag filled with red liquid and asked, "What is that?"

Gregory smiled. "Food for Victor."

I frowned. "What the hell is it?"

Gregory shook his head smiling. "I'm not spilling the beans on this one."

Ares and Victor walked in whispering, but when they saw me they stopped. I scoffed. "Real subtle, I have no idea you were talking about me just now."

Ares smiled and walked towards me. "What else should we talk about?"

I shrugged and stood on tiptoe to kiss his cheek. "Whatever you want great Prince."

Ares laughed. "You're a smart ass? Great."

"I *was* raised by a man." I said with a smile.

Victor frowned and asked, "How long have you been together?"

Ares kissed my cheek then went and grabbed food from Greogry. "Two days."

Victor's eyes opened in surprise. "Then she really is your *passt genau.*"

Ares took a bite out of the piece of raw steak he was holding and nodded his head. "I wouldn't lie about that. She answered my call from a state away."

Victor turned to me and for the first time I noticed his eyes, solid black like the pupil had taken over. Victor asked, "Is it true that you haven't changed yet?"

I nodded my head and licked my lips. "Can I ask you something?" He nodded his head. I cleared my throat, "Why are your eyes black?"

He laughed making me moan in pleasure. Ares growled loudly and rushed to stand between me and Victor. "Knock it off! You are my friend, but don't push me too far."

Victor bowed at the neck. "I apologize to you both."

I grabbed Ares' arm and pulled him back to me. "I'm sorry to cause drama between you two."

Victor smiled. "It's not your fault. And I'll let Ares explain my eyes later."

I groaned. "Why is it that everyone makes Ares tell me things? I'm not going to freak out and run away if one of you tells me."

Ares frowned. "What else are you waiting for me to tell you?"

I pointed to the bag of red liquid. "What that is?"

Ares' eyes widen and he turned to stare at Gregory. "You didn't tell her?"

He shook his head. "Nope, I thought you should be the one to explain about Victor. She obviously has no clue."

I snarled. "I'm not stupid."

Gregory shook his head. "I didn't say that. I just meant that you have no idea what Victor is."

Victor frowned. "Why doesn't she know what I am?"

Ares answered before I could. "Her idiot father decided he wasn't going to tell her about being a werewolf until she changed for the first time. Problem is that she has been fighting her change since elementary school and he stopped her change when she answered my call. She was never taught about us or you or any of the others."

I stared in shock at Ares. "Others? What do you mean others? Oh, wait like the witches?"

Victor shook his head angrily. "What a fool. We don't have very much time to teach her though."

Ares sighed. "I know. I was hoping you would help."

Victor smiled. "I would be honored to."

I walked to Gregory and asked, "Do you have any real food?"

Gregory frowned. "You really should eat one of these steaks. Especially if you are going to continue to fight your change."

I sighed and nodded my head. "All right, fine. But can you at least warm it up?"

Gregory smiled and nodded his head. "Sure."

I walked back over to Ares and put my hand on the inside of his arm. I suddenly felt scared and pressed my body to his arm. He stopped talking to Victor and looked down at me. "What's wrong?"

I shrugged. "I'm not sure, I just suddenly got really scared."

Ares sniffed the air then picked me up in his arms holding me tight against him. "Someone is here. Victor, did you bring anyone with you?"

Victor shook his head sniffing the air. "No, but I know who it is." Victor walked quickly towards the front door throwing it open. I stared at the tall man standing on the porch looking in. He looked like Victor's twin, but without the black eyes. Victor hissed. "What are you doing here?"

The man frowned. "Is that any way to treat your father and your king?"

I stiffened in Ares' arms and wrapped my arms around his neck so that I was pressed tighter to him. Ares rubbed my leg with the hand that was holding them and whispered, "It's alright, you don't have to be scared of him while I'm here."

I nodded my head and pressed my forehead to his cheek inhaling his smell and calming my nerves.

Victor's father walked into the house and bowed at the waist to Ares and me. "Greetings Ares, Prince of the Werewolves."

Ares set me down beside him and bowed at the waist to him. "Greetings Maurice, King of the Vampires. To what do we owe the pleasure of your visit?"

I gasped as he said the word, "vampires" and moved a step closer to him so that I was touching my entire left side to his entire right side. *How come I didn't guess that? Fangs equals vampire. Duh.* Maurice stared at me in confusion then looked up at Ares. "Did I do something wrong?"

Ares laughed and shook his head. "No King Maurice..."

Maurice shook his head. "Just Maurice, Ares."

Ares smiled. "Of course. No, Maurice. She is, well...I would like to speak with you and Victor about this in private if you wouldn't mind."

Maurice stared at me second before inhaling. "She's a werewolf, but that other smell and those eyes. I know them, but can't think of where. Let's go talk before I figure it out and give something away you did not want her to know."

Ares started to walk to the living room with Maurice and Victor and I grabbed his arm pulling him back to me. I whispered, "Don't leave me alone."

He sensed the worry in my voice and smiled. "It's alright, Koda and Matt will protect you." He looked up at Koda and Matt and smiled, "Right?" Koda and Matt nodded their heads in unison with serious faces on. Ares snarled. "And you both know that if anything happens to her that I *will* have to punish you."

Koda smiled. "I would have it no other way."

Matt snarled. "Death may be a good punishment for that much of a failure."

I stared in shock at them. "Why are you so willing to be punished if something happens to me? It makes no sense. You don't even know me."

Ares sighed and shook his head. "I have to go. Keep her safe." I watched with growing nervousness as Ares walked from the kitchen to the living room. Once he was out of my sight I started to shift from foot-to-foot.

Matt sighed. "Artemis it's okay. Victor and Ares have been friends since they were born and Maurice will not do anything to any of them because of that."

I sighed and walked towards Koda. Koda stood perfectly still as I leaned my head against his chest. I exhaled a shaky breath and said, "I know you don't know me and I don't have any right to ask, but could you just hold me for a second? I would ask Bret, but he is not allowed to be alone with me and I don't fully trust him."

Koda exhaled the breath he was holding and said, "I'm sorry about Bret. And I will do whatever you ask me to do."

I wrapped my arms around his waist as he wrapped his arms around my shoulders. I whispered, "I'm sorry for causing so much drama here. I really am not a drama queen, by any means."

Matt snorted. "You apologize too much Artemis. We know you aren't a drama queen and the drama that has been happening is not your fault."

I turned to him and could see the jealousy in his eyes. I pulled away from Koda and walked towards him. "Why are you jealous? I did not pick Koda over you, I just assumed Ares would feel less threatened if he found Koda hugging me then you."

Matt rolled his eyes. "I think Ares would be mad to find any of us hugging you, but if you are in need of consoling he would get over it. And I am jealous, but I'm trying to get over it."

I stood one foot from him and looked up at his handsome face. "I swear I did not pick Koda because I favor him."

Matt smiled. "Love, it's alright. I am just jealous when it comes to my brothers."

I frowned. "Brothers? Who is your other brother?"

Matt frowned and looked over my head at Koda. "Shit."

Koda sighed. "Yes, shit is right."

I sighed. "Just let Ares tell me. I'm used to it by now."

Matt smiled and placed his hand against my face. "Thanks, Love."

I frowned at him. "Why do you call me Love?"

He shrugged. "I call most girls Darlin or something like that, but you are definitely Love. Mine or not, that is who you are."

I blushed and looked down at my hands. Matt laughed and whispered, "I love that you blush."

I pulled away from him and walked towards my bedroom. I heard them following me and sighed. "Can we go outside?"

They both answered, "No," in unison.

I groaned. "Fine, then can we sit at the dining table and play a game?" I turned around and looked up at their matching faces.

Koda shrugged. "Sure."

I smiled and walked back to the table and sat down at the head. Koda and Matt sat across from each other staring at me. I smiled. "We're going to play one hundred questions."

Matt groaned. "You tricked us."

I smiled and nodded my head. "Sort of. So, I'll go first. Why am I so attached to Ares already?"

Koda smiled. "You are his *passt genau,* his perfect match. Only the strongest of our kind get one. You are born with a sort of mental and physical connection to him. Almost like you were literally *made* for him."

I asked, "How many before have had a match?"

Matt tapped his chin in thought for a moment. "Just one set that I know of, the Mother and Father."

"Who are they?" I asked.

Matt sighed and put his hand against his forehead. "I can't believe your father never told you any of this. The Mother is Asena..."

I interrupted him. "Oh, yeah, the she-wolf that saved the baby then ended up mating with him to create werewolves."

Matt nodded his head. "Yes, and the boy she saved is who we refer to as the Father."

I nodded my head. "I understand that part, but how do you know that they were born for each other? What if it was just a coincidence?"

Matt shook his head. "It was not a coincidence. The boy sent out a call like the one Ares did and Asena answered."

I shook my head. "But he was human, not a werewolf."

Matt shrugged. "I don't make the stories, I just tell them. That's what happened according to Asena."

I shrugged. "If you say so. Okay, your turn."

Matt and Koda looked at each other for a moment then Matt asked, "Have you ever slept with Bret?"

I felt my eyes widen and shook my head. "No, never. I'm a virgin."

Koda smiled. "Have you ever kissed Bret?"

I shrugged. "Not like a boyfriend type of kiss, but a friend kiss. He did kiss me the night Ares called to me, but I didn't kiss him back."

Koda and Matt exchanged a look then Matt asked, "Have you ever done anything with Bret or any other boy?"

I shook my head. "I haven't even touched another boy besides Bret well and Billy, but I didn't do anything then either."

Koda asked, "Why not?"

I stared at him for a second then sighed. "I've always been the outcast in my town. Bret was the only one who would be my friend, let alone touch me. And Billy was only talking to me and stuff towards the end. I think he was just trying to...well you know."

Matt frowned, "Your dad never explained why to you?"

I stared at him in shock and asked, "He knew why?"

Matt and Koda nodded their heads in unison. Koda said, "It's because you're a werewolf. Humans can sense that we are predators and fear us. Bret must have just ignored the feeling because of your physical appearance."

I felt the first tear fall down my face and asked, "What's life like when you are raised with others of our kind?"

Matt shrugged. "Like the humans except that we are much closer, like a family. I firmly believe that your childhood would have been a lot easier if you had been around your own kind."

I felt the tears falling and asked, "How close is the nearest group?"

Koda whispered, "This one and it's about one hundred miles."

I stood up and started to walk towards my bedroom when Ares walked into the dining room. He frowned at me and walked quickly to me wrapping his arms around me. "What's wrong?"

I shook my head. "It's nothing Ares."

He growled. "What did you two say to her?"

Koda said. "She asked us about why she was an outcast with the humans and what it would have been like to grow up around us."

Ares sighed. "Sorry Koda."

Koda laughed. "Don't worry about it Ares."

Ares pushed me back and said, "I'm sorry about your father. If I could change time for you I would."

I nodded my head and wiped at the tears on my face. "I know Ares. It's alright."

He snarled. "It's not alright. I'm going to find your father."

I shook my head. "You can't leave me again. PLEASE!" I grabbed both of his arms and gripped as hard as I could.

Ares stared in shock at my face and Matt cleared his throat making me release my hold a little. Matt said, "She is starting to show the symptoms Ares."

Ares looked over my head at Matt. "Describe."

Matt said, "She started to panic when she watched you walk away from her and grew increasingly nervous when you were out of her sight. She had to have Koda hold her to stop her panic."

Ares looked down at me and asked, "Is that true?"

I felt the blush on my cheeks, looked down and lied, "No."

"You have no reason to be embarrassed. It's part of what we are. It means that you are finally letting go and soon you and I will be fully connected."

I shrugged still looking down. "So, I was a little nervous."

Matt gave a short bark of a laugh. "You were about to run after him."

"Shut up Matt."

Ares shook his head smiling. "It's really alright Artemis. I promise I won't leave you unless I have to."

I felt my heart pick up and shook my head. "That's not a good enough promise." I growled. "I don't like this feeling."

Ares nodded his head. "I understand Artemis. I feel the same way."

I stared at him and said, "You don't act like it."

He smiled. "I hide it. Wouldn't you think I was a little odd if I got all nervous when I walked away from you?"

I nodded my head. "Ya, I guess you're right."

He hugged me against him. "We'll get through this first part and get on to the easier parts soon. I came in here to get you though. Will you come with me to speak with Victor and Maurice?"

I shrugged. "As long as I can touch you while I'm near them."

Ares nodded his head. "Deal. I'm not sure why you are scared of them though. Your werewolf side should make you feel safe around them."

I shrugged. "Maybe it's my other side."

Ares frowned. "Yes, probably. I hope Maurice and I are wrong about what you might be."

I frowned. "What is that?"

Ares shook his head. "I can't tell you right now. Come on." I let him lead me by the hand to the living room where Maurice and Victor sat in chairs facing the couch. Ares sat down on the couch pulling me down with him. I scooted as close as I could without being in his lap.

Victor smiled. "I promise we won't hurt you or Ares."

I nodded my head and licked my lips nervously. "Okay."

Maurice smiled making his face look less frightening. "How old are you?"

"Eighteen."

He frowned. "How old were you when you stopped your first transformation?"

I shrugged. "I think ten."

His eyes widened a little bit, almost unnoticeable if you weren't watching for it. "Have you ever changed?"

I shook my head. "No, I almost did when Ares called to me or whatever, but my dad threw me in the creek and stopped it."

Victor asked, "Do you remember hearing Ares' call?"

"When he howled on TV? If that was his call, then, yeah."

Victor asked, "Do you remember answering?"

I shook my head. "No, I was watching the TV and thinking how gorgeous he was in wolf form and that it was strange that I wasn't afraid of him at all when I saw him killing people, then I started convulsing. Then my dad threw me in the creek and put me to bed. When I woke up I felt something was wrong, no, I thought wrong, but it was more like I felt drawn outside and there was Ares and Koda and Matt."

Maurice asked, "Why don't you want to change?"

"I don't want to answer that in front of Ares." I said softly.

Ares groaned. "You might as well, because I'm going to be asking you anyway."

I groaned and scooted a little ways away from Ares, not looking at him. "I don't want to change yet. If there is a chance that I could be human..."

Maurice interrupted me. "No. I'm sorry child, but even if you don't change you are still half werewolf and half..."

Ares cleared his throat stopping Maurice from finishing. I growled and glared at Ares. "Why won't you let him tell me?"

Ares smiled. "It is too dangerous for you to know."

I snarled at him. "Just tell me."

He snarled back. "No and watch yourself. I will not allow you to challenge my authority."

I sighed and pushed down my anger, staring down at my hands. "Sorry Ares. It's hard to control my anger sometimes."

He sighed. "I understand. If you would change it would be a lot easier."

I groaned. "I get it alright. I need to change. Just give me some time."

Ares titled my head up and smiled at me. "I'll give you however much time you need."

I smiled back at him and then looked at Victor and Maurice who were watching us intently. I pulled away from Ares and blushed. "Sorry. I forgot you two were here."

Maurice spoke softly, "She is delightful Ares, but you must teach her how to act properly."

Ares nodded his head. "I'm sorry Maurice. I didn't know you were coming otherwise I would have."

Victor laughed. "I think you should leave her be. It's nice to have someone not treating you different."

Ares smiled. "She's good at it."

I stared at the three of them. "I think I missed something?" They all nodded their heads and I shrugged. "Whatever."

Maurice asked, "Do you remember your mother?"

I shook my head. "No, she left when I was five years old."

Maurice's eyes widened considerably from shock. "When you were five? Exactly?"

I nodded my head. "I remember it because it was the day before my birthday."

Victor asked, "Did your father ever tell you about her?"

I shook my head. "At first he said she was going on a trip, but the more years that passed he just said that he didn't want to talk about it. I have seen a picture of her, but that's it. I stopped asking Darren about her when I turned ten."

Victor asked, "When you started having the seizures?"

I nodded my head. "Yeah, but I guess that was really me trying to change."

Maurice nodded his head. "Yes, it was."

I sighed and said, "My mother left because of me and I know that. I don't know why, but someday I will."

Maurice smiled. "I'm sure you will. Now, what did your father tell you about yourself? How did he explain your purple eyes?"

"I didn't know I had purple eyes until Ares came to get me. I always had contacts in and we didn't have a mirror in the house. He always made me change out my contacts in the bathroom too. It's why Bret didn't know either."

Victor asked, shock evident in his tone, "You didn't have a mirror?"

I shook my head. Ares explained, "She didn't even know what she looked like until she came here and I made her look in the mirror."

Maurice rubbed his chin. "I'm beginning to understand Ares' desire to find your father. To not tell your daughter about her heritage or to let her meet others of her own kind is monstrous."

I looked at Maurice. "Can I ask you a question?"

"Of course."

I whispered, "What are you?"

Maurice smiled and looked at Ares. "May I?"

Ares nodded his head. "Of course. I was going to have Victor tell her later anyway."

Maurice smiled and said, "Do not be frightened child, I will not harm you, alright?"

I nodded my head and moved closer to Ares. He held my hand and smiled. I watched as Maurice looked down at the ground and inhaled. I could feel a strange pressure, like the tide pulling at my legs, moving towards him. He looked up at me and I gasped, jumping over the back of the couch behind Ares.

Maurice's eyes were solid black like Victor's and he smiled revealing long fangs where his small canines used to be. He said, "I told you not to be frightened."

I nodded my head and swallowed. "I know, but I couldn't help it."

Maurice smiled flashing his fangs again. "I will not hurt you, I have already eaten today."

I felt my heart speed up and asked, "Please tell me what you are."

He looked down and I felt that tide push past me, leaving his body. He looked back up and his face and teeth were back to normal. "I'm a vampire."

"Like Dracula?" I asked curiously.

Maurice groaned and rolled his eyes. "Honestly, Vlad was always looking for attention. That bastard."

I stared at him in shock. "Dracula was real?"

He nodded his head. "Of course."

I asked, "The fog that was killing people that was vampires wasn't it?"

He nodded his head again. "Yes. We were trying to hide our existence."

"Why are vampires and werewolves working together? I thought they hated each other?"

Ares laughed and said, "That's a story we made up so the humans would not hunt us both at the same time."

I frowned. "What do you mean?"

Victor smiled. "Vampires and werewolves have been allies since we found out about each other. The original vampires could not go out in the sunlight so the werewolves became our daytime body guards. It was mutually beneficial because they would protect us during the day and then the vampires would work at night and pay for everything for the werewolves.

SONG OF THE MOON

When the witch hunts of the seventeenth century and werewolf hunts of the eighteenth century happened, we decided it was time to go into hiding and wait for our chance to take over the world."

I nodded my head. "I understand about waiting to take over, but I had no idea about you guys being allies."

Victor laughed. "Neither do the humans. It really is a great plan. So far the humans just think that the wolves are so fast that when a human walks in the fog they just ran over and kill them."

"I remember seeing the video. It was creepy to see the fog move." I stared at Victor for a second until all of the pieces clicked into place. "You can change into fog! You can shapeshift!"

Victor and Maurice smiled. Maurice said, "She is very smart."

Ares nodded his head. "Yes. Smart like a werewolf."

"Is that how he formed out of the shadow?" I asked curiously,

Ares nodded his head again. "Yes. They can shift to shadow, mist, wolves, fog, bat, rats and some others I don't remember."

My eyes widened in shock at the extensive list. How would you even be able to tell the difference between a vampire in animal form and a regular animal? They could have been around me all of my life and I never knew it. "Good thing you are on our side."

All three men laughed at me causing me to blush and looked down at my hands. Maurice asked, "Do you know what a vampire is?"

I shook my head. "Only what I've seen in movies."

Maurice said, "We are no more than a cursed soul. Like the werewolves are cursed with lycanthropy."

I looked up at him in shock. "So, you aren't a living dead monster?"

Maurice frowned, wrinkles appearing on his forehead. "Of course not. I can't believe humans even believe that kind of thing."

Victor sighed. "It's not like they came up with it on their own. One of us told them that."

"Okay, so you just have a curse which gave you fangs and the ability to shapeshift and you have to eat blood to survive?" Victor and Maurice nodded their heads. I shrugged. "Okay. So, is that all? Can I go eat?"

Ares raised one of his eyebrows. "You aren't scared, nervous or going to ask questions?"

I shook my head. "I can't be prejudiced. I mean it's not like they chose it."

Ares smiled. "Well that's refreshing to hear."

My stomach growled loudly. "Can I please get some food?"

Ares nodded his head. "Sure."

I stood up and quickly walked to the kitchen. Koda stood by the fridge holding a piece of steak. I took it from him and threw it in the microwave turning it on for forty seconds. I watched as the steak rotated inside the microwave. Koda cleared his throat behind me making me turn to him. "Are you alright?" He asked.

I shrugged. "Yeah, why wouldn't I be?"

He frowned and started to reach a hand out towards my face. "You're pale."

I focused on my body and noticed that I was shaking. I held up my hands and felt my eyes widen as I saw them shaking uncontrollably. Koda grabbed my hands and stared into my eyes. "What's wrong, Artemis?"

"It's that feeling again. Like the one I had when Maurice was at the door. I'm just suddenly *terrified*."

Koda picked me up in his arms and ran into the living room. Ares snarled when he saw me in Koda's arms, but stopped when he saw my face. He asked, "What's wrong?"

Koda said, "She's scared. Her hands are shaking real bad and she said it's the same feeling she got when Maurice was at the door."

Ares turned to Maurice. "Did you bring someone with you?"

Maurice stood up and shook his head. "No." He inhaled and then spit. "That's not a vampire. It's an..."

Before he could finish his sentence the wall to the living room smashed into pieces. Koda turned his back to the wall and crouched down to protect me from the flying pieces. I heard the popping and snapping of bones telling me that someone was changing into a wolf and tried to look, but Koda was suddenly running through the house. I held on to his neck as hard as I could as he ran with me. He turned his shoulder towards the bedroom wall and smashed through it. I gasped as the sun shone in my eyes. We started running through town, in a blur of colors. Koda kicked open the door to the concrete warehouse, never missing a beat. "Bret!" He yelled.

Bret appeared in front of us out of nowhere and stared at my face. "What happened?"

I tried to frown, but suddenly couldn't move. I gasped for air and stared at Bret's worried face. Koda looked down and growled, "Shit!" He set me down on the floor on my back and ripped open my shirt.

I tried to protest, but couldn't do anything. Bret held down my arms, although unnecessarily, and whispered, "This is going to hurt."

I tried to look down at what was happening, but my entire body was numb. Koda inhaled then I felt something rip out of my chest. I screamed in pain and then couldn't breathe again. I gasped for air and started to flail, but a short man with glasses squatted down beside me and spoke in a soothing tone. I stopped flailing and sat still as I felt him poking below my chest. He pushed down on one spot and I cringed, but still couldn't get any air. A sharp snap startled me, then I inhaled and air rushed down my throat and filled up my lungs. I breathed in deep and held the air in for a second as my throat burned from the oxygen it finally received.

Bret stroked the side of my face as I relearned how to breathe. Koda's face appeared above mine. He asked, "Are you doing alright?"

I whispered, "Better now. What happened?"

His face was guarded as he tried to hide his true emotions from me. "A piece of wood pierced your lung."

I stared at him in shock. "How am I breathing then?"

He smiled. "You aren't human, Artemis. We heal a lot faster than humans."

"Well I guess it's a good thing I'm not human then. Ares would be really mad at you."

Koda groaned. "Don't remind me. He's already going to be pissed that I let you get hurt at all."

I sat up and saw the children huddled in the back corner with two large wolves standing in front of them. I looked up at Koda. "What's going on?"

His lips twitched as he snarled. "Ogres are attacking the village. That's why you got scared, because you could smell them. Stupid creatures. Come on, we have to get you out of the village."

Large explosions and screams sounded outside of the warehouse. I stared at the children and shook my head. "Not if the children are staying here."

Koda groaned and bent down so that our cheeks were touching as he whispered in my ear, "They are not as important as you. We can make more children, but we cannot replace you."

I gasped and pulled away from him. "That's horrible! I won't leave."

Koda snarled and reached down to grab me, but Bret pulled me backwards and crouched down in front of me in an attack stance. Koda shook his head. "Back off Bret. I'm not going to hurt her. I just want to take her to safety."

"She doesn't want to leave," Bret said with clenched fists.

Koda growled, his eyes turning solid black. "Do you want her to die Bret?"

Bret slowly stood up and sighed. "No."

Koda nodded his head. "Neither do I. Now come on and help me protect her while we leave the village." The sounds of fighting continued outside as they talked.

Bret turned towards me and I jumped up and backwards out of his reach. "No. I'm staying here. Someone has to protect these children."

Koda motioned at the wolves and children. "There are two guards in front of them already."

I shook my head fiercely. "What if that's not enough? If I leave and then find out later that these kids were killed I won't ever be able to forgive myself."

Koda smiled, his eyes back to his natural blue. "You said you wouldn't forgive Ares for turning Bret, but you seem to be getting along just fine."

I snarled. "Only because Bret is okay with being a werewolf."

Bret laughed. "Okay? I'm ecstatic! These new abilities are wonderful!"

"Anyway, it's not fair to compare that to the current situation. It's almost impossible for me to harbor hard feelings for Ares. It's so frustrating!"

Koda nodded his head and I realized that he and Bret had moved closer to me while I was ranting. I started to jump backwards, but Koda grabbed my arm and held me against him. I struggled as hard as I could, but he held on to me. He picked me up in his arms and looked back over his shoulder. "You coming Bret?"

"No, I'm going to stay here to help guard the kids," Bret answered.

I leaned over the top of Koda's shoulder to look at Bret. He smiled at me and I shook my head. "Bret, you don't have to. You can come with us." A loud explosion made me jump in Koda's arms.

He shook his head. "Koda can protect you. I'll help the kids."

"Thanks Bret."

He nodded his head and pushed Koda. "No problem Chicky. I'll see you soon."

My throat was dry and it was becoming difficult to get words out. "Alright."

Koda whispered, "Now tuck into as small a ball as possible against me and hold on." I wrapped my arms around his neck and did as he asked. He wrapped his arms around me and ran out of the warehouse through the door Bret held open.

I gasped at what I saw as we came out. All of the houses were on fire and bodies littered the ground. Most were thankfully ogres, but there were some werewolves. Koda pushed my face down and started running as fast as he could. I felt the air whipping around us and knew we were going much faster than humanly possible. The sound of fighting and screams slowly died away until the only sound I heard was the beating of Koda's heart. His heartbeat did not speed up as he ran, but stayed a constant steady thrum. I felt my eyes beginning to close and shook my head, but it wasn't enough. Slowly sleep won and I slept without dreaming.

CHAPTER SIX

I opened my eyes slowly and found myself lying on top of Koda in a parallel line with him, with my head on his chest and the rest of our body parts lining up. I lifted my head up slowly and looked around. We were lying in the middle of a forest in the dark of night. The forest was too dense to be able to see any stars as I looked up. Koda whispered, "The ground is really hard and this was the only way I could think to keep you comfortable."

I smiled at him. "Thanks, but you really didn't have to do that. It's not fair that you are uncomfortable."

He shrugged. "I'm fine. I'm used to sleeping on the hard ground. Although it would have been better in wolf form, but I didn't want to scare you."

I laughed at the image. "That would have been interesting. Would you like me to get off you now?"

He smiled at me seductively. "Only if you want. I'm pretty happy." I smiled back at him, unsure what he meant until I felt him flexing under my lower body.

I hopped up off of him and turned away as the blush spread over my entire face. Koda laughed.

"Wow. I didn't expect that reaction out of you. Hasn't that ever happened with Bret before?"

I groaned and stayed facing away from him. "Yes it has, but you aren't Bret. You're Koda and I barely know you."

Koda sighed. "Well you better get to know me fast because we are going to be spending the rest of our lives together."

I turned around and stared at him. "What do you mean by that? Did something happen to Ares?"

He smiled. "Calm down. Nothing happened to him. I just mean that I am Ares' pack and guard and I'm guessing yours too and that I will be alive hopefully as long as you, which is going to be hundreds of years."

I stared into his blue eyes and whispered, "Are you only protecting me because you are afraid of Ares' discipline?"

He stared back into my eyes and whispered, "No. I'm protecting you because I can see what you will become' and I have spent time with you and I couldn't bear the thought of you being hurt or...or dying. I fear it would tear me apart as much as it would Ares."

He sat up, pulled me down so that I was now sifting in his lap with my legs around his sides and stroked the side of my face softly. "I promise to protect you from whatever tries to cause you harm, whether it be another person or even Ares."

I nodded my head unable to speak. He leaned forward and kissed my lips. I felt a spark flare up in the core of my body, but ignored it, suddenly overwhelmed with a strange sensation. I kissed Koda back, forcing his mouth open with my teeth. He groaned in pleasure and wrapped his arms around me, pressing us together as he kissed me back. He leaned forward making me lie backwards on to the ground and pressed himself against me. I moaned and bit his lip playfully. I pulled back from him and lay on the ground catching my breath. He smiled back for a second and then turned his head to the side. He started to stand up, but was suddenly flying through the air with a wolf on his back. I started to go after them, but Matt grabbed my arm. "Love, you better just wait here."

I shook my head as I realized Ares had tackled Koda. "No, Ares might hurt him and it wasn't his fault. Someone is messing with our emotions, I can feel it." I pulled away from him and ran through the forest after them. I yelled, "ARES ! ! ! Please stop. It's not his fault. Someone is messing with our emotions!"

I heard snarling and ran toward the sound and found Ares snarling over Koda who was lying in human form on his back with his hands to his sides. I ran up and reached toward Ares, but he turned to me and snapped his teeth. I stopped walking and stared at him. "Would you really hurt me, Ares?"

Ares' wolf face softened and he walked backwards off of Koda. I whispered, "Someone is manipulating our emotions Ares. I can feel it."

He changed back to human and stood perfect and naked in front of me. I licked my lips and fought to keep my eyes above his chest. He snarled. "Why were you kissing him?"

"I just told you that someone is manipulating our emotions and I'm not lying. I swear Ares that I would not have kissed him under my own mind."

"Thanks. I guess I'm just chop liver," Koda said playfully.

Ares growled. "Don't push me Koda!"

I laid my hand on Ares' arm and whispered, "I'm sorry I kissed him. I promise it won't happen again."

Ares turned to me and for the first time I saw the pain in his eyes. "Don't promise something you can't keep."

I shook my head and wrapped my arms around his upper body. "I promise Ares. I am sorry that I lost control."

He sighed and hugged me back. "It's alright. I know you're telling the truth. Matt, go find who has been manipulating them."

Matt ran off into the woods without a word. Koda stood up and walked toward Ares. He dropped to his knees and said, "Please forgive me Prince Ares. I did not know what I was doing and I swear it will not happen again. I will work to gain more control over myself."

Ares spoke in a stern voice, "You are forgiven. Stand."

Koda stood up and smiled. "Thank you."

Ares looked down at me and smiled. "And of course I wouldn't hurt you. I was just upset at finding you eating each others mouths."

I cringed. "I already apologized and you don't have to rub it in."

"I'm sorry. Are you alright?"

"Of course I am. I mean we had a little issue, but..."

Ares interrupted me. "What issue?"

Koda groaned. "You couldn't have waited Artemis? I mean shit, I just got his forgiveness and now you are throwing me under the bus again."

"Sorry," I said sympathetically.

Ares spoke through gritted teeth, "Someone better tell me what happened."

Koda dropped to the ground on his hands and knees in front of Ares and said, "I failed you my Prince. When the ogre smashed through the wall I was not fast enough to turn away. A piece of wood pierced her lung, collapsing it."

Ares looked down at my body just below my bra and traced the scar with his fingertip making me shiver. I was suddenly very aware of the fact that I didn't have a shirt on. "It's alright Koda. You got her out of the village as quick as you could and that was the best thing to do."

I gasped. "Oh my God. Bret and the children are they okay?"

Ares nodded his head. "Bret was actually very helpful in protecting the children. They are all calling him their protector. I don't think he is going to be leaving with us."

I smiled, but felt a twinge of sadness at the news. "That's great." I turned away from Ares and started walking through the trees.

He grabbed my arm and stopped me. "I'm sorry he won't be coming with us."

I shrugged. "'S alright. It's better for him this way."

Koda stood beside us. "When did you get that tattoo?"

Ares glared at Koda. "How have you seen it when I haven't yet? Is that something else you did before I came?"

I could see the anger building in Ares and sighed. "You just didn't pay attention to where it was or you would have seen it already too."

Ares' frown evened out and a twinkle of intrigue returned to his eyes. "Can I see it?"

I shrugged and turned my back to him. He traced his fingertip across the snarling wolf head in the center of my lower back. Ares asked, "When did you get this?"

"Two years ago."

"Did your father see it?"

I shook my head emphatically. "No, he would have killed me for getting a tattoo."

Ares smiled. "It's actually very nice."

I blushed. "Thanks."

Koda shook his head. "I can't believe your father never said anything to you even though you had such a fascination with wolves."

I shrugged. "My fascination with wolves was normal compared to other girls' fascinations with horses or whatever other animal."

"I think we should find some clothes before we leave," Ares said quietly. I realized I was staring at Ares' lower body and blushed looking away from him. He hugged me tightly, "I love that you blush. I hope you always do it."

"I don't."

Matt ran back through the trees and frowned. "I couldn't find anyone."

I sighed. "Great. Well let's get back. I'm still hungry."

"Sorry about that. Those damn ogres attacked without warning. Lucky that you got scared in time for me to change," Ares said.

I remembered Maurice and Victor and asked, "Are Victor and Maurice alright?"

Ares nodded his head. "Maurice managed to get to cover before the sun got him. Both were a big help in defeating the ogres actually. From now on all werewolf posts are going to be assigned two vampires. We're going to be taking a vampire along with our group as well."

I frowned. "Why?"

Ares answered instantly, "For better protection of you. Plus he wants to observe our relationship anyway."

I groaned. "Great. Now I'm an experiment? Why don't you just hand me over to the humans?"

Ares snarled. "I would never do that. Those monsters would torture you worse than you could imagine."

I stared at him and wondered if he had been tortured by humans. I almost asked, but knew it would probably just make him angrier. "So what's the vampire's name that is joining us?"

"Victor."

My throat felt dry again. "Great. Well let's go."

I started walking and Ares cleared his throat. "You're going the wrong way." I giggled and followed behind him staring at his muscled back and butt as he walked. I felt proud of myself that I had managed not to stare at his crotch while we were talking. I could hear Koda and Matt whispering behind me, but couldn't understand what they were saying. I tried to ignore them, but curiosity got the better of me.

I turned around, stopping in front of them. "What? What are you two whispering about?"

Koda and Matt stopped walking and stared at me for a full minute. Matt finally sighed. "Love, we would appreciate it if you wouldn't make us tell you."

I growled. "Why? Because Ares is here and would get mad?"

I felt Ares beside me, but didn't look over at him. Matt groaned. "Alright. We wanted to know why it is that you say you have never been with a man before, but you are so comfortable walking around in your bra and with Ares being naked if that's true?"

I stared at them in shock for a minute as I added up what they had said. *Why am I so comfortable being in my bra around them? And why am I not blushing with Ares walking naked in front of me?* I shook my head. "I...I don't know why I'm comfortable. I mean Ares being naked might be because of our weird connection thingy, but I've never even worn a two piece bathing suit in front of anyone before. I...I should be embarrassed, but strangely I'm not."

Ares smiled. "You're probably just adjusting to being around us. Also, wereanimals generally like to wear as little clothing as possible. You know, the whole shapeshifting thing? We lose a lot of clothes the first year because we end up shifting while dressed and human clothes don't fit very well on large wolves."

Koda rolled his eyes. "Tell me about it. I've shredded more jeans than I can count."

I wrapped my arms around my stomach. "Well whatever it is now you boys have your answer." I felt the blush rush up my cheeks and I groaned. "And now I'm properly embarrassed. Can we go?"

Matt smiled. "We didn't *want* to embarrass you, we were just wondering if you might have been lying to us."

I shook my head. "I'm only eighteen for crying out loud."

Koda laughed. "Shit, eighteen was the beginning of my man-whore days."

Ares groaned. "Don't remind me. You weren't very discreet about it either. I still haven't forgiven you for screwing that girl in my room while I was sleeping in there."

"Ew," I said wrinkling up my nose. "This is why I tried to hide from everyone. Girls are catty and cynical and guys are gross and only think about one thing."

Matt said, "Food."

Ares said, "Hunting."

Koda said, "Fighting."

My mouth gaped open at them for a moment. "Seriously? Sex! All men think about is sex. And obviously Koda is a prime example," I said, pointing towards him.

Koda rolled his eyes. "Don't ask about Ares then."

I looked sideways at Ares and wondered how many women he had slept with. *He is really old. Probably best not to ask.* I shook my head. "Let's go guys. I'm hungry."

Ares smiled. "If you would change, we could take you on a real hunt."

I shook my head. "I'm not going to change."

Ares groaned. "You'll have to change eventually Artemis. Just because you don't change doesn't mean you aren't a werewolf."

"Whatever. I'm not changing yet."

Ares snarled. "You know, I could force you to change."

I snarled. "Don't even try it."

Matt stepped between us. "Calm down. Everyone calm down. Let's get home and find some food."

Ares stopped snarling and shook his head. "Whoever is messing with us is very powerful. I'll need to speak to Victor right away." I squatted down in an attack stance as Ares took a step towards me. He sighed. "Artemis, I promise I am not going to try to change you right now. I just wanted to carry you so that we could get back to the village faster."

I shook my head. "Let Matt carry me if you are telling the truth."

Ares snarled. "Would you rather Matt or Koda carry you than me touch you? If I hadn't come when I had, would I have found you and Koda doing other things?"

I stopped snarling and stared at him, seeing the hurt in his eyes. I stood up and shook my head with my hands on top of my head. "I'm sorry. This isn't like me. You're right, we need to get back soon because this person is screwing with me really bad."

Ares picked me up in his arms and ran without another word. He ran through the thick forest dodging trees and jumping over fallen logs like it was a flat surface. I enjoyed the feel of his hot naked flesh against my arm and face. I rubbed my face in the crook of his neck as he ran. He shivered and slowed down. I kissed the point where his neck and shoulder met and kissed my way up his neck to his ear. He moaned and grabbed my face with the hand that had been holding my legs. I dropped to the ground and he snarled at me making me lie flat on the ground, waiting for my punishment. He growled into my ear. "Do not tease me. I understand it is hard to control these emotions, especially since you have not had them before. My control is waning though and I do not want to try to finish what you are starting if that is not what you want. So stop teasing me and sit still until we get back."

I glanced down his body and saw what he meant about his waning control. I swallowed hard and looked back up at him. "I'm sorry." I leaned up and licked his cheek short and quick. I gasped and lay back down, shocked by what I had just done.

Ares smiled. "Don't worry, that's a submissive apology that wolves do to each other. It's natural that you would do that to me in this situation." He licked my cheek back and said, "You're forgiven." He stood up and turned to Matt. "You need to carry her. I fear that my control has been extremely diminished."

Matt laughed. "I can *see* that." Matt walked over and held out his hand to me. "Come on, Love. I'll carry you the rest of the way."

I took his hand and let him help me stand up. He picked me up in his arms and ran faster than any of them had carried me before. The wind whipping my hair and face excited me and I suddenly had the urge to run. I tore his arms away and fell to the ground on my feet. I started running as fast as I could, blowing past Ares and Koda. I yelled in joy and felt a burst of energy and began running even faster.

I could hear Ares, Koda and Matt behind me, but I didn't care about anything except running. It was the freest feeling I had ever experienced. I dodged around the trees, which I could see surprisingly well for how fast I was going. It was more like I could sense them. The night air spilled around me and I could suddenly smell everything. The birds and small animals in the trees, the three men/wolves behind me and the larger animals a few miles away. I had no idea how I knew everything, but I did.

We ran into the clearing of the village and I gaped. Houses were burned to the ground and the warehouse had a gigantic hole in the side of it big enough to fit a whale in. I ran to what was left of Gregory's house. The living room was now nothing more than a covered patio and the kitchen was completely gone. I screamed, "No!" And ran to where the kitchen used to be. I found the fridge on its back a few feet away and pulled it open. Meat and various other groceries lie on the back of the fridge defrosting. I reached in and grabbed as much meat as possible and pulled it out. I looked around for the microwave and found it under what used to be the kitchen sink. I looked at Matt. "Can you grab that?"

Matt picked up the microwave and followed me into the house. I walked to the bathroom and pointed at the plug. "Plug it in there please." He did as I asked and opened the door to the microwave. I pushed the meat inside and shut the door and turned on the microwave for twenty seconds to heat up the meat. I waited anxiously shifting from one foot to another as the meat twirled inside the microwave. The "ding" of the microwave made me jump and I hurried to grab the meat out, shoving an entire steak in my mouth and chewing. I moaned in pleasure and talked around my full mouth of food, "This is so good."

Ares walked into the bathroom and stared at my pile of meat in my arms. "Hungry?"

I snarled as much as was possible with a full mouth. "Don't make fun of me."

His lip twitched slightly as he tried to hide a smile. "Sorry. Can I have a piece?"

I grumbled, but handed him one of the smaller steaks. Matt laughed. "At least she is generous."

I snarled and swallowed the piece of meat that was in my mouth. "You shut up." I plopped down on the closed lid of the toilet and ate my meat quickly. Matt and Ares walked away sharing the piece of meat I had given them.

Victor walked in and smiled at me. "Hey." I frowned and continued to eat my meat without saying anything. He laughed. "I can see that you are eating, but I just wanted to formally introduce myself now that I am going to be joining your little faction."

I nodded my head and pushed the food in my mouth to the side. "Nice to meet you. I'm usually not this rude, but I'm really hungry."

Victor nodded his head. "I understand completely. It must take a lot out of you to stop your changes."

I shrugged. "Don't know. Just always do it."

Ares came back in. "You need to rest."

I nodded my head and kissed Ares cheek as I walked to my bedroom and laid down on the bed, rolling on my side to face away from the door. I heard the door open and someone come in and assumed it was Ares. I ignored him closing my eyes. I started to fall asleep when someone grabbed my arms and forced me on my back with my arms stretched and held above my head on the bed. I opened my eyes and saw Gregory standing over me with a knife in his hand. I swallowed hard. "What's going on?"

Gregory snarled, "I'm doing what should have been done the night you were born, but your father was too much of a coward to do."

I stared at the knife in his hand and asked, "Are you going to kill me?"

He nodded his head smiling. "Yes, and I'll love every second of it. If that boy hadn't been here before, you would already be dead."

I looked backwards and saw a man I had never seen before holding my arms. "You both know that Ares will kill you when he finds out, right?"

Gregory laughed quietly. "He won't know who did it because we are going to take your body out in the woods and make it look like suicide."

I rolled my eyes. "I would never kill myself. He won't believe it."

Gregory smiled. "Oh I think he will." He raised the knife and started to plunge downwards towards my chest and I rolled to the side of the bed tearing my arms out of the other man's hold. Gregory snarled, "Grab her!"

I ran around the bed and towards the door, but Gregory grabbed me. I screamed, "ARES!!!!" as Gregory threw me back on to the bed and picked up the knife he had dropped. I kicked as hard as I could at Gregory, but he moved out of the way. The other man grabbed on to my arms again and I screamed as loud as I could.

The wall beside me burst into pieces as Bret ran through it. He grabbed the other man and threw him out of the room and against the house across the street. Ares ran through the bedroom door and tackled Gregory, pulling the knife from his hand and stabbing it into Gregory's stomach. I jumped off the bed and ran to Matt who had come into the room behind Ares. He held me against him, his muscles strained as he fought to control himself. Ares grabbed Gregory's throat and squeezed then pulled backwards ripping his throat out. Blood sprayed over Ares and the bedroom. Ares tossed the piece of Gregory's throat outside the bedroom and into the street then grabbed Gregory's head and twisted and pulled ripping his head off his body. Ares threw Gregory's body and head out of the bedroom and into the street next to his piece of throat.

Ares turned to me and his eyes were amber wolf eyes. I felt no fear though he was covered in blood and I had just watched him rip Gregory's head off. I pulled away from Matt and walked towards Ares. Ares took a step back from me and shook his head speaking in a voice which was more of a growl than natural. "If you touch me you'll change. I have no control over my power right now."

I shook my head and continued to walk towards him. "I won't change." I reached out and touched his face and felt my body twitch hard once. I groaned and fought to control myself.

I stared into Ares' eyes and felt lust, admiration and...love. My body cooled and released its tension. Ares eyes cleared as I felt power flow into my body. He stared in awe at my face and whispered, "I knew you were perfect, but this is remarkable. Even I do not have this power." I stood on tiptoe and kissed his lips softly. He kissed me back and whispered, "I will protect you at all costs."

I smiled and nodded my head. "I know you will."

Bret growled. "I saved you too! Why does he get all of the attention?" He squatted down and I saw his body beginning to change. I walked to him and he snarled at me.

Ares started to come towards us, but I held up my hand walking towards Bret. "You are not my alpha, Bret. You cannot snarl or growl or try to show dominance that you do not have. If you try to attack me I will hurt you. Friend or not, I am your alpha."

Bret snapped his teeth at me and started to change. I reached into him with my power and felt the power of the moon and wolf in him. I pulled those powers into me absorbing them. Bret fell to the ground completely human and asleep.

Matt whistled. "Wow. I've never seen anyone but Ares do that."

I smiled then felt exhausted. I put my hand out for the bed, but missed and started to fall. Ares caught me and picked me up in his arms. He whispered, "You have to learn to pace yourself. Using too much magic too quickly will drain you."

I shrugged. "I'm a newb what can I say?"

He tilted his head to the side in confusion reminding me of a canine once again. "A newb? What is that?"

"It means I'm a newbie. Some of Bret's nerdy friends used to say it when talking about video games." I said quietly.

Ares shook his head. "The humans have used a lot of different slang over the years. Most of it I think is ridiculous. Like groovy. What is groovy? Stupid, that's what it is."

I giggled and asked, "Where am I going to sleep now?"

He winked. "How about my room?"

I blushed and Ares smiled. "I was just teasing. We'll put you in Koda's room and make him sleep on the couch."

Koda groaned. "Why me?"

Ares snarled. "You kissed her, remember?"

Koda groaned. "Fine, if that's my punishment, then alright."

Ares shook his head. "That's only the beginning of your punishment. You still have lots of punishing left."

I sighed. "It wasn't his fault Ares."

Ares shook his head again. "Spells like that can't put thoughts in people's heads. They can only intensify what they are thinking."

I looked at Koda and blushed. I turned my face into Ares' neck and said, "Okay take me to his room."

SONG OF THE MOON

Ares walked quickly to Koda's room and laid me down on the bed. "I know this must be hard for you, but I assure you that I will do all that I can to make you happy." He bent down and kissed my cheek then hurried out, shutting the door behind him.

I groaned and rolled on to my side closing my eyes. *Great, I am falling in love with him at a ridiculously rapid pace. Of course my life would be complicated like this.*

CHAPTER SEVEN

Two knocks on the bedroom door woke me from my peaceful sleep. I groaned and stood up from the bed walking clumsily towards the door. I reached for the light, but couldn't find the switch. The person knocked again, louder this time. "Hold on, I'm trying." I groaned. I finally opened the door no longer trying to find the light. The light from the hallway blinded me for a second and I had to wait for my eyes to adjust. I blinked three times then finally saw who was there. "Bret? What's wrong?"

Bret walked into the bedroom flipping on the light switch and closing the door. I stared at the light switch, angry at not being able to find it. Bret turned to me and demanded, "Why did you humiliate me yesterday?"

I stared at his face as I tried to remember what he was talking about. It was odd to see his face, the one I had seen for years and thought handsome and now I thought was only average. I smiled. *I guess when you are dating the God of War that it's hard to compare anyone else to that.*

Bret snarled. "Why are you smiling?"

I sighed. "Look Bret. In the world of werewolves you have to have a pecking order. Sure you can be friends and lovers, but you have to keep the order and you tried to break it. I didn't mean to humiliate you, but you challenged me in front of others. I had to remind you who your alpha is."

Bret growled. "You aren't alpha, you are just screwing the alpha!"

I growled back at him shoving my finger in his chest. "You don't know anything! I'm not screwing anyone and I *am* your alpha. Do you need a reminder?!"

Bret snarled. "Try it and see who the real alpha is."

I felt my body temperature rising with my anger and felt my body starting to twitch. I looked at Bret's body and saw him beginning to change as well. I groaned, "Fuck it!" I let my body take over and transform. I could feel the bones popping and sliding around to change my shape. My skin split apart, making a disgustingly wet sound as it ripped into pieces and then started falling below me. I closed my eyes and inhaled holding my breath as I finished the transformation. I slowly re-opened my eyes and looked out with much clearer, much sharper eyes with a muzzle between them that surprisingly didn't interfere with my view. I picked each foot up and wagged my tail then pulled my lips up in a smile.

I shook my body and turned to look at Bret. He was bigger than me in height, width, and weight, but I knew I could still defeat him. It was too cramped in the bedroom to move around easily though. He snarled at me and I snarled back. I sighed in happiness, finally finding a body that felt right. This body was like home for me. I no longer cared to school Bret, I just wanted to run. I ran through the bedroom door breaking it into pieces and ran down the hallway. Bret barked and growled as he ran after me, but I didn't care. As I turned from the hallway towards what used to be the living room I saw Ares, Koda and Matt in the kitchen. When they saw me their mouths dropped open in shock. Ares ran towards me, but I couldn't wait for him because Bret was right behind me.

I ran through the giant opening and towards the closest set of trees. The early morning air was crisp and clean as I breathed through my new mouth and nose. I ran faster into the trees dodging and weaving through them. I could feel the energy in the trees and plants and asked their permission to frolic among them. The trees seemed to anticipate my moves, leaning out of the way to give me more room to run faster and enjoy my new found freedom. I could hear the others running after me and it made me smile. For once I was in charge. I ran through the forest and inhaled the smells for what seemed like the first time. I could feel Ares gaining on me and turned to watch him. His black fur glistened in the dawn light as his muscles bunched and stretched to run to catch up to me. He was truly magnificent and I knew he was alpha. He was much larger than Bret and extremely larger than me. His majestic head tilted to the side as he caught my eye. I lolled my tongue out to the side in a playful show.

His voice whispered through my head. *Why are you a wolf?*

I snapped my tongue back inside my mouth and stopped running staring at him in shock. *How can I hear you in my head?*

He snorted. *All wolves can communicate through mind-to-mind telepathy. Some, like me, Koda and Matt can do it while in human form.*

I sighed. *Bret was challenging me again and I decided to let myself...*

Bret slammed into the side of me sending me head over heels. My head missed a nearby trees by only a few inches. I wasn't sure if the trees had moved or not, but I thanked them anyway. I jumped up and snarled, but Ares already had Bret on his back on the ground. *What is your problem, Bret?! She didn't do anything to you.*

Bret snarled. *She humiliated me yesterday.* He turned his head to look at me. *And I'm right about the alpha thing.*

SONG OF THE MOON

I snarled and launched myself so that I pushed Ares off of Bret and took his place above Bret, snarling with my teeth by his throat. *Do you want to die Bret? I will kill you if you don't stop trying to fight me. I am alpha as much as Ares.*

Bret snorted. *Ares is alpha, but you are just his bitch. The only reason no one will challenge you is because of him.*

I shook my head shaking my mane. *I am alpha with or without Ares. I don't want to kill you Bret, but you are leaving me little choice.*

Ares, Koda and Matt surrounded us. Matt growled softly. *Don't kill him. Let the loser go back to the village and live there with them. He is only pissed because you chose Ares over him. And he doesn't believe you aren't screwing Ares because what other reason would you chose Ares over him? Right Bret?*

Bret snarled and I bit down into his throat. He yelped loudly as blood began to leak down his coat. *You better knock it off Bret. I don't care what you think because I know I am alpha. With or without Ares I am your alpha.*

I released my hold on his neck and stepped backwards to join Koda, Matt and Ares. Bret hopped up to his feet and shook his head. *You are definitely not the same girl I fell in love with.*

I snarled. *Because you fell in love with a lie my father had set up. This is the real me and if you don't like it then too bad. I'm already taken anyway.*

Bret coughed. *Ya, good luck being his slut. Although you seem pretty good at it so far.*

Ares charged forward knocking Bret to his side. *Enough! You cannot talk to her that way. She is not a slut and she is your alpha. Now go back to the village before I kill you.*

Bret stood up and ran back to the village without another word. I walked forward and turned around so I could look at the three wolves with me. I giggled internally at the thought that they were wolves now and not men. I could see Koda, Matt and Ares having some type of dialogue among them, but had no idea what about. I snarled, making them all look at me. *It's not nice to talk about me when I can't hear you and am standing right here.*

Matt tilted his head to the side. *You should be able to tap into our conversation if you want to.*

I shook my head. *Nope, I can't. So what are you talking about?*

They looked at each other and Ares finally turned to me. *We were discussing how beautiful you are in wolf form and how much like the Mother you look. You are exactly as she is drawn and described, except for the purple eyes.*

I frowned. *I still have purple eyes? I thought your eyes were supposed to change to wolf eyes?*

Koda nodded his head. *They're supposed to, but it may have something to do with you being half.*

I nodded my head and looked around the forest. I wished the moon was out, but it was my own fault for not changing sooner. We walked back to the house in silence, or at least I was in silence. I waited while the others changed and walked into the house. I was about to start to change when Ares walked back out wearing a pair of pants. He smiled at me. "You alright?"

I nodded my head feeling my ears flop as I did. I sat on my butt and pictured my human self. My bones popped and I felt myself shrinking in size until I could feel the cold wood porch beneath my butt. I curled into a ball trying to hide my body as Ares handed me a large blanket. "It's all I could find quickly."

I wrapped my self up in it and stood up. "Thanks."

Ares smiled. "You need to put some clothes on though because we're leaving."

I frowned. "Where are we going?"

He shook his head. "It's a secret."

I sighed. "Like everything else in my life."

Ares took a step towards me and my heart beat instantly picked up speed. I swallowed and he smiled. He reached out slowly and stroked my cheeks softly. "I'm very lucky to have gotten you as a match."

I opened my mouth to say something, but Ares stopped me with a kiss. My legs felt like jelly and Ares wrapped his arms around my waist to keep me from falling. I pulled back from his kiss and whispered, "It's not fair that you make me feel this way and I have no effect on you."

Ares laughed and shook his head. "You have a great deal of an effect on me. I just am better at hiding my emotions."

Koda cleared his throat making us turn towards him. "Ares it'll be getting dark soon."

Ares sighed and nodded his head. "Of course."

He pulled away from me and it felt like a scab being pulled off. I bolted inside and to Koda's bedroom where a pile of clothes were lying on the bed. I changed faster than I ever had before and walked out to the porch where Ares, Koda, Matt and Victor were talking. I leaned against the porch railing and stared out at the abused town knowing it was my fault. Matt walked to stand next to me and smiled. "How are ya doin' Love?"

I shook my head, "So much fighting and death and damage all because of me? It doesn't make sense. I'm not special."

The other men stopped talking and I turned around to face them. Ares shook his head. "You are special. You and I are special together. There are going to be people trying to get you and use you for themselves, but you must never think it's your fault."

Two black SUV's pulled up in front of the house and Koda smiled. "Time to go."

I walked towards the SUV's ignoring Ares and Victor as best as I could. They were both whispering too quietly for me to hear their conversation, but obviously they were talking about me. I climbed into the first SUV and crawled into the center seat looking out the side window.

Ares sat down beside me and placed his hand palm side up on my knee. I stared at it for a moment then sighed giving into my desire and placed my hand in his. My heart picked up tempo and I felt content. I closed my eyes and Ares sighed happily beside me. "Thank you."

I rested my head against his shoulder. "It's getting much harder to fight. Plus, it's not like I don't *like* holding your hand."

Ares laughed and kissed the top of my head. "I like holding your hand too. You should sleep now. It'll be a while before we reach our destination." I closed my eyes and enjoyed the feel of his hand holding mine, but sleep wouldn't come.

I shifted on the seat and Ares released my hand so he could pull me down into his lap. I started to protest, but knew I would be more comfortable. I laid my head in his lap and he draped his left arm across my stomach and began stroking my hair with his right hand. I rubbed my cheek against his pant leg and sighed happily. For once it felt right to do this. With Bret it had always felt wrong somehow. *Could it have been because I was meant to be with Ares?*

Time dragged on, but Ares never stopped rubbing my hair. The vehicle finally stopped and I sat up stretching my arms above my head. Ares frowned. "You didn't sleep?"

I shook my head. "No, but it was relaxing."

He smiled at me and it was so gorgeous that my heart skipped a beat. Koda cleared his throat pulling me out of my trance. "I'm hungry."

Ares sighed. "You're always hungry."

I looked out the window and gasped, "My town!"

Ares smiled. "We need to rest for a day and I thought you might like to get some of your other things from your house."

I climbed out of the SUV and looked around the deserted streets. The only lights were coming from the pub and I could hear everyone talking loudly from inside. I turned to Ares and hugged him. "Thank you."

He kissed my cheek softly. "I'll have to remember to do things like this more often."

I looked at his naked chest and frowned. "Maybe you should find a shirt first?"

Ares frowned. "Are you embarrassed by my body?"

I laughed. "Definitely not! I just don't want to have to beat all of the girls off of you when we go inside."

He smiled. "Aw, you're jealous."

I snarled. "Don't patronize me."

Koda tossed Ares a shirt from inside the car and Ares quickly put it on. I started walking towards the pub before Ares could tease me anymore. I turned around before opening the door to make sure that Matt, Koda and Ares were fully clothed then walked into the pub. Everyone ignored me as they watched the news of another attack. I walked to an open booth and waved at the waitress Darcy. She smiled at me and nodded her head. I waited until all of the guys sat down then sat on the edge seat beside Ares. He smiled at me and continued whispering to the others. The news story ended and Jason, Skankzilla's dad, turned off the television.

Darcy hurried over and smiled at me. "Hey Darlin'! I was worried about you and your dad when you both disappeared."

I smiled. "Oh we just went camping. You know how Darren loves camping."

She laughed. "So what do ya'll want?" I rolled my eyes and Darcy laughed. "The usual?"

I nodded my head. Ares nudged me and I sighed. "Darcy this is Ares, my boyfriend."

Darcy looked him over with lust in her eyes. "You do know how to pick them. Well what do the rest of you want?"

I looked around the pub as the others ordered and caught Skankzilla glaring at me and storming towards me. I tensed and felt my lip pull up in a snarl. I quickly pulled my lip back down and smiled at her. She put her hands on her hips and glared at me. "Where's Bret?!"

I batted my eyelashes. "Why would I know that, Skankzilla?"

She growled at me and it sounded so pathetic that I almost laughed. "Listen you hooker trash. I've taken your crap because of Bret, but if you've done anything to him..."

I stood up an inch away from her face. "You'll do what?"

She stuttered and took a step back. "I...I..." Ares cleared his throat and Skankzilla looked around me to him. Her breath caught in her throat when she saw him. "Oh, hi."

He smiled. "Bret moved. He said to tell you he's sorry he didn't say goodbye."

She stepped around me and flipped her hair over her shoulder. "Oh, well I'm Trish."

Ares winked. "I'm Ares, Artemis' boyfriend."

Skankzilla's eyes widened in shock and disbelief. "You're dating *her*?!" Ares nodded his head and she asked, "What did she have to do to date you?"

I reached back to punch her when Billy grabbed my arm. "Calm down Artemis. She's not worth it. You know she's just mad that Bret left without saying bye to her."

Ares glared at Billy's hand on me, but stayed perfectly still in his seat. I pulled my arm away from Billy's hand gently. "You're right Billy."

Skankzilla turned to talk to Koda, but he waved his hand dismissively at her. "Beat it, Skank."

Billy looked at the four men sitting at the table with me and frowned. "Who're they?"

I smiled. "Billy this is Ares, Koda, Matt and Victor."

Billy nodded his head at them. "So, are you staying or you on your way out?"

Ares was still glaring at Billy angrily and I remembered that Billy had tried to shoot them while they were wolves. I shook my head. "Just stopping at my house for some things and staying the night. We'll be leaving tomorrow morning."

Billy smiled at me. "So, you'll be here tonight? You could come over..."

Ares shook his head. "She's taken, boy."

I glared at Ares. "Ares, I can handle this."

He folded his arms across his chest and continued to glare at Billy. Billy frowned. "What's he talking about?"

I sighed. "Ares is my...I'm dating Ares."

Billy looked Ares up and down. "How long?"

I frowned. "What?"

Billy looked at me. "How long have you been with him?"

"Not long."

Billy shook his head. "Artemis he's..." He pulled my arm gently turning me away from the table. I heard Ares grow softly, but it was too low for Billy to hear. "Artemis I don't like this guy."

I smiled and patted his back. "Good thing it's not up to you then. It was nice seeing you Billy, but my food's here."

I turned to sit down and Billy grabbed my arm hard, pulling me back toward him. "What's does he have that I don't?"

I stared down at his painful grip on my arm and opened my mouth when Ares spoke slowly beside me. "Manners for one. Release your hold on her before I lose my temper."

Billy smiled smugly. "And why should I worry if you lose your temper, huh freak?"

Ares smiled and the promise of pain was plain on his face. "Try me."

Billy started to tighten his grip and I punched him in the face with my other hand. He let me go and stumbled backwards falling against the bar. Ares pulled me back against him. I glared at Billy. "You were always so jealous. I thought it was just of Bret, but you're just too insecure."

Billy glared at me. "You've always just been Bret's pet freak!"

Ares moved across the aisle faster than I could see and picked Billy up by his throat holding him up with one hand. "I would prefer it if you refrained from insulting my girlfriend. As you can see I lose my control when that happens.'

Ares dropped Billy to the ground and Billy gasped for breath. J.D. started to move towards us, but Jess grabbed his arm and shook her head. I smiled at Jess and she smiled back. She pointed at Ares then put two thumbs up nodding her head smiling. I smiled back at her and pulled on Ares' arm. "Come on, let's eat before it gets cold. He's just a loser like Bret."

Ares looked at my arm where a small red mark still sat from Billy gripping me. He kissed it softly. "Do you see what I've told you? I'm fast, but not fast enough at times."

I kissed his cheek. "It's alright."

He sat down and I could see the judgmental eyes of the others in the pub glaring at me. I sat down and we ate in silence. The noise started up again in the pub, but I could hear every painful comment from everyone talking about me. I finished my burger and chocolate shake and walked out of the pub.

Jess walked out behind me and smiled. "Hey."

I smiled at her. "Hey. Sorry about that."

She shrugged. "Why are you apologizing to me? That's the most excitement we've had in a long time! And your boyfriend is sexy! Man! I couldn't believe how he held Billy up with one hand." She said in awe.

I giggled nervously. "Yeah, he gets real angry when people hurt me."

She sighed. "I'm sorry about how we treated you before Artemis. You don't have to leave you know?"

I shrugged. "No worries."

Ares walked out of the pub and wrapped his arms around my waist. The feel of him holding me released all of the tension in my body. Ares asked, "So, have you told her your good news?"

I frowned. "Um...no."

Ares started pouting. "Well that's one way to hurt my feelings."

Jess gasped, "Are you pregnant?"

I yelled, "Hell no!"

Ares frowned. "What she meant to say is that we're engaged."

Jess looked at my hands. "I don't see a ring."

Ares sighed. "I told you to let me get you a ring."

"No you..."

He pinched my stomach and smiled. "She was very worried about Darren finding out. But we're eloping."

Jess frowned. "Eloping? I thought you said you haven't been with him for very long?"

Ares laughed. "We've known each other a while, but we've only be dating a little while. We're family friends."

Jess smiled. "Oh. That's cool. Well I hope you have fun. Maybe we'll see each other again soon?"

I shrugged. "Maybe."

I walked away from her and Ares followed me silently. Koda, Matt and Victor caught up with us when we were at the feed store. I stopped and turned around to glare at Ares. "What the hell was that?!"

He frowned. "What?"

I yelled in frustration, "Eloping?! What is it with you and making sure everyone knows I'm yours?! Can't you just let me deal with them?! I mean its bad enough that I'm stuck with you..." I gasped. "Ares, I...I didn't mean that."

He shook his head. "Yes you did. I'm sorry. That boy just set me off."

"We better get to the house. I've got a lot of hunting to do." I said, happy for the subject change.

Koda asked, "Hunting?"

I smiled. "Come on." Ares walked back with Matt and Koda talking quietly to them.

Victor walked beside me and whispered, "You shouldn't be so hard on him. He's trying."

I scoffed. "So am I Victor. This isn't easy."

Victor nodded his head. "Think how hard it is for him."

I frowned. "What do you mean?"

He sighed and rubbed his temples. "Ares is the second fiercest warrior of all of the werewolves in the *world*. He doesn't bow to anyone except the King and now he's got you to deal with. You're pigheaded, strong willed and he's been bending over backwards to try to make this easy on you when it's tearing him up inside."

I stopped and stared at Victor. "How?"

Victor sighed again. "Being tied or having a match requires almost constant touching in the first few months and most often requires you to seal the bond. You're young and inexperienced so Ares isn't pushing you, but you keep pushing him away and refusing to touch him and we all know you would refuse to seal the bond. It's eating at his control. If we aren't careful he could snap."

I frowned. "So, I'm causing him pain?"

Victor nodded his head. "More pain than you could imagine."

Ares frowned when he saw us standing still. I whispered, "What do we have to do to seal it?"

Victor smiled. "I'm sure you can figure that out."

I groaned. "No! No way Victor!"

He shrugged. "Would it be so bad?"

I watched Ares walking gracefully towards us and felt my lower body tighten. Ares stopped walking and stared at me in shock. I groaned and covered my eyes with my hands. "No, anything, but that. Not yet. Can't we just cut each others palms and press them together or something?"

Victor laughed quietly. "This is why he is giving you space, but just think about the pain you're causing him. I'm not telling you to do it tonight, but it will need to be done soon. The sooner you seal your bond the safer you both will be."

Ares frowned. "What are you two talking about?"

Victor smiled. "Nothing."

I shook my head and jogged towards my house. Headlights raced down the street towards me. I stopped jogging and the truck skid to a stop in front of me spraying gravel. Ares pulled me backwards and I sighed. "He wasn't going to hit me."

Billy climbed out of the truck with Jake and Jeff. Ares shook his head. "We need to go."

I saw the seriousness on his face and wondered what was wrong. I looked at Jake and Jeff and noticed they were holding bats. I asked, "What are the bats for boys?"

Jeff smiled. "In case things get out of hand."

I smiled. "Do I really scare you that much, Jeff?"

He frowned. "What?"

Jake, one of Bret's other good friends laughed and tossed his bat into the truck bed. I smiled. "Thanks Jake."

Jake winked at me. "You ever need a change of men, call me."

I rolled my eyes. "You know you couldn't handle me."

He sighed. "Too true."

Ares frowned. "Is there something I don't know about?"

I shrugged. "Just that I'm too scary for the boys here to deal with."

Ares snorted and stroked my cheek. "Scary? Not hardly. Sexy? Definitely."

Billy asked, "Artemis what's happened to you? This isn't like you? Why are you with these scumbags?"

I frowned. "Nothing's happened to me. And they aren't scumbags."

Billy rolled his eyes. "They are obviously much older than us and I'm sure Ares is really after your *heart*."

Ares snarled and I put my hand on his chest stopping him from moving forward.

Jeff smiled. "Silenced by the bitch? Wow, that's a new low."

I pointed at Jeff. "You! You sleazy jerk. You have no room to call me names. I've seen the girls you go out with and the diseases you give them. And I didn't silence him. He is just letting me fight my own battle. And whatever Ares is after is none of your..."

Jeff smiled. "So you've already given him what he wants. Interesting."

I snarled and leapt towards him. He swung at me with the bat and as I put my hands up to block it Ares moved forward grabbing the bat from Jeff's hands. Jeff's eyes bulged as Ares took the bat from him and tossed it into the truck. Ares pushed his finger into Jeff's chest making him step backwards. "Just because she has better taste then to date you does not mean she's given up anything, which, not that it's your business, she hasn't. If you ever try to lay a finger on her again, I'll kill you."

Billy pointed at Ares. "And he's better than me how?"

I swung around and punched Billy in the face knocking him to the ground. "I'll be leaving tomorrow and you'll never see me again. So just shut up." I turned to Jeff. "And do something useful with your life. Football is useless."

Victor frowned. "I like football."

I sighed. "Not now Victor."

We walked the rest of the way to my house and I stared up at the porch steps. This had been my strange, but cold home. The house used to be a place of fun, but now it only brought me sadness. I walked into the house and straight to the cupboard under the sink. I pulled out Darren's hidden bottle of whiskey and took three giant gulps before Ares jerked it away from me. The burning of the liquor distracted me as I wiped my mouth. "What?"

Ares snarled. "What are you doing?"

I shrugged. "It's not like I can get drunk easily."

Koda laughed. "No. Wait, how do you know that?"

I smiled. "I drank with Billy and Jess and J.D. one night, but nothing happened. They were smashed, but I wasn't."

Ares snarled. "Did he do anything?"

I rolled my eyes. "No."

Victor opened the fridge and I watched in astonishment as he flipped a switch and a hidden compartment slid forward. Victor grabbed two bags of blood and closed the compartment again. Victor smiled at me. "It's customary for werewolves to keep blood on hand in case a vampire comes to visit."

I turned to Ares and asked, "So, now what?"

He smiled. "We rest here tonight."

The desire to touch him started intensifying and I remembered Victor's words that it hurt Ares more. I walked forward slowly and leaned my head against his shoulder. The pain receded and Ares sighed. I walked into the living room and sat down. "So, when you told Jess we were engaged you weren't just being possessive were you?"

Ares shook his head. "How many times do I have to tell you this? You and I are the perfect couple."

"I'm an eighteen year old girl tied to a man I barely know who likes to kill people." I said irritably.

Ares frowned. "I don't *like* to kill people. It's just necessary."

Koda snorted. "Unless it's a sidhe, then you like it."

Ares snarled at him and I asked, "What's a sidhe?"

Ares sighed. "Another preternatural I do not want to discuss with you until necessary."

I frowned. "Why not?"

He spoke in clipped words. "Because I refuse to. I refuse to acknowledge their existence. Now moving on, when we get to Victor's place there are going to be other werewolves there. Don't look at the alphas or betas in the eyes and you have to act submissive to them. The females are very aggressive towards each other, so for now, try not to make any contact with other females. You're especially going to be a target."

I frowned. "Why me?"

Koda smiled. "Because Ares was the hottest bachelor when we left. They've been drooling for him to come back and now you've taken him. So, they'll try to kill you so that he'll want them more."

I felt my jaw drop open and looked at Ares. He was gorgeous, but worth killing someone over? I tried to imagine him with another woman and a large growl ripped through my chest. My wolf stretched in my body and I pleaded for her to go to sleep. Ares stared at me in shock and I giggled in embarrassment. "Sorry, just testing a theory." I sighed. *Dammit I can't be willing to even think about killing someone over a man. It's so...true. Dammit. I barely know him and the thought of him with another woman makes me want to rip her head off!*

Ares smiled. "You have any questions?"

I nodded my head. "Do you have alpha females?"

Ares nodded his head. "We have ranks like the vampires. King, queen, prince, etcetera. To get to a place of high rank for werewolves we have to defeat the current person in that rank in a battle. Vampires are all about bloodlines and crap, but our method is that the strongest and most powerful are the rulers. Survival of the fittest at its best."

I asked, "Are werewolves like vampires, where they get stronger or more powerful the older they are?"

Victor looked at me curiously. "I never told you that."

I smiled, "You can learn a lot from movies."

Ares nodded his head. "To a certain extent. Darren is very old, but not very powerful. It depends on your aura and abilities."

"But as a new werewolf, I'll be pretty much helpless against older ones?" I concluded.

Ares nodded his head and smiled. "That's why you have me. No one will be able to defeat me to get to you."

"If I am ever going to gain the respect of anyone in the pack I have to fight my own battles!" I said angrily. Ares was frowning at me and I could tell he wanted to order me not to get into battles ever. I rubbed my eyes. "I think we've talked enough tonight. I have a lot to think about and I'm tired." I started walking down the hallway to my room when I felt him behind me. "What Ares?"

He laughed softly. "How'd you know it was me?"

I shrugged and turned around to face him. "I can smell you. Plus you have a weird feeling about you, like I want to bow to you." I groaned realizing I had said the last part out loud. "I didn't mean that."

Ares smiled. "It's normal for all wolves. As beta I have a lot of authority and it gives me a powerful aura."

I frowned remembering Darren discussing auras with me when I was younger. "Do you have an aggressive aura?"

Ares frowned. "What do you mean?"

I shrugged. "Darren said that people with aggressive auras are more likely to go on a rampage."

Ares shrugged back at me. "You can't see your own aura so you'd have to ask someone else."

"Well I can't see anyone's aura." I said. Ares smiled at me and put his hand against my face. I instantly started to lean into his hand and jerked back. "I don't like that I'm like this."

Ares smiled. "What? That all you can think about is me touching you? I told you that you're my *passt genau*. We are destined to be together, forever."

I frowned. "What if I don't want to be with you forever?"

His smile slipped away into a look so filled with rejection, that I instantly regretted my words. He asked softly, "Am I not pleasing you? Is there something you would like me to change?"

I looked at his sculpted body and his handsome face and knew nothing needed to be changed. The girls I knew would do almost anything to be with a man like him. And here I was trying to throw it away before I even gave him a chance. I spoke softly. "It's not that Ares. I'm just really overwhelmed by my feelings for you and the fact that I don't know you. Maybe you could tone down on reminding me that I'm stuck...I mean that I'm supposed to be with you forever. I've never even had a boyfriend and to be told I'm destined to be with you seems like a sentence, not a blessing."

Ares nodded his head and smiled a little. "I'll try. Just know that I'll do anything for you. No matter the cost."

I smiled and nodded my head. My hands ached to touch him and I gave in, letting my body rush forward and hug him quickly. I pulled away before I kissed him and darted into my bedroom and on to my bed. I listened to all of the new sounds I could hear with my heightened senses and smiled as the sound of the creek at the other end of our property gurgled. I drifted in and out of consciousness, but couldn't get the feeling that someone was going to attack me out of my head. I decided I needed sleep and even if I looked like a child, I would ask one of them to sleep in the room with me. I opened my door and screamed. Victor, Koda and Matt ran down the hallway then sighed in relief when they saw Ares sitting on the floor outside my door.

Ares frowned. "I'm sorry. I didn't mean to frighten you. I just didn't want to be too far away."

I finally regained my composure. "It's okay, you just startled me." He looked at me as if waiting for me to continue and I looked at the ground. "Could you sleep in here tonight. I'm just..."

Ares jumped up and smiled. "Of course. I would prefer it actually, but I didn't want you to get the wrong idea."

I smiled at him and nodded my head. Victor winked at me making me blush. I walked to my bed and heard him close the door quietly. I quickly took my shoes off and climbed into bed closing my eyes. Ares climbed in behind me and I tensed. *Not exactly what I had meant about sleeping in here.* He put his arm around my stomach, but kept space between our bodies. As much as I wanted to object, it was comforting to have him with me. I pulled the blanket around me tighter then realized I was sweating.

Ares whispered, "Having two werewolves in a bed at once usually makes blankets obsolete." I nodded my head and kicked the blankets off. We settled in once again and my brain shut off. The sound of arguing woke me up. I opened my eyes and was instantly lost in Ares' sky blue eyes. He smiled at me. "Good morning."

I swallowed the lump in my throat at the realization that I had just technically slept with a man. Okay, okay, I know it's not the same thing, but he was in my bed because I asked him to sleep with me. "Morning. Who's fighting?"

"They're discussing politics. Nothing important." He rubbed my back slowly with his hand. "Did you sleep well?" He rolled on to his back and I scooted over laying my head on his warm bare chest. I inhaled his now familiar smell and nodded my head. "Very well."

He asked, "Are you feeling better?"

I sighed. "I'm realizing that being a werewolf isn't as scary as I first thought. I'm still worried I could go on a killing spree..."

Ares stroked my back with long even movements. "I won't let you do that."

I smiled and looked up at his face. I had expected him to be smiling, but he was serious. He stared into my eyes with a desire I had never seen before and then I felt it. I reached up slowly, fearful of his reaction and ran my hand down his face. A small smiled played at the corners of his lips and I couldn't hold myself back. I moved up on the bed and kissed him on the lips. The instant our lips connected fire shot through me and I moaned. Ares' responding moan let me know that he was feeling the same thing. He kissed me back with a need of his own and wrapped his arms around me.

I ran my hands over his chest as we kissed and felt my lower body tighten. I gasped and tried to pull away, but Ares had repositioned us so that he was lying on top of me. I ran my hands through his thick black hair and kissed him harder, grabbing a chunk of his hair in my hands and pulling him to me. He moaned again and thrust his tongue into my mouth. He kissed my lips once more than moved down my jaw to my neck. My breathing sped up and he smiled at me. The smile was perfect. Admiration, desire and happiness all in one. He kissed my lips one more time then jumped off me.

I frowned. "Where are you going?"

He smiled at me from the bedroom door. "I want you for your heart, not your body, but if I stay any longer with you kissing me like that, I don't know if I can hold myself back." He walked out of the room and my face erupted into a blush. I grumbled to myself as I changed clothes and went through my morning routine.

I walked out into the living room and stared at the pile of dishes in the sink. I opened the fridge and growled. "What happened to all of the food?"

Koda laughed. "You have three male werewolves in your house and you wonder where your food went? It's in our stomachs!"

I glared at him. "And you didn't think to leave some for me!" Koda's smile faded and I sighed. "I'm sorry, I'm just hungry." I tapped my foot then sighed. "Well I guess we'll just have to go to the pub."

Ares asked, "Do you have money for the pub?"

I laughed. "You don't know Darren very well do you? I told you I had to go hunting." I walked to the bottom middle kitchen cabinet and pulled all of the canned food out on to the floor. A piece of tape held down a tiny white string and I pulled on it opening the small compartment Darren built into the cabinets. He always hated banks and being a couple hundred years old explained it better. I reached into the compartment and pulled out the long slender bag hidden inside. I shut the compartment and put the canned food away then tossed the bag to Ares. I walked quickly into Darren's room and tried to move the bed, but it was too heavy. I turned to see Koda in the doorway smiling at me. "Can you move this?"

He shrugged and walked over to the bed. He put his foot against the base and with a slight movement sent the bed flying across the room and into the wall. Ares ran in the room and sighed. "Koda."

Koda smiled. "Sorry. Couldn't help myself."

I rolled my eyes at him and walked to where the center of the bed used to be and sat down. I traced my fingertip along the edge of the two boards and smiled when I felt the air coming up on the edge of one. I pressed against the very end of the board and it popped up. The boards were only three inches wide so I had to turn my hand sideways to get it in and down. When my hand was in down to my wrist I had an evil idea. I hid my smile and then screamed as if in pain and acting like I was trying to pull my arm out. Koda rushed over to me and started trying to pull my arm out. He looked at my face and I smiled. "Sorry couldn't help myself."

Koda sighed. "Shit."

Ares laughed. "Looks like she'll be a handful for you too, Koda.

Koda groaned. "Damn, a prankster and a smart aleck like me. Wonderful."

I finished reaching in the hold and pulled the bag up. Darren must have added more while it was in the hole because it wouldn't come out. I stared at the small space and didn't want to ask for Koda's help again. I am a werewolf so shouldn't I be able to break it apart? I made a fist and punched the board next to the open one and smiled as it broke apart. I punched the board on the other side of the hole and it broke open, too. Koda watched me with a small smile on his face. I cleared the piece of the board and grabbed the bag. I gasped when I realized how heavy it was. What used to be a three inch by three inch bag was now a ten inch by ten inch bag. I smiled and tossed it to Ares. "I think we have enough for a while."

He opened the two bags and smiled. "Darren didn't like banks did he?"

I shook my head. "Not one bit."

Koda frowned. "What's in the bags?" Ares tossed him one and Koda's eyes lit up. "Damn, that's a lot of money."

I stood up then frowned at my hands. A couple of pieces of the boards were sticking out of my hand and it was bleeding. Ares rushed over to me and tossed the other bag of money to Koda. He picked my hand up gently and sighed. "This is why you don't punch wood."

"Thanks for telling me now." I said through gritted teeth. He started to pull a piece of wood out of my hand and I groaned. "Ow. Ow. OW."

He sighed. "You're going to have to let me pull these out."

I gritted my teeth. "Fine, but do it fast."

Koda laughed. "That's what he's best at."

I turned to him and wanted to ask what he meant, but Ares snarled. "Shush. Let's get this over with so she can eat." He smiled at me and then kissed my lips softly. Fire exploded on my lips and I stared into his blue eyes. *Maybe being tied down to him wouldn't be so bad. I mean, man is he gorgeous.* He kissed my cheek, then dropped my hand. "That wasn't so bad now, was it?"

I frowned and looked down at my hand. All of the pieces of wood were out and the wounds were already healing. "Wow."

Koda snorted. "She's easily impressed."

I shook my head. "I've never really been injured so I never knew we could heal so fast."

"There are downsides to that." Koda said.

"Like what?" I asked curiously.

He smiled. "Healing too fast and having to cut out the pieces of wood."

I cringed. "Ow."

Koda nodded his head. "Definitely."

Ares asked, "Are we ready to go eat?"

I looked at him wearing Darren's jeans and t-shirt and smiled, "Almost. I need to pack some stuff." I took the money bags from Koda and walked to my bedroom finding one of my backpacks. I shoved clothes and hygiene products into it, slung it on my back and then walked out to the porch where the three men were talking quietly. I started to walk down the steps when Ares cleared his throat. I stopped and turned around. "Yes?"

He sighed. "Don't laugh, but can I hold your hand?"

I stared at him in shock for a second, then looked at Victor's face. He tilted his head to the side and I smiled at Ares. "Sure." I held my hand out towards him and he gave me his perfect smile again.

He interlaced our fingers and we walked through town toward the pub. It felt good to be holding his hand. No it felt, perfect. He picked our hands up and kissed the back of my hand quickly. "Thank you."

I rubbed my face against his shoulder and sighed in contentment. "No problem."

The pub was slow as usual so we got a seat right away. I looked around for Darcy, but a new waitress I had never seen before, walked over to our table. The instant Ares saw her, his entire body tensed. She smiled and spoke with a thick southern drawl. "How y'all doin? What type of drinks can I start ya' off with?"

I smiled. "You're new here. I'm Artemis."

She laughed. "Oh, I know who you are honey. I'm Sally."

I frowned. "You know who I am?"

She nodded her head and tilted her head towards the bartender. "He talks a lot about you and yer dad."

I smiled. "Oh. Well I'll have a soda." The men stared in frozen shock at her. I frowned. "What do you guys want?"

Ares shook his head. "It's time to leave."

I frowned. "Why?" I looked more closely at the waitress and didn't see anything out of the ordinary except that she was very attractive. I shrugged. "Guess we aren't eating here."

I started to stand up and she frowned. "Why her? Why not me?"

I stared at her in shock and Ares sighed. "Sally, she's my *passt genau*."

Sally's eyes widened and she shook her head. "I don't believe you. You're just with her because she's younger. I'm not that old." She lowered her voice. "I'm only a hundred. You know that's young and you know I'm better."

Ares shook his head. "Sally, it wouldn't have worked between us even if I didn't find Artemis."

Sally snarled. "Let me kill her and prove I'm better."

Ares anger exploded from his body and his authority as beta beat against me like a wave of fire. He pushed me gently out of the booth and Koda grabbed me wrapping his arms around my body. The instant Koda touched me Ares' anger and authority stopped pressing against me. Ares spoke slowly, "Sally. She is my *passt genau*. You know the rules about that. If you kill her it's an automatic death sentence. What would you gain?"

She smiled. "It's not a death sentence if she agrees to the fight."

Ares arms flexed and she fell to her knees. "You will not speak of fighting or killing Artemis again. If you do, I will let the King judge you for attempted assassination."

She whimpered. "I just want to be yours."

Ares temper faded and the pressure released as he squatted down and looked into her eyes, "You can find many others that would willingly be with you. I'm sorry, but I'm taken." Ares stood up and reached out for me. Koda released his hold on me and I walked quickly to Ares. He led me past the weeping waitress and outside.

We were almost to the SUV's when she burst out of the pub. "No! No I won't let her win. She's only a pup and not fit to be your mate."

I stared at the furious woman and could see the bloodlust in her eyes. Ares started to let go of my hand and I grabbed his bicep. "Please. Please don't kill her."

Ares frowned. "She wants to kill you."

I shook my head. "Being shunned for another woman younger than you, is defeat enough. Let's just leave. Order her as beta to go to the nearest wolf town and stay there."

He stared at me in shock. "You want to spare her life, even though she's admitted that she wants to kill you?"

I nodded my head. "It's not worth it. Please Ares."

He sighed and rubbed his temples. "Alright Artemis." He kissed my cheek and walked towards Sally who was staring at me with a look of utter hatred. I turned to face Matt and he put his arm around my shoulders. Ares picked my hand up and whispered, "It's done."

I turned to see Sally stand up and give Ares one last pain filled look, and me, a look of contempt before running into the forest. "Thank you." I stood on tiptoe and kissed his cheek. We started walking again and I couldn't get the look of pain she had had out of my brain. *How many women would I have to deal with?* I stopped Ares. "How many women have you been with?"

He frowned. "What?"

I sighed. "How many Ares? How many women am I going to have to deal with that are like Sally?"

He sighed. "I'm not sure."

I swallowed the lump in my throat and fought the tears away. *How can you not know for sure?* "More than fifty?" He nodded his head. I asked, "more than a hundred?"

He groaned. "I'm not sure."

Tears started to leak out and I wiped them quickly. "At least I know." I walked away from him as quickly as I could towards the SUV's. My stomach growled loudly and I scolded it, "We'll eat soon enough, just wait."

Ares spoke from beside me. "I didn't know I was going to have a match until you were born."

"I'm sure that stopped you." I said angrily.

He grabbed my arms and turned me towards him. I looked to my right avoiding making eye contact with him. He whispered, "Artemis. Artemis look at me." I turned my face and looked at him with the best frown I could muster. "I've been alive a long time and only when you were born, did I know that you might be my match. It wasn't even a positive thing then either. Once I felt you, I couldn't be with another woman again."

I frowned. "What do you mean felt me?"

He smiled. "The instant you were born my heart no longer looked at women. It was like they stopped being female and were just another wolf. I didn't know what was happening, until I talked with Darius."

I looked at Koda. "Is he telling the truth?"

Koda nodded his head. "He wouldn't even go to strip clubs with me."

Matt sighed. "We left Germany for America so he could get away from the females he had been with."

I frowned. "So they think you've deserted them for eighteen years, but are hoping that you will come back, and then they can start up with you again?"

Ares nodded his head. "I'm afraid so. If I had been positive about you, I would have told them the reason, but at the time, it was easier to just leave. Women can be very aggressive when they think you're choosing another over them."

I shrugged. "I guess I understand." I walked to one of the SUV's and climbed into the middle seat. I kept looking out the side window not wanting to talk to Ares anymore. I knew it wasn't his fault, but it didn't hurt any less to know that he had been with so many women. We drove in silence through the smaller towns until we reached a drive thru window.

Ares asked, "What do you want?"

I sighed. "Don't laugh. Five cheeseburgers extra ketchup and a large chocolate shake."

Ares smiled. "Why would I laugh?"

Victor ordered food for everyone and Ares handed him money from my bag. Koda poked my arm from the back seat. I turned around and he smiled. "How are you doing?"

I looked from Ares to him and shrugged. "Fine."

Koda sighed. "Come on. We're pack now."

I frowned. "Pack?"

Ares nodded his head. "Koda, Matt and I are a pack. And now that you are my mate you are part of our pack."

I stared at them in shock. "You only have one female in your pack and that's only because it's me?"

Ares shrugged. "Matt and Koda haven't found mates yet."

Matt snorted. "Not looking either."

I frowned. "Isn't it like a natural instinct to find a mate?"

Matt shrugged. "You can fight your natural instincts. I don't feel like being with a crazy female just because my *instinct* says I should."

Victor tossed back the bags of food then handed Ares the drinks. I grabbed my burgers and shake and dug in no longer wanting to engage in conversation. Victor continued driving and after I was done eating, my eyelids started to droop. Ares put his arm around my shoulders and pulled me against him pushing my head against his shoulder, "You need to rest."

I shook my head. "All I do is sleep or eat."

He kissed my forehead. "Your body is adjusting. It needs time to rest and recuperate."

I looked down at the wolf burn on my hand. "How come this hasn't gone away?"

Ares rubbed the small burn on my palm, then picked it up and kissed it, making the spot tingle. "Silver permanently scars us."

I groaned. "Great." I closed my eyes as I leaned against Ares. He hugged my shoulders and rubbed his chin against my forehead.

We drove with the radio on for a few hours and then Victor groaned, "Traffic."

I looked up and saw the line winding into the airport. "Where are we going?"

Victor turned around and smiled. "France."

I gasped and turned to Ares. "France?! Do we get to visit the Eiffel Tower?"

Ares laughed. "Sure." My wolf seemed to wake inside me and stretched. I gasped and Ares inhaled loudly. "She wants to hunt."

I stared at him in shock. "How'd you know?"

He smiled. "I could feel her and smell her."

I frowned. "But I can't even tell what she wants. She just woke up and stretched."

Matt laughed. "They never wake up unless they want something."

I looked at Ares. "Is she another personality?"

He shook his head. "No, she is you with some different instincts. She's a more primitive version of you. Of course you still think, but sometimes her instincts will take over. Which is why you need a strong alpha nearby to help you."

I smiled. "Which is why it's good to have you?"

He kissed my cheek. "Yes."

Victor finally pulled up to the front of the airport and we all climbed out. Koda took my bag from me and we walked toward the counter. Ares held my hand and, even in the crowd of people I felt completely safe. The woman at the counter asked for our ID's. Victor handed her ID's and then waved his fingers. Her face went slack then she smiled and handed him our tickets. Ares pulled me towards the gate and when we were far enough away whispered, "Vampire powers come in handy with humans quite often."

Victor handed me my ID and plane ticket. I stared at my ID in shock. "Artemis Lupine? Lupine isn't my last name." I said.

Ares smiled. "Lupine is my last name."

"Oh." I said in shock. He was already making changes that married couples make. I couldn't say my name with his last name though. It didn't seem right yet.

I looked at the plane tickets and my hands started to sweat. Ares frowned. "What's wrong?"

I licked my lips nervously. "I...I've never been on a plane and well..."

Koda laughed loudly. "She's scared!"

I growled at him and my wolf snarled inside me. Koda's eyes flicked with golden specks and he growled back. Ares grabbed both of our arms and his power hit me like a tidal wave of hot water. "Enough."

I kept my gaze even with Koda's ignoring Ares as best as I could. Ares snapped his teeth at me and my wolf disappeared, leaving me weak. I started to fall forward and Ares put his arm around my waist holding me up. I whimpered, "I..."

Ares shook his head and I looked up to see the golden tint to his eyes. "Be quiet."

Ares handed our tickets to the stewardess who smiled at me. "First flight?" I nodded my head and she waved. "Have fun."

Ares led me inside the airplane and to our seats. I pulled away from him and stared out the window. Ares sighed. "Artemis, I wasn't trying to upset you."

I sighed. "I know. My wolf doesn't like the idea that Koda is dominant to me."

Ares rested his hand on mine and whispered, "All wereanimals hate enclosed metal places. It's natural for us to hate what amounts to a flying cage."

I looked up at his sincere face and asked, "Does it bother you?"

Ares nodded his head. "Very much, but when you're as old as me, you learn to hide the things that bother you. When enemies learn what bothers you, they use it against you."

The plane began moving down the runway and I gripped Ares' hand tightly. He rubbed his thumb across my hand and whispered, "I won't let anything happen to you."

I closed my eyes as the plane increased speed and began tilting upwards and lifting off the ground. "Would we survive a plane crash?" I asked quietly.

Ares laughed softly. "Well, it depends, but most likely." The plane leveled out and a high pitched ding made me open my eyes to look at the sign allowing us to move around the airplane. Ares picked my hand up to his lips and kissed the back of my hand softly. "You alright?"

I looked at the blood trickling down his hand and gasped. "Ares, I'm...I'm sorry." I tried to let go of his hand, but he held on to me.

"Calm down, Artemis. Look." He repositioned my hand in his so that he was still holding mine, but I could see the wounds I had made from my fingernails. The half circles that were filled with blood slowly stopped bleeding and then the skin closed completely with no sign of the cuts except the blood staining his hand.

Victor leaned over the back of our seats and handed Ares a handkerchief. "Would you mind? I'm hungry and I don't think you want another incident like Bosnia."

Ares rolled his eyes. "You should have eaten before we left and Bosnia wasn't my fault. Koda bit me."

Koda sat down in an empty seat across from us. "I was only ten and you were being rude."

Victor scoffed. "It took me three *days* to heal from that crash and my father spent five thousand dollars on outside help to finally convince the humans that it had been a lightning strike."

Ares rolled his eyes. "That's pocket change to your father and besides it would have been fine if you had eaten *before* we got on the plane with two hundred humans."

I looked at Victor as the pieces of what they were talking about fit into place. "You ate two *hundred* humans?"

Victor shushed me and whispered, "No, I tried to eat Ares and he changed and the humans freaked and I *killed* the two hundred humans."

I looked at Ares. "You killed them?"

Ares shook his head. "No, I was fighting with Koda because he was trying to eat the humans. Victor killed them."

Koda shrugged. "I'd only changed twice and humans smell *very* good when you're a pup."

I wrinkled my nose in disgust. "If you say so."

"You don't think they smell good?" Asked Koda.

"They smell like humans, not food." I said seriously.

Ares smiled at me. "Really?"

I blushed and looked down. "Something else that makes me not normal?"

Victor was tapping his chin with his finger loudly. "It must be because she was raised around them and that boy was so close to her when she was fighting the changes so many times. She must have just associated their smell with friends. You know the wolves', friend, foe or food mentality."

Koda scoffed in the seat across from us. "Food can be foe or friend also."

I looked up at him in shock. "You'd eat a friend?"

Ares shook his head smiling. "Not a friend as in another wolf, but like a friendly dog."

I stared at Ares then saw the smile Victor had to the side of me. "That's really not funny."

Victor and Ares laughed loudly and the overweight woman in front of us turned her head and shushed us. I stuck my tongue out at her and she turned back around whispering loudly to the balding man beside her about "disrespectful youth".

Ares reached across me and my heart sped up instantly at the nearness of his body to mine. His smile widened as he pushed up the window cover so we could see outside the plane. I closed my eyes as he and Victor looked out the window. Ares whispered, "Artemis, just look. It's very beautiful."

I shook my head and squinted my eyes closed harder. "No thanks. I'll pass."

Victor sighed. "And here I thought the Great Ares would get an adventurous mate, but it looks like he got a wimp."

I nodded my head with my eyes still closed. "Yep, sorry Victor, not falling for the bait."

The plane bounced around as we hit a patch of turbulence and I gripped the arms of the seat and squealed in fear. The arms began moaning in protest of my grip and Ares pried my left hand off the arm between us and held my hand. "Artemis, do you think I'm a liar?"

I turned my head towards him and opened one eye. "What?" The plane was jolted again and I closed my eyes squeezing tightly on his hand and the right chair arm.

He whispered, "I told you that I wouldn't let anything happen to you and yet you're destroying the plane in your fear of the plane falling. Do you think I'm lying when I tell you that I'll protect you?"

SONG OF THE MOON

The pain and sincerity in his voice made me open my eyes and loosen my grip. I looked at him and it caused my stomach to knot up at the sight of his pain. "I don't think you're a liar, but you couldn't possibly protect me from everything."

Ares frowned. "So you do think I'm a liar? I'll just have to prove it to you." He leaned towards me and cupped my face with his hands. His skin was warm and his breath was hot as he kissed me on the lips. Fire exploded in my body and I wrapped my arms around his neck. He pulled away from the kiss and whispered, "Nothing matters to me now except you. This plane could fall on my mother's house and my only worry would be your safety. Trust me to protect you."

I nodded my head and licked his cheek. "I'm sorry."

He smiled. "You licked me again?"

I shrugged. "I am a wolf."

He whispered, "Will you accept your place in my pack now?"

I frowned. "What do you mean?"

Matt whispered from behind me, "He means will ya' accept him as yer' mate and me and Koda as yer' packmates?"

I turned my head so I could see Matt through the crack in the seats. "What happens?"

Matt smiled. "We go on a hunt and you finally sleep with us."

My eyes widened and Matt shook his head. "Love, your mind is filled with dirty thoughts. I only meant that we sleep in the same bed with you, not *sleep* with you."

Ares growled. "No, not the latter."

Koda sighed. "Ares has never been good about sharing."

Ares sighed. "We hadn't eaten in four days and I killed it! Besides I apologized the next day."

I smiled and asked, "What happened?"

Koda leaned around Ares and talked just loud enough for me to hear, but not for the humans on the plane. "We were running through Germany and hadn't been able to find a house or food for a few days. Well as you can imagine we were ravenous. Ares here sees a lone stag and takes off after it killing it in like three seconds. I walked over to eat my share and he attacks me!"

I gasped, "No!"

Matt stood up and leaned over the tops of our seats. "So, while Ares is chasing Koda around, I run over and started eating off the stag. As you can imagine that wasn't alright with Ares. So he leaves Koda and charges after me!"

Koda laughed and shook his head. "We had to keep drawing him away and then sneaking into eat like that for two hours before we got our fill and then we both ran off and let Ares eat."

Ares sat back in his seat and frowned. "I apologized afterwards. Besides I'm supposed to eat first and you both know it."

Matt asked, "When are we going to test the new dominance layout?"

"It depends on how she feels. I don't want to push her too soon." Ares said softly.

"You're talking about me like I'm not here." I scolded.

Ares smiled and rested his hand on my knee and closed his eyes. "Sorry, baby."

I smacked his hand off my knee and snarled, "Don't call me baby!"

Ares opened one eye and looked at me with a completely calm, neutral face. "What would you like me to call you?"

I frowned. "I don't know, but not baby or darling or...well I can't think of anything you could call me."

Ares closed his eye again and replaced his hand on my knee. "I'll think of something."

Matt smiled. "Glad I took Love already."

Ares scoffed. "Yeah, thanks."

I relaxed back into my seat and noticed the window still open from the corner of my eye. I closed my eyes and reached over searching along the wall for the window cover. I finally found it and pulled the cover down and then opened my eyes again, only to find Ares, Koda and Matt watching me. I blushed and looked down at my hands in my lap. Koda sighed. "You think she'll ever stop blushing?"

Ares rubbed his thumb across my kneecap. "I hope not."

More blood rushed to my face and Victor whispered from behind Ares, "I can smell her from here. Knock it off."

Ares laughed softly and pulled his hand off my leg. "My apologies, Victor. We should all rest. It's going to be a *long* night once we arrive."

The absence of his hand was like a bee sting. I pushed up the middle arm, scooted closer to Ares and leaned my head against his shoulder. I closed my eyes and reveled in the happy electric current thrumming through my body. Ares kissed the top of my head and then laid his head on top of mine.

CHAPTER EIGHT

I pulled myself out of a dreamless sleep as I heard the stewardess talking quietly to Ares in another language. Instnatly my anger began to well up. I opened my eyes and found myself inches from her breasts. I sat up quickly and was about to snarl when Ares grabbed my hand and the anger disappeared. I stared at his hand as though it were a bear trap and asked, "How'd you do that?"

The stewardess handed me a pillow and then walked away. Ares whispered, "I wasn't doing anything with the stewardess and I very politely explained that we were getting married. I had no idea she would start discussing it with me and then she insisted on getting a pillow for you even though we're about to land."

The pillow fell off my lap as I moved back into my own seat and faced the closed window. "I didn't say anything."

Ares whispered, "You didn't have to. I could feel your anger like a growing forest fire."

I looked at him and asked again, "How'd you do that?"

He smiled. "I took your anger from you. It's a handy trick you learn when you become an alpha."

SONG OF THE MOON

The stewardess stood in the front of the plane and picked up the intercom. She began speaking in fluent French and I felt my anger rising again. She was pretty and thin, model thin. Ares sighed. "I would never cheat on you."

My anger rose at the thought of Ares with another woman and my body temperature began rising. Matt growled softly behind me and Ares growled back. Koda whined softly and I took a giant breath then let it out slowly. The anger vanished and my body cooled down. Matt snorted and Koda sighed. Ares thumped my arm softly. "Cool down."

I smiled and looked at his golden eyes. "I am. You seem to be upset still though."

Ares shook his head and the gold faded. "To feel your strong emotions is hard on me. Our connection is still new and not finished yet. The connection between our emotions is designed this way to keep you safe, but you're a little more volatile than most your age."

His words stung as I deciphered between the lines and got the unspoken word of "immature". The light to put your belts on chimed over our heads giving me a chance to look away from Ares and put my belt on. The plane began to descend and I gripped on to the arm rests tightly. Ares held out his hand, but I ignored him by closing my eyes and leaning back against the seat as the plane landed on the runway. I kept my eyes closed until the attendant got back on the intercom and I could hear people beginning to stand up. I unbuckled my seat belt and stood up facing the front of the plane.

Koda walked up from the back, where his assigned seat had been, carrying my backpack. I held out my hand and he shook his head smiling. "I'll carry it."

I wanted to argue, but Ares was watching me and we were next to walk out of the plane. "Thanks." The desire to touch Ares was growing stronger, but I refused to give in. There was no reason I had to touch him *all* the time. Victor led the way out of the airport and to a waiting limousine. I smiled at Victor. "I've never gotten to ride in a limo before."

He smiled at me. "Well then get in."

I ducked into the limo and climbed over on the seat to look out the large side windows. The others climbed in behind me and the driver started the limo. I moved from one side of the limo to the other as we drove through France. The Eiffel Tower loomed over us as we drove by it and I asked, "Do we get to go see it?"

Ares frowned. "If we have time."

I was about to pout when Koda said. "Matt and I will take you tomorrow while Ares is in meetings."

Ares shook his head and folded his arms across his chest. "Absolutely not. She's not to be away from me while we're here."

Matt glared at Ares. "You think we wouldn't be able to protect her?"

Ares growled. "I think there are too many leeches, no offense Victor, in this city."

Victor frowned. "Why would any vampire want to bother Artemis? There are only a few people that have seen her and those are either in America or my father."

Ares shook his head. "I'm alpha of this pack and I say that I don't want her out of my sight."

"Ares you're being overprotective. No one would want to take Artemis or hurt her. Gregory was just psycho and an exception and Darren was supposed to have killed her years...uh oh." Koda stopped talking, looked down at the ground and rubbed the back of his neck.

My eyes were bulging out of my skull as I looked at each of the four men who were quickly averting their gazes from me. "What do you mean Darren was supposed to have killed me?"

Ares looked up. "You're a mixed blood, Artemis. Mixed bloods aren't supposed to be made let alone allowed to live. Your father was ordered by the king at the time you were born to kill you. As we can see he never did though."

The words sunk in slowly until the painful truth hit. "He'd been planning it for after Bret left."

All of the men looked at me in shock. Ares asked, "What do you mean?"

Tears began running down my cheeks and I hugged my knees to my chest. "I heard Darren talking on the phone a few times about his plans. He would tell the person that it was going to be harder to do than he originally thought and to just give him until after Bret left. He always told me that I didn't need to worry about trying to find friends after Bret left and I thought he meant that I'd find others, not that I'd be dead."

Ares growled and rushed across the limo picking me up and holding me in his lap. "He won't hurt you now. I won't let him."

I buried my face in his chest and inhaled his scent that was fast becoming familiar and comforting. In a matter of minutes the sorrow at my revelation disappeared and I was relaxed again. Deciding to ignore the news about my father, I whispered, "Can I go see the Eiffel Tower tomorrow?"

Ares sighed. "Dammit."

I lifted my face and licked his cheek. "Please."

Ares groaned. "Alright! But you have to stay with Koda and Matt at all times, even bathroom trips."

I kissed his lips quickly and jumped across the limo to look out the window. "I can't wait!"

Matt turned on the seat beside me and started pointing out places we would visit as the limo drove on. The city faded into countryside and I sat down in my seat sighing loudly after thirty minutes. "When are we going to be there? I'm hungry."

Victor smiled showing his fangs. "Care to make a bet on who's hungrier?"

Ares growled. "Don't test me Victor."

My legs began to go numb from sitting so long and I slid to the floor kicking my feet. "Dangit, my legs are falling asleep."

Victor smiled. "We're almost there. I'd say five more minutes, tops."

I folded my legs into my body and asked, "What's it like?"

Victor shrugged. "You'll see."

Ares held his hand out towards me and I took it giving into the pain I'd been trying to ignore for the last hour. He pulled me up on to the seat beside him and I laid my legs across his lap. He started massaging my legs and I moaned in pleasure. "Wow, you're really good at that."

"I'm very good at a lot of things." Ares winked at me and I blushed, closed my eyes and enjoyed the massage.

Koda asked, "Do we have to dress up tomorrow?"

I opened my eyes to see the interaction. Ares nodded his head. "Of course. I don't want to go before them dressed in Darren's clothes."

Koda sighed. "I know. I just hate wearing a jacket all the time."

Victor shrugged. "You could wear dress casual instead."

Matt shook his head. "If we dress at all we will dress formal. It's how Ares likes it."

Ares shrugged. "If I'm going to try to look good I might as well look great."

"When don't you look great?" I gasped as the words slipped out of my mouth. I yanked my legs away from Ares and curled up into a ball trying to hide my blush.

Ares picked me up in my ball position and set me on his lap. "Thank you."

I mumbled, "You're welcome," from inside my ball.

Ares rested his head against my shoulder and whispered into my ear, "You always look great too."

SONG OF THE MOON

Part of me wanted to climb out of Ares' lap, but a larger part of me enjoyed his arms around me. I gave into the larger part and relaxed out of my ball to wrap my arms around his shoulders and rest my face in the crook of his neck. The temptation to bite him gnawed at me so I nipped his throat lightly. He growled, "No."

I whined and nipped his neck again letting the wolf instincts take a little bit of reign over my human ones. Ares growled at me again and bit my shoulder hard enough to make me gasp, but not hard enough to really hurt. I nipped his chest and jumped out of his arms to crouch on the floor of the limousine. Ares was crouched on top of the seat smiling at me and I swore I could see an image of a tail wagging behind him. Koda yipped excitedly behind me and jumped towards me. I rolled away from him and Matt jumped on top of me. I nipped his arm and rolled away from him running into Ares who bit my bottom. I snarled and jumped around biting his shoulder and then jumping on top of the seat beside Victor. Victor shook his head and sighed. "Wolves. You're all so silly."

I looked down at the crouched position I was in and plopped down on my butt sitting like a human and blushing at the things I had just done. Ares was staring at me with golden eyes. "You don't want to play anymore?"

I shook my head and blushed. "No."

Koda whined. "Play." Matt nodded his head vigorously.

Victor sighed. "Point a sharp object at them and they'll rip your head off without a second thought, but offer to play tag and they become children pouncing around like fairies." Ares growled and Victor smiled "You know what I meant." A large rod iron gate with swirls and flowers decorating it came into view and Victor sighed. "Finally."

Ares, Matt and Koda shook their heads and sat down on the seats normally. Koda and Matt folded their arms across their chests angrily and Ares stared out the window ignoring me. They were mad at me. The gate opened and we drove past rows and rows of grapes. "The vampire capitol of the world is in a vineyard?" I asked.

Victor shook his head. "It's a winery."

I rolled my eyes. "You know what I meant."

Victor smiled. "There are hundreds of miles of tunnels below us and we earn money from the winery to sustain a comfortable way of life. The humans get great tasting wine and we get a place of solitude. It's a win-win situation for everyone."

I frowned. "Except the people you eat."

Victor shrugged. "Eat a few, release a thousand. It's still a good deal."

The mansion we pulled up in front of was easily three times the size of any of the celebrity's in the United States I had ever seen on TV. Two muscular men stood beside two giant wooden doors that must be the front entrance. I looked closely at their bodies and noticed the low percentage of body fat and extra ounces of muscle. I turned to Ares. "The vampires use werewolf guards?"

Ares smiled. "I'm surprised you could tell they are wolves from here."

"Low amounts of body fat and high amounts of muscle suggest steroids or inhuman metabolisms. I figured the vampires would feel safer with werewolves than steroid using humans."

Victor laughed making me shiver in delight. "You are very perceptive."

Ares frowned. "You need to eat, Victor."

Victor cleared his throat. "Sorry about the voice thing. As Ares said I need to eat or...well let's not discuss that." The driver opened the door for us and Victor climbed out first, smiling at the driver flashing his fangs and walked up the steps towards the werewolf guards and the entrance. Koda and Matt climbed out next waiting a few feet away from the limousine.

Ares smiled at me. "It'll be alright. No one will harm you, especially not with me beside you." I nodded my head, but licked my lips nervously. Ares asked, "Would you let me hold your hand? It'll make me feel better."

He climbed out of the car before I could answer and I sighed in relief. *All I want is for him to hold my hand.* I climbed out of the car and reached for his hand. He squeezed my hand reassuringly and we started up the steps. The two guards at the door placed their fists over their hearts and bowed at the waist to us. Ares mimicked their gesture and smiled. "Greetings brothers."

The guards smiled and spoke in unison, "Greetings Prince."

Ares pointed at me. "My *passt genau* is with me during this visit. If she needs anything you come to her aid. Her needs are the most important out of anyone's here."

The guards sniffed the air and Ares face went neutral as he waited. I stared at the two guards who were at least six and a half feet tall and built like walls. My feet started to move towards them and Ares nodded his head, simultaneously letting my hand go. I walked slowly up to the guards and inhaled the smell of forest, fur and also getting their individual smells mingled in as well. They inhaled deeply and smiled wide. They both spoke in unison again, officially creeping me out, "Greetings sister."

I smiled. "Greetings brothers."

Ares took my hand and pulled me away from the guards and into the mansion. The mansion was dimly lit and there were only a few servants running around in uniforms. Ares whispered, "The vampires are all downstairs since it is still daylight. When the sun sets they will all come up here to mingle."

I asked, "Do I have to dress up tomorrow too?"

Ares nodded his head and kissed my cheek. "Don't worry. One of the seamstresses will have something to fit you."

I wanted to protest, but a beautiful woman walked up to us speaking in rapid French. Ares nodded his head and then spoke back to her in French. She looked down at me and frowned, slowly letting her eyes travel up my body from my feet. She looked back at Ares and spoke again quickly pointing rapidly at me then back to herself and then at Ares. Ares sighed and shook his head. "Sophe..." His words were French again so I couldn't keep up, but at least I knew her name.

Koda ran his hand down my right arm and my body relaxed a little. He smiled at me. "It's alright. He's just explaining who you are."

I frowned and looked at the beautiful French woman. "She's one of the women he's slept with, isn't she?"

Ares turned to me and frowned. "Artemis..."

I pulled my hand out of his and smiled. "It's alright. Talk to her and I'll talk to Koda."

Ares looked like he wanted to object, but Sophe was speaking angrily to his back trying to get his attention. Koda opened his arms and I stepped forward into his body. Matt walked up behind me and hugged me from behind wrapping his arms around Koda in the process. I asked, "Aren't you going to make a comment about him hugging you?" I asked Koda.

Koda shook his head. "We're pack and the touch of our pack mates is soothing. Like Ares' touch to you, but not the sexual part. Matt is my brother."

Matt kissed the top of my head then stepped back. "Don't be so upset Love. He's simply trying to calm 'er down. Angry female werewolves are not fun to deal with."

I pulled away from Koda and stared at the animated conversation that was going on between Ares and Sophe. "She loves him."

Koda nodded his head. "She does, but she also knows that he never loved her."

"I can't handle this." I started to walk away, but Koda and Matt walked beside me. Ares watched me out of the corner of his eyes, but was trying to pay attention to the yelling French woman in front of him.

Luckily she kept his attention while we started on our way. Koda gave me a tour of the main floor of the mansion, which consisted of a dining room, a living room, a kitchen bigger than my house, a game room with poker tables, pool tables and two giant televisions, and six bedrooms. We were about to walk out to the back patio and to the pool that Matt said was just beyond when Ares caught up to us. He whispered, "I'm sorry Artemis." He held out his hand and I accepted it. He hugged me against him. "Are you alright?"

I shook my head. "No, but there's not much that can be done."

He tilted my chin up and kissed my lips. "Would an hour back massage make up for it?"

I smiled. "It'll help." Ares smiled at me and I couldn't stay mad at him. I groaned. "It's not fair that I can't stay mad at you."

Ares kissed me again. "Not fair at all."

Matt cleared his throat. "Could we continue now?"

Ares bowed at the waist. "Of course, my liege. Forgive my rude interruption."

Matt rolled his eyes. "Jerk."

Ares smiled. "Baby."

Matt opened the patio door for me and continued the tour of the acre patio with dining tables and candelabras, then onto the two-acre wide pool. Ares and Koda debated over whether it should technically be considered a pond or lake, since it was so large, but Matt argued that the fact that they used a pool pump and chlorine made it a pool. I tried to engage in their debate, but there was a strange weight resting on my chest and back. I tried to figure out what it was when the words popped into my head on their own: powerful darkness. The presence became heavier as the sun moved down towards the horizon. Ares rubbed my arm and kissed my cheek, as we walked back towards the mansion.

Koda led the way down the hallways as if he owned the place and into a large bedroom. The bedroom had one giant bed, which could sleep at least five people comfortably. A desk and chair as well as a couch sat against the walls on the room. One door led to the bathroom with Jacuzzi tub and open shower. The second door led to a walk-in closet bigger than my bedroom had been. Ares stopped at the entrance to the bedroom and spoke quickly to a maid in French. The maid left and then Ares walked to stand beside me at the large bed. "We had these specifically made for those wishing to sleep in packs."

I jumped up on to the bed and sank into the cushions, sighing in pleasure. I started to push the mound of pillows off the bed, but decided it might be rude. I buried myself under the pillows instead. The bed moved and I smelled Ares before he pulled the two pillows that were covering my face off. "Does this mean you like it?"

I nodded my head and took the pillows back, recovering my face with them. The men were talking about something serious and boring, so I decided to take a shower. I climbed off the bed and rearranged the pillows as close to the original shape as I could remember, then walked toward the bathroom. Ares asked from close behind me, "Are you taking a shower?" I nodded my head then froze when I felt him behind me.

"Ares, please." Ares shrugged and picked me up in his arms walking towards the bathroom. I gasped, "No! Ares, that's not what I meant!"

He set me down and frowned. "Why are you scared?"

My heart was beating faster than it ever had before. "Ares, you can't come in there with me."

He sighed. "Oh, I see. I was raised better. I'm sorry."

I hurried into the bathroom and showered quickly. I wrapped myself in a towel and peeked my head out the door. "Can one of you bring my bag?"

SONG OF THE MOON

Koda started towards the door with the bag, but Ares took it from him and handed it to me. Koda stuck his tongue out at Ares behind his back making me giggle. Ares turned around, but Koda sucked his tongue back in and winked at me. I quickly changed into my bathing suit and turned on the giant tub and its jets. I walked back to the bathroom door and opened it before hopping into the large tub. A few moments later Ares stuck his head inside then smiled. "You know that is a tub, right?"

I shrugged. "It looks and feels like a spa to me. Plus it's big enough to fit me and at least three other people." He walked in and sat on the edge of the tub trailing his hand in the bubbling water. I swallowed the nervousness I was feeling and asked, "Would you like to join me?"

He smiled at me and then disappeared from the bathroom. I heard low quick whispers and then he was back in the bathroom wearing a pair of swimming shorts. I stared at his muscular body and couldn't help the reaction of my lower body. I sat up straighter as he climbed into the spa. He frowned. "Isn't this a little hot for you?"

I shook my head. "No, but if it's too hot for you I can turn it down." I reached behind me to the complicated controls and hit the down arrow to decrease the temperature. Sometimes modern technology is a Godsend.

He smiled at me. "You look great in that bikini."

I blushed and looked down at the water. "Thanks." I started swirling the water with my hands and felt the water move as he shifted across the tub.

He sat down beside me and whispered, "I know this is all new to you and I'll try to be as well behaved as I can."

I turned to him and saw the desire in his eyes. I suddenly reached up and kissed him on the lips. He kissed me back and heat exploded between us. He wound his hand through my thick hair and gripped the back of my neck pulling me against him.

I wrapped my arms around his shoulders and ran my hand through his hair. His hair was as thick as mine. Our kiss grew until he pulled back to gasp for air. I smiled at him and ran my hand across his sculpted chest. He flexed his chest, but it didn't appear to be on purpose, simply a reaction to my touch. I leaned forward and kissed his lips again and he stayed perfectly still. He slowly released his grip on my hair and slid his hand away from my neck to rest beside him in the water. I could see the need in his face and could tell just how much he was holding back by the stiff posture and the white of his knuckles as he made a fist. I hadn't ever been with a boy or man before and didn't know what to do or not do. I kissed his cheek then his lips and climbed off of him to sit beside him. He exhaled and I realized that he had been holding his breath. I stared at the water and wondered what he thought of me and my moments of hormonal insanity.

He stayed very still for a few minutes then turned to me. His eyes blazed with power and he asked deadpan, "Why did you stop?"

I smiled at him. "You were holding your breath and I didn't want you to die."

He smiled. "With you touching me I would fight death to the end.

I frowned at him. "You can't die."

His smile faded and he wrapped his arms around me holding me against him. "I won't die as long as I have you."

I sniffed and realized I was crying. "You're all I have."

Someone cleared their throat and Ares and I turned around slowly, with Ares keeping his arm around my shoulder the entire turn. I wiped my face with the back of my hand, but that only spread the water from my hand on to my face. Koda and Matt stood in the doorway smiling. Koda spoke with a soft voice that had an Irish lilt to it. "You have more than Ares. You have us too. We're pack now and if Ares leaves or dies we will still be with you."

SONG OF THE MOON

I stared at him in shock, realizing that he was opening himself up to me. I waved at him to come closer and Matt and Koda jumped into the tub still wearing their jeans and t-shirts. Water splashed over the sides of the tub and on to the floor. I moved forward and hugged them both at the same time. They inhaled and I did too, taking time to memorize the smell of my pack. They both smelled like the forest and underneath lingered a scent of crisp clean grass. Koda and Matt hugged me for a while then let go and pushed me back towards Ares. Ares put his arm around my waist and squeezed me against him. "See Artemis, you aren't alone anymore and you won't ever be again."

I started to cry again and they all held me in the center of them in a group hug. My wolf swirled inside me and reached out with some invisible force to touch each of their wolves. I could see all of their wolves staring at me and I wasn't afraid. *These wolves won't hurt me. These wolves are my pack and they will do everything to protect me and keep me happy.* I realized it was my wolf's thinking and frowned at her, but she was too happy to pay attention to my feelings. We sat in our huddle for a few minutes longer as my tears faded and then everyone got out. I dried off then sighed at my now wet bag on the floor. I started to pull everything out when something cold fell into my hand then began burning. It felt like acid burning my skin, but it was solid, not liquid. I dropped to my knees and screamed in pain trying to pull my hand out.

Ares, Koda and Matt surrounded me and started growling. Ares reached towards the bag, but jerked his hand back at the last second. "Victor!" Ares yelled.

Victor appeared over me and hissed, flashing his fangs. The others moved back a ways to give him room. Victor reached down and pulled the bag off exposing my hand and what was attached to it. I stared at the silver photo frame with a picture of a tall slender woman with purple eyes and wondered how it had gotten into my bag. Victor started to pull the frame from my hand, but it was burned into the skin and hurt like hell. Ares growled and Victor frowned. He spoke in soothing tones to the wolves surrounding me, "I have to get it out of her hand before this enters her blood and kills her."

Ares nodded his head, but was still snarling at Victor. Koda had dropped down and was cradling my head in his lap. Apparently I had fainted at some point. Matt held my other hand as Victor yanked the frame from my hand. I screamed and blacked out.

CHAPTER NINE

I woke up surrounded by heat and tried to kick the blankets off, but kicked empty air. I was fully clothed when I had previously been in a bikini. I turned my head and realized I was surrounded by Koda on my right, Ares on my left and Matt at my feet. I started to sit up when searing pain made me whimper and stare at my bandaged hand. All three men sat up at once and stared at me. They were all wearing blue jeans and no shirts, making me look from one muscled chest to another. Ares stroked my face and frowned. "You're sweating."

I nodded my head. "It's too hot."

He gave a single quick nod and Matt and Koda climbed off of the bed, letting a cool wave of air hit me. I inhaled and then coughed, nearly gagging. "What is that smell?"

Ares stroked my cheek. "Your burnt flesh."

I groaned as I remembered the picture frame. "I didn't even pack that. I'm guessing it was silver and that's why it burned me?"

Ares nodded his head. "Silver is our weakness. I'd like to know how it got into your bag."

I frowned. "I don't know, but I think it was a picture of my mom. Can I see it?"

Ares shook his head. "Victor had to destroy it."

"What?!" I gasped. "He couldn't have just taken the picture out and then destroyed the frame?"

Victor spoke from behind me, "I did not have time. Your pack's instinct to protect you was on overload. They might have attacked me if I took too long."

I whimpered. "I didn't even get a good look at her. I only remember fragmented memories. Enough to know that I look like her."

Victor sat one hip on the edge of the bed beside me. He was wearing a pair of black slacks and a dark blue button up shirt that looked like silk. He smiled. "I am sorry that I did not think about what you would have liked. I just wanted to get it away so I didn't have to fight your pack."

I nodded my head and turned my gauze wrapped hand around. "Thank you."

Ares asked, "Why would Darren have had a silver frame anyway? He wouldn't have been able to hold it."

I smiled. "It was my mom's frame."

"How do you know that?" asked Ares.

"Dad said he only had one thing of hers and never let me see it, so I'm guessing the picture frame was it," I responded quietly.

Ares whispered, "I'm sorry we didn't keep the picture for you."

I shrugged. "It's alright." I felt something tingling on my hand under the gauze and squeaked like a scared mouse. "What the hell?" I started unwrapping my hand and Ares and Victor tried to stop me. Once I had it unwrapped I stared in shock at the mutilated skin that used to be my hand. The tingling increased and the burned skin shed off on to the floor as a new layer of skin replaced the old. "What happened?" I asked in shock.

Ares smiled. "Interesting."

Victor said, "It must be because of her other..." Ares growled, stopping him from speaking further. Victor bowed his head and continued, "It must be from her mother. Perhaps silver is not a permanent problem for our little Goddess."

I frowned at Ares. "Why won't you let me know what my mother is and what I am?"

He smiled. "I will soon, but for now it's best if you don't know."

I didn't believe him, but decided not to press the matter. I ran a finger over my newly healed skin and smiled. "Wow."

Koda walked over. "The seamstress is here with the clothes for Artemis to choose from."

I looked around Koda to see a girl, no older than twenty, standing beside a rolling clothes rack filled with dresses. I looked at Ares and groaned. "A dress? You're making me wear a dress?"

"Don't you want to look nice for the King and Queen of the Vampires?" Ares asked.

I folded my arms across my chest. "The King has already met me. I've never even worn a dress before."

Ares kissed my cheek. "Then this will be a good learning experience for you. Besides, don't you want to look nice for me?"

There was no winning this argument, so I sighed and walked towards the girl. She looked from my toes to my head and then back again, frowning nonstop. "She is the one I am supposed to dress?" Her thick accent caught me off guard and it took me a moment to decipher what she had said.

Ares bowed at the waist to the girl. "Hello, Lucy. It's always an honor to see you."

Lucy folded her arms across her chest. "Flattery will not win you any points with me, Ares. I'm not a magician you know." She looked at me in disgust again. "Am I to bring our beautician in as well? She looks to need it."

I opened my mouth to call her one of the rude names I could think of, but Ares spoke before I could say anything. "Lucy, it would be wise to remember your place as well as what mine is. She is my *passt genau*, treat her with respect. Your insults of her are direct challenges to me."

Lucy's bottom lip quivered, but then she shook her head and straightened her back before turning back to me. "I apologize for my insults. I'm old and 'ow you say? Cranky, yes, 'zats the word."

I looked at her face and frowned. "Old? You don't look old."

Lucy smiled. "That is one of the benefits of being a dhampir." She saw my puzzled face and frowned at Ares. "You bring 'er to the vampire's 'ome without training as to what we are?"

I waved my hand at her. "I know what a dhampir is, half vampire and half human. I've just never seen one before. And I thought you were supposed to be enemies with vampires?"

Ares said, "I have much to teach her Lucy. I only found her a few days ago."

Lucy turned back to me. "Dhampirs and vampires are enemies, but my father is very powerful and 'as enough pull to keep me alive and 'appy as long as I don't kill any of the vampires."

"I understand," I told her.

She sighed heavily. "Let's get started. We 'ave only an 'our to prepare you."

She walked to the dress rack and tapped her chin thoughtfully. Ares walked towards her and she hissed. "Go get ready. I do not want you breathing down my neck while I prepare 'er. I will do my best to make 'er perfect for you." Her French accent seemed to grow stronger whenever she spoke to Ares.

Ares sighed. "Fine. Koda will stay in the room with you, Artemis."

Lucy stared at Ares in shock. "You do not trust me?"

Ares smiled. "I don't trust anyone to be alone with her." Ares walked over and kissed my lips quickly before hurrying to the bathroom. My skin began itching and I began breathing faster.

Koda walked over to me and touched my shoulder. The smell of forest and wolf slowed my breathing, but the desire to run after Ares was still very strong. Lucy smiled. "Interesting." She turned back to the dresses and picked out a purple dress and held it up to my face. "It matches your eyes, but I am not sure if it will work. Put it on."

I pulled off my jeans and t-shirt, trying hard to ignore the fact that Koda was right behind me, and pulled the dress on over my head. The bust was a little tight, but manageable and the material was soft against my skin. I spun in a slow circle for Koda and Lucy. Lucy tapped her chin and turned to Koda. "What do you think, Wolf?"

Koda smiled. "It's perfect."

Lucy frowned. "Hmm...per'aps I will like it more once the makeup and 'air is done. I'll fetch the beautician."

She pushed her cart out of the room leaving me alone with Koda. The bathroom door cracked open and Ares asked, "Did you find a dress?"

Koda answered, "Yes and it's very nice."

Ares asked, "Did Lucy leave?"

"Yes," I answered.

Matt walked out of the bathroom with a towel tied around his waist. I found myself staring at his abdominal muscles and remembering what it felt like to touch Ares' in the tub. Ares growled softly. "Artemis, what are you thinking about?"

I swallowed. "Uh, nothing."

Matt laughed. "It's alright Love. And that dress looks amazing on you."

Ares groaned. "I want to see it."

I yelled, "NO! You can't see me until you're ready. Plus, I'm not *ready* yet."

Ares sighed. "Fine, but stop thinking whatever it is that you were thinking."

I blushed and looked towards the bedroom door. Two soft knocks brought Koda's attention to the door as well. He opened it to reveal a tall, thin French woman in a business suit and four inch heels. She winked at Koda. "'Ello 'andsome."

Koda smiled. "Hey there, Madeleine. You're looking scrumptious as ever."

Madeleine walked to me and frowned, crossing her arms over her small breasts. "Let's get started. I 'ave much work to do."

I growled softly. "Why are the French so rude?"

She shrugged. "We're French, it's in our blood to 'ate Americans." She grabbed my forearm and led me to the desk, carrying a large suitcase that I was sure held torture devices in every imaginable shape. I sat down in the chair and she opened the suitcase to reveal the devices which were much worse than I had imagined. Ares walked out of the bathroom and Madeleine spread her arms out to hide me. "What are you doing?! Get out of 'ere!" She yelled.

I looked through her arms to see Ares averting his eyes. "I'm not even looking at her Madeleine. Artemis, I'm going out for a little bit. Matt will stay here with you."

My stomach cramped and my pulse started beating in double time. "When will you be back? Where are you going?" I asked nervously.

Madeleine sighed happily. "Aw, it's so nice to see true love."

Ares ignored Madeleine. "I'm just going out for a little bit. I'll only be gone thirty minutes and Koda is coming with me."

"Hurry, please."

Ares sighed happily. "Of course." Koda blew me a kiss then followed Ares out of the room.

Matt sat down on the desk and was thankfully wearing a pair of shorts and a t-shirt. Matt placed his hand on mine on the desk and smiled. "He'll be back before you're even ready."

I picked his hand up and inhaled the back of it. I could still smell wolf fur and his smell, but the soap he had used took away the forest. "I don't like feeling like this. I understand he's my match and we're pack, but I *really* don't know him. My wolf is getting harder to ignore too."

Madeleine watched me curiously. "How long 'ave you known you're a wolf?"

Matt answered for me as I continued to inhale the smell of his skin. "Only a few days. As long as she's known Ares."

Madeleine's eyes widened. "She must be at least sixteen. 'Ow 'as she not known?"

Matt sighed and rubbed my hair softly. "Her father chose to not tell her and kept her away from our kind."

Madeleine looked at me with pity in her eyes. "That must 'ave been very difficult. Come, let me make you gorgeous for your mate."

I growled. "Don't call him that."

Matt shook his head at Madeleine. "Don't ask."

Madeleine sighed. "Wolves are always full of drama." Matt held my hand as she worked on my face. My nervousness increased as the minutes ticked by without Ares near me. Madeleine brought in another woman who brushed and fixed my hair into a half up and half down style, with everything lightly curled. Ares came in just as they made the final touches to my makeup and hair. The two women and Matt covered me as Ares walked by to the closet. I thanked Madeleine and the other woman and then walked to the bathroom to use the restroom. Madeleine had refused to let me go while she was working.

I started to come out of the bathroom, but Koda blocked my exit. "Ares is finishing getting ready. It's your turn to wait."

I looked over Koda's new outfit of a tailored suit that fit all of his muscles nicely. His Mohawk was gelled up and the gel made the green dye seem even brighter. "You look nice," I said honestly.

He spun in a slow circle. "Thank you." He smiled at me. "You look great too, very beautiful."

I blushed and then asked, "How much longer is he going to take? I'm hungry." A chill swept over my body as the sun set and the powerful presence I had felt the previous afternoon caused fear to close my throat. I wrapped my arms around myself and shivered.

Ares spoke from outside the bathroom. "What's wrong Artemis? Why are you so frightened?"

"It's a strange...I know I'm going to sound stupid when I say this, but there is this powerful darkness I've been feeling since we came here. It got really strong just now, when the sun set."

Koda smiled. "It's alright dahlin' it's just the vampire King."

Ares spoke from farther away in the room. "I'm almost done, just finishing my hair."

I turned and looked at the mirror in the bathroom and stared at the woman looking back at me. I still couldn't believe it was really me. I raised my hand up to my face and pushed on my cheeks. Koda smiled at me, but stayed quiet as I stared at the purple eyes my mother had given me. Ares spoke from near Koda, "Are you ready?"

I scoffed. "I've *been* ready." I turned around and instantly felt self-conscious. *What if he thinks I look horrible? What if he decides I'm not good enough for him to be with? He's got so many attractive women vying to be with him and I'm just...*

Ares interrupted my thoughts by stepping into the bathroom and staring at me with wide eyes. He looked perfect. His suit looked like it had been stitched to him and his black hair gleamed with the gel in it and looked spiked, but still natural somehow. His blue eyes sparkled and I wanted him to want me, to approve of me.

He smiled and walked forward slowly. "Artemis, you look..."

I blushed and looked down at my hands. "Don't..."

Ares wrapped his arms around me and kissed me on the lips, hard, squeezing me against his muscular body. He smelled like wolf, Ares and cinnamon. He pulled back from me and whispered, "Perfect. Beautiful. Delicious."

The worry fluttered away and I smiled. "You look great, Ares."

He shook his head. "Nothing can compare to your beauty." I blushed a darker shade of red and he smiled. "I got you something." I stared at him in shock as he pulled out a white box. He opened the lid to reveal a beautiful diamond heart necklace. Ares took the necklace out and whispered, "So that you will know that my heart is yours alone."

I shook my head as I stared at the shining diamonds on the necklace. "That's too expensive. I couldn't..."

Ares raised his hand and I stopped talking. He walked to stand behind me and put the necklace on. "Nothing is too expensive for you. Besides, I have quite a bit of money saved up and I can spend it however I like."

I touched the heart lying on my upper chest and smiled at Ares. "Thank you. It's beautiful."

He kissed the side of my neck sending chills down my spine. "You're welcome. Are you ready to meet the vampires?"

I curtsied to Ares and spoke with a deep voice trying to sound seductive, "Is my lord ready?"

Ares bowed at the neck and smiled. "Always for you, m'lady." He extended his bent elbow to me and I put my hand on the inside of his arm. He asked, "How do you know what to say?"

I shrugged. "I watched a lot of renaissance movies."

He kissed the back of my hand. "You're the most beautiful Princess in the lands."

I frowned. "Wait. In order to be Princess wouldn't I have to fight the others?"

Ares shook his head. "As my mate you become my equal in power."

I frowned harder. "So since you're Prince then I am Princess? What if someone else wants my position?"

Ares sighed. "That's something we'll discuss much later. For now, let's focus on the task at hand."

I curtsied again. "Of course, my lord."

"You really are perfect," he said as he squeezed my hand and led the way out of the bedroom. Koda walked in front of us while Matt walked behind us silently. There were a lot of people walking down the hallways and all stopped to stare or moved aside to let us pass, while others whispered. Koda led us downstairs and into a well lit underground portion of the mansion. Koda maneuvered around the confusing hallways, going in what seemed to be circles. Ares squeezed my hand reassuringly, as we stopped in front of two large ornate doors.

Victor walked up to us with two identical looking male vampires and stepped in front of us. "You all ready?"

Ares nodded his head. "As ready as I ever am to walk into a room filled with vampires."

Victor winked. "We've already eaten for the night."

I asked, "What are they celebrating tonight anyway?"

Victor smiled. "They are celebrating the return of the Prince of the Vampires and the continued alliance with the werewolves."

I nodded my head. "That's right. You're a Prince, too."

Ares scoffed. "It's more impressive when you have to get it for being the strongest, but Victor is one of the most powerful vampires."

Victor sighed. "Yes, you are truly a powerful wolf, Prince Ares."

I shook my head smiling. "This is all so strange."

Koda rolled his eyes. "Tell me about it."

Two werewolf guards opened the doors and we walked inside behind Victor. The room was by far the largest room I had ever seen. Twelve long tables with bench seating filled up most of the room. Crystal chandeliers hung from the ceilings and gave a soft reflective light from the hundreds of candles that hung on the walls and sat on the tables in elegant holders. In the center of the room sat a thick wooden table with three thrones in the center. The vampire King looked like Victor's twin, but unlike Victor, he was wearing a puffy pirate shirt that was open to the middle of his hairy chest. His pants were black and looked like a replica of pirate's pants too. A beautiful woman, wearing a blood red dress, sat beside him on his right side. Victor walked down the center aisle, which was adorned with a dark red rug, and bowed to the King and Queen. The twin vampires dropped to one knee beside Victor.

The King held up his hand and the room silenced. He stood up and smiled. "Welcome Prince Victor of the Vampires. It has been too long since you have returned to your home."

Victor stood up straight then bowed his head at the neck. "Greetings, King Maurice and Queen Isabella. I am glad to return home."

Maurice still smiling said, "Stand, faithful guards of the Prince, Jean Pierre and Francois." As he said each of their names they stood up as though puppets and the King the puppeteer.

Victor spoke just loud enough for everyone to hear, "May I introduce our allies, Prince Ares of the Werewolves, his mate Artemis and his two guards Koda and Matthew."

Ares began walking forward and I stayed beside him as we walked. He moved his arm to the side so he could bow and I curtsied as low as I could, staring at the ground. Maurice spoke with a voice that caressed around my body like a warm hand. "Greetings Prince Ares and his wolves." Ares stood up and I stood with him, all the while keeping my hand on his arm. Maurice continued, "I see that you are still convinced that she is your mate."

Ares spoke loud. "She is my *ivraie vivace*. My perfect match."

The room was filled with gasps and then whispers of shock. Maurice raised his hand and the room silenced. Maurice stared down at me and for a moment I returned his gaze. I felt his power and quickly averted my eyes to his chin. He spoke in a soothing voice, "I had not thought it was true. Could you tell us how you found her?"

Ares spoke loud enough for everyone to hear, with a voice of power, and yet it was soft at the same time. "I felt her presence when she was born and all other women paled before me. None held my interest any longer and I craved no woman's caress. I searched for a long time, all over the world, until I had my first dream of her and her of me. By chance we met and the dreams continued. I sent out my call shortly after meeting her and she answered in half transformation, and then subdued her wolf."

The crowd began whispering loudly again. Isabella raised her hand and the crowd silenced, but more slowly than they had for Maurice. She smiled and asked, "Are you to tell me that for the past eighteen years you, the Prince of Wolves, have restrained from the temptations of a woman's bosom?"

Ares smiled. "I have."

She continued as if he had not spoken, "You, the most powerful bachelor, have not so much as craved a woman's touch or the sweet words of a female for eighteen years?"

Ares turned his head to me and smiled. "Not until I found her."

Maurice walked down from the throne he was sitting on, to stand in front of me. My wolf's fear spiked through me, making my heart beat faster. I forced myself not to step back and instead squeezed Ares' hand. Maurice smiled. "You have no need to fear me child. I will not harm you."

I said nothing and stared at his chin. I wasn't sure if the movies were right, about the vampires being about to take control of you with a look in their eyes or not. It wasn't a chance I was willing to take. Maurice inhaled. "Obviously she is not full blood as we discussed previously, but she also does not smell of *you* Ares."

Ares nodded his head. "She is young and I am giving her time to adjust. And I would still ask your courtesy in not divulging her bloodlines."

Maurice nodded his head. "Wise of you in these times. She looks like someone..." He gasped, "You are the daughter of Darren?"

I nodded my head and spoke softly, "I am." The room filled with loud murmurs and Maurice raised his hand to silence them.

He spoke again and his voice filled me with warmth and brought a smile to my face. "What is your father's view on this?"

Ares spoke with obvious hatred. "Her father is an outlaw, whose punishment when found will be severe."

Maurice smiled. "I see. How do you feel about this, Artemis?"

I frowned because it didn't sound like a question the King of the Vampires should ask. "It's a lot to deal with at first, but I love my pack and am pleased to be the Prince's match."

Maurice frowned. "You are not sure though."

I frowned in response. "As I said, it is a lot to deal with and I have only known this all for a few days."

Queen Isabella asked, "You did not know what you are?"

I shook my head. "Until Ares found me, I thought I was human."

The room was filled with shock responses and she asked, "How could you have not known what you are? Your kind changes before eighteen."

Ares shook his head. "Not all of us, great Queen. A few have been known to fight the change until their eighteenth birthday, but they had at least changed one part and knew. The Princess did not change any part and her father made her believe she was having human's seizures."

Isabella gasped. "She was around 'umans while fighting the change?"

Her change in accent was disturbing, but I answered her. "I went to school with humans and some would even hold me, while I fought the changes."

Isabella raised her hand to stop the others from speaking before she got a chance. "You fought off your change while in the presence of 'umans?" I nodded my head. She asked, "'ow many times?"

I tried to calculate, but math was not my best subject. "About six times a month since I was ten years old."

The crowd erupted in conversation so loud that I couldn't hear myself think and yet I couldn't make out what any of them were saying. The cartoon where all the kids hear is "Wa Wa" suddenly made sense. Maurice raised his hand to quiet the crowd. He spoke in a voice that no longer caressed me, but scared me. "You fought your change surrounded by humans with them touching you and then did not attack them?"

I nodded my head. "I never felt the urge to attack them. Usually I would be angry when I started the seizure...I mean attempt to change. I would calm myself down and it would stop. Then I would eat red meat and be fine."

Maurice turned to Koda and Matt. "Have you two witnessed this?"

Matt and Koda both nodded their heads. Koda responded, "Her wolf was not present during the times she tried to change around the humans. Her father made sure to keep her away from other wolves and even hid his wolf from her."

Maurice asked, "Is her wolf present now?"

Ares nodded his head. "Yes. Her wolf exposed herself to Artemis on the day I sent my call."

Maurice stared at me with an expression that made me want to run. The look of need was not like Ares' passion-filled gaze, but instead a look of needing power. The look bore into me until I sensed his hostility and realized he would kill me if he could. I stepped back towards Koda and Matt and they pressed their chests to my back. Victor saw my face and our stance and turned towards his father. "Perhaps we could end the discussion for today and allow our guests to sit for food?"

Maurice's face changed back to his politician's smile and he nodded his head. "Of course. Please take a seat."

Ares walked with me pressed against his side, so close that I stepped on his shoes a few times until we were at the table. They sat us beside the King and Queen's table and faced us towards the center of the room. Koda and Matt didn't sit beside us, but stood behind to keep guard. Once we were seated, Ares leaned over and whispered, "What happened to make you so nervous?"

I flipped my hair to the other side of my face and pretended to be merely leaning my head on Ares' shoulder. I whispered as quietly as I could, "The look he gave me was not friendly. I know you probably think I'm full of crap, but I could feel his need and then his hostility."

Ares kissed the top of my head. "I don't think you're full of crap, but let's not discuss this until later, when there aren't so many ears to hear." I kissed his cheek and sat up straight. Victor was now sitting beside his father and speaking very quietly to him. Was Victor a bad guy? Servants brought out bottles of wine and then plates of meat. The servants looked scared more than pleasant. I sniffed one as he passed by and realized he was human. I turned to Ares and he shook his head. I ate my food in silence until the King and Queen stood up. Everyone in the room including Ares stood up, so I did too.

Maurice smiled at everyone. "Thank you for coming my friends, but I must bid you *adieu*, the sun is rising soon and I need my beauty sleep." He took Isabella's hand and together they walked out of the room through the door we had come through. After they had disappeared through the doorway, Victor and Ares led me hurriedly back to our bedroom.

I jumped on to the bed and sighed. Ares laid down beside me on his side facing me and smiled. "That was fun, right?"

I scoffed. "About as fun as cleaning poop out of fifty horse stalls in the middle of a hot day in summer."

He ran his hand up and down my arm slowly with just his fingertips touching me. "I'm sorry you had to deal with that, but being my mate means that you will be forced to do that many more times with many different races. Can you handle that?"

I smiled. "I don't know. What's in it for me?" He leaned over and gave me a very chaste kiss. I frowned. "Definitely not worth it."

He smiled. "Really? Then how about this?" He rolled on top of me and kissed my lips with the need I had seen in his eyes from the tub. I kissed him back and power exploded inside me and ran into him. He grunted, but didn't stop our kiss as warmth built between us. He rolled us over so that I was lying on top of him and ran his hands down my back and over my rump. He squeezed lightly and the power in me slammed into him, making him grunt in pain and grip me harder. I moaned in pain and he deepened the kiss. The kiss grew and I felt increasingly woozy. He slid his hands father down until they were at the bottom of my dress and pushed it up so he could put his hands on my bare butt. Thongs are good for not showing lines in your dress, but they do expose many things when your dress isn't on. He snarled and bit my lower lip. I gasped and kissed him with my own bites and nibbles of his lower lip. We were so busy with each other that we didn't pay attention to anything else. Cold water splashed over us and made me gasp. I spun around in a crouching attack position and snarled at the water throwers. Koda and Matt stood smiling together, holding two empty buckets. Ares stood up beside me and frowned. "What was that for?"

Koda said, "You told us not to let you get too carried away with her until she was ready."

I snarled at him. "I wasn't pushing him away, was I?"

Matt shook his head. "No, but you aren't ready either."

I took a step towards them growling and felt my wolf ready to come out. Koda squatted down and growled back at me. I snapped my teeth at him. "You aren't alpha!" I yelled.

Koda snarled at me. "Neither are you, but I am beta."

I shook my head. "No I am."

Matt squatted down and growled at both of us. "Knock if off you two."

I snapped my teeth at him and saw his wolf's anger. He dropped his left hand in a crouching stance mimicking both Koda and me and snarled at me. Ares stared at us frowning. I felt my wolf wake up and smiled. I pulled my dress off over my head and took my shoes off. Ares sighed, "Artemis." I unhooked my bra and pulled my underwear down while keeping eye contact with the two others and then let her come. My body stretched and my bones cracked as she rose from my body in four quick steps. When I was finished changing, I felt the soreness that would be present when I returned to human shape, but I didn't care. Matt and Koda stood before me in their wolf forms and I suddenly realized how much smaller I was. They were both at least one and a half times my size whereas Ares was twice my size. Koda took a step towards me and I ran forward slamming into him. He skidded backwards, but did not fall. I bit into his side, pulling a piece of flesh off, and jumped away as Matt ran at me. They turned to face me and I realized they were fighting together.

Ares snarled from behind them and dropped his clothes. I stared at his naked perfection and waited anxiously for him to be wolf too. He changed in one fluid motion like in my dreams and walked forward to snarl at me. I stared at him in shock as he stood between Koda and Matt. I took a step back from him and then shook my head. I snarled and snapped my teeth against the three who were against me. The door opened, but I didn't want to risk looking away so I stayed staring at the other three. Koda turned towards the door and I saw my opening. I threw myself forward and bit into his neck, but he shook me off. I jumped back and tried to hit him with my paw, but Ares blocked me snarling. I backed away from him and sat on my butt. Why was he attacking me? Ares took a step towards me and Francois and Jean Pierre appeared in front of me. Their faces looked terrifying as they hissed flashing their fangs with their fingers elongated into claws. Ares stared at them in shock as they protected me from my own pack.

One of the twins, I couldn't distinguish between them, spoke with a deep voice, "Why are you attacking your mate?" Ares barked and the vampire shook his head. "Dominance battles are between them, you know this. How dare you interfere?"

Ares moved forward and I did too. The vampire twins and werewolf twins began fighting each other and I stared at Ares in shock. He snapped his teeth at me and snarled. I knew he was alpha, but he had no reason to be interfering in my dominance with the others as the vampire had said. I decided to do the only thing I could, submit. I dropped to my side and rolled on my back, exposing my neck and stomach to Ares. He continued to snarl and growl as he walked forward and stood over my body. His teeth were inches from my neck and he opened his jaw, when Victor ran in and flung Ares aside.

Victor stood between Ares and me and then raised his hands. "Silence." The wolves stopped growling and stared at him. Victor said, "You are under a spell. Please listen. Change back."

Ares changed back quickly and frowned. "What is going on?"

Victor smiled. "You owe me now, friend. You were about to take her life."

I changed back and stared at Ares in shock. Ares shook his head. "I wouldn't have killed her."

Victor shrugged. "Perhaps not, but I did not wish to take that chance."

I stood up and ran to the bathroom, shutting the door behind me and locking it. I shivered with the cold tile touching my feet and turned to the tub. I turned it on and heard Ares knock. "Artemis, please let me in." I stared at the water as it filled up the giant tub. "This door isn't very hard to break down. I'll do it if you don't let me in."

I sighed and walked over to the door unlocking it, then ran and hopped into the halfway filled tub. I turned on the jets and stared at the bubbling water. My sore body began to relax and I asked, "Were you going to kill me?"

Ares sighed and knelt beside the tub to look at me. I kept my gaze on the water waiting for his reply. "Of course not. I wouldn't kill you no matter what spell I was under."

I asked, "Why did you interfere? I have to prove my dominance in order to have a place in the pack."

Ares shook his head. "No, you get your place in the pack from your mate."

I looked up at him and frowned. "So, I could be the weakest wolf in the pack and become the alpha's mate and be alpha female?"

Ares nodded his head. "Yes."

I scoffed. "That's ridiculous."

Ares shrugged. "Sort of, most alphas only choose strong mates anyway. We wouldn't choose the weakest, because she may not give us strong offspring."

I stared at him in shock. "Offspring?"

He looked down obviously embarrassed. "Some do have offspring."

I rolled the idea over in my head of having children and scoffed. "No thank you."

He looked up at me and frowned. "You don't want kids?"

I laughed. "Werewolves having kids? That's crazy. What if you go all insane one day and kill one?"

He smiled. "You wouldn't kill your offspring."

I frowned. "No, but someone else might."

His smile faded and he nodded his head. "Rival alpha's have been known to kill other's offspring, but not very often, and definitely not mine."

I shook my head. "I don't want to talk about it."

He nodded his head and reached towards me. I moved away and he sighed. "I told you I wasn't going to kill you."

I blushed. "I'm naked."

He looked down at the water, then himself and frowned. "So am I."

I looked at his face and saw the need there again. I shook my head. "I'm not ready for that. Not yet."

He sighed and nodded his head. "I understand. I'll leave you to your bath." He walked slowly from the room and I couldn't help but stare at his muscular glutes. He looked back and winked, then walked out of the bathroom and shut the door. I exhaled a breath I hadn't realized I had been holding and groaned. I couldn't be this caught up in him already? How can he have such an effect on me? I groaned again and dunked my head under the water. Had I imagined Maurice's reaction to me? I pictured his face and shook my head. No, I was right. I climbed out of the tub and pulled on clothes out of my bag. I frowned at a wet pair of jeans lying on the floor and reluctantly pulled them on, then pulled on a blue t-shirt over my head. Wet jeans suck to walk in.

I walked slowly out of the bathroom and sat down between Jean Pierre and Francois and whispered, "Thank you." They both nodded their heads. The one on the right patted my shoulder in response, but they were both staring at Victor who was speaking to Ares. Koda and Matt stood in front of the bed staring at me. I frowned at them then stood up. "What?"

They both looked down then back up at the same time. Twins are freaky. Koda said, "I'm sorry." I stared at him in shock not believing what I just heard. He smiled. "I'm sorry for trying to fight you."

Matt nodded his head. "And I'm sorry for ganging up on you."

I frowned. "Yeah that was odd. I didn't even want to fight you, but you had to jump in."

Matt smiled. "Koda is my twin and we always fight together, so it was really mere instinct."

I continued to frown as my emotions built. "So it was instinct for you two and Ares to try to fight your newest pack member? Nice. Now I know whose side you're on and that I need to watch my own ass!" I crossed my arms over my chest and looked at the ground. Koda groaned and moved to sit in front of me, but one of the vampire twins hissed at him making him stop. "Leave her alone, wolf. She needs time to adjust."

Koda snarled. "I agree Francois but she also has to know that we aren't her enemies and that we are sorry."

Francois, the one on the right, shook his head. "Later. Leave her be." He put his arm around my shoulders and I leaned against him resting my head on his chest. It was odd to be so comfortable around him so quickly and yet still have the urge to run and the hair on the nape of my neck standing up. It became easier to ignore the urge to run around vampires though.

Koda growled and took a step towards us, but Ares shook his head at him. "Leave it alone." Koda groaned and stormed off to the bathroom, slamming the door shut behind him. Ares walked towards me and for the first time, I felt nothing for him. He squatted down in front of me and sighed. "Artemis. Please forgive us. I would not have hurt you and the others didn't mean it personally."

I stared at him and sniffed the air and listened to his heartbeat. Dammit, he was telling the truth. "You can't expect me to be fine with it, when you may have hurt me if Victor hadn't come."

Ares smiled. "I understand how you feel and do not expect you to be over it immediately, but quickly would be best. We have to decide our next move." He looked at Francois then sighed. "And also, it would probably be best if you did not appear so friendly with vampires. It's not natural for our kind to be so cozy with theirs."

I smiled. "I am not *cozy*, but I just feel comfortable with Francois and Jean Pierre."

Francois nodded his head. "I would never harm the little goddess."

I groaned and stood up. "I need to go for a walk." Jean Pierre and Francois stood up and smiled at me. I sighed. "Dammit, can't we go somewhere that I won't need babysitters?"

Ares smiled. "You will always have guards Artemis. You are too valuable not to be protected."

I whispered, "Valuable to whom?"

Ares frowned and grabbed my arm and pulled me against him. Fire burned where his hand touched against my skin as he stared into my eyes. "You are valuable to me and your pack. Don't you understand yet?"

I sighed. "I did not mean it that way. I simply meant that it seems that I am *valuable* to more people than I should be and that my value to them is probably not what you would approve of."

Ares fury settled and the fire vanished. "Who are you talking about?"

I shook my head. "You said I shouldn't speak of it until there weren't 'ears to hear'."

Ares face lifted in shock. "Can you be so perceptive to have seen an expression on his face that I did not?"

"It was more than that. I could see his need and its nothing like the look of need you have towards me." I blushed as I finished saying it and looked down.

Ares kissed my cheek softly. "My needs can wait, but we must speak with Victor regarding this new problem." He turned around with his hand on my arm, but I stayed still. Ares sighed and turned back to face me. "You have to describe what you saw to Victor."

I frowned. "Fine, but after this I'm taking a walk with whichever person I choose as my guard."

Ares smiled. "As you wish."

I felt my face relax from its frown and spread to a look of shock. "You know the movie Princess Bride?"

Ares smiled. "Of course. Who doesn't?"

Koda called from behind the bathroom door, "Rodents of unusual size? I don't think they exist."

I smiled. "Koda."

Koda peeked out from the bathroom. "You rang?"

I inhaled and spoke quickly so I wouldn't lose my nerve, "I forgive you and Matt for ganging up on me since I am a new pack member, but if it happens again don't expect me to be so willing to forgive you."

Koda smiled and ran from the bathroom to me. He picked me up in a big bear hug, squeezing the air from my lungs and kissing my cheek repeatedly. He set me down then nodded his head. "You'll do great here."

I scoffed and Ares frowned down at me. "So you'll forgive them, but not me?"

I shrugged. "I expect more of the alpha as anyone would." His face deepened to sadness and I couldn't stand to see that look on his face. I hugged him and kissed his cheek. "I forgive you."

He shook his head. "No you're right. I should've had more control than that. I would've never stopped a dominance fight before and I don't know why I stopped yours. And turning on you was extremely unacceptable. Such an indiscretion would have resulted in a punishment that would have lasted many days."

I kissed his lips softly and whispered, "We all make mistakes. I'm sure I'll make a ton in the first years with you. Besides wolf pups are always getting scolded in the wild, so it's only natural for us to make mistakes."

He finally smiled and kissed my lips back. "You're a fascinating person, Artemis. I'm more than lucky to have you as my match."

I pulled away from him so he wouldn't see my blush and walked over to Victor who was sitting at a desk on the far wall by the fireplace. I sat down on the fireplace and looked up at him. He smiled at me, set his pencil down and spoke with a voice filled with a fluid French accent, "'ow may I 'elp you *mon papillon*?'

I frowned. "What does that mean?"

"It's my new pet name for you."

"Okay, well I need to talk to you about something that happened in the ceremony and it's something no one else can hear."

His eyes widened with understanding and he nodded his head, speaking without the French accent again. "Francois and Jean Pierre, go and make certain that there are no ears to hear nearby." Francois and Jean Pierre hurried out of the room together. Victor repositioned his chair so that he was facing me and smiled. "How are you feeling?"

I shrugged. "Overwhelmed, but I'm just trying to deal with it one part at a time."

He nodded his head thoughtfully. "So, you are over the shock of being told you are a werewolf?"

I nodded my head. "I can't change what I am and there is no sense in dwelling on something that I cannot change. I am still upset that I am something else besides werewolf and do not know though."

"Ares only keeps from you what will harm you. He cares very much for your safety."

I blushed and looked down. "I know."

Victor leaned forward and whispered, "And how are you feeling about your alpha?"

I sighed and whispered back, "Honestly it's really weird. I understand him being my alpha and that I am his match, but it seems wrong to feel so strongly for him. And the whole mate thing is just too much to think about so I try not to."

Victor tapped his chin thoughtfully. "So, you feel strongly for him and believe you should not because you have only known him a few days?" I nodded my head and Victor smiled. "That is easily fixed. No one will judge you for your feelings towards him because legend tells that a matched pair is instantly in love. Besides, who would argue that being in love is a bad thing?"

"My father."

Victor hissed. "Your father is a stupid man. Forget him. He *would* put such vile concepts into your head. Sweet *papillon*, your feelings are just that, your feelings. Do not let others decide how you should feel. If you hate Ares, then hate him and tell him. But if you love Ares, then love him and tell him. Love is a wonderful thing, little *déesse*. Do not waste it."

I sighed. "Are you going to tell me what the last thing you called me means?"

"Déesse means Goddess. If I wanted to be more accurate I would call you *déesse lunaire*."

I smiled. "Moon Goddess, right?" He nodded his head. "Most languages have a few words that sound similar. I figured *lunaire* was like lunar."

Victor nodded his head happily. "Perhaps I will teach you some French."

Ares scoffed from behind us. "No thank you."

I jumped at his voice, not realizing he was standing there. I stared at Victor's chest and asked, "How long have you been standing there?"

He replied, "When you asked what the last thing he called you meant. Why? Were you talking about me?"

I looked up at him with my smart ass remark on the tip of my tongue and froze. His face was openly fearful and sad. "We were talking about you, but nothing you need to worry about. Actually Victor was helping me."

Ares looked at Victor suspiciously. "Are you trying to stake a claim?"

Victor put a hand to his chest with his mouth open in an O shape trying to look innocent and shocked. "*Moi*?! Of course not!"

Ares snarled. "Because if you are, then I'll be forced to fight you."

Victor laughed softly. "You have been away too long *mon ami*. I would never think of trying to do such a thing. She is yours as you are hers and I would not dream of interfering."

Ares sighed obviously relieved and smiled. "Thank you. I do not want to imagine how difficult it would be to kill you."

Victor rolled his eyes. "It would be impossible because you wouldn't be able to do it."

I waved my hands at them. "Enough. Let's not discuss something that won't happen."

Ares stood a little ways from us to make a triangle of our group. Jean Pierre and Francois walked in and bowed. "All is clear," they said in unison.

Victor nodded his head. "Good, now you and the wolf twins go monitor so new ears do not wander close." Francois and Jean Pierre bowed again and walked out of the room. Koda and Matt bowed to Victor then to Ares and walked out. Victor turned to me and smiled. "Now, begin from the beginning."

I inhaled and described to him the way the king had looked when every bit of new information hit him and the final look that I swore was hostility. Victor nodded his head as I spoke and then sighed when I finished. I whispered, "If I'm wrong then I'm wrong, but that's how I felt and what I saw."

Victor shook his head. "You are not wrong per se, but if this is true then it is a bad thing indeed."

Ares groaned. "So you think she's right?"

Victor nodded his head. "He has been searching for a way to increase his power. I think we should heed this as a warning to keep Artemis guarded at all times."

Ares frowned and I could see his anger building. "Do you think he will try something?"

Victor rubbed his temples. "I don't know. I don't think he would risk a full out assault for her because the wolves are still important to us. But he hasn't been king for so many years because he's stupid. He's a smart man. He might try something discreetly."

Ares nodded his head and reached his hand out towards me. I swallowed quickly, knowing that as soon as I touched him his power would wash over me. I slowly reached out and took his hand and then frowned. Nothing happened. He smiled at me. "I can control my powers when I think about it."

I smiled and looked at the ground. "I'm sorry."

He tilted my chin up and looked into my eyes with such a serious face that I couldn't turn away. "I will protect you. You know that, right?" I nodded my head and his anger began to build again. "No one will take you from me."

I whispered, "Damn, and here I thought I was going to get an out."

A small smirk tilted up one corner of his mouth. "Even if you ran of your own free will, I would find you. You're mine."

I put a hand on each side of his neck just below his chin and pulled him down to me. "And you are mine." I stood on tiptoe and kissed his lips hard. He responded by putting one hand on the back of my head and one around my waist to pull me against him. Our kiss deepened until I heard Victor clear his throat. I had forgotten he was even there. I blushed and pulled away. "Sorry Victor."

Victor laughed. "Do not apologize. You did nothing wrong. I will be leaving to my room now.

Jean Pierre and Francois will come to you in the morning, Ares." He stood up beside me.

Ares frowned. "We need to discuss our plan..."

Victor waved his hand interrupting Ares. "Later. I am tired and need rest. Tomorrow, let your guards take Artemis out to enjoy the town, and we will discuss business then." Victor bent down and kissed my cheek softly. "Good night *mon papillon*. May your dreams be as sweet as you are." He left the room in the floating gait vampires had.

Koda and Matt came back in the room smiling at us. I asked, "I take it that I don't get to take a walk tonight?"

Ares shook his head and kissed my lips softly. "Not tonight, sweetheart." He dropped my hand slowly and walked to the bathroom. The click of the lock echoed in the still room.

Koda scoffed, breaking the silence. "What pissed him off?"

I walked over to the bed and bent down to get inside my bag. "Someone wants me and he is afraid that they might attack you to get me." I grabbed my favorite pair of pajama pants that were covered in pictures of a wolf staring at you with the line, "Bark Off" under his feet. I reached farther in and grabbed the night shirt that matched it. I started to undress to put them on when I remembered Koda and Matt. I sighed. *I'll have to get used to indecent exposure eventually.* I stripped my jeans and t-shirt off and put the pajamas on. When I turned around Koda and Matt were staring at me in shock. I frowned. "What?"

Matt smiled. "You changed in front of us?"

I shrugged. "What's the big deal?"

Ares walked out of the bathroom and frowned at us. "What's going on?"

Koda pointed at me. "She changed in front of us."

Ares frowned. "You changed clothes in front of them?"

I shrugged. "I'll be naked a lot in front of them if I keep changing to my wolf form and besides I had a bra and underwear on and was facing away from them."

I folded the dress and set it on the bedside table to return to Madeleine. Ares was speaking quietly to Koda and Matt so I hopped up on the bed and pulled one of the pillows down to lay my head on. I felt the bed move, but stayed staring at the bedroom door. Koda stood in front of me and waved his hands at me. "Move over bed hog."

I frowned. "What?"

He sighed. "We're a pack and a pack sleeps together. We did it last night. Now move over."

I smiled. "So this must have looked really awkward when it was just the three of you?"

Ares nodded his head. "Yes, there were many questions floating around."

I backed up on the bed until I touched someone's body and repositioned my head on my pillow. Koda took his shirt off and climbed onto the bed facing away from me. I felt someone at my feet and sat up to see Matt along the bottom of the bed. I frowned. "Why does Matt always have to sleep down there?"

Koda turned his head and body so he could see me. "It's a pecking order thing."

I shook my head. "Come on. At least trade every night."

Koda frowned. "You don't want me to sleep beside you?" Ares growled softly and Koda shook his head. "You know what I meant Ares."

"It has nothing to do with who it is, it's just not fair that he has to sleep at our feet all the time. Tonight you can sleep here Koda, but tomorrow Matt gets to sleep up here."

Ares asked, "Are you going to try to make me sleep at the foot of the bed too?"

I shrugged. "Why shouldn't you? We're all a pack, right? And that means that your pack mates wouldn't try to make a move on me anyway. Right? So then you should be a gracious alpha and sleep at the foot of the bed every third night."

Ares frowned and Matt laughed. "Oh I love this'n."

I smiled at him and rolled over to face Ares for a second. "Am I overstepping boundaries?"

Ares kissed my lips softly. "Definitely, but for you, I will concede this issue to you. We will rotate sleeping patterns, except for you. You must stay at the center of us."

I frowned. "Because you're worried about someone trying to get me?"

Koda leaned over us. "It's a lot harder to take someone from the center of the pile than the outside."

I sighed and nodded my head. "Fine." I kissed Ares' lips one more time and rolled over to lie on my back. Ares and Koda spooned themselves to me and Matt wrapped himself around us all. The heat started to become too much, but I quickly fell asleep to the sound of my pack's breathing.

CHAPTER TEN

As Victor had instructed, Ares left early the next morning to strategize with Victor and the twin vampires while Koda and Matt took me out to explore Paris. We took a limo from the mansion to the heart of the town nearest the Eiffel Tower. It was a three hour drive from the winery, so we walked everywhere once in town. The shops were cute and I bought a few souvenir shirts with the money I had taken from Darren. We also ate at a lovely outside diner. Koda ordered snails just so we could look at them. As we walked from the diner towards the Eiffel Tower, I felt someone watching us and looked around, but there were too many people looking at us for me to be certain. My purple eyes didn't help our tourist looks, but Matt spoke fluent French so we were left alone and didn't have to ask for directions. I moved closer to Koda when I still felt the threatening presence nearby. Koda looked down at me with the smile he had had on all day, but quickly vanished into a frown when he saw my face. "What's wrong?"

I whispered, "Someone's watching us."

Koda looked around and smiled. "There are many people watching us."

I shook my head. "No, it's...it's like I can taste their aggression, their threat."

Matt sniffed the air and sighed. "There are too many bloodsuckers living in this city for me to be certain, but I can sense a little of the aggression she is speaking of."

Koda rubbed the back of his neck. "Maybe we should go back."

I groaned. "Dammit. And we're so close." I looked longingly up at the Eiffel Tower and sighed. "Alright, let's go back."

We turned around and started down the road towards the other town we had started from. Matt pulled out a cell phone and spoke quickly in French. He whispered, "The driver is still at the town waiting for us."

I nodded my head and tried to breathe slower. We turned down another road which was nearly deserted and walked faster. We were almost to the end when three people stepped into the alley, blocking our path. Koda pushed me behind him and Matt pressed himself against my back. Koda asked, "What do you want?" I peeked around Koda's arm so I could see what was happening.

The three men continued to walk towards us and I watched their feet, but they didn't float like the vampires. The man in the center spoke in a deep voice, "You know what we want. Just hand her over and no one dies."

Koda growled. "You're pack! You can't betray us!"

The man shrugged. "The leeches pay higher, and besides, after we kill you no one will know what happened."

Koda took a step forward and I grabbed his hand. He spun around and stared at me in shock. "Koda, please don't. I don't want you to die."

Koda snarled. "If I let them take you I might as well die! You are my pack and what they will do to you will make you wish you were dead."

The man laughed deeply. "Oh, we'll be extra nice to the little pup. Won't we men?"

The other men nodded their heads, smiling wickedly. I swallowed hard and stepped back into Matt's arms. Koda stepped forward and exhaled. The two men, who hadn't spoken, ran forward and started attacking Koda. Koda dodged and countered their attacks faster than I could keep track of. Grunts and cracking sounds made me cringe and hope Koda was alright. I watched in amazement as Koda grabbed the smallest man and threw him at the man who had spoken originally. The impact was as loud as a car crash, as their bodies slammed to the ground. Koda grabbed the last man's throat and squeezed tight.

I started to move forward to stop him, but Matt put his arm around my chest and whispered, "This is the only way. Either we kill them now, or Ares will order us to kill them later. They have admitted to trying to kidnap you, the Prince's mate. It is unacceptable."

I watched in horror as Koda dug his fingers in and ripped out the front of the man's throat, exposing bone. The man fell to the ground convulsing and the other men stared in shock. Koda reached into his pocket and pulled out a long black bag. He opened the bag to expose a silver stake inside. Making sure not to touch it himself, he drove the stake into the convulsing man's body then yanked it back out. The body stopped twitching and his veins turned black. The two men who had been watching started to get up, but Matt let me go and ran over to them. He grabbed them by their throats and mimicked the attack Koda had done reaching into his own pocket to take out a similar black bag. I stared in shock at the three dead men with their throats ripped out, holes in their chests and black veins lying in the alley. Koda and Matt took out black handkerchiefs and wiped the blood off their stakes. When done, they carefully closed the bags and put them back in their pockets.

Koda walked back towards me and reached his hand out. I flinched away from him and he smiled. "It's alright. They're dead now."

I whispered, "You killed them. Why?"

Koda squatted down and stared into my face. "Artemis, they were going to kidnap you. Do you know what they would have done between the time they took you and the time they got you to whoever wanted you?"

I shook my head. "You didn't have to kill them. Don't you have werewolf prison or something?"

Koda shook his head. "We kill men who are this dangerous to our packs or they will just come out of prison even angrier than before. If I hadn't killed them, they would have come back for you. They wouldn't have stopped until they had you, or they were dead. I couldn't let them have you." He extended his hand to me again.

I frowned, but took his hand and let him lead me past the dead men. We were almost to the street when three more men stepped in our way, making us stop. I turned around and gasped. "Koda, there's more behind us." Koda turned to the three other men walking behind us. Matt came to stand beside me so that I was in the between him and Koda. I sniffed the air and frowned. "More wolves."

The men held long hammers with silver heads as they walked towards us. I grabbed Koda's arm and whispered, "I don't want you to die for me."

Koda shook his head. "I won't let them take you, Artemis."

I shook my head. "No! Please Koda."

Matt grabbed me around the waist and pulled me back against him as the six men circled around us. Koda frowned. "State your intent."

The six men looked at each other for a few seconds until one of them finally stepped forward. He was tall and muscular and scary. A scar over his right eye made him look even tougher. "We are here for the girl."

Koda shook his head. "Not going to happen."

The man smiled. "We are here for the girl and your lives don't matter. We will kill you and take her."

Koda leapt forward and began attacking the man. I watched as they punched and kicked and realized that Koda knew some type of martial arts. The other man however knew some as well. As Koda and the leader fought the other five men moved forward. Matt started to attack them, but there were too many and after a minute three of them were holding Matt down. Koda punched the leader as hard as he could knocking him back into Matt, but the leader had recovered and with one of the other men they grabbed Koda and tackled him to the ground. The last man took his hammer and held it up as if ready to kill them with it. I ran forward and held my hands up in front of them. "Wait!"

The man put his hammer down and the leader asked, "What are you doing? Someone grab her."

I turned to the leader and spoke in a voice barely audible to human ears, "If I go willingly, will you let them live?"

Koda thrashed on the ground. "No! Artemis! No!"

The leader frowned at me then nodded his head. "We will knock them out so they can't follow us, but we won't kill them."

Koda got one guy off of him, but the leader pinned him down with a knee to his face. I cringed. "Please! Please don't hurt them. I'll go with you, but you have to promise that you will only knock them out and not kill them or hurt them severely."

The leader turned to the other men and nodded his head. They all stood up holding Koda and Matt who were trying to fight. I felt tears falling down my face and whispered, "Tell Ares that I'm sorry, but I can't let you die."

Matt shook his head. "No! Artemis you don't understand. You don't know what they'll do to you!"

I wiped at the tears on my face. "You'll be alive and that's all that matters."

Koda snarled and his body started to twitch. "If you do anything to her I will find you all and kill you!"

The leader smiled and shook his head. "We won't harm a single hair on her head. Knock him out before he changes!"

The man that was left took out a small black object and walked up behind Koda. He swung the object and hit Koda in the lower back of the head knocking him out instantly. Koda's body slumped forward and they lowered him to the ground carefully. Matt trashed and snapped his teeth. "No! Artemis!"

I smiled. "You'll be alright Matt. It's a small price to pay to keep you alive."

Matt began twitching and the man hit him with the black object making Matt's body go limp. They set him on the ground next to Koda and turned towards me. With all of their eyes on me I suddenly realized that it may have been smarter to run, but it was too late. The leader grabbed my arm and led me from the alley towards a large black van with tinted windows. "Why do bad guys always drive vans to kidnap people?" I asked myself.

I looked back once at Koda and Matt and let the tears fall down my face. They would live and that's all that mattered. The leader opened the doors to the van and I climbed inside. After everyone was in they drove off in silence. I stared out the window, watching the scenery go by and hoped I might remember how to get back. The leader who was sitting next to me frowned at me. "Why did you come willingly? Did you believe they didn't have a chance against us?"

I frowned. "I don't know if they could have taken you or not, but I don't want their deaths on my hands. I'm not important enough to die for."

SONG OF THE MOON

The leader shook his head and took out a black handkerchief. He held out the handkerchief to me. "Put it on."

I folded it and wrapped it around my eyes and tied it so that I couldn't see anything but darkness. I leaned back against the seat and closed my eyes, hoping that whatever was in store for me wouldn't be as bad as I imagined. We drove for hours in silence and then finally stopped. I heard the doors opening and closing and then the blind fold came off. The leader stood in front of me. "Come on. Bathroom break."

I followed him out of the car and made sure not to make eye contact with any of the other men. They were all wolves and all dominant, which seemed wrong. We were at a gas station. I followed the leader to the side of the gas station building and walked into the bathroom. I shut the door and sighed. *What had I done?! What are they going to do to me?* I went to the bathroom then washed my hands in the sink. I stared at my reflection at the stranger in the mirror and sighed. *Would Ares think I betrayed him? Would he even try to find me?* I pictured his furious face when Koda and Matt came back without me. *Would he kill Koda and Matt?* I shook my head. *No, he wouldn't kill them because they had tried. Would he kill me if he found me?* I saw the tears brimming in my eyes and quickly wiped them away. I inhaled deeply and walked out of the bathroom.

The leader asked, "Better?" I nodded my head and followed him back to the van. He climbed in beside me and frowned. "What are you feeling?"

I frowned back at him. "What?"

He shook his head. "I can't understand your feelings. They're mixed."

I glared at him. "Why do *you* care?"

He sighed. "I know you must think the worst of us, but I swear that I will not harm you. We are just taking you to the leader."

I frowned. "Who is the leader and why does he want me?"

He shrugged. "We aren't told those things. We just get our money, a person and instructions."

I sighed. "Great." *Could the vampire king be the one kidnapping me? These guys wouldn't have been told that though.* "What's your name?" I asked the leader.

He smiled. "Jesse."

"And you're a wolf?"

He nodded his head. "Bitten wolf."

I frowned. "A who?"

He stared at me in shock. "You don't know the difference?"

I rubbed my temples. "I only found out that I was a werewolf a few days ago. I'm not really up on the details."

His look of shock increased. "How old are you?"

I sighed. *Why did I have to go through this all the time?* "I'm eighteen and didn't change until after...yes *after* my eighteenth birthday. I'm pretty sure I changed part way when Ares called me, but we aren't sure."

Two men up front gasped and spun around. "Ares?!" they exclaimed in unison.

I frowned at them. "How did you know to get me and not know whose I am?"

Jesse stared at me in shock. "What do you mean whose you are?"

"You really should find out more information before you go on a mission. I'm Artemis Lupine, daughter of Darren, *passt genau* of Ares." The van jerked to a stop and everyone stared at me in shock. I frowned. "Didn't you figure out I was Ares', when his two pack mates were with me?"

Jesse groaned. "Dammit, no wonder he got the better of me at first. Koda's a freaking martial arts nut. Shit."

The man in the front passenger seat asked, "What are we going to do Jesse? We can't separate a match."

Jesse snarled. "It's done. We can't just go hand her back to Ares and hope he doesn't kill us. You know him, he'll kill us before he asks questions. He didn't get the nickname, 'God of War', for being a sweetheart."

I asked, "Is he really that ruthless?"

Jesse smiled. "You do not understand the ways of the wolf yet. He is ruthless because he must be. If he wasn't, he wouldn't be Prince, and if all of us weren't we wouldn't be alive." I sighed and Jesse frowned, "We'll need to find a place for the night and figure this all out."

I turned to him hopeful. "If you take me back I'll make sure Ares doesn't kill you."

All of the men laughed. Jesse shook his head. "No. He won't allow us to live after this.

"Then take me back close by and I'll walk. I'll say I snuck out and they won't have to know it was you. I don't even know you guys so I won't be able to tell them who you are." I pleaded.

Jesse shook his head. "Koda saw us and Ares will smell us on you and his brothers."

The man in the driver's seat said, "It's probably a really good thing that we didn't kill them. If Ares had found them dead he would have started the hunt immediately. Now he won't know until Koda and Matt make it back after waking up."

Jesse nodded his head. "Let's find a hotel." The driver started driving again and then pulled into a motel a few minutes later. Two of the men went to the clerk and paid for a hotel for the night. We drove to our room and everyone piled out and into the room. Jesse held the door open for me and gave me a friendly smile. *Aren't kidnappers supposed to be mean and violent?* My stomach grumbled and everyone looked at me. Jesse said, "Mark, go buy some food."

The driver of the van walked out of the room quickly and shut the door behind him. I turned to Jesse and asked, "What are you going to do?"

He shook his head. "I'm not sure yet. For now you just go sleep on that bed." He pointed at one of the two twin beds. *I'm not tired yet and how could I sleep when my life was being discussed?* I walked to the bed anyway and lied down on it. I could hear them whispering together, but they were too quiet for me to hear. A few minutes later Mark came back with five bags of fast food and drinks. He handed me a drink and two cheeseburgers before going to the other men and separating the food between them. I ate my food and stared at the men holding me captive. They were all scary looking and yet the fear that was painted on their faces made them seem less intimidating. I wondered if Ares was really so bad that they should fear him this much. They were still talking an hour later, so I curled up on the bed and went to sleep. If I was going to try to get away tomorrow I needed my sleep now. I closed my eyes and tried to get comfortable, but without my pack sleeping around me I was freezing.

I awoke to find two hands on me. A small whimper escaped my lips before I could stop it and a man laughed softly. "I ain't gonna hurt ya. I just wanted to ask if ya was cold?" I nodded my head, not looking at the man. He said, "I'll get a blanket from the car. These hotels are nastay." I heard the door to the room open and close, and then a car door and then the room again. I frowned. *Had my hearing really improved that much?* He shook out the blankets and then laid it on me. "There ya go. If ya need anything else, just ask."

I turned to look at him and asked, "Why are you being nice to me?"

He frowned wrinkling his forehead and asked, "Why wouldn't we be nice to ya?"

I sat up. "You kidnapped me. Koda and Matt seemed to think I was in more danger of you all than anything else."

He smiled showing two identical dimples. "We're hired help, but we aren't scum. We were told to bring you to the leader alive and that was all. Why would we hurt ya?"

I frowned. "So, you aren't going to torture me?"

He laughed loudly and shook his head. "Naw. We aren't. Darn kids watch too much television." He walked over to the other bed and lay down.

I curled up in the blanket and closed my eyes. *Maybe I could survive this.* I had just started to fall asleep hearing the soft sounds of snorting when the bed moved. I opened my eyes, but stayed still. The bed groaned softly as someone climbed on to it next to me. I started to sit up, but a large hand covered my mouth and the man whispered in my ear, "Now you be real quiet, girl, or I'll kill you." I frowned. Hadn't the other man just said they weren't going to kill me? He ran his hand down my face and neck and towards my chest. I slapped his hand and he grabbed my wrists in one hand, keeping the other hand on my mouth. "It'll be easier on us both if you don't resist."

He kissed my neck and then licked my upper chest. He moved my knees apart and pressed himself against my jeans. I whimpered, realizing what he was doing. He rubbed himself against the front of me and I lost control. I reached my leg up and kicked him in the side. Sometimes being flexible is a great thing. He grunted, but didn't release his grip. He slammed his lower body against mine and I started crying. I realized now that this was what Koda and Matt had been worried about. I felt my body starting to shake and welcomed my wolf. She glared at this man trying to take advantage of me and fury radiated from her as she took over my body. My mouth changed to teeth as he started to kiss down my chest again. I bit into his hand drawing blood and making him scream. I kicked him backwards and finished my change without any pain. I rolled over and snarled at him.

He held his hand up and growled. "You dumb bitch! I'll kill you for that!" The lights for the room turned on, temporarily blinding me, and the five other men stared at us in shock. I jumped forward and bit into my attacker's crotch tearing through his jeans and into his flesh. He screamed in pain and tried to hit me, but I jumped back before he could land his punch. The other men rushed forward and grabbed him.

Jesse glared at him. "What the hell do you think you're doing?"

The man whimpered. "She bit me."

I snapped my teeth at him. Jesse stared at me in shock. I jumped up on to the bed and sat down. Jesse asked, "Artemis?" I rolled my eyes and barked at him. The other men were staring at me with open mouths. Jesse shook his head. "Am I the only one seeing this?"

Mark shook his head. "She looks like Asena."

Jesse smiled. "I knew I wasn't the only one seeing it."

Someone knocked on the door loudly, making everyone jump. I glared at the man who had tried to rape me and smiled as he fell to the ground from pain and blood loss. This was one man I wouldn't mind killing. I sniffed the air and snarled. Vampires. Two figures in black cloaks floated into the room and stopped in front of the bed. One of them spoke and I almost barked in joy. "Is this the girl?"

Jesse nodded his head. "That's Artemis."

The man lifted his hood back just enough for me to see his face and wink at me. Francois! He put his hood back down. "Why is she in wolf form?"

Jesse looked nervous and started stuttering. "Www...well you see..."

Francois held up his hand. "Enough. I see the wounded man on the floor. You are lucky that we are in a generous mood today." Francois took out a pair of jeans and a t-shirt and tossed them on the bed. "Change girl so that we may take you."

I changed back to human form and pretended to be upset, putting on my clothes and glaring at the man on the floor. I asked, "Could I take him as a souvenir? I'm sure your leader will be hungry so early at night."

Francois nodded his head. "You were told not to harm her and so he will be the price." Jesse started to move forward, but Francois held up his hand. "It is done." The other vampire, who I guessed was Jean Pierre, picked up the man and carried him outside. I followed them out to their silver car and climbed into the passenger seat. The second vampire stuffed the injured man into the trunk, then climbed into the backseat.

Once all the doors were closed Francois pulled his hood back and the other man did too. I stared at the other man for a second then asked, "Who is he?"

Francois smiled. "An accomplice. Now you stay quiet and we can all stay pleasant."

I frowned. "What do you mean? Aren't you taking me to Ares? How did you find me so quickly?"

Francois drove down the road without another word. I watched where we were going, but had no idea where we were. After a few miles I asked, "Francois, why aren't you talking to me?"

He shook his head. "I am sorry for this Artemis, but I must obey my maker."

My mind clicked and it felt like liquid was in my brain. "You aren't here to save me are you?"

The other vampire laughed. "Save you? We are here to take you the rest of the way!"

I glared at Francois. "Why? Why are you doing this?"

"I told you that I must obey my leader. She is my maker and I can't rebel against her. I'm sorry." He said softly through gritted teeth.

I frowned. "But you're a born vampire, you went out in the sun just now. How can you have a maker?"

He smiled. "You're perceptive. I was on death's bed, and she offered me her blood, but in doing so I became as enthralled to her as any made vampire."

I stared at the window letting my mind numb itself. "Am I going to die?"

Catherine Banks

"No. She wants you alive." We drove the rest of the way in silence and I found myself becoming more and more upset. I clenched my teeth to keep from flying off the handle and pressed my cheek to the cold glass. We stopped in front of a small cottage in the middle of nowhere and the two vampires got out. I climbed out with them and followed them to the house. It was fully dark now and I could feel the presence of a powerful dark force. I swallowed, as I stepped inside the cottage and saw Isabella.

She was still as beautiful as I remembered and still as scary. She smiled. "Welcome Artemis. I have been waiting for you." She waved her hand at the table, which was covered in food like a buffet.

I licked my lips hungrily and shook my head. "No. What do you want Isabella?"

She laughed, making me shiver in delight. "Straight to the point. I like that." She walked to a small living room and sat in an overstuffed chair. I sat on the chair opposite her and frowned. She smiled wider. "As soon as I heard that Ares had a match, I knew it must be you. Your father disappeared so long ago, that it was apparent that he failed in his duty and kept you alive. I guess it worked out for the best, because now you are here."

I shook my head. "Why do you want me? I'm not special."

She frowned, somehow making herself even more attractive. "But you are special and that's why I went through so much trouble to get you away from that horrid Ares. He wouldn't use your abilities like he is supposed to."

She was confusing me. "Abilities? You mean changing to a wolf?"

Isabella gasped. "You do not know? You are not simply a wolf, but also sidhe."

I frowned. "What's that?"

She smiled. "The humans call them fairies, I believe."

I stared at her in shock. "Fairies? Like, wings and magical powers, fairies?"

She nodded her head. "Yes. Your mother is a very powerful sidhe warrior. I knew when I saw your eyes who you were and I knew I had to have you."

I glared at her. "Why would you want me? You're a woman."

She laughed again, making me think of nefarious things. Vampires' voice powers are no joke in real life. "I do not want you for children, silly girl, but for your powers. You are going to help me take over this pathetic planet and push the wolves back to their proper place of servants."

I stared at her in shock. "Does Maurice know what you are doing?"

She waved her hand dismissively at me. "Do not worry about the King. Francois here will be working with you on your powers. As soon as you have gained them, we will move to the next step."

The second vampire brought in the man who had attacked me and threw him down on the ground between Isabella and me. I snarled at him and she smiled. "You seem displeased with this man."

I nodded my head. "He tried to rape me."

She hissed. "I gave them specific instructions not to harm you." She stood up and picked the man up off of the floor. I stared in shock at her strength, as she easily held him with one hand, and stared into his eyes. "Did you harm her?"

The man whimpered. "Please beautiful Queen, do not kill me."

She frowned. "Your lack of denial is an omission." She stood him up and smiled. I felt her power pulsating against him and groaned. She ran her fingertip along the man's cheek. "You disobeyed me wolf." The man smiled happily, as though she called him her favorite pet name. She kissed his cheek then leaned his head back. I watched in horror as her fangs extended and she plunged them into his neck. He stayed still as she drank from him. I put my hand over my mouth to keep from vomiting and forced myself to watch. The man's eyes grew dimmer and dimmer until, with one last suck, the light disappeared from his eyes. I gasped as she let his body ago and it crumpled lifeless to the floor. "Clean that up, please Francois." She turned back to me and smiled, showing her bloody fangs. "Consider that retribution for the stress and pain he caused you. Now I must leave, but you must work hard and focus on your powers." She started to walk away and I cleared my throat.

She turned around and frowned at me. I asked, "What if I refuse to help?"

She laughed making me think of nefarious things. "That is not an option. You will help me or you die. It's as simple as that, *mon cheri. Adieu.*"

I watched her retreating back and felt hopeless. *How could I have powers besides my werewolf ones? Could I really be a fairy?* I looked over my back and frowned. No wings. The second vampire took the dead man's body out of the house. Francois smiled at me. "You should eat Artemis."

I glared at him, but walked over to the table no longer able to resist my hunger. I ate the food quickly, then folded my arms on the table. "What if I don't have powers?"

Francois frowned. "Then you will die. For now let's think positive thoughts."

I scoffed. "Positive? Like I might escape and get to watch Victor tear you into pieces?"

Francois sighed. "I know you do not understand about my kind, but we have no choice but to do as our maker tells us. I am sorry, but we must begin your training." He sat across the table from me and frowned. "Put your palms face up and focus on them. You should be able to put energy in your palms and make fire."

"Fire in my hands?" I asked doubtfully.

He nodded his head. "You should be able to make fireballs."

I smiled and then frowned. *Why didn't I get to learn the cool stuff when I was with Ares?* I stared at my palms and pictured a flame. I clenched my eyes tight and wished for warmth or fire to my hands. I sat still for a few minutes, but nothing happened. I exhaled and looked at Francois. "Nothing's happening."

He nodded his head. "Perhaps fire is not your element." I was beginning to hate hearing French accents. He tapped his chin thoughtfully. "Try picturing the ocean and see if you can make a water ball."

I raised an eyebrow. "A water ball? How is that useful?"

He sighed. "Just do it!" I frowned at him, but focused on my hands. Then minutes later, I groaned. He frowned in thought. "Hmm...maybe too much has happened today. Perhaps you should go to bed and try again tomorrow."

I sighed. "Great." I walked up the stairs and then stopped at the top. "Uh, where's my bedroom?"

He smiled. "Second door on the left." I nodded my head and started up again when he called to me. "And Artemis, don't even think about trying to escape. Andre and I have excellent hearing and are very light sleepers."

"Whatever. Stupid bloodsuckers." I mumbled the last as I walked into the bedroom that served as my prison. I plopped down on the bed and stared at the wood ceiling. Would Ares find me? Would he even be looking? I heard the front door open and shut, but ignored it. I rolled onto my side and closed my eyes, finally getting a peaceful night's rest. I awoke the next morning to the front door opening and closing again. I sat up and stretched my arms over my head. What now? Go downstairs and try to gain powers I don't have? Perfect. Maybe death would be better. I walked down the stairs and sat in the head chair of the dining table. "I'm hungry."

Andre frowned at me, but went into the kitchen. Francois sat down at the table wearing a new pair of clothes. He smiled. "How are you feeling this morning?"

"Like a captive who's hungry," I grumbled. Andre walked back into the room carrying a large tray of pancakes and bacon. I smiled. "Andre, if you weren't one of my prison guards, I would kiss you."

He set the tray on the table, flashed his fangs at me and walked away. I ate the food until I couldn't eat anymore and relaxed against the chair. Francois smiled. "Ready to begin your lessons again?"

I sighed. "Wouldn't it be better if someone with experience helped me? You know, someone who was also sidhe?"

He frowned. "The sidhe are not exactly friendly with the vampires. Besides, you can do it without their help. Just focus."

Although I didn't think I had the powers they were talking about, I was curious to try. Darren should have taught me about this, or Ares. Why did the bad guys have to be the ones to teach me?

I put my palms face up on the table. I focused on them and thought of fire, but after an hour with nothing happening I grew tired. "I can't do it. Maybe I don't have magic."

"Well, it is lunch time, so maybe you just need food."

I groaned and stood up, stretching my body. Andre walked in carrying a tray of food and two wine bottles. Although by now I knew it wasn't wine in the glasses. I ate my food in silence and stared at my prison guards. "How long will she keep me alive, if I don't have magic?"

Andre shrugged. "Your fey magic isn't all that she wants."

I frowned. "What did you call my magic?"

Andre looked at me as though I'd just asked what a foot was. "Fey is another term for the sidhe or fairies. I can't believe Darren never told you about all of this. It is somewhat important."

"You knew my father?" I asked in shock.

Andre nodded his head. "I fought with him in a battle once. He was a good fighter, but a bastard."

I scoffed. "Tell me about it."

Andre looked at me then and studied my face. I squirmed in my chair at his inquisitive stare. "Did you live with the humans like they say?" He asked.

I nodded my head. "I did. I went to school with them and played with them. I thought I was one of them."

Andre asked, "What are they like?"

I shrugged. "Most of the other students didn't like me. Ares said it was because they instinctively knew I was a predator. But there were a couple who accepted me for me and were great." I sighed remembering Bret.

I finished eating and leaned back in my chair. I snapped my fingers and imagined a flame like a lighter. Nothing happened though and no matter how good my imagination was I just didn't feel magic in me. My wolf stirred inside me, making me gasp. Francois frowned. "None of that."

I shook my head. "I can't control her yet."

Francois frowned. "I forgot you have only changed recently. Your wolf needs an alpha to control her."

I frowned. "What? Why do you need Ares to control me? He hasn't yet." My wolf stirred harder in me and I felt her trying to change me.

Francois hissed. "Stop it!"

I screamed in pain as a few of my bones separated trying to remake my shape. I yelled, "I'm trying! But I can't stop her!" More bones and muscles separated and expanded. I fell to the floor screaming in pain. The change hadn't been this painful before. Andre jumped over the table and grabbed me, throwing me on the ground and pinning me. I snapped my teeth at him and shook my head. "You aren't helping Andre! She doesn't like you."

He got off of me and my body finished the transformation. I lay still on the ground panting and hurting. The pain started to subside and I rolled over. Francois and Andre's faces were now that of the vampires I had nightmares of. Their fangs extended and their fingers turned into daggers. I growled at them softly, but stayed back. I suddenly knew how I could tell Ares I was captured. I ran to the front door and burst through it. I knew Andre and Francois were right behind me, but I had to do it. I stopped outside the door and raised my snout to the sky and howled as loud as I could. Andre reached for me and I jumped to the side, continuing my long howl. Dogs in the neighborhood near us began howling with me, and soon our songs filled the night air.

Within seconds I lost my breath and Francois tackled me. I didn't fight him and instead submitted to him. He frowned down at me, and then the faintest howl drifted on the wind to my ears. Ares had heard me and he was answering my call. He was coming for me. The thought made me happy and sad at the same time and if I had been in human form I would have cried. Francois dragged me by my scruff back into the house and hissed at me. I laid on the ground averting my eyes and staring at his shoes. He had on running shoes that were covered in mud.

Francois hissed again. "Change back."

I tried to change, but my wolf wouldn't let me. She liked being in control and didn't want to go back. I whimpered and Andre sighed. "Dammit. She doesn't have control over the wolf to change. You should have warned us that she was so new!"

Francois sighed. "The mistress did not care about her being new. Neither of us foresaw this as a possible reaction."

I watched them bicker and relaxed on the ground. Ares had heard my call and answered me. He was coming for me. I just had to wait for him. Andre grabbed me by my scruff while I was lying down and threw me across the room. My instincts kicked in and I pushed off the wall with my feet and landed on the ground. Andre's fangs were extended past his bottom lip and he screamed at me. It was a scream so full of rage and fury, that I flinched. He started towards me, but Francois stood in his path. "Our mistress ordered us not to kill her."

Andre hissed. "I won't kill her, but I'm going to make her wish she was dead."

I remembered Koda telling me that they would do that and I growled softly. Apparently rape hadn't been the only thing they'd been worried about. I started moving around the table so it was between us, and Andre followed me. Francois let Andre go, and then began to come at me from the other side. It seemed that he liked Andre's reasoning and the thought of causing me pain wasn't a bad one. His fangs extended and he hissed at me. I snapped my teeth at them both and prayed Ares would come sooner rather than later. Andre jumped across the table at me. I had a second to decide my course of action and the wolf took over. I dove under the table and out the other side, while Andre tried to reach underneath.

I ran for the stairs and up into my bedroom. I focused on my human form and my body transformed faster than I had ever been able to before and with no pain. I ran forward and shut the bedroom door and locked it. I knew it was silly to think the small wooden door could keep the vampires out, but it was all I could think to do. I heard them move up the stairs and smelled them closing in on me, but the door didn't open. I curled up on the bed and waited for what they would do to me, because there was nothing else I could do. A few minutes passed and nothing happened. I listened harder and heard fighting downstairs. Had Francois come to his senses and begun to fight Andre? I strained to listen, but all I could hear was the thudding sound of fists hitting each other. I started to walk towards the door and decided it was better to stay here, until I knew who the winner was.

Five more minutes passed and then I heard footsteps up the stairs. I frowned because they were heavier than the vampires had been originally. Could they only float when using magic? I waited tensely as someone stopped in front of my door and inhaled. I suddenly wished I was in my wolf form, but she was too scared to move. There were soft whispers, then a knock on the door. I frowned. Why would they knock on the door? A familiar male voice asked, "Artemis? Are you in there?"

I jumped off the bed and ran for the door, throwing it open. "Victor!" I ran into his arms and hugged him. "Oh Victor you're here." Victor patted my back, then pushed me away. I felt something hot and wet on my face and put my hand up to feel blood. I looked at Victor and gasped. "Are you hurt?"

He shook his head. "It's not my blood."

I looked around. "Where is Ares?"

He smiled at me. "He is not as fast as me, but he should be here in a moment. He wanted me to come ahead and to ensure your safety."

I nodded my head then turned to my left to see Jean Pierre's sad face. I reached my hand out to him and he took it pulling me against him in a hug. "I am sorry for the pain my brother caused you *mon ami.*"

I shook my head. "It is not your fault. You came to save me."

He pulled back and I saw the tears running down his face. "I had feared the dark mistress had taken control of him, but I had not dreamed he would do something so despicable."

I shook my head. "He did not hurt me. He was probably the only reason Andre did not hurt me." I frowned then. "Are they..."

Victor nodded his head. "They are dead."

I exhaled in relief and began to shiver, thinking of what Andre had wanted to do. I heard someone come in the house and pressed myself against Victor, praying it wasn't Isabella. Soft bone popping sounds traveled up the stairway and then loud footsteps followed. I inhaled and smiled wide. I ran from Victor's arms towards the man I loved. I frowned at the realization and then quickly smiled again. Ares held his arms out to me, a look of relief on his face as I jumped up on him. He held me against his body and I kissed his lips. I felt his tense body and remembered what I had done. I pushed away from him and knelt on the ground in front of him, with my head turned to the side offering my neck. I whispered, "Please forgive me. I did not go with them to betray you."

Ares squatted down and lifted my chin up. "There is nothing to forgive. What you did was stupid, but I did not think you betrayed me."

I felt the tears falling down my face and asked, "You aren't angry with me?"

He nodded his head looking very serious. "I am angry with you." I let a few tears fall down my face and he sighed. "But I am more happy that you are alive and that my brothers are alive, as well."

I gasped. "Are they okay?'

Koda and Matt walked up the stairs naked and smiling. I only glanced at their lower bodies because the nakedness was still so new to me, then ran to them. I hugged them at the same time and kissed each of their cheeks. Matt kissed my cheek back and Koda licked the tears from the side of my face he could reach. "Don't cry, Darling."

I shook my head. "I'm sorry Koda. I know I am supposed to listen to you, but they wanted to kill you. They didn't even know who you were. I couldn't let you die for me. Please forgive me."

Matt put his hand on my cheek softly. "How could we not forgive you when you saved us? We are in your debt it seems now."

Koda snorted. "Don't tell her that."

I kissed Koda's cheek and whispered, "Now you'll never hear the end of it."

Koda sighed. "At least I'll hear it. We were so scared that you were..." Tears ran down his face and he dropped to his knees. "Forgive us for failing you."

Matt dropped to his knees beside Koda. "Forgive us our Prince and Princess."

Ares walked to stand beside me and asked, "Shall we forgive them my Princess?"

I extended my hands to Koda and Matt. "There is nothing to forgive. You fought, and there were simply too many."

Matt shook his head. "We could have taken them."

I shook my head. "No more. I do not forgive you for there is nothing to forgive. You did your best at the time and that is all we can ask of you."

Matt stood up and kissed the back of my hand before smiling. Koda shook his head and looked up at Ares. "What of you, my alpha? Am I to be punished for this unforgivable offense?"

Ares picked my hand up and placed it against his cheek. "We have our pack mate back unharmed. I think if she can forgive, then for this instance so can I."

Koda stared in shock at Ares then stood up and kissed my cheek. "As Matt said, we are in your debt."

I smiled and kissed his cheek. "Then repay your debt by taking me away from here."

Victor sighed. "We must find another refuge it seems. The lion's den is too full for us to hide safely."

We started down the stairs and Ares picked me up in his arms, cradling me against his chest. I frowned. "Why are you carrying me?"

He laid his head against mine and said, "So that I know you are safe. I will not let you out of my sight again."

I smiled and kissed his lips softly. "As my alpha wills it."

He rolled his eyes. "Isn't it supposed to be as my *king* wills it?"

I shrugged. "Alpha, king, same thing."

We were almost to the door when Koda yelled, "Get down!"

Ares turned and squatted down so that his body was shielding me from whatever was attacking us. I could hear a woman shouting and knew it was Isabella. I tried to get free of Ares' arms, but he held me. "I will not lose you again."

I stared at him in shock and for the first time saw the sadness on his face. "Ares, you have to help them."

"Can you stay here, out of trouble?" He asked.

I nodded my head. He kissed my lips as though it were the only thing he needed to survive, and then disappeared out of the house. I sat on the stairway stunned from the kiss. I could hear them fighting and her rage-filled screams, and then everything went silent. I ran down the stairs and stood in the open doorway, staring in shock at what I saw. Maurice stood covered in moonlight over his dead wife's body. His dagger like fingers glistened with blood. I swallowed as he looked up at me with eyes burning with power. He asked, "Have you been harmed?" I shook my head. He asked, "Do you feel we have broken our treaty?" I looked at Ares and he nodded. I shook my head in response. Maurice smiled and it made me smile back at him. "Then my job is done." He turned and floated across the lawn, towards a limo and climbed in.

Ares rushed to me and glared at me. "You promised to stay there."

"I promised to stay out of trouble, and when I came to the door there was no trouble," I said with a smile on my face.

He sighed and Koda laughed. "She's quick."

Ares snarled. "Don't encourage her!"

I pressed my naked body against his and felt his body respond against me. "I think encouragement is what we all need."

He stared down into my eyes and then shook his head taking a step back from me so that our bodies no longer touched. "No, not tonight. Tonight I want to just hold you, while we sleep. To be a united pack again."

I frowned, but nodded my head. "Alright." I walked towards the second limo that I figured was waiting for us, and climbed inside.

Victor climbed in after me and frowned. "You are bothered?"

I wiped at the tears building in my eyes and knew I was being stupid and irrational. "No."

Koda climbed in next and frowned at me. "What's wrong?"

I pressed myself against the seat and stared out the window of the car. Once the door was shut and everyone was inside, the car drove off. I could hear the others whispering quietly, but ignored them trying to console myself for the stupid feeling I was having. Ares had rejected me, but not because he was mad or didn't want me, and yet it was still rejection. I brought my knees up, hugged them against my body, and buried my face between them. I felt a hand on me and knew it was Ares and did not look up. I stayed in my ball, as I tried to convince myself of how stupid I was being, and yet the sting of his rejection was too much after the drama I had been through. Ares tried to pick me up in his arms and it was too much.

I moved across the limo as fast as I could to sit beside Jean Pierre. Ares snarled at Jean Pierre and he shrugged. "I did nothing Ares."

Ares asked, "Then why did she run to you?"

I hid my face behind Jean Pierre's arm as I answered. "He is not wolf and I need a second to clear my head."

Ares voice was short as he asked, "Why?"

I opened my mouth to tell him and then stopped. I asked instead, "Why didn't you tell me I am half sidhe?"

Everyone instantly stopped moving, so much so that I couldn't hear a heartbeat. Ares asked, "Who told you?"

I whispered, "Isabella. It is one of the reasons she wanted me. They were trying to force me to learn my powers."

Ares sighed. "I did not tell you because the fey are not our allies right now. If they learned of your existence, they might join in the hunt for you."

I chanced a look at Ares and asked, "Why does everyone want me dead?"

"Everyone wants you because you're valuable," Ares said with a sympathetic smile. He then held his hand out to me. I stared at it and then turned my face into Jean Pierre's back. Ares snarled. "Why are you refusing me?"

I asked still pressed against Jean Pierre, "Why did you reject me?" Ares laughed softly and I looked up to glare at him. "You think this is funny?" The car stopped at the mansion. I hurried out of the car before Ares could stop me and ran up to the doors. The guards stared at me in shock at first. I realized that I was still naked. I straightened my shoulders and spoke in as firm a voice as I could, "Open the doors for your Princess."

The guards bowed their heads and hurried to open the doors. Ares was close behind me now. I ran inside as fast as I could into the bedroom. It surprised me that I remembered how to get there. I ran straight to the bedroom and locked the door behind me. I turned the shower on and climbed in letting the hot water beat against me as I cried for a reason I knew I shouldn't be. Sometimes being a woman means that your emotions don't always make sense. I heard the door crack and knew Ares had broken the door down. I didn't look at him. I continued to cry and face the back corner of the shower stall.

I felt his anger as he came closer to me and cringed as he opened the shower. I whimpered as his anger hit me like a waft of hot steam. He inhaled, then exhaled, and the anger was gone. He turned me around to face him and I dropped my gaze immediately. He tilted my chin up and kissed my lips, but I pulled away. He whispered, "Artemis." He said it almost chiding and I turned away from him to face the corner again. He wrapped his arms around me and whispered into my ear, "Silly woman. I did not reject you."

I whimpered. "You did. You said you just wanted to..."

He nodded his head against my hair. "That I wanted to hold you and be a united pack. Not that I didn't *want* you. Artemis." He turned me around and stared at my face. His small smile vanished and he put his hands on either side of my face. "Artemis, I could never reject you. You are all I want and more. I just did not want sex with you tonight, because the thought of losing you was too much..."

Koda answered from outside the shower. "You should see the dining room."

Matt sighed. "It will take many days for the holes to be repaired."

Ares growled. "Who invited you?"

Koda and Matt stepped into the shower and stood on either side of us. Koda smiled. "She is our pack mate too."

Ares frowned. "You see? Even if we had wanted time alone, we would not get it."

I smiled a little and then shook my head. "But you did reject me."

All of the men sighed. Ares asked, "Are you ready for that step? Are you sure that you want to do that?"

I thought about it and asked, "Why wouldn't I be?"

Ares smiled. "You have only known me a few days."

I smelled Victor come near the room and spoke loud enough for him to hear, "A good friend of mine said that love is not something that we should waste. That if I love then I should love. I have realized that... I do." I looked into Ares' shocked eyes and said the only thing I knew truly in my heart, at that moment, "I love you Ares. All I could think about when I let those men take me was how angry you were going to be at me and how hurt you were going to be... because I left..." I began to cry again and Ares hugged me.

He kissed my cheek and said, "I was not angry or hurt, just, well...okay I was angry, but not how you thought. I'm just happy that you are alive and safe." He pulled back from me so I could see his face and I realized that everyone else was gone. He smiled at me. The look in his eyes said it before he did. "I love you too, Artemis. More than you will ever know." He kissed my lips and I kissed him back. I let my hands travel up his body and into his hair and he pressed me up against the glass of the shower stall.

Ares' hands ran along my sides, but traveled no where else, as though he were worried of what I would and wouldn't allow. I grabbed his hands and brought them forward to cup my chest. I whispered, "I want to finish our connection, to truly be your mate. I want to be Artemis *Lupine*. I want *you*, Ares."

He stared into my eyes, his face full of conflict. Then his need took over and he kissed me back.

What started in the shower, ended on the floor. It is a wondrous thing to have someone make love to you. I knew without a doubt in my heart that Ares and I loved each other. In those moments, it didn't matter to me that I had been destined for him or that he was a killer at times. He was mine and I was his. That was all I needed to know. We lay breathing heavily on the floor, as our bodies tried to calm down. I turned my head and stared at his handsome face. He smiled at me, making his eyes shine with the happiness he felt. It was the first full smile I had seen on him. I asked, "Will it be like that every time?"

He shook his head and I frowned. He laughed and pulled me against his body, proving that he could go again if I wanted to. He said, "It's better, the longer you are together."

I smiled at him, then Koda cleared his throat. I looked over the top of Ares' body at him and frowned. "How long have you been there?"

Koda smiled. "Do not worry, we just came in."

Ares sighed. "Koda, what is it?"

Koda blushed a little and spoke in a voice barely above a whisper, "I do not mean to interrupt, but we too have craved the attention of our pack mate." I stared at Koda in shock. He shook his head and waved his hands back and forth, "Not like that! We just want to sleep with you." I opened my mouth in shock and Koda groaned. "Artemis! To sleep with you, you know SLEEP!"

Matt tossed two robes at us. Ares quickly put his on and faced his two pack members. I slipped mine on and stood beside Ares. "Are you asking for me to come to bed so we can sleep in our pack?" Koda and Matt nodded their heads in unison. I smiled. "Very well." We walked quickly to the bed and I hopped up in the center. Ares climbed in on my left side and I laid my head down on his chest, while Koda climbed in behind me and molded himself to my back. Matt lay down at our feet and wrapped his arms around my legs. I smiled happily and closed my eyes. "I love you all."

Koda kissed my cheek softly. "I love you as well."

Matt kissed my foot. "Me as well."

CHAPTER ELEVEN

We left France early in the morning, but without Victor or Jean Pierre. They were forced to stay behind to discuss some impending threat, which I assumed was regarding the attacks on the other countries. The connection between Ares and me was stronger than ever. I needed to have constant physical contact. We grabbed the first flight and I felt my worry ease as we left France.

"Where are we going, Ares?" I asked as I relaxed against the seat.

Ares smiled happily. "My home, in Germany."

I stared at him in shock for a minute and then smiled. He did have German features as did Koda and Matt.

My smile left as a thought came to mind. "Great. Big, German, werewolf women. You couldn't have come from a country with small women, could you?"

Ares kissed my cheek. "You'll be fine."

I smiled evilly. "Maybe I'll just toast them with a fireball."

Ares shook his head. "You aren't allowed to use your sidhe powers unless absolutely necessary. No one must know that you have them."

I groaned. "Great. I finally get powers and now I can't use them." After a little accident this morning, where I'd torched a hand towel, we realized I was able to use my sidhe powers.

The plane touched down and we walked through the airport to the waiting vehicle. A man, standing at least seven feet tall, leaned against the hood of a strange European vehicle. He smiled at Ares and bowed at the waist. "Greetings Ares."

Ares bowed. "Greetings Brother."

The man turned to me and smiled as he spoke to Ares. "I see your taste in women has improved."

My lip twitched in a snarl and Ares wrapped his arm around my shoulders. "This is my mate, Ulger and your Princess."

Ulger dropped to one knee in front of me. "Forgive me, Princess, I had not heard that Prince Ares took a mate."

I looked at Ares for help, but he just smiled. "Uh, you're forgiven," I said awkwardly.

Ulger stood up and kissed the back of my hand. "Thank you, Princess."

Ares cleared his throat and Ulger turned to him. "Darius wanted me to tell you that Darren has escaped our trackers. We aren't sure where he has gone, but we've sent additional trackers to pick up his trail."

"My dad got away? He's still alive?" I asked in shock.

Ares wrapped his arm around my shoulders and whispered, "I won't let him hurt you."

His words and touch calmed my nerves and I relaxed against his side. "I know."

Ares opened the back door and smiled brightly. "Are you ready to meet more of our kind?"

I shook my head. "No, but what choice do I have?"

We drove in silence for a few hours and my mind began wandering. *What were these women like? Were they all as beautiful as the ones I had seen?*

Ares tried to pull me into his lap and I resisted, pulling away from him. He frowned. "What's wrong?"

I saw the look of concern on his face and forced the words out before I lost my nerve. "If I let you, would you leave me, for these women?"

Ares smiled, his blue eyes sparkling. "Not a chance. Artemis, I love you. I thought you were over this?"

I shook my head. "I'm sorry. I'm just nervous." I leaned against him and closed my eyes.

He whispered, "You are the only woman for me. Whether you feel the same for me or not, I will always love you."

I looked up at him and saw the pain in his eyes. He thought I was trying to tell him that I didn't truly care for him. I whispered, "I do love you, Ares."

Ares whispered, "It's our destiny to be together. Are you rehashing old issues because you don't want to discuss the new ones with me?"

"I don't know what you're talking about," I said indignantly and looked out the window to my left.

Ares whispered, "I know it's hard to deal with the fact that you aren't a virgin anymore, but isn't it satisfying to know that you'll be with the one that you gave it to, the rest of your life? Not many humans can say that."

I turned to him and kissed his lips. "I love you Ares. I'm just insecure."

He shook his head. "You have no reason to be insecure. I only have eyes for you."

Koda groaned and turned around from the passenger seat. "That was so cliché Ares. You're how old and you couldn't come up with something better than that? I mean, you did work with Shakespeare!"

Ares frowned. "I was trying to be cute. Thank you for ruining our moment."

Koda winked at me. "Just here to help."

We drove for hours through a thick forest on an unmarked dirt road, until finally coming to a small gate with two male guards. Ulger rolled down his window and spoke in a foreign language, I assumed was German to the guards. The guards opened the gate, bowing to our vehicle as we drive past. The trees began thinning and we came to a large wood barn. Ulger stopped the car and we all climbed out. I stretched my arms up over my head, squealing as I stretched.

Ares wrapped his arms around my waist and kissed my cheek. "You keep doing things like that and we won't make it to the village."

I blushed and tried to step out of his arms. "Ares, don't tease me."

He licked my cheek, holding on tightly to me. "I believe I was just saying that to you."

Ulger parked the car inside the barn and then walked back to us. "Ready?" he asked as he cracked his neck from side to side.

Ares nodded his head, smiling wide. I asked, "Ready for what?" Koda pulled his shirt and pants off, and then dropped to his hands and knees shifting forms flawlessly in seconds. His wolf form was more beautiful than I remembered. I fought the urge to run my hands through his fur and turned towards Ares, who was taking his shirt off.

I sighed. "Fine, but I'm not changing back until we're somewhere I can get dressed. I don't want to parade around naked."

I took my shirt off slowly, noticing Ares watching me and folded it nicely on the ground. I slowly pulled my pants off, wriggling my butt excessively. Ares took a step towards me and Koda stepped between us, whining and barking. I stripped my underwear off quickly and changed shapes. It felt good to be a wolf again. My wolf felt ecstatic at being let out and we stretched from head to tail. Ares sniffed my shoulder and I wagged my tail. *Let's run!*

Koda's tongue lolled out the side of his mouth. *Loser has to run around the house naked?*

Matt snorted. *No one wants to see you run around naked, anymore than we already have to.*

Ares whined. *Loser has to give the winner a backrub!*

We all ran down the dirt road kicking up dust behind us. My muscles stretched and my blood pumped harder as I ran. The boys were lengths ahead of me when a familiar scent tickled my nose. I jumped into the forest to my right and ran through the trees towards the smell. *Mom.*

I could hear Ares, Koda and Matt barking for me, but they could wait. I had to find my mom. Ares spoke through my head. *Where are you going? What's wrong?*

I ran faster trying to follow the scent before it disappeared. *My mom's here. I can smell her.*

I jumped over a fallen log and the forest quieted. I strained my ears to listen to Ares' approaching barks, but not even the wind whispered through my ears. I changed back to human and crossed my arms over my chest. "Hello?"

A bright light darted through the trees coming towards me. I lifted my arm to cover my eyes and the light dimmed. A man with pale skin and blue vines etched in his arms and across his chest walked towards me. He wore only a pair of pants and was sleeker muscled than Ares, built more like a runner or swimmer. I swallowed in fear. "Who are you?"

He spoke and the leaves rustled. "I am Achilles."

"What are you?" I asked in the silence.

"I'm Sidhe." The leaves rustled again as he spoke making me shiver involuntarily.

"What do you want? Why are you here?" I asked growing more and more nervous and wishing Ares was here.

He smiled and held out his hand, his body glowing slightly as though a light was turned on inside of him. "I'm here for you. I'm your fiancée and I'm here to take you," he said in a soothing voice.

Ares touched my shoulder and the sounds of the forest crashed into my ears deafening me. I dropped to the ground covering my ears with my hands and moaning in pain. Ares voice boomed like thunder, "YOU'RE NOT TAKING HER ANYWHERE!"

Made in the USA
Charleston, SC
09 July 2013